SAVING SORYA

CHANG AND THE SUN BEAR

WRITTEN BY **TRANG NGUYEN**

ILLUSTRATED BY **JEET ZDUNG**

DIAL BOOKS FOR YOUNG READERS

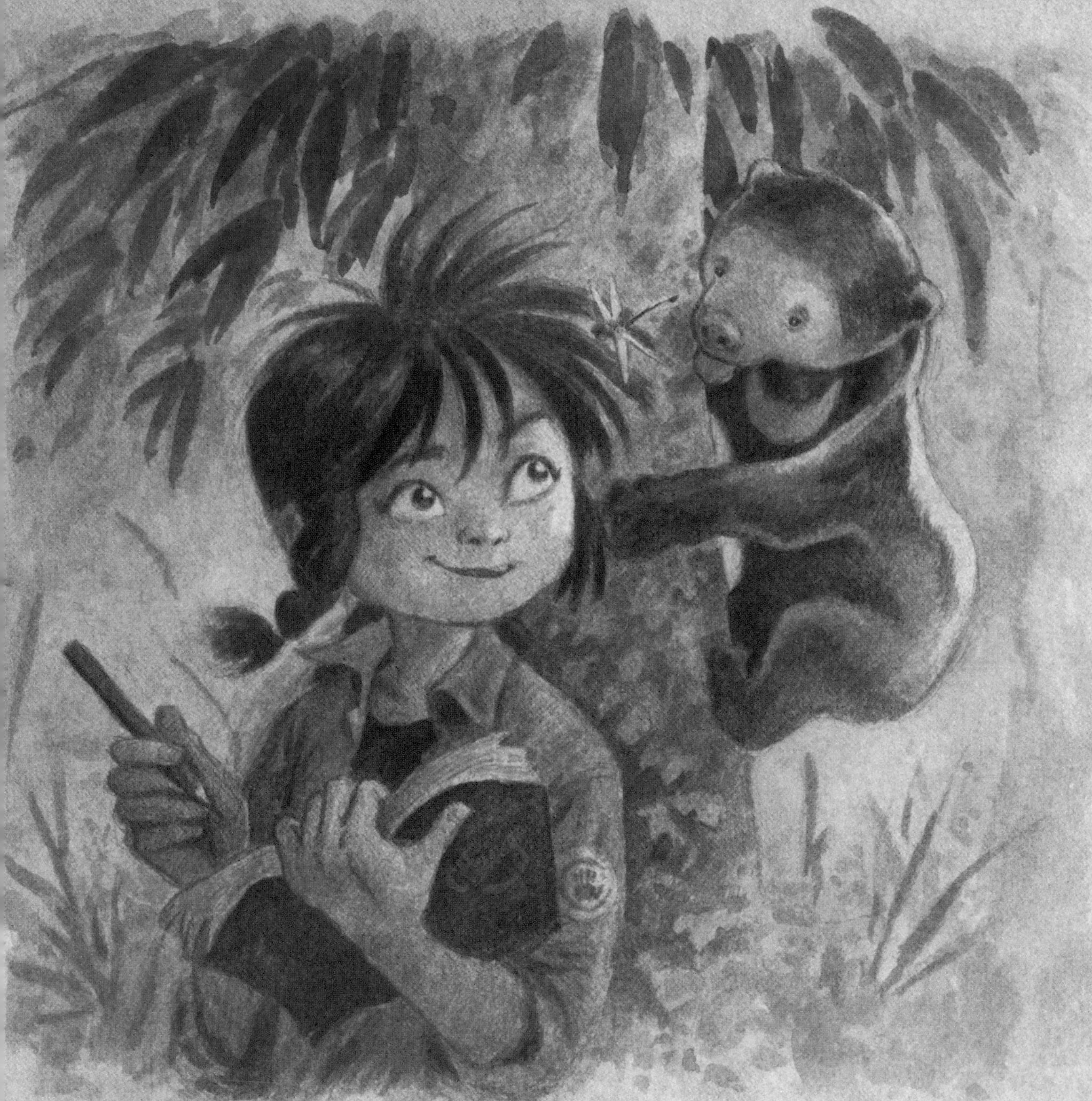

TO DAISY, LINH ĐAN,
AND ALL YOUNG
ANIMAL LOVERS
EVERYWHERE.

HELLO READERS,

MY NAME IS TRANG, AND I AM A VIETNAMESE WILDLIFE CONSERVATIONIST. *SAVING SORYA: CHANG AND THE SUN BEAR* IS THE STORY OF CHANG, A LITTLE GIRL WITH A HUGE DREAM TO PROTECT AND CONSERVE WILD ANIMALS WHO ARE BEING PUSHED TOWARD EXTINCTION BY HUMANS. CHANG WORKS HARD TO FOLLOW HER DREAMS, AND SHE IGNORES PEOPLE WHO SAY WILDLIFE CONSERVATION IS NOT A GOOD CAREER FOR HER.

WHEN CHANG MEETS SORYA, A SMALL AND TIMID SUN BEAR, CHANG DECIDES SHE WILL DO EVERYTHING SHE CAN TO RETURN SORYA TO THE RAINFOREST. THIS IS A STORY INSPIRED BY REAL CHARACTERS AND EVENTS: CHANG IS BASED ON ME. MY LIFE CHANGED WHEN I ACCIDENTALLY WITNESSED A MOON BEAR WHOSE BILE WAS BEING EXTRACTED. AT THAT MOMENT, I DECIDED THERE WAS NOTHING ELSE I WANTED TO DO MORE THAN BECOME A CONSERVATIONIST AND CREATE A BETTER, SAFER WORLD FOR WILD ANIMALS.

SORYA IS A REAL SUN BEAR WHO WAS RESCUED FROM THE ILLEGAL BEAR TRADE BY A WONDERFUL ORGANIZATION IN SOUTHEAST ASIA CALLED FREE THE BEARS. BUT HER JOURNEY IN THIS BOOK IS BASED ON THE STORY OF A MOON BEAR NAMED POLA. POLA WAS RESCUED IN 2008 AND REINTRODUCED TO THE WILD.

IN READING THIS STORY, YOU'LL LEARN MORE ABOUT AN AMAZING CREATURE--THE SUN BEAR--AND ITS IMPORTANT ROLE IN THE FOREST, AS WELL AS THE LIFE-SAVING CONSERVATION WORK THAT'S HAPPENING TO PROTECT THESE ANIMALS AND THEIR HOMES. I HOPE THIS STORY GIVES YOU THE ENCOURAGEMENT AND INSPIRATION TO FOLLOW YOUR OWN DREAMS, WHATEVER THEY MAY BE, AND TO NEVER GIVE UP.

TRANG

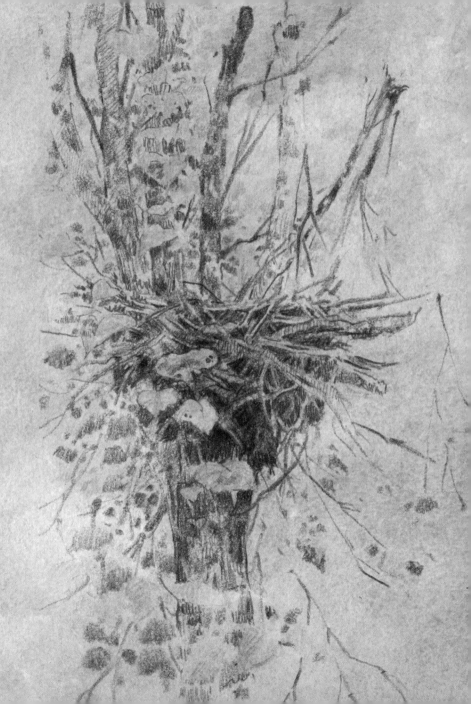

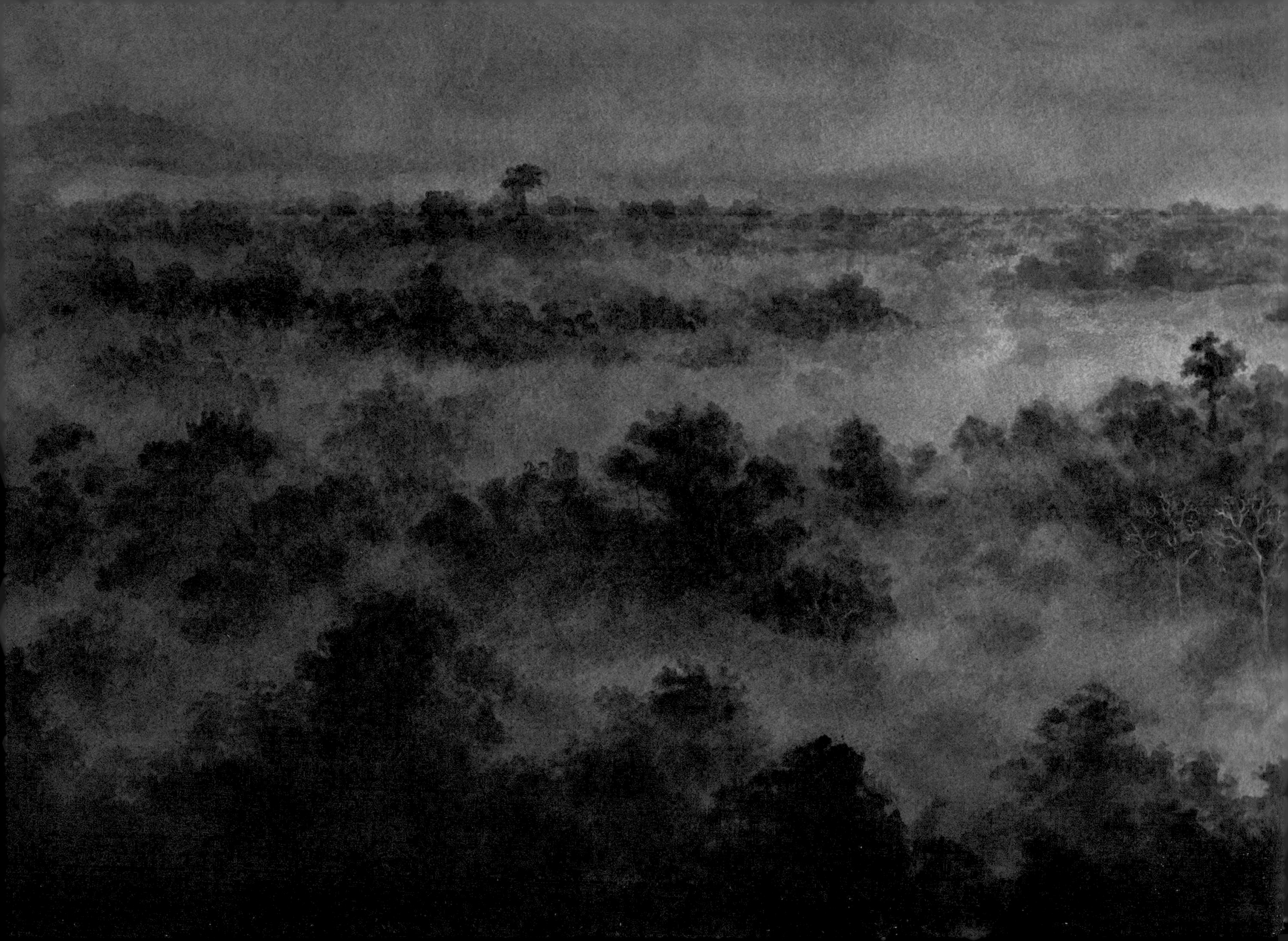

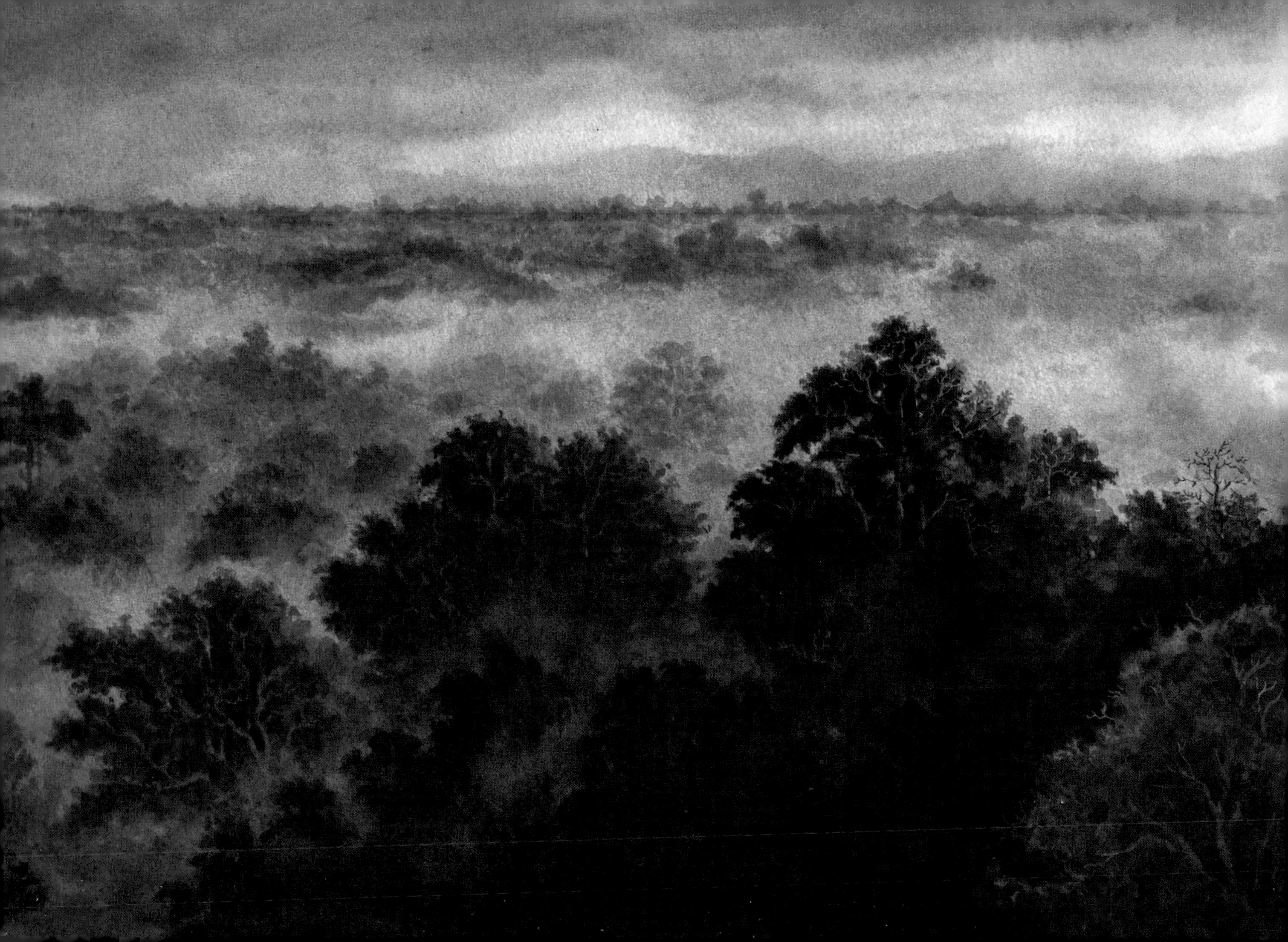

CHAPTER ONE

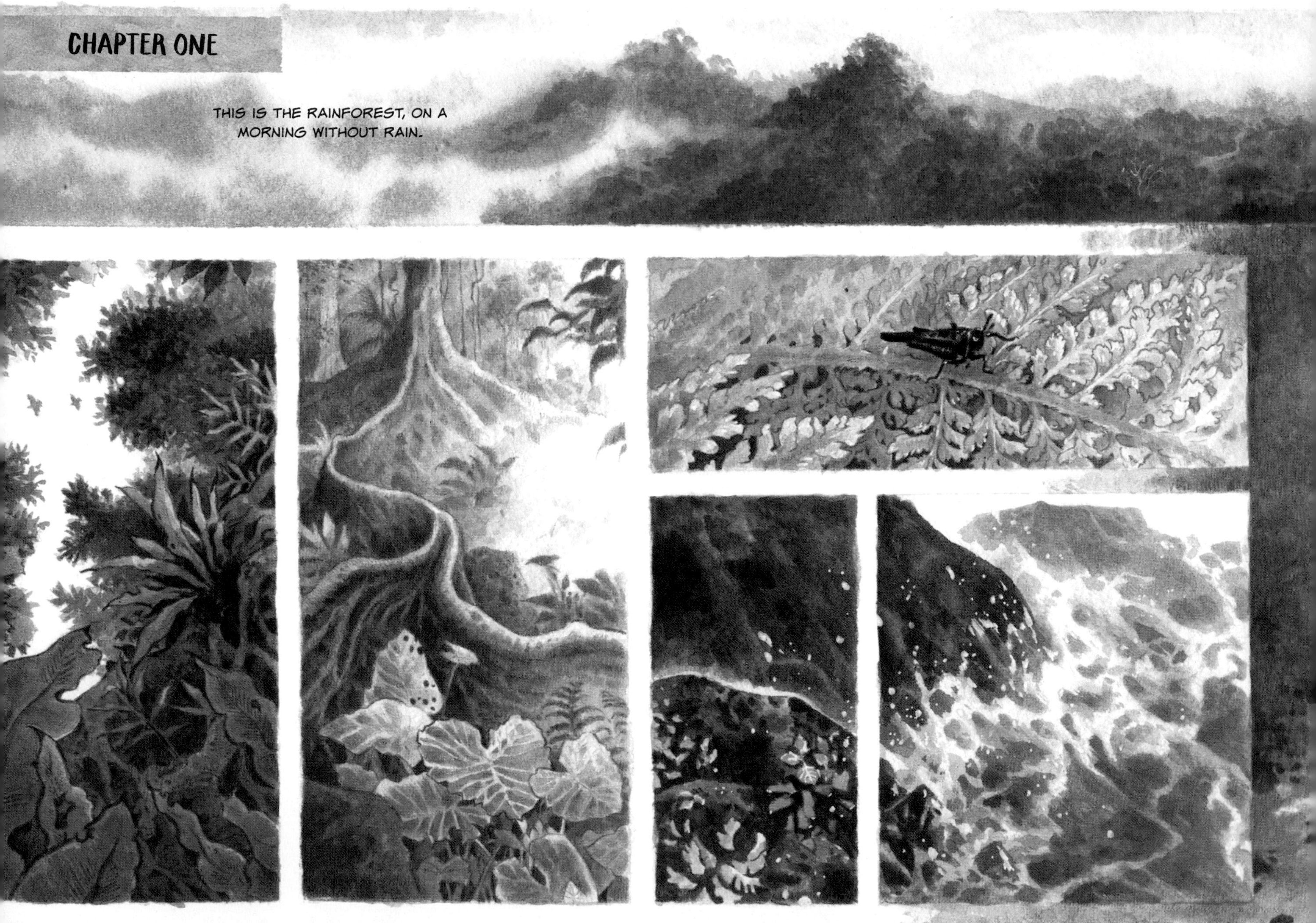
THIS IS THE RAINFOREST, ON A MORNING WITHOUT RAIN.

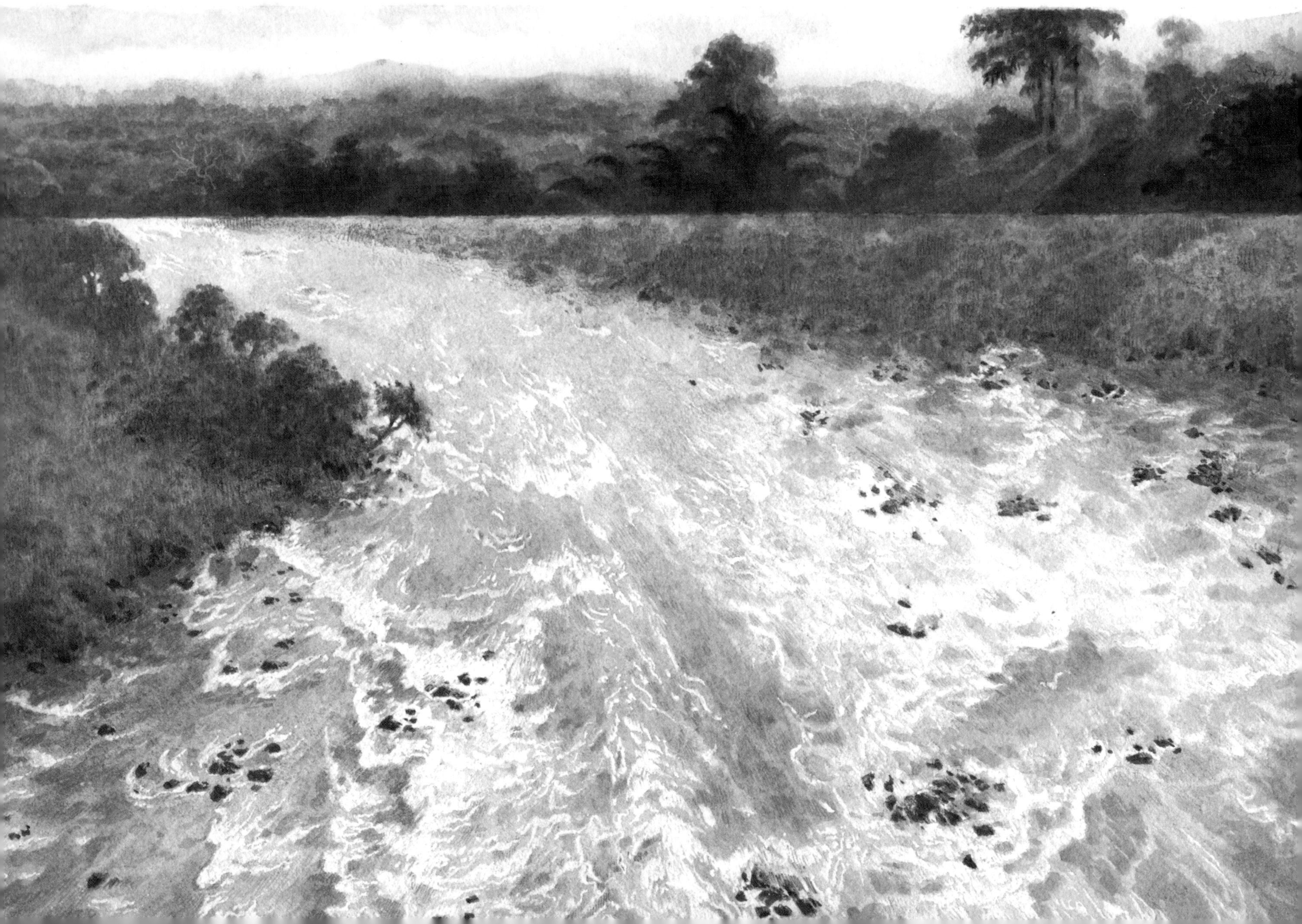

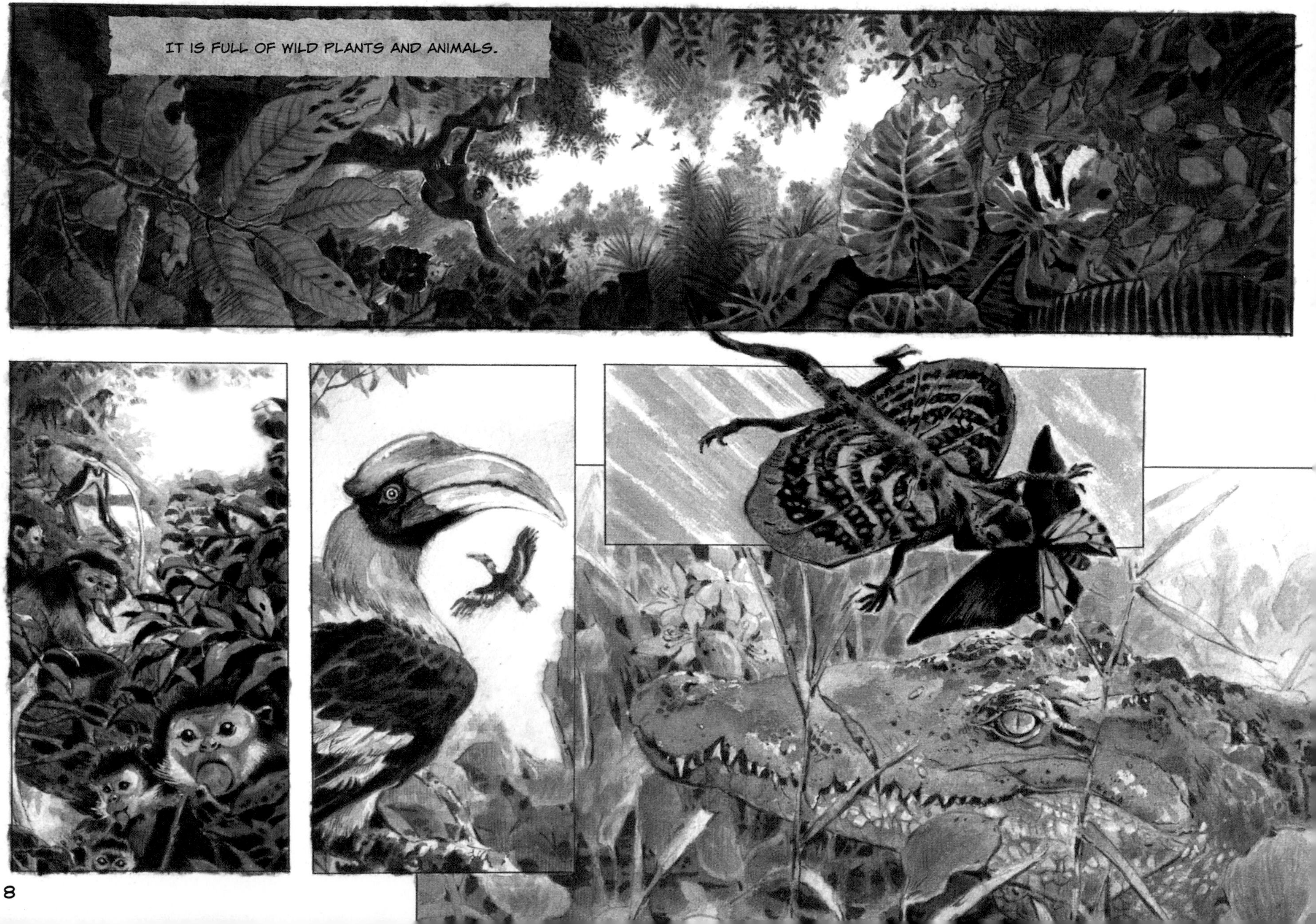
IT IS FULL OF WILD PLANTS AND ANIMALS.

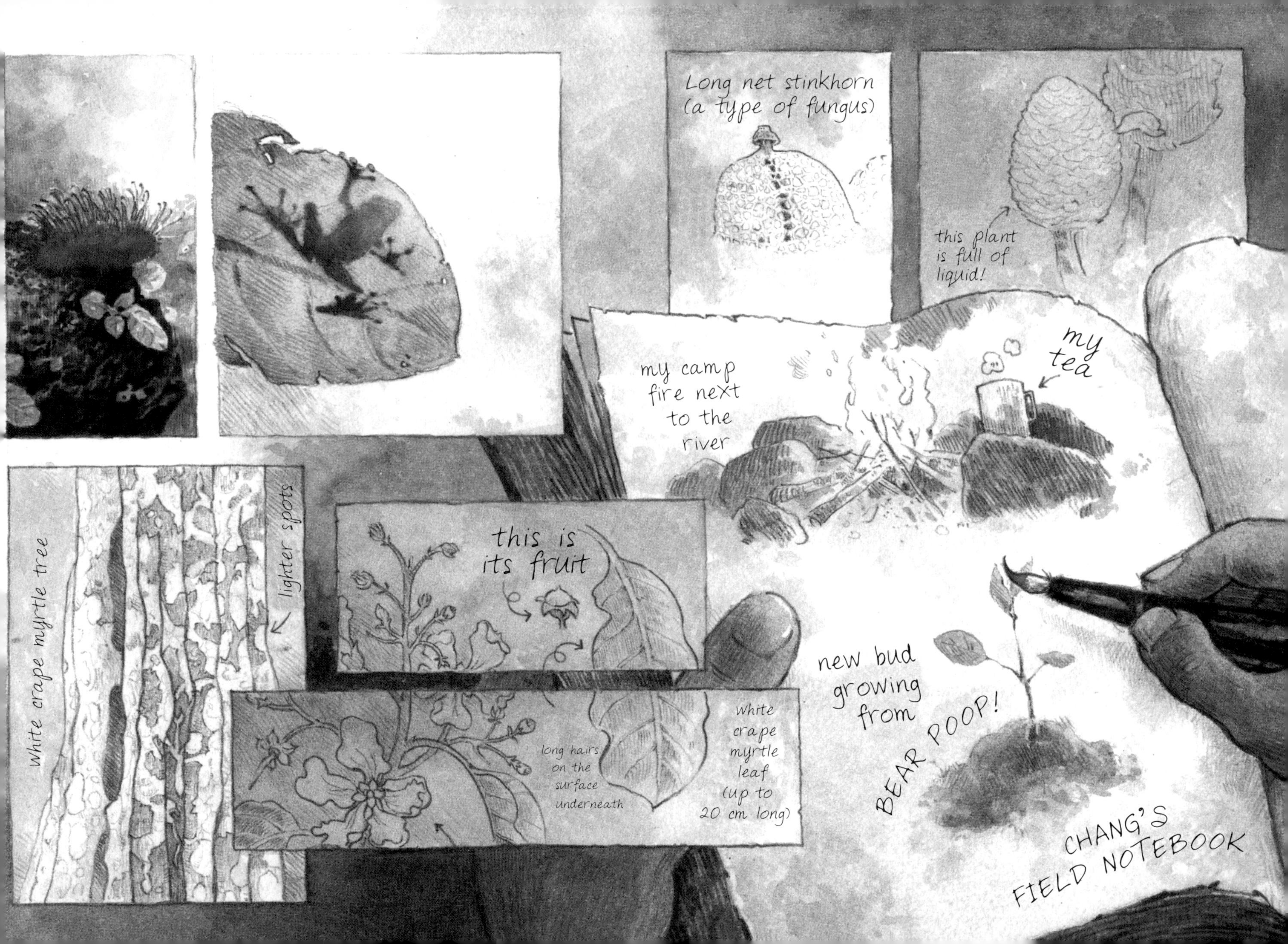
Long net stinkhorn
(a type of fungus)
this plant
is full of
liquid!
my camp
fire next
to the
river
my
tea
white crape myrtle tree
lighter spots
this is
its fruit
new bud
growing
from
BEAR POOP!
long hairs
on the
surface
underneath
White
crape
myrtle
leaf
(up to
20 cm long)
CHANG'S
FIELD NOTEBOOK

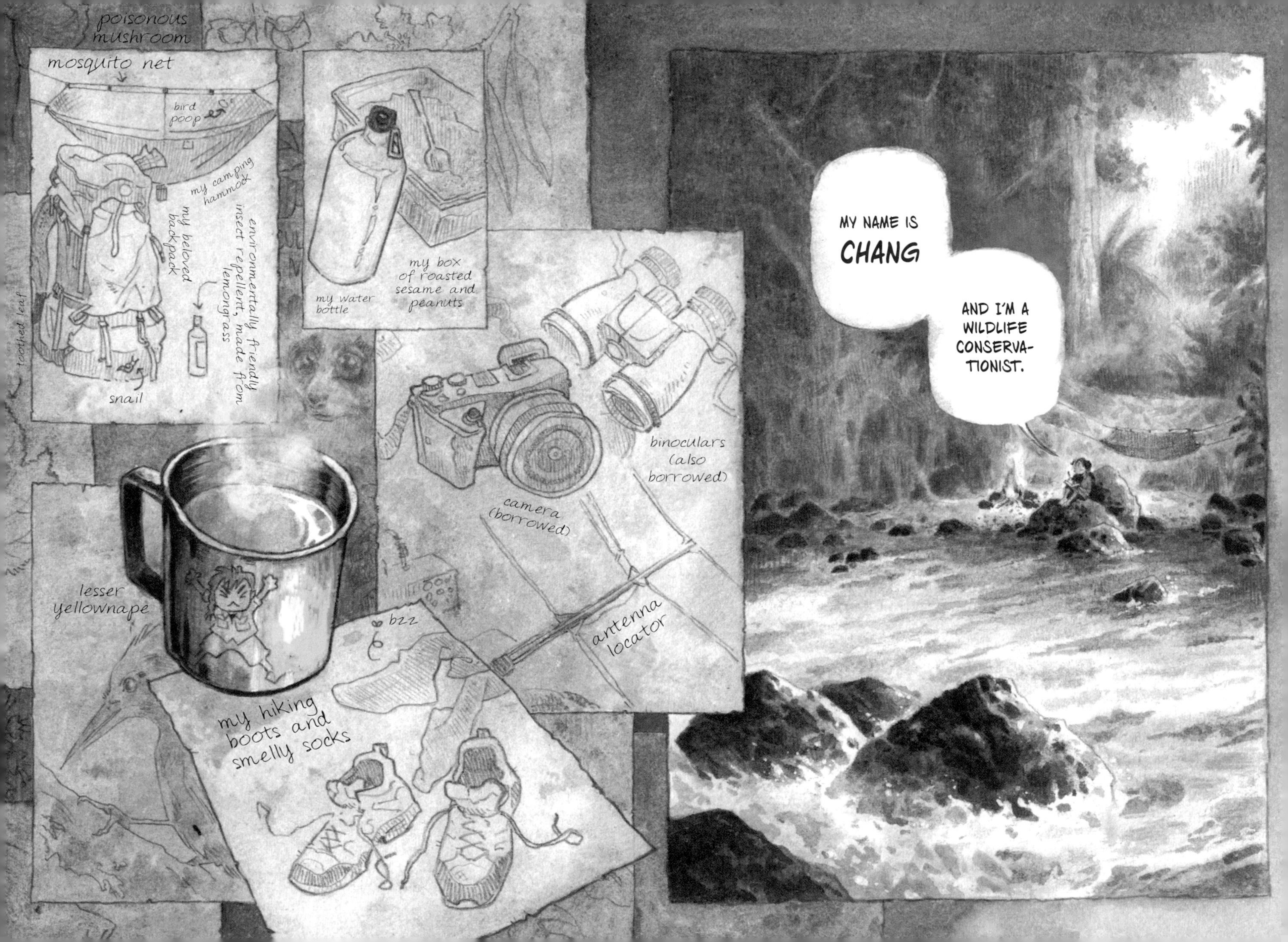
poisonous mushroom
mosquito net
bird poop
my camping hammock
my beloved backpack
environmentally friendly insect repellent, made from lemongrass
snail
toothed leaf
my water bottle
my box of roasted sesame and peanuts
binoculars (also borrowed)
camera (borrowed)
antenna locator
lesser yellownape
bzz
my hiking boots and smelly socks
MY NAME IS CHANG
AND I'M A WILDLIFE CONSERVATIONIST.

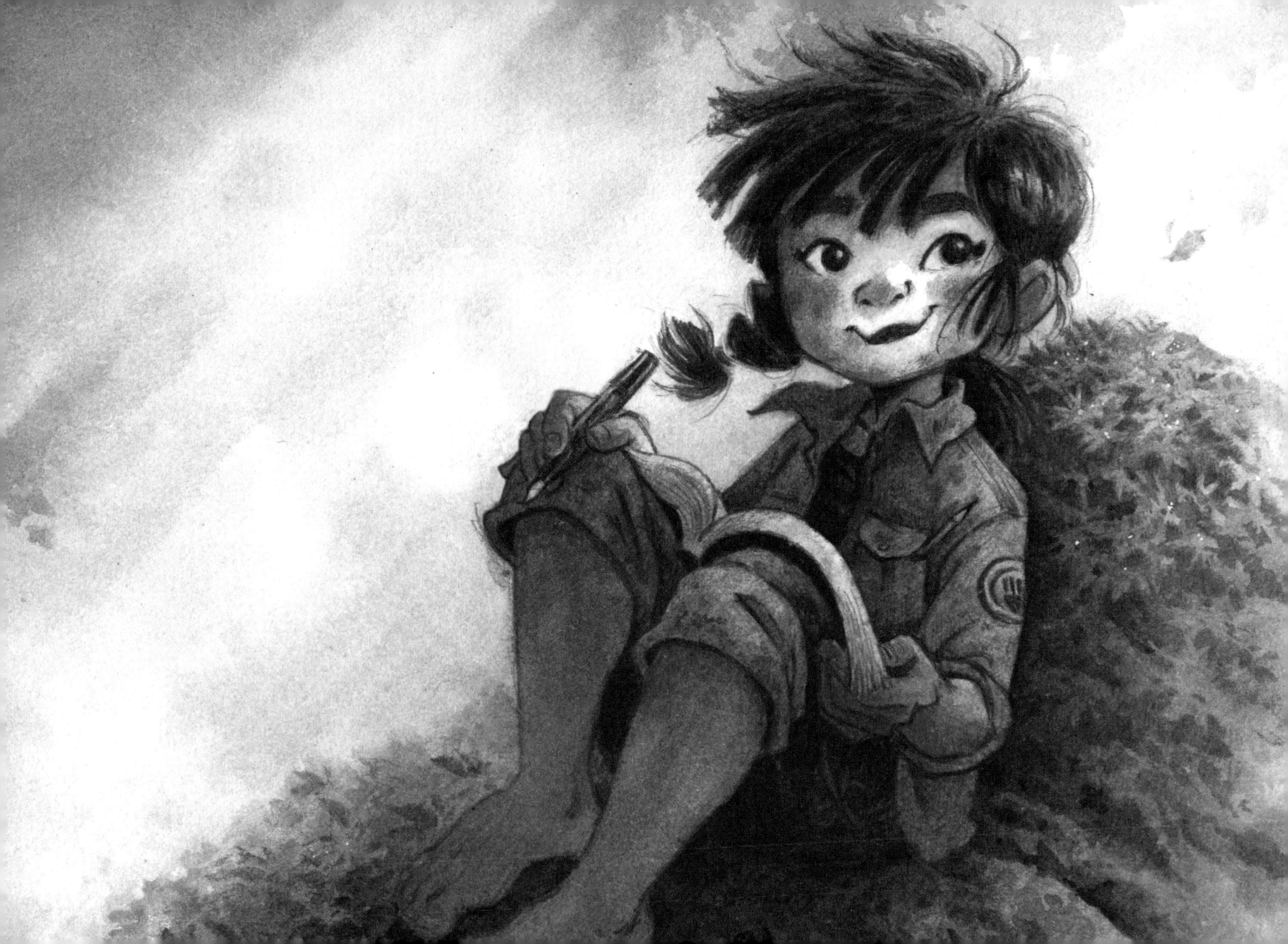

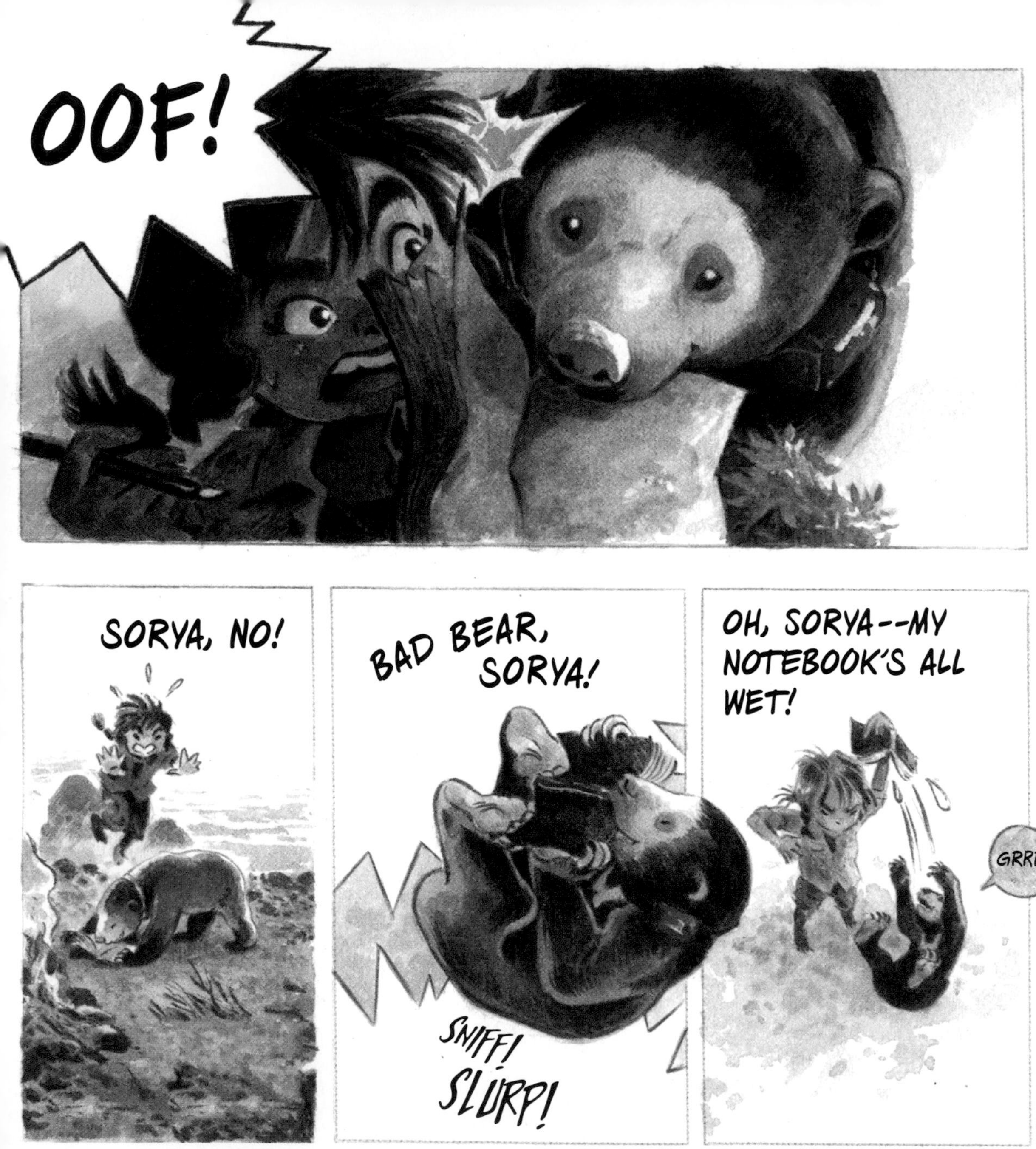
OOF!
SORYA, NO!
BAD BEAR, SORYA!
SNIFF! SLURP!
OH, SORYA--MY NOTEBOOK'S ALL WET!
GRRR

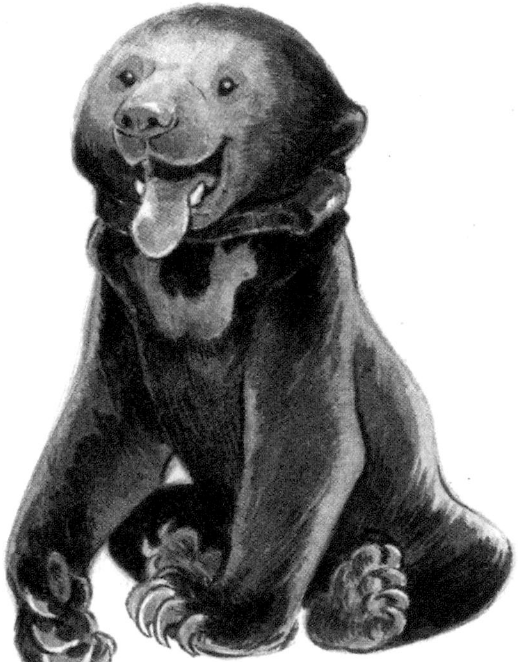

THIS IS SORYA, A LOVELY LITTLE SUN BEAR.

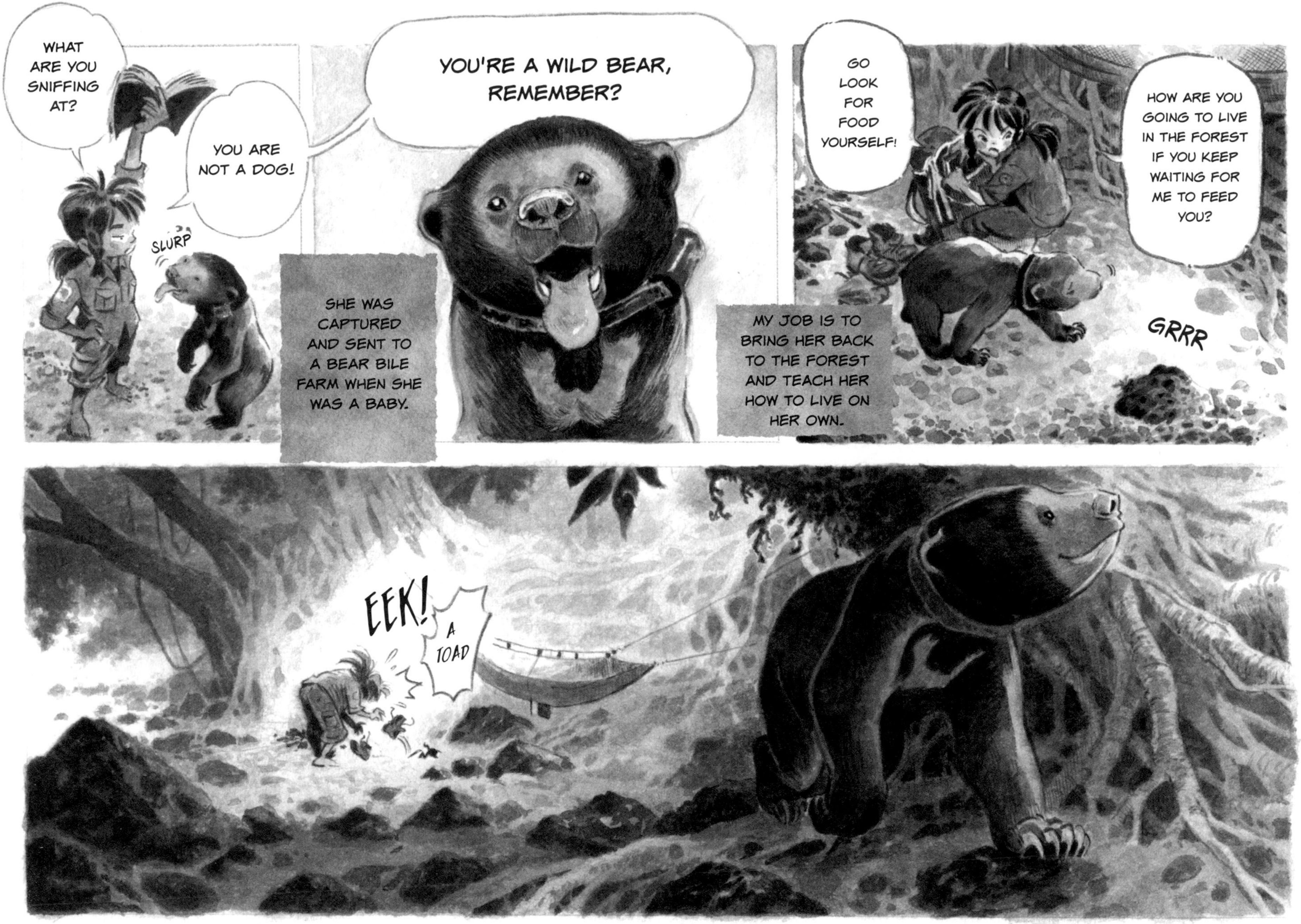
WHAT ARE YOU SNIFFING AT?
YOU ARE NOT A DOG!
SLURP
YOU'RE A WILD BEAR, REMEMBER?
SHE WAS CAPTURED AND SENT TO A BEAR BILE FARM WHEN SHE WAS A BABY.
GO LOOK FOR FOOD YOURSELF!
HOW ARE YOU GOING TO LIVE IN THE FOREST IF YOU KEEP WAITING FOR ME TO FEED YOU?
MY JOB IS TO BRING HER BACK TO THE FOREST AND TEACH HER HOW TO LIVE ON HER OWN.
GRRR
EEK!
A TOAD

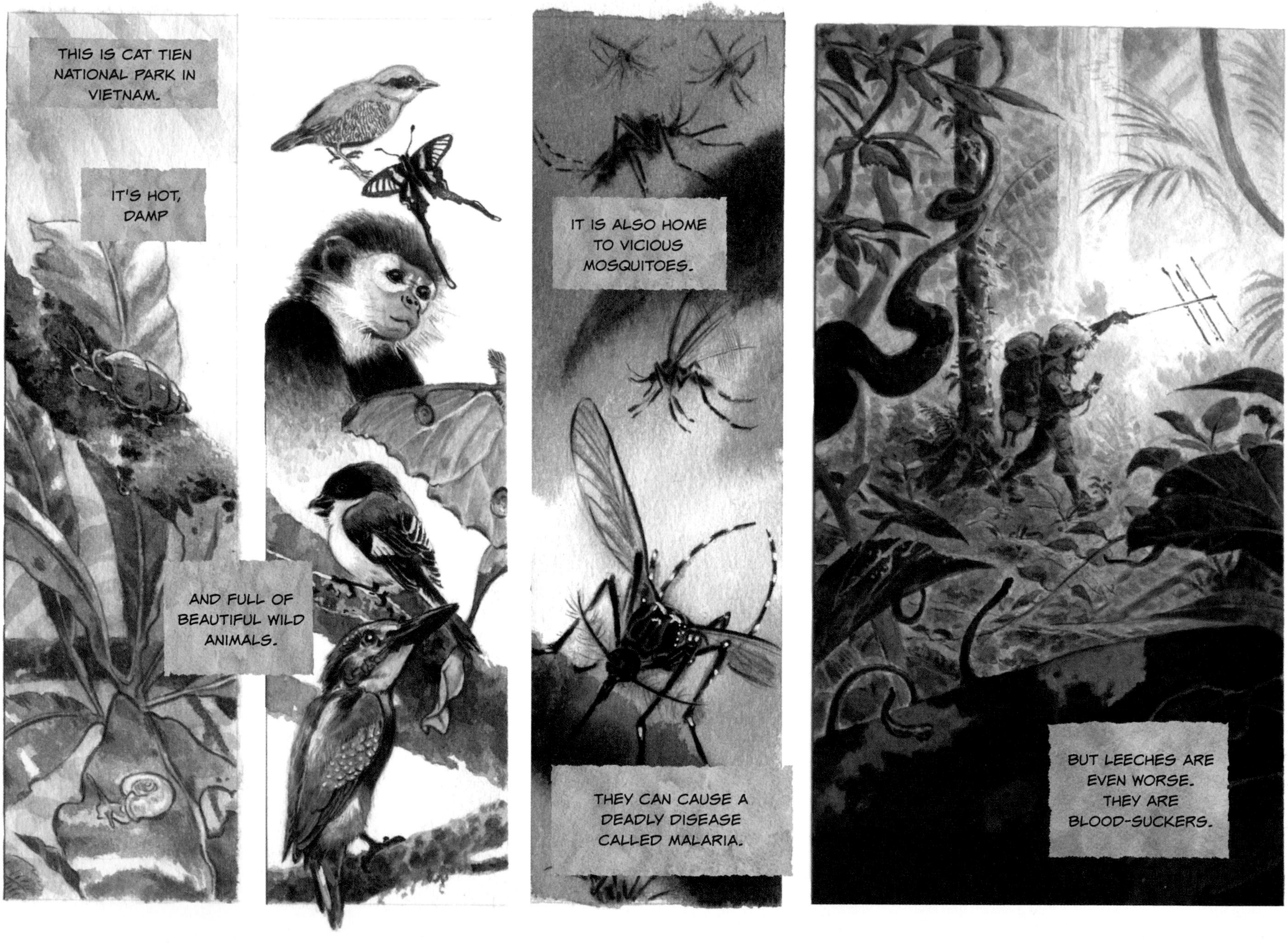
THIS IS CAT TIEN NATIONAL PARK IN VIETNAM.
IT'S HOT, DAMP
AND FULL OF BEAUTIFUL WILD ANIMALS.
IT IS ALSO HOME TO VICIOUS MOSQUITOES.
THEY CAN CAUSE A DEADLY DISEASE CALLED MALARIA.
BUT LEECHES ARE EVEN WORSE. THEY ARE BLOOD-SUCKERS.

LEECHES CRAWL...

EVERY-WHERE!

My natural insect repellent scares the mosquitoes and leeches off.

organic lime and lemongrass

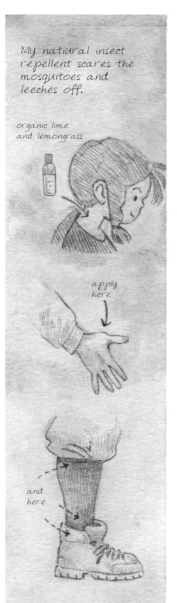

apply here

and here

I ALSO USE A STICK TO FLICK THE LEECHES AWAY.

FLICK...

CRACK!

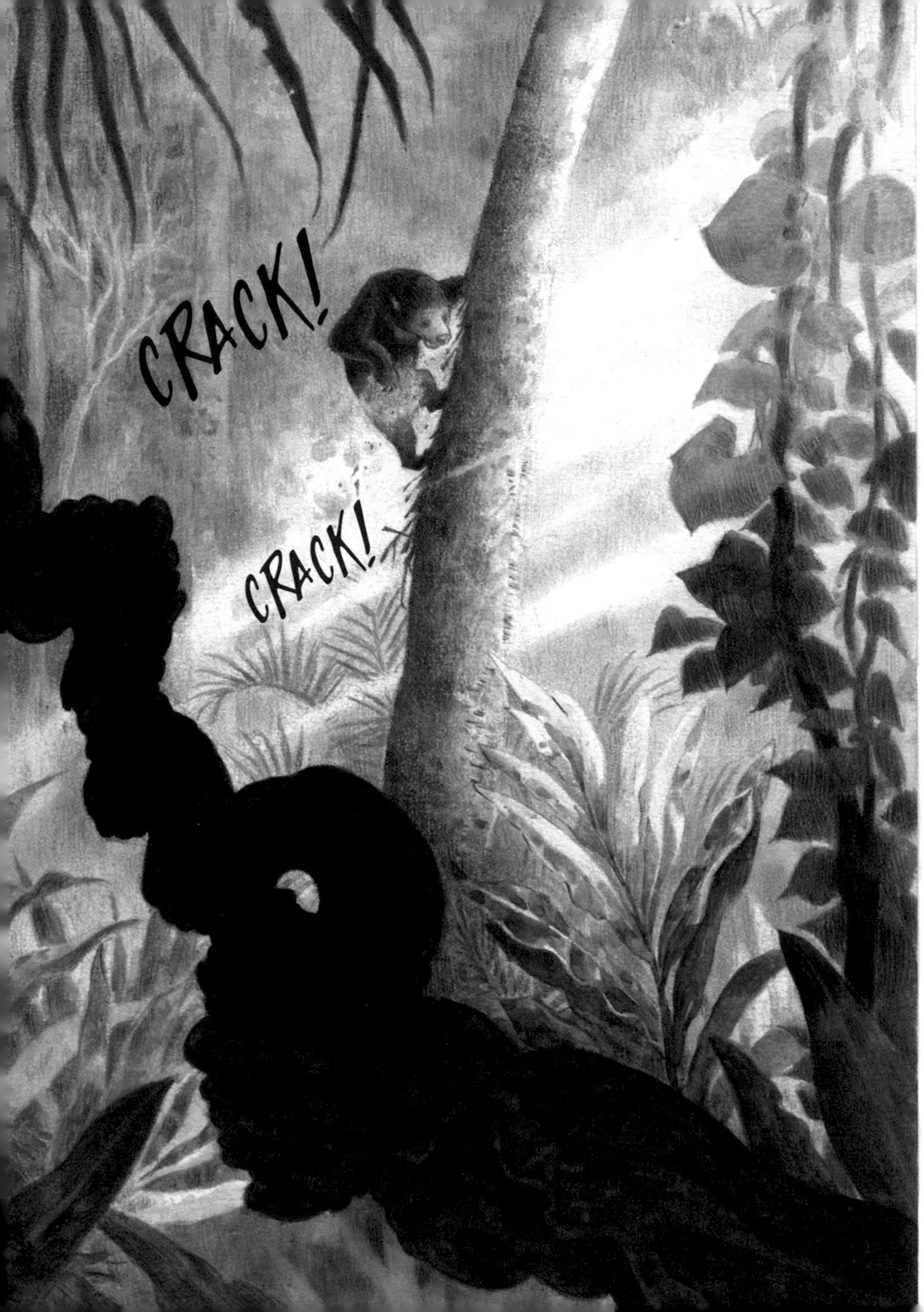
CRACK!
CRACK!

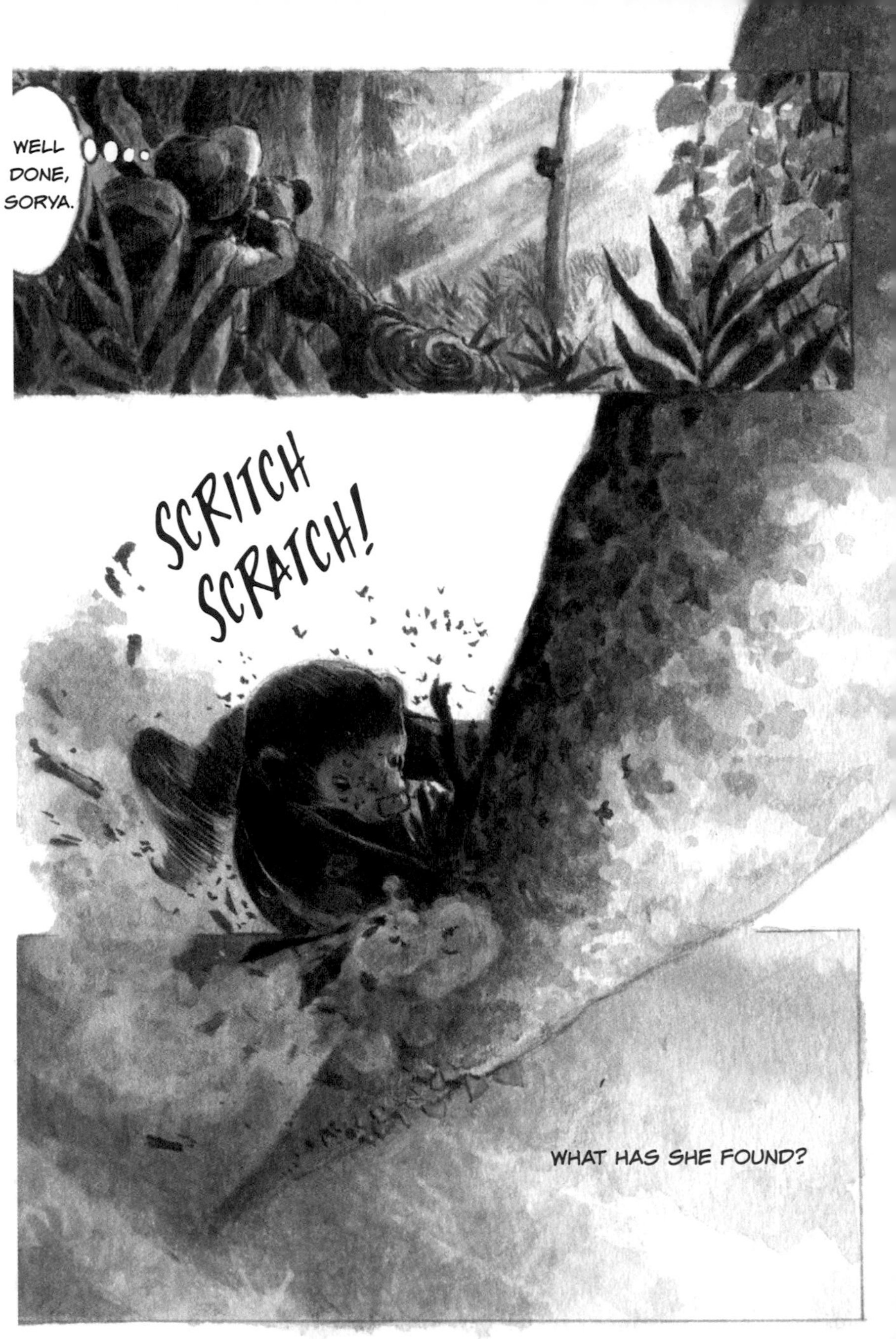
WELL DONE, SORYA.
SCRITCH SCRATCH!
WHAT HAS SHE FOUND?

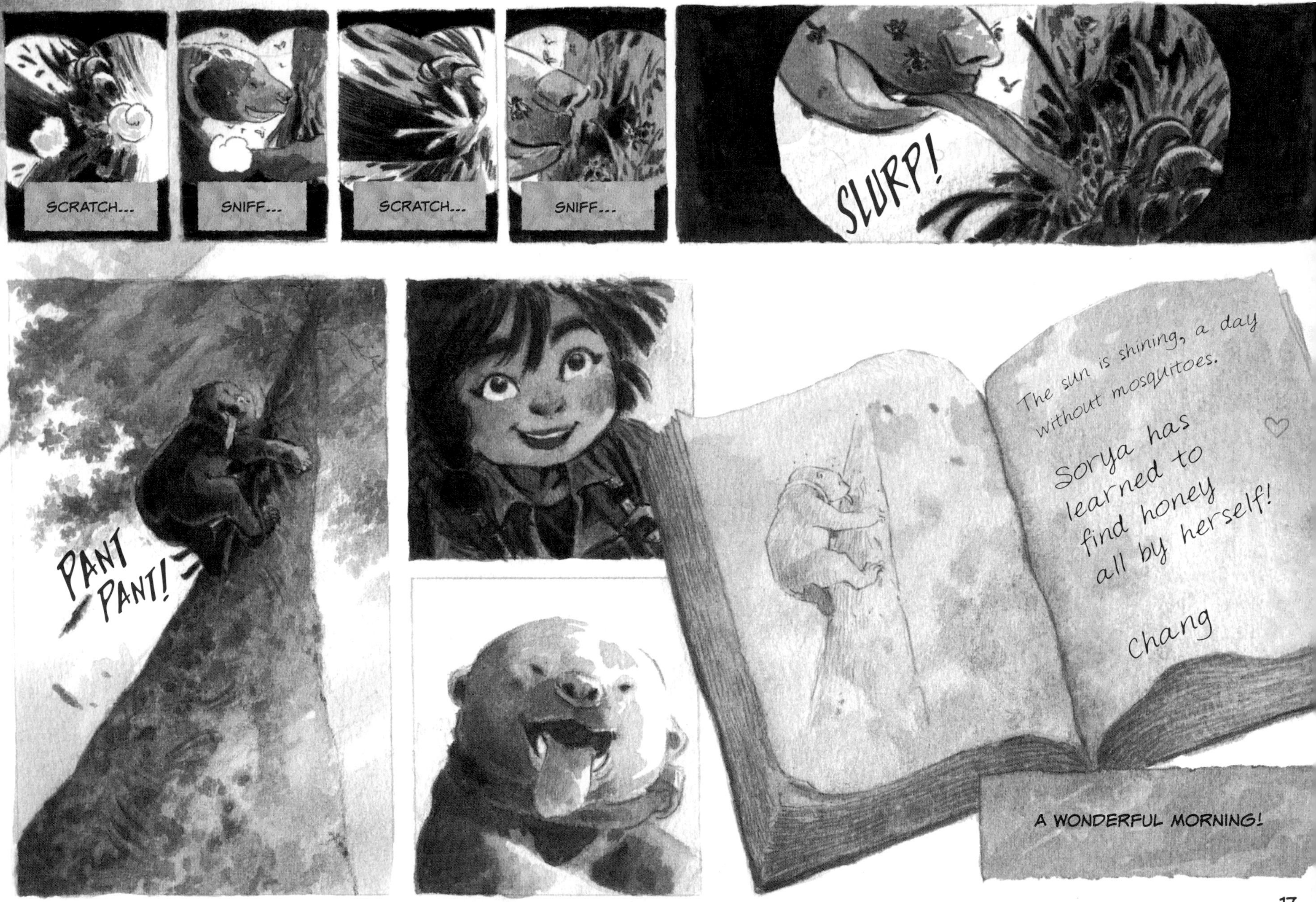

SCRATCH...
SNIFF...
SCRATCH...
SNIFF...
SLURP!
PANT PANT!
The sun is shining, a day without mosquitoes.
Sorya has learned to find honey all by herself!
Chang
A WONDERFUL MORNING!

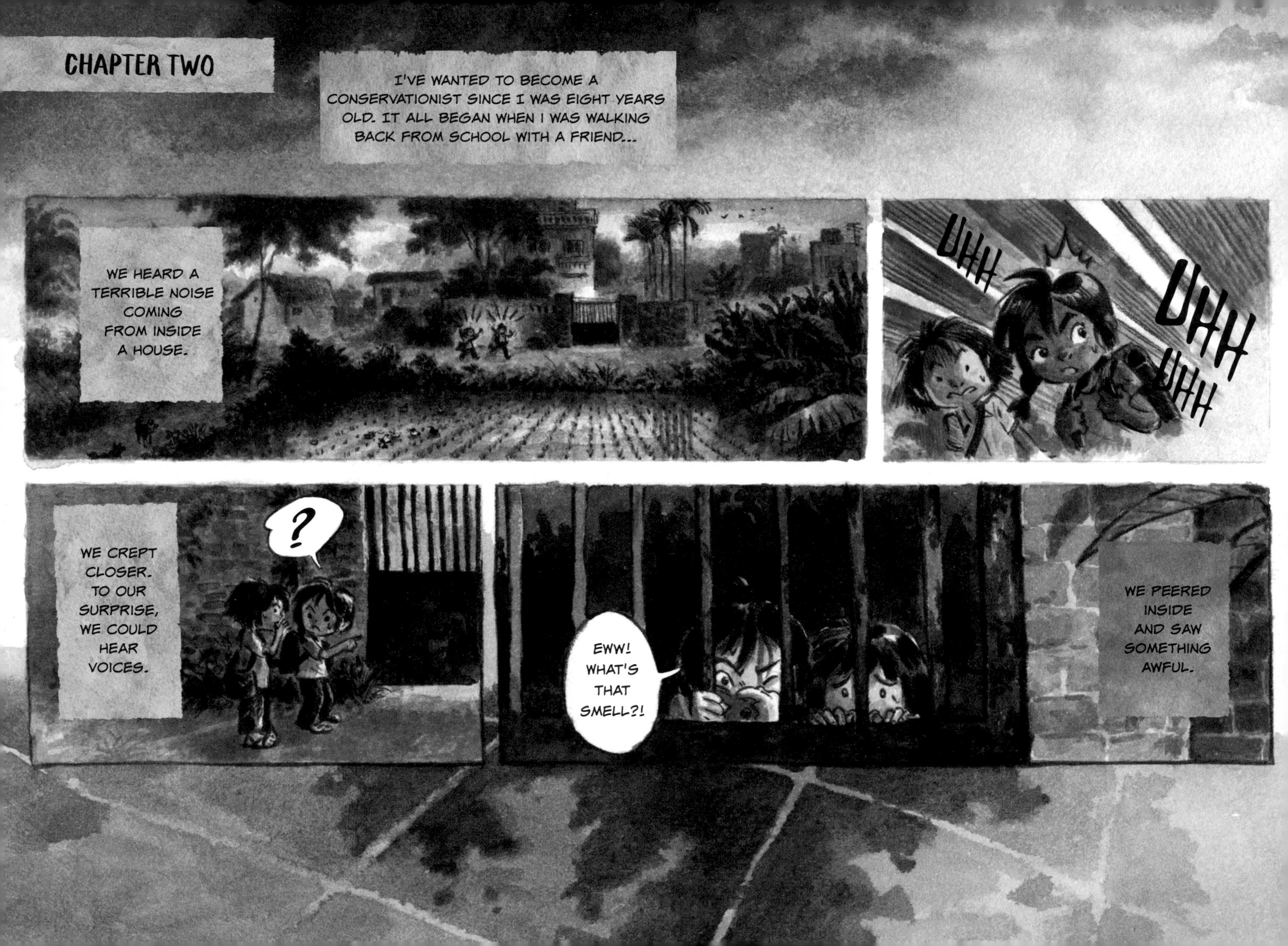
CHAPTER TWO
I'VE WANTED TO BECOME A CONSERVATIONIST SINCE I WAS EIGHT YEARS OLD. IT ALL BEGAN WHEN I WAS WALKING BACK FROM SCHOOL WITH A FRIEND...
WE HEARD A TERRIBLE NOISE COMING FROM INSIDE A HOUSE.
UHH
UHH
UHH
WE CREPT CLOSER. TO OUR SURPRISE, WE COULD HEAR VOICES.
?
EWW! WHAT'S THAT SMELL?!
WE PEERED INSIDE AND SAW SOMETHING AWFUL.

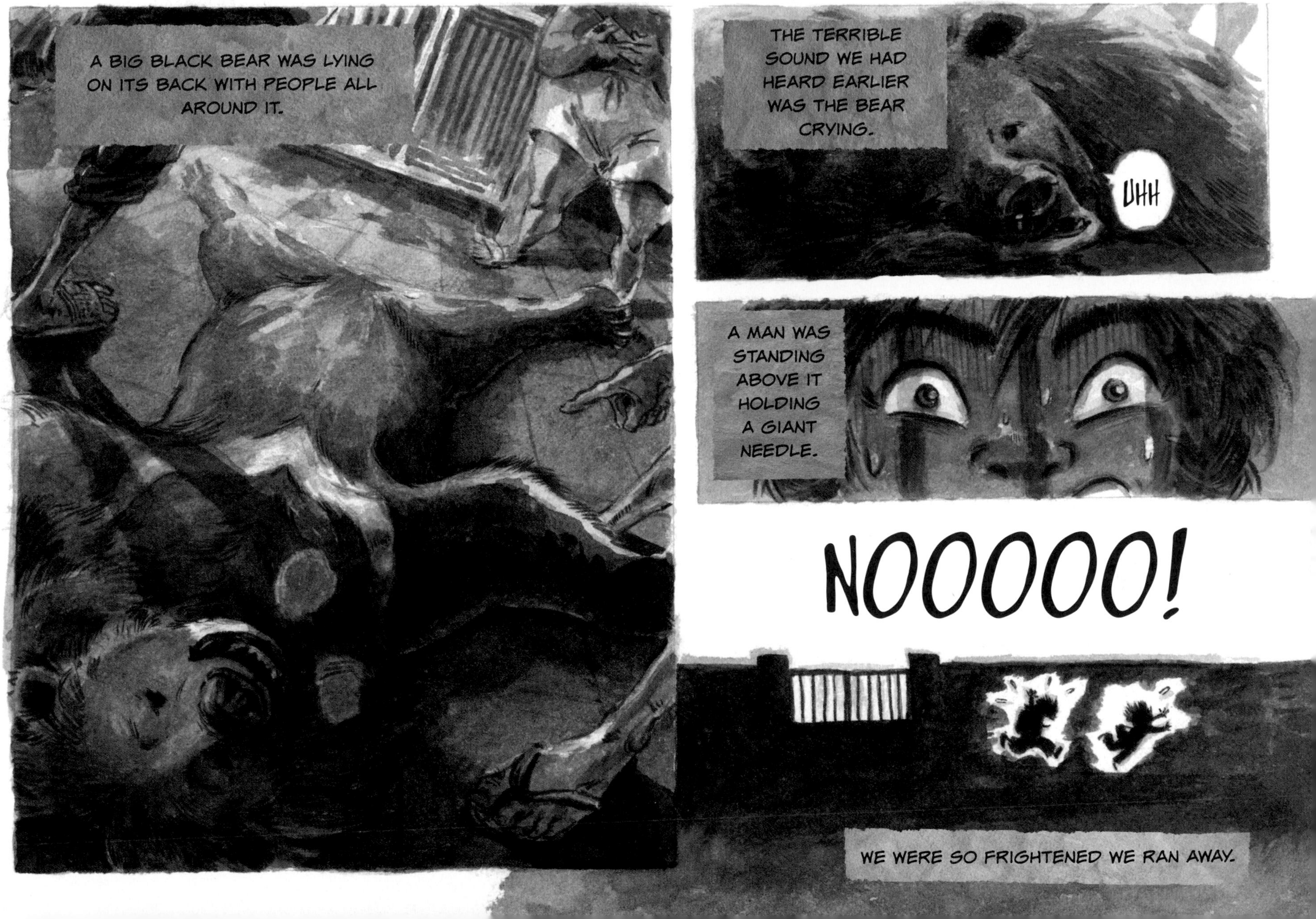
A BIG BLACK BEAR WAS LYING ON ITS BACK WITH PEOPLE ALL AROUND IT.
THE TERRIBLE SOUND WE HAD HEARD EARLIER WAS THE BEAR CRYING.
UHH
A MAN WAS STANDING ABOVE IT HOLDING A GIANT NEEDLE.
NOOOOO!
WE WERE SO FRIGHTENED WE RAN AWAY.

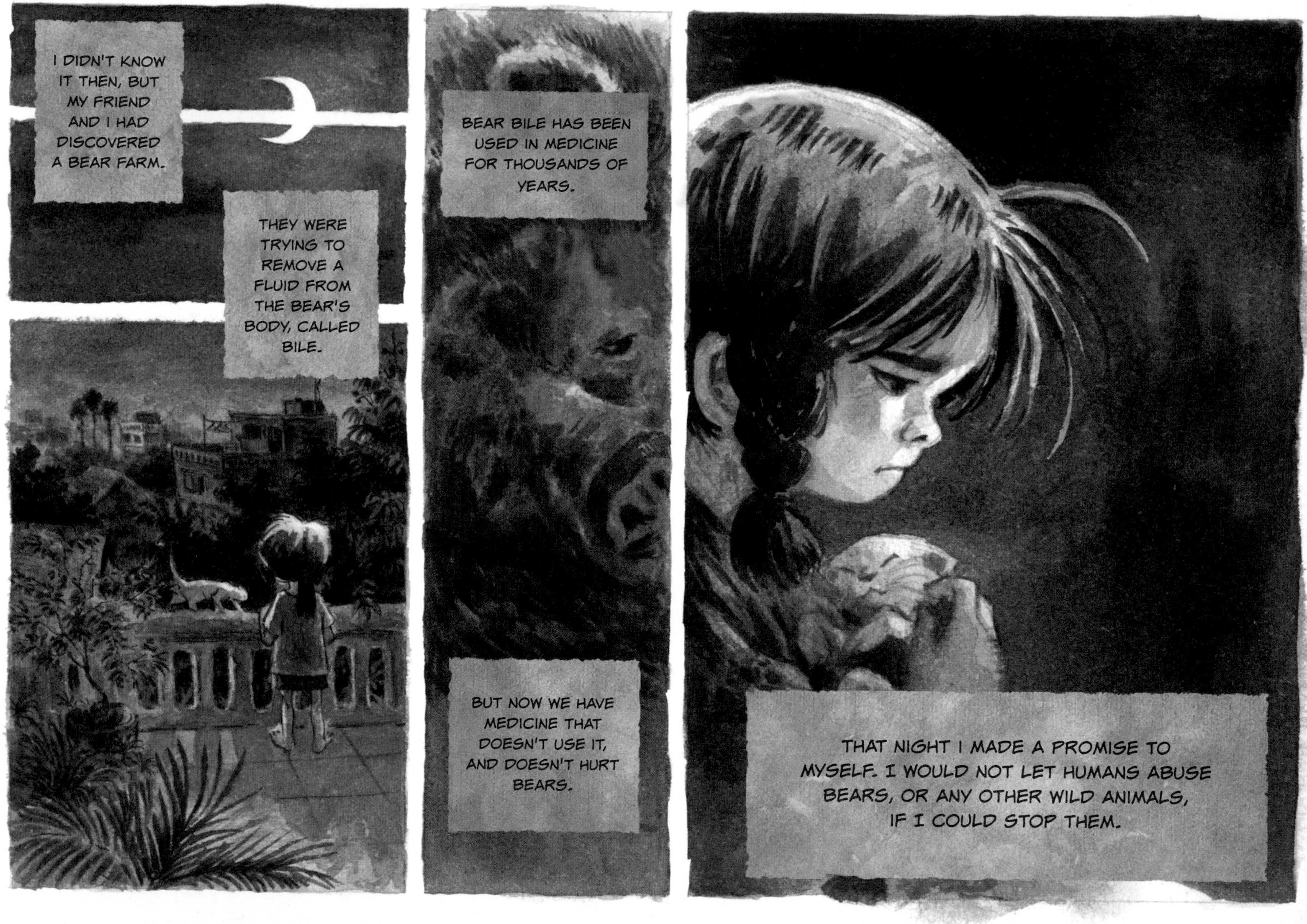
I DIDN'T KNOW IT THEN, BUT MY FRIEND AND I HAD DISCOVERED A BEAR FARM.
THEY WERE TRYING TO REMOVE A FLUID FROM THE BEAR'S BODY, CALLED BILE.
BEAR BILE HAS BEEN USED IN MEDICINE FOR THOUSANDS OF YEARS.
BUT NOW WE HAVE MEDICINE THAT DOESN'T USE IT, AND DOESN'T HURT BEARS.
THAT NIGHT I MADE A PROMISE TO MYSELF. I WOULD NOT LET HUMANS ABUSE BEARS, OR ANY OTHER WILD ANIMALS, IF I COULD STOP THEM.

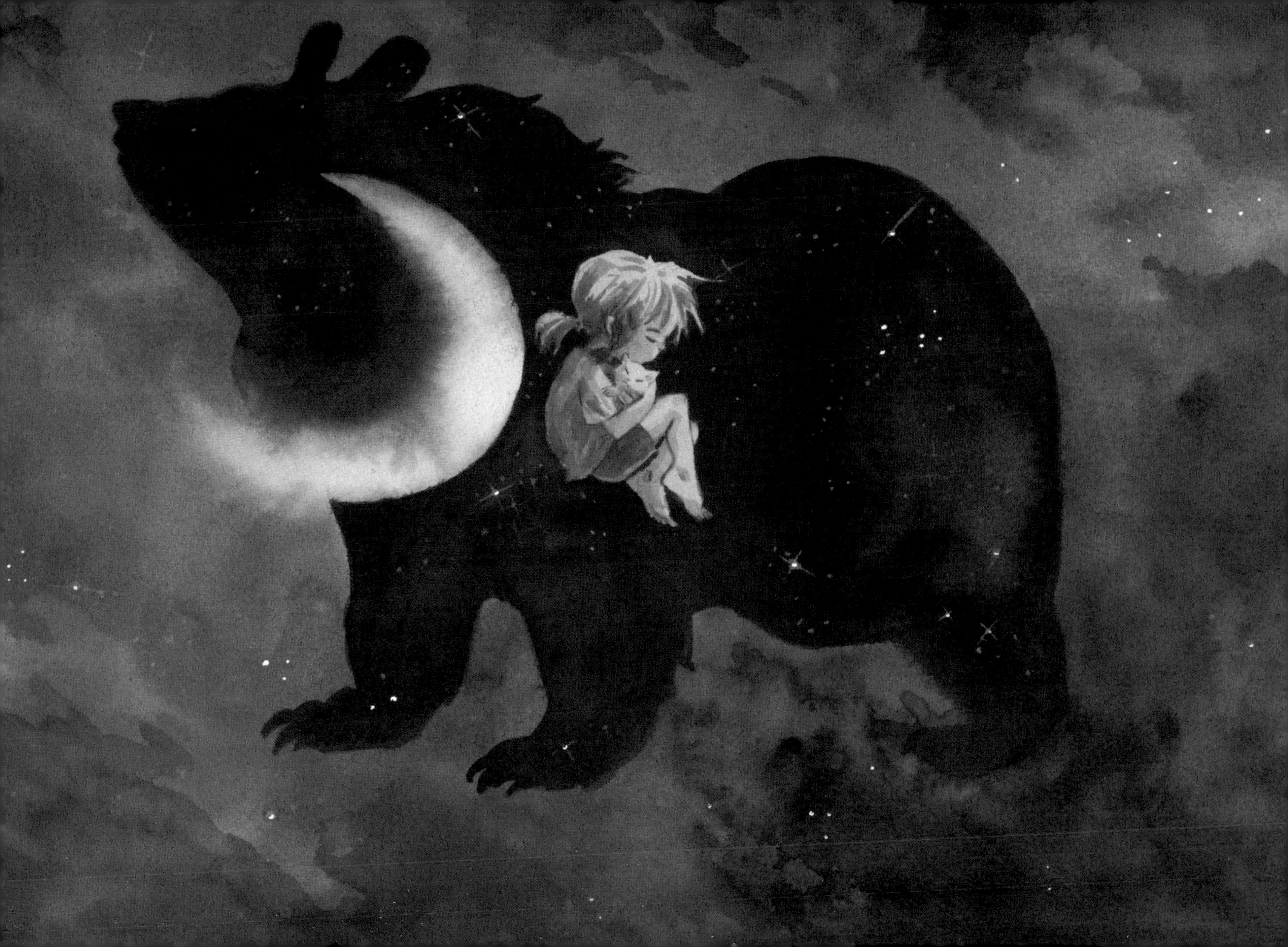

SO, THE VERY NEXT DAY,
I DECIDED TO BECOME A
WILDLIFE CONSERVATIONIST.

I HAD HEARD
ABOUT
WILDLIFE
CONSERVATIONISTS
ON TV.
THEY ARE
PEOPLE WHO
PROTECT NATURE ALL
OVER THE WORLD--
IN DESERTS, NEAR
OCEANS, AND EVEN
INSIDE CAVES.

THAT'S WHEN I
REALIZED:
I COULD
PROTECT THE
RAINFOREST
NEAR MY HOME!

NOTHING'S
GOING TO
STOP ME!

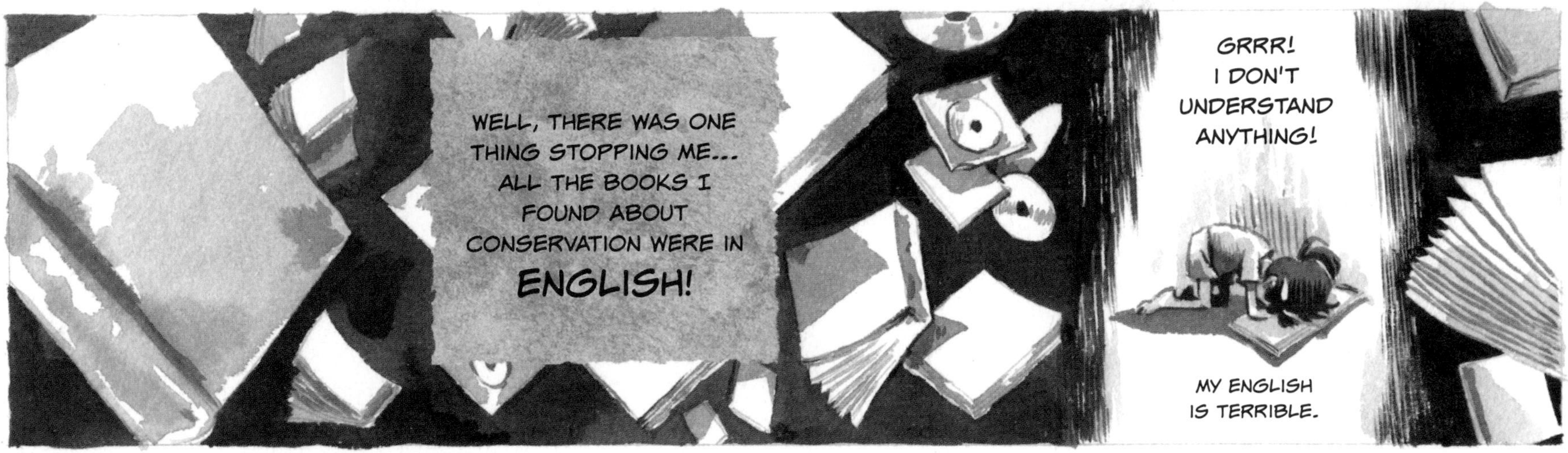
WELL, THERE WAS ONE THING STOPPING ME... ALL THE BOOKS I FOUND ABOUT CONSERVATION WERE IN ENGLISH!
GRRR! I DON'T UNDERSTAND ANYTHING!
MY ENGLISH IS TERRIBLE.

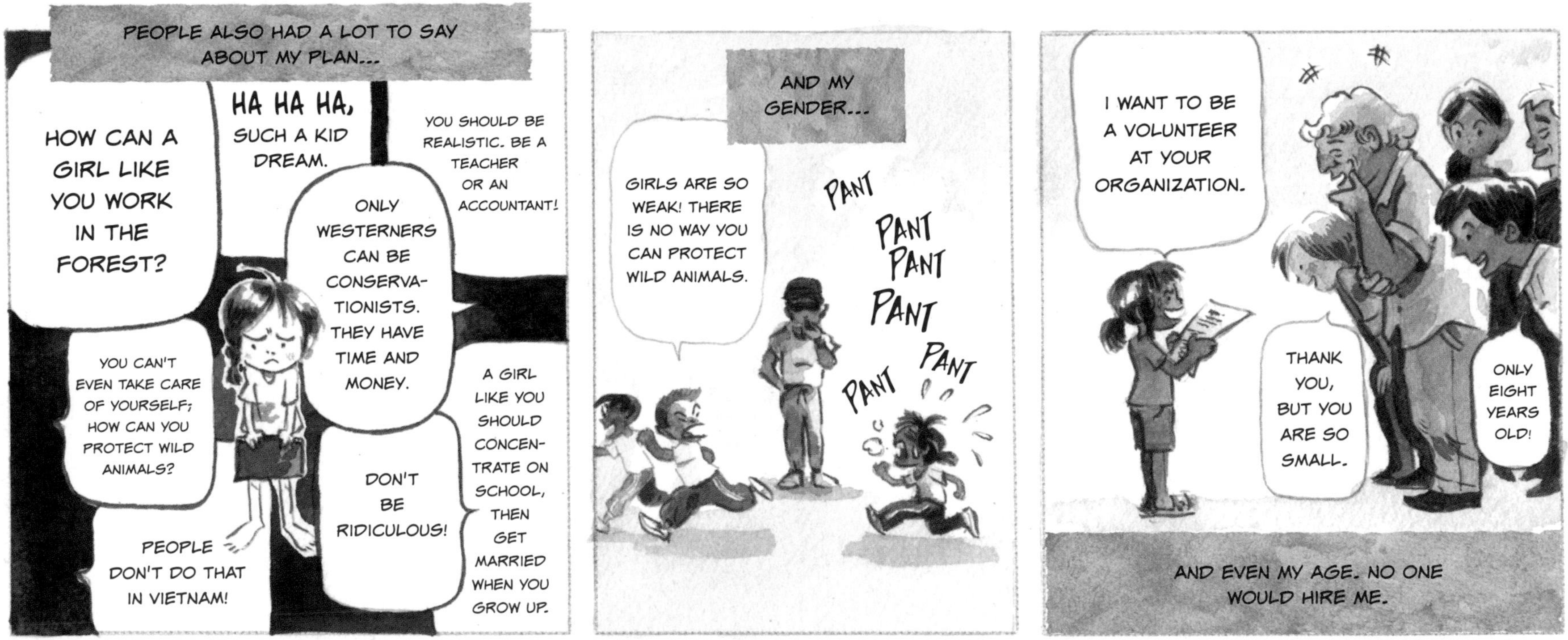
PEOPLE ALSO HAD A LOT TO SAY ABOUT MY PLAN...
HOW CAN A GIRL LIKE YOU WORK IN THE FOREST?
HA HA HA, SUCH A KID DREAM.
YOU SHOULD BE REALISTIC. BE A TEACHER OR AN ACCOUNTANT!
ONLY WESTERNERS CAN BE CONSERVA-TIONISTS. THEY HAVE TIME AND MONEY.
YOU CAN'T EVEN TAKE CARE OF YOURSELF; HOW CAN YOU PROTECT WILD ANIMALS?
A GIRL LIKE YOU SHOULD CONCEN-TRATE ON SCHOOL, THEN GET MARRIED WHEN YOU GROW UP.
DON'T BE RIDICULOUS!
PEOPLE DON'T DO THAT IN VIETNAM!
AND MY GENDER...
GIRLS ARE SO WEAK! THERE IS NO WAY YOU CAN PROTECT WILD ANIMALS.
PANT PANT PANT PANT PANT PANT
I WANT TO BE A VOLUNTEER AT YOUR ORGANIZATION.
THANK YOU, BUT YOU ARE SO SMALL.
ONLY EIGHT YEARS OLD!
AND EVEN MY AGE. NO ONE WOULD HIRE ME.

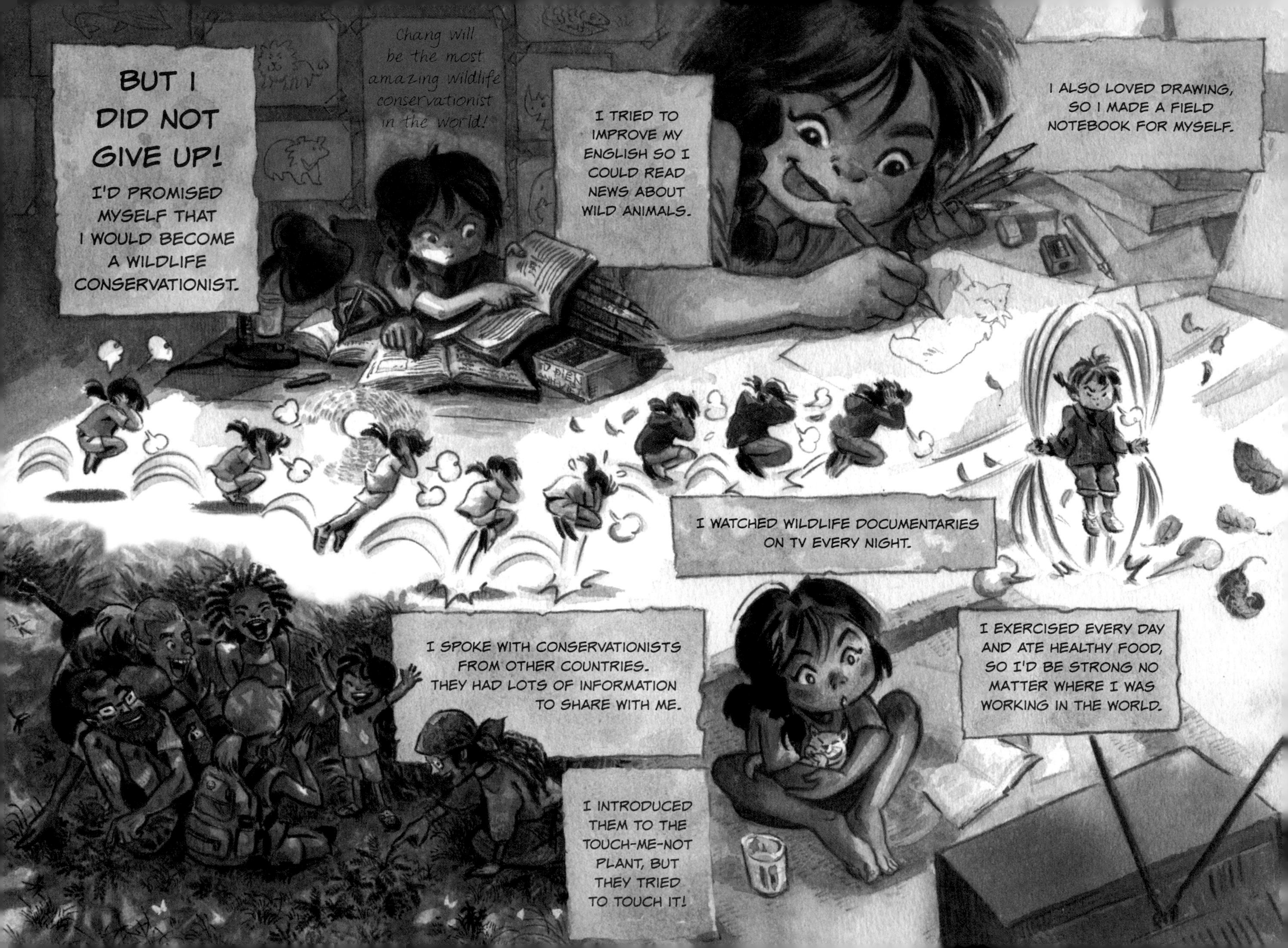
BUT I DID NOT GIVE UP!
I'D PROMISED MYSELF THAT I WOULD BECOME A WILDLIFE CONSERVATIONIST.
Chang will be the most amazing wildlife conservationist in the world!
I TRIED TO IMPROVE MY ENGLISH SO I COULD READ NEWS ABOUT WILD ANIMALS.
I ALSO LOVED DRAWING, SO I MADE A FIELD NOTEBOOK FOR MYSELF.
I WATCHED WILDLIFE DOCUMENTARIES ON TV EVERY NIGHT.
I SPOKE WITH CONSERVATIONISTS FROM OTHER COUNTRIES. THEY HAD LOTS OF INFORMATION TO SHARE WITH ME.
I INTRODUCED THEM TO THE TOUCH-ME-NOT PLANT, BUT THEY TRIED TO TOUCH IT!
I EXERCISED EVERY DAY AND ATE HEALTHY FOOD, SO I'D BE STRONG NO MATTER WHERE I WAS WORKING IN THE WORLD.

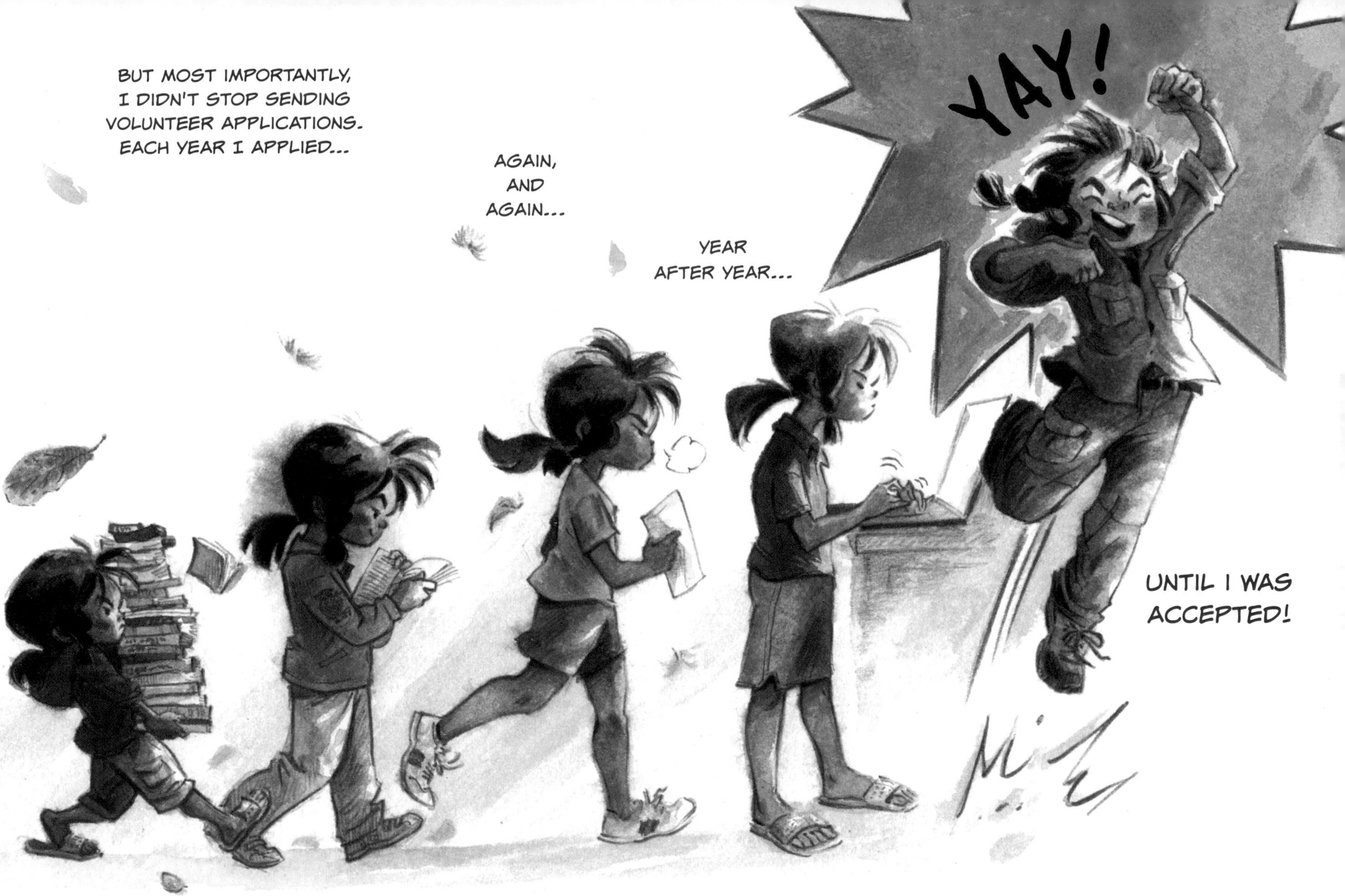
BUT MOST IMPORTANTLY, I DIDN'T STOP SENDING VOLUNTEER APPLICATIONS. EACH YEAR I APPLIED...
AGAIN, AND AGAIN...
YEAR AFTER YEAR...
YAY!
UNTIL I WAS ACCEPTED!

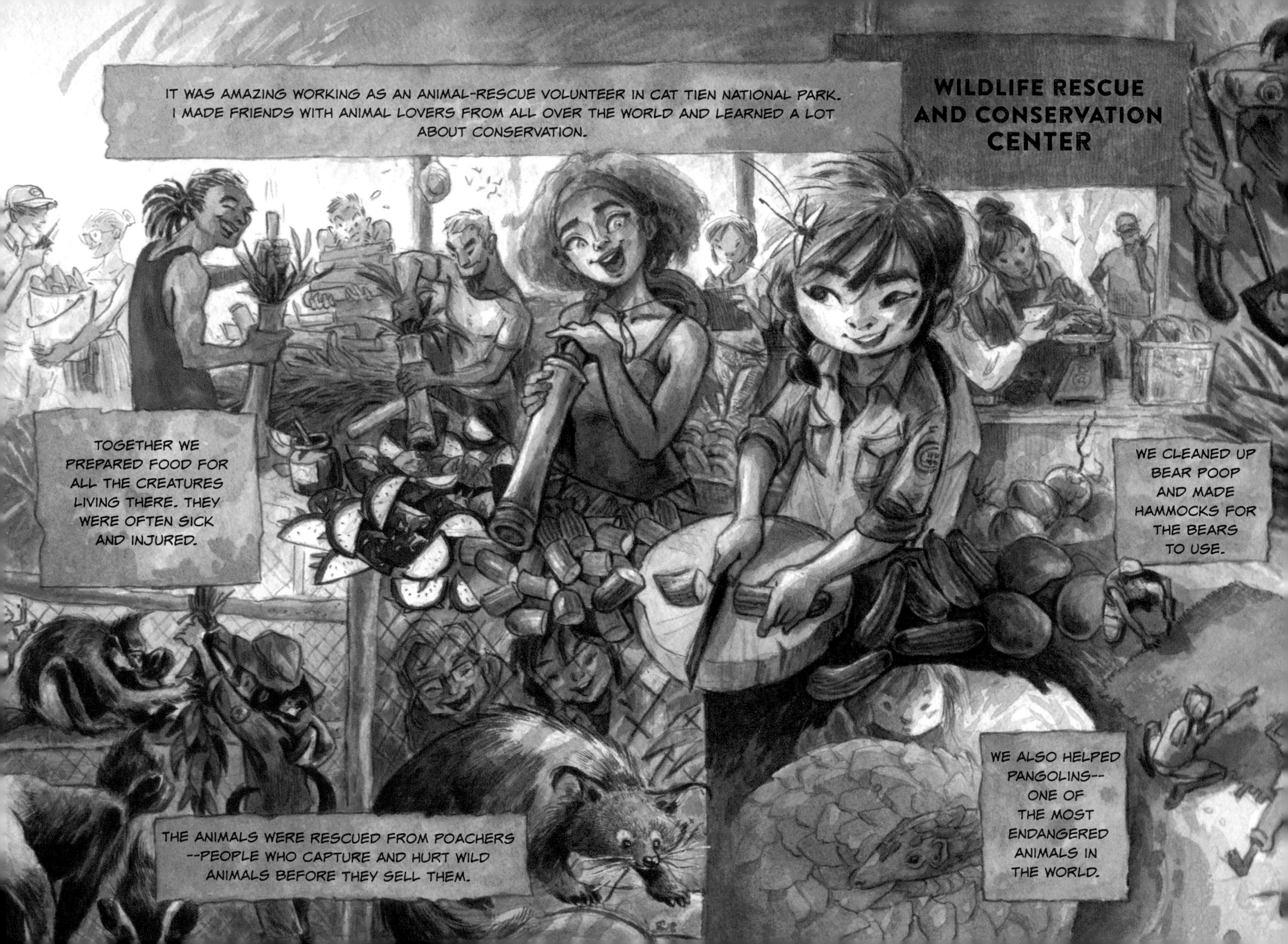
IT WAS AMAZING WORKING AS AN ANIMAL-RESCUE VOLUNTEER IN CAT TIEN NATIONAL PARK. I MADE FRIENDS WITH ANIMAL LOVERS FROM ALL OVER THE WORLD AND LEARNED A LOT ABOUT CONSERVATION.
WILDLIFE RESCUE AND CONSERVATION CENTER
TOGETHER WE PREPARED FOOD FOR ALL THE CREATURES LIVING THERE. THEY WERE OFTEN SICK AND INJURED.
WE CLEANED UP BEAR POOP AND MADE HAMMOCKS FOR THE BEARS TO USE.
THE ANIMALS WERE RESCUED FROM POACHERS --PEOPLE WHO CAPTURE AND HURT WILD ANIMALS BEFORE THEY SELL THEM.
WE ALSO HELPED PANGOLINS-- ONE OF THE MOST ENDANGERED ANIMALS IN THE WORLD.

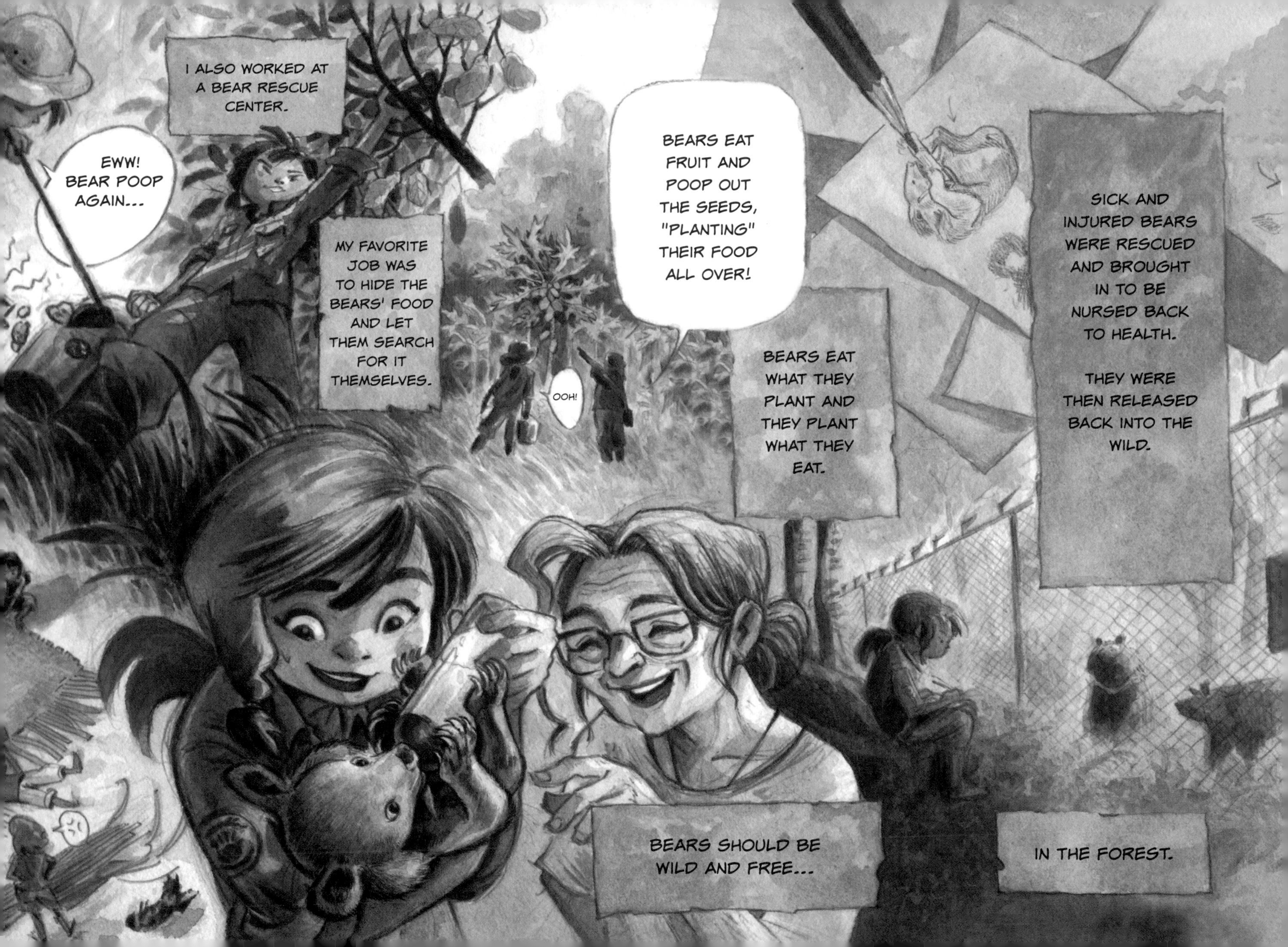
I ALSO WORKED AT A BEAR RESCUE CENTER.
EWW! BEAR POOP AGAIN...
MY FAVORITE JOB WAS TO HIDE THE BEARS' FOOD AND LET THEM SEARCH FOR IT THEMSELVES.
BEARS EAT FRUIT AND POOP OUT THE SEEDS, "PLANTING" THEIR FOOD ALL OVER!
OOH!
BEARS EAT WHAT THEY PLANT AND THEY PLANT WHAT THEY EAT.
SICK AND INJURED BEARS WERE RESCUED AND BROUGHT IN TO BE NURSED BACK TO HEALTH.
THEY WERE THEN RELEASED BACK INTO THE WILD.
BEARS SHOULD BE WILD AND FREE...
IN THE FOREST.

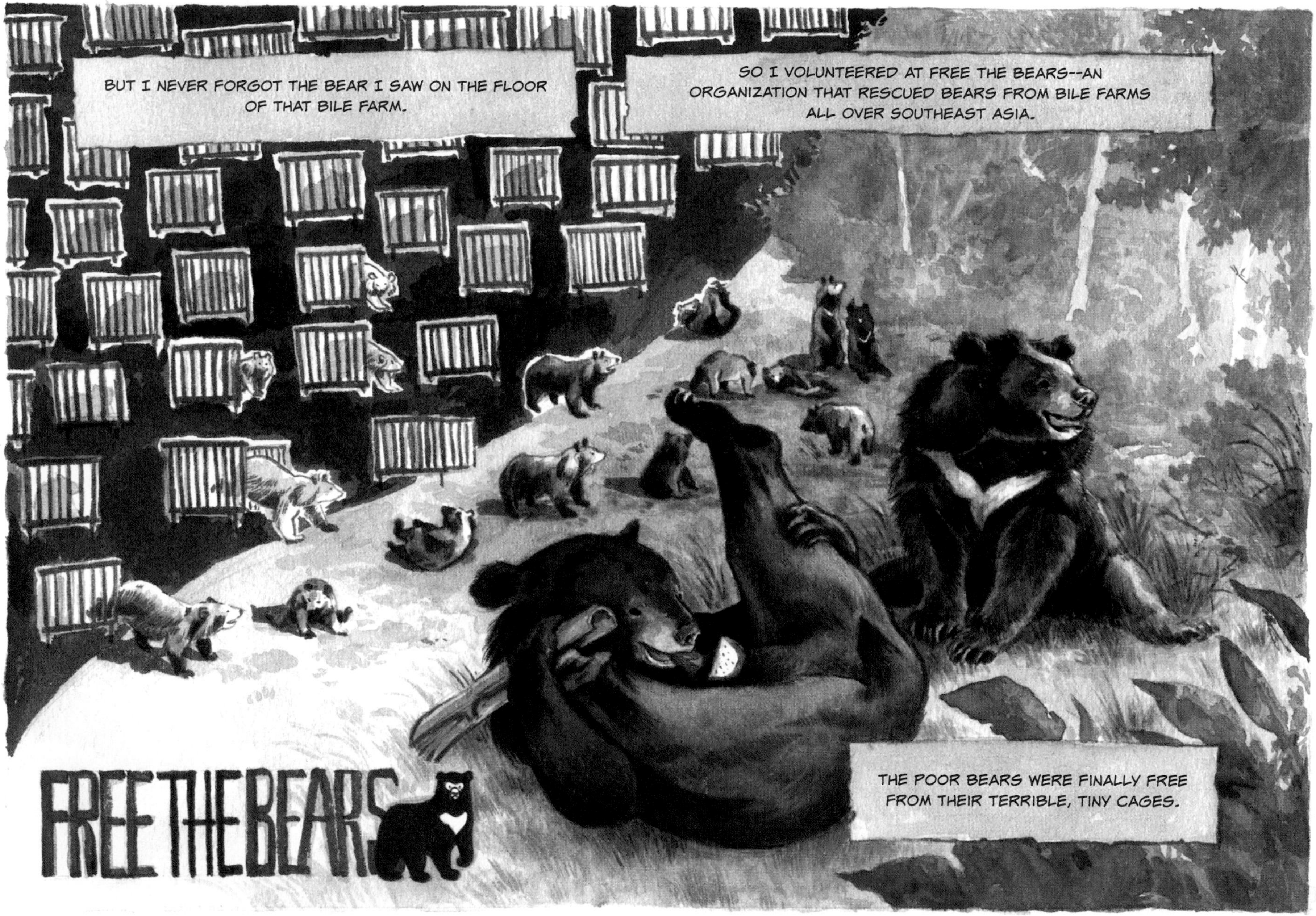
BUT I NEVER FORGOT THE BEAR I SAW ON THE FLOOR OF THAT BILE FARM.
SO I VOLUNTEERED AT FREE THE BEARS--AN ORGANIZATION THAT RESCUED BEARS FROM BILE FARMS ALL OVER SOUTHEAST ASIA.
FREE THE BEARS
THE POOR BEARS WERE FINALLY FREE FROM THEIR TERRIBLE, TINY CAGES.

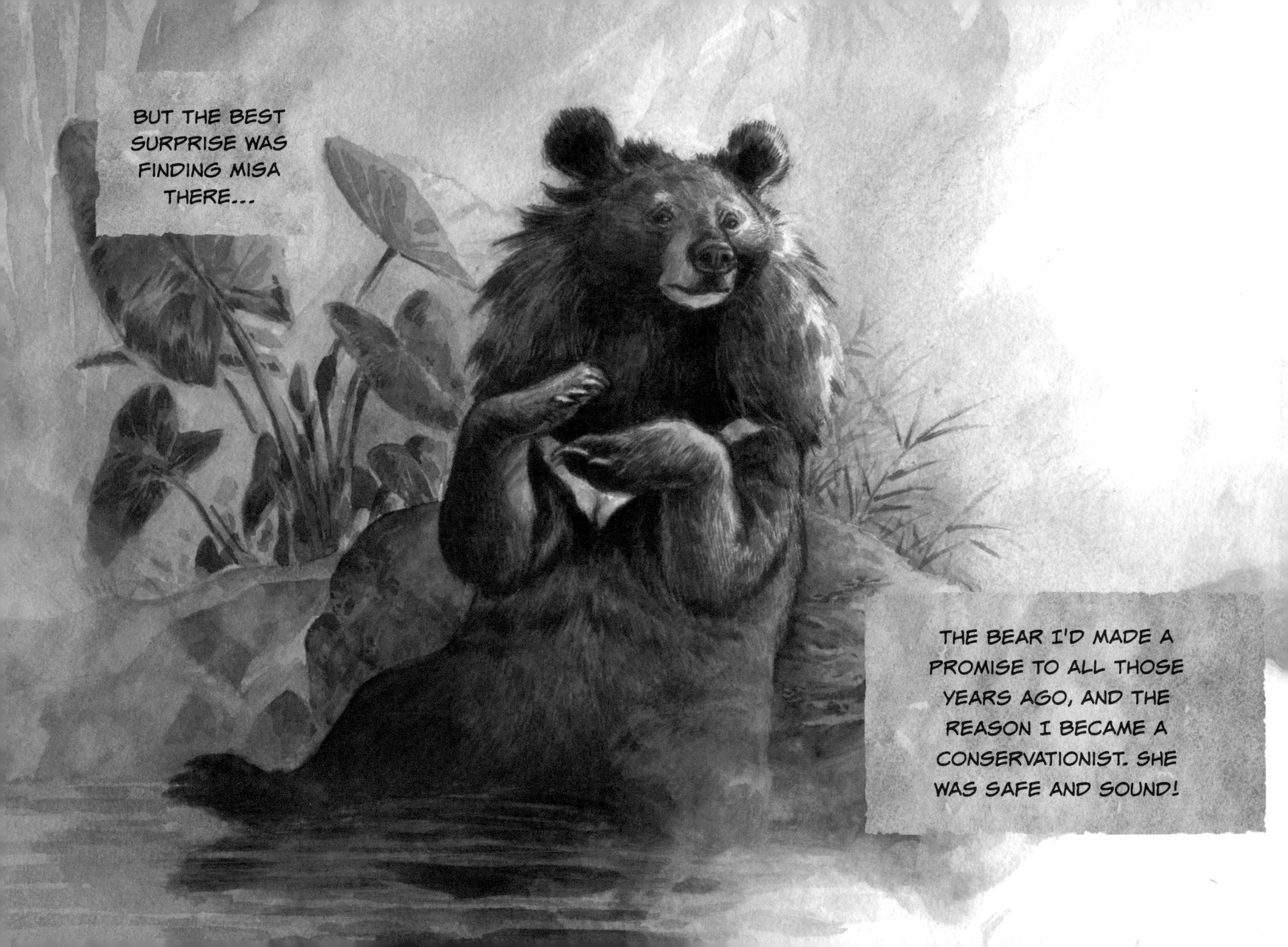
BUT THE BEST SURPRISE WAS FINDING MISA THERE...
THE BEAR I'D MADE A PROMISE TO ALL THOSE YEARS AGO, AND THE REASON I BECAME A CONSERVATIONIST. SHE WAS SAFE AND SOUND!

CHAPTER THREE

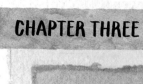

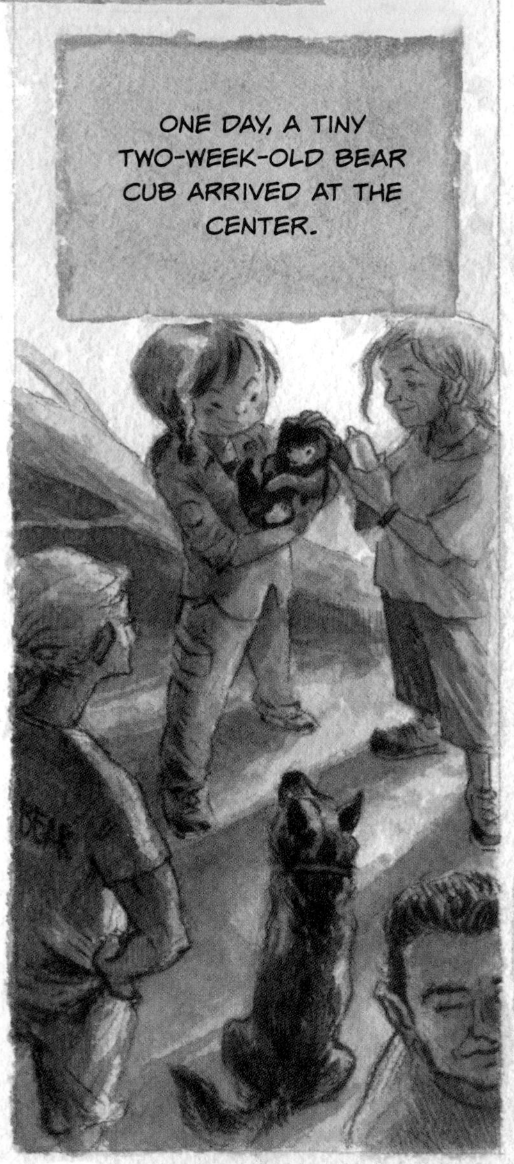
ONE DAY, A TINY TWO-WEEK-OLD BEAR CUB ARRIVED AT THE CENTER.

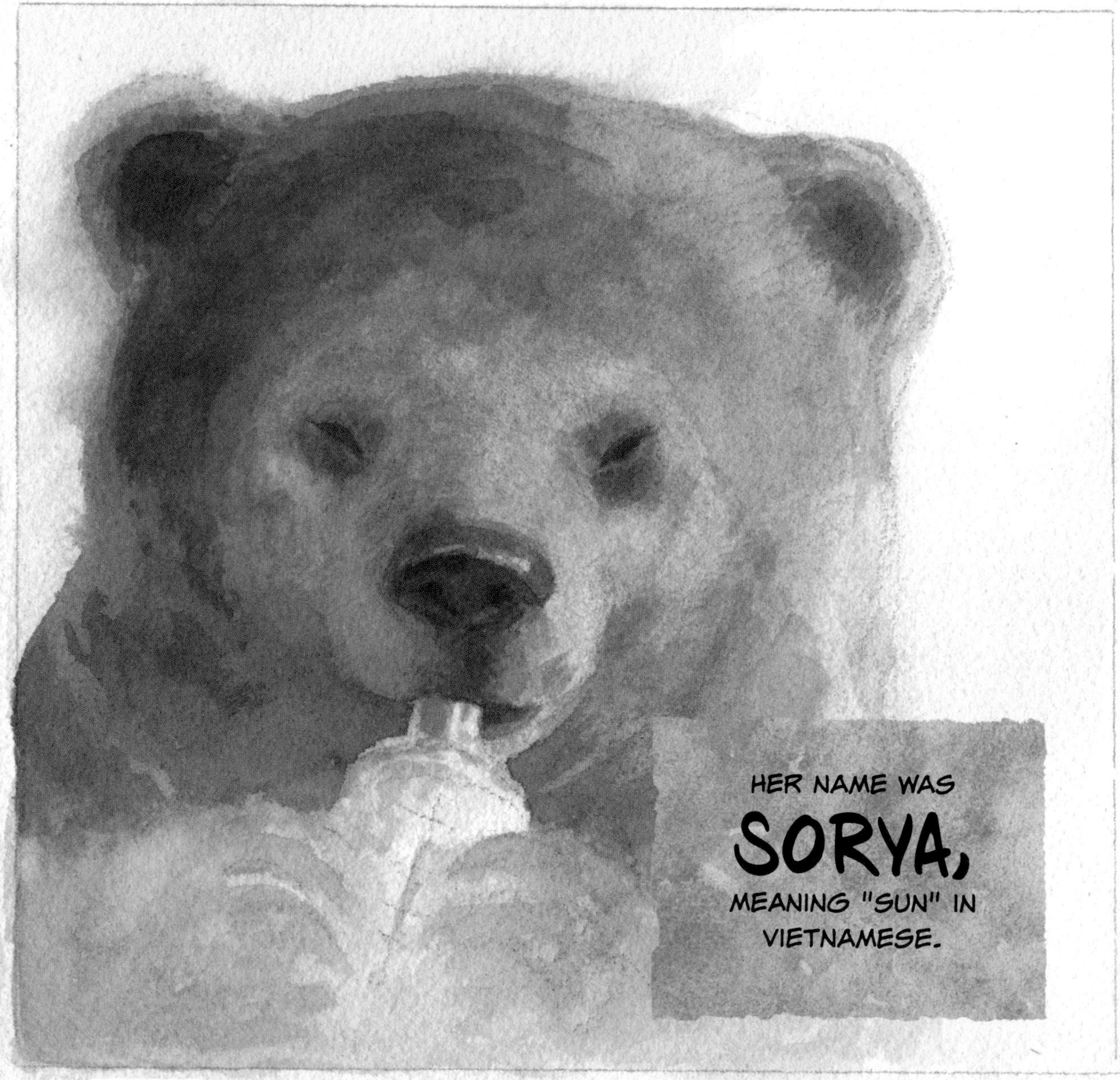
HER NAME WAS SORYA, MEANING "SUN" IN VIETNAMESE.

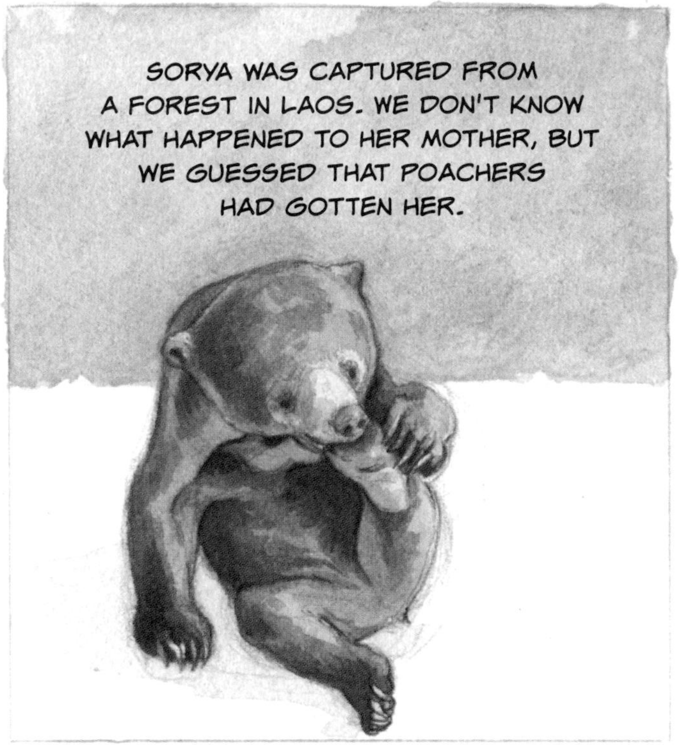
SORYA WAS CAPTURED FROM A FOREST IN LAOS. WE DON'T KNOW WHAT HAPPENED TO HER MOTHER, BUT WE GUESSED THAT POACHERS HAD GOTTEN HER.

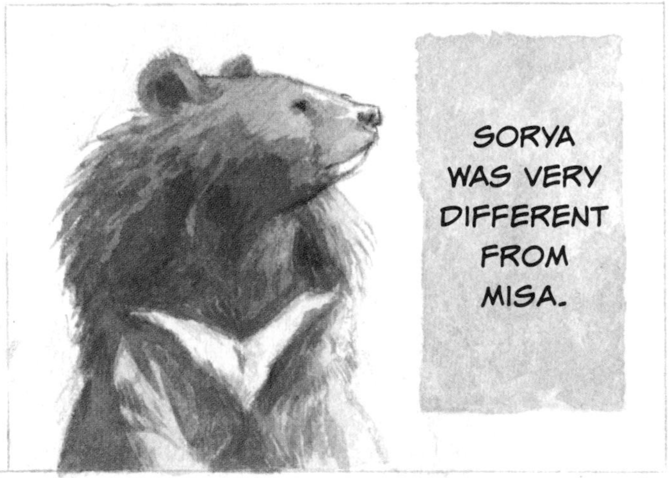
SORYA WAS VERY DIFFERENT FROM MISA.

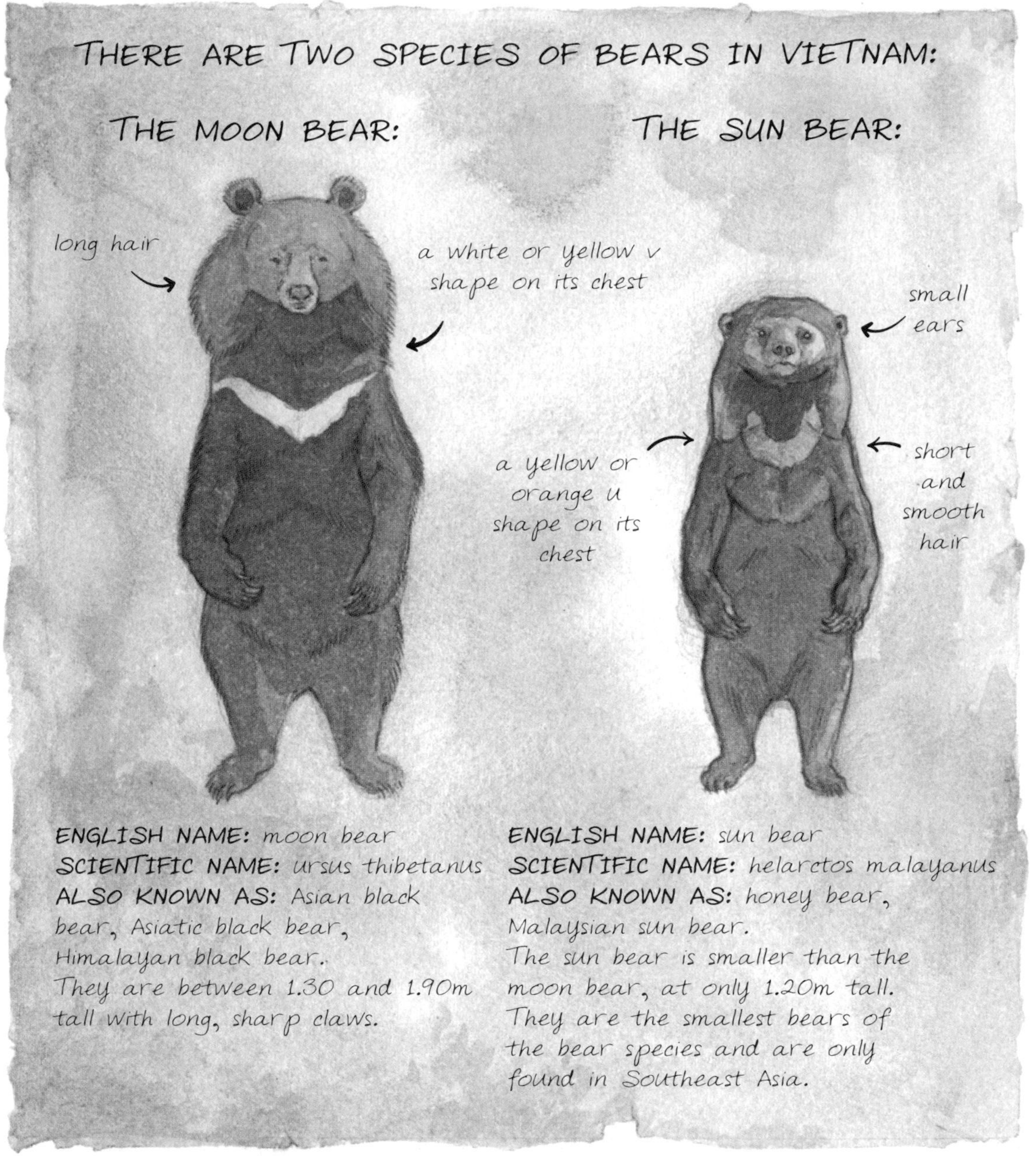
THERE ARE TWO SPECIES OF BEARS IN VIETNAM:
THE MOON BEAR:
long hair
a white or yellow v shape on its chest
THE SUN BEAR:
small ears
a yellow or orange u shape on its chest
short and smooth hair
ENGLISH NAME: moon bear
SCIENTIFIC NAME: ursus thibetanus
ALSO KNOWN AS: Asian black bear, Asiatic black bear, Himalayan black bear.
They are between 1.30 and 1.90m tall with long, sharp claws.
ENGLISH NAME: sun bear
SCIENTIFIC NAME: helarctos malayanus
ALSO KNOWN AS: honey bear, Malaysian sun bear.
The sun bear is smaller than the moon bear, at only 1.20m tall. They are the smallest bears of the bear species and are only found in Southeast Asia.

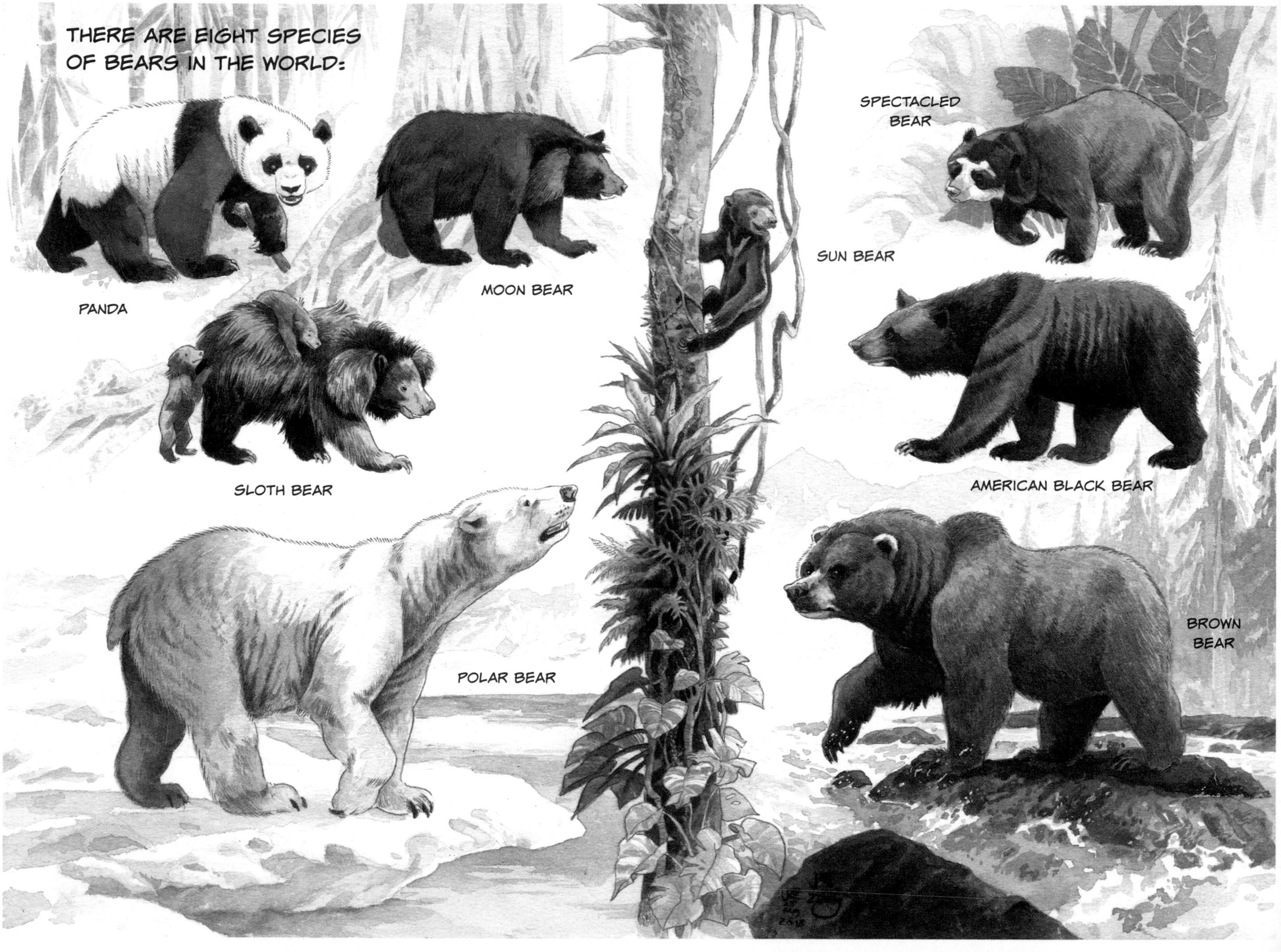
THERE ARE EIGHT SPECIES OF BEARS IN THE WORLD:
PANDA
MOON BEAR
SUN BEAR
SPECTACLED BEAR
SLOTH BEAR
AMERICAN BLACK BEAR
POLAR BEAR
BROWN BEAR

I LEARNED EVERYTHING I COULD ABOUT SUN BEARS...

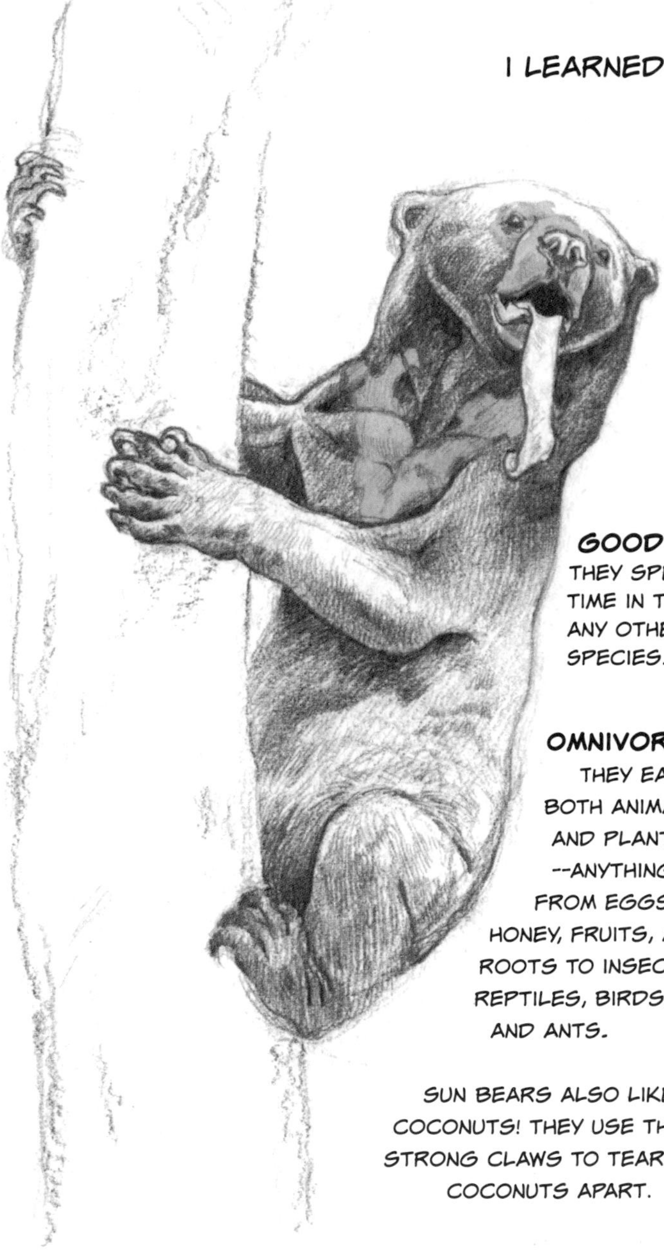

GOOD CLIMBERS:
THEY SPEND MORE TIME IN TREES THAN ANY OTHER BEAR SPECIES.

OMNIVORES:
THEY EAT BOTH ANIMALS AND PLANTS --ANYTHING FROM EGGS, HONEY, FRUITS, AND ROOTS TO INSECTS, REPTILES, BIRDS, AND ANTS.

SUN BEARS ALSO LIKE COCONUTS! THEY USE THEIR STRONG CLAWS TO TEAR THE COCONUTS APART.

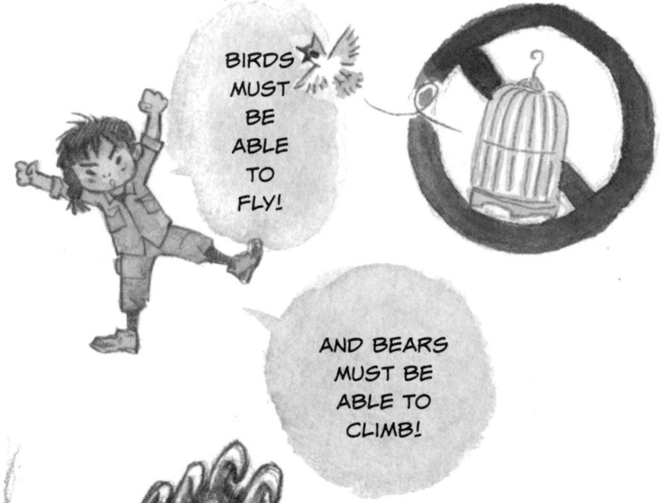
BIRDS MUST BE ABLE TO FLY!
AND BEARS MUST BE ABLE TO CLIMB!

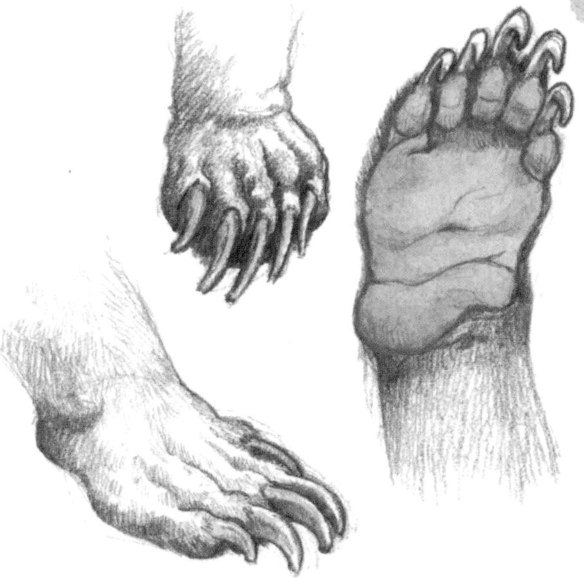

AGILE FEET:
SHARP CLAWS CURVED LIKE HOOKS, AND THE BOTTOM OF THEIR PAWS DON'T HAVE FUR.

THEIR FEET POINT INWARD, SO THEY HAVE A VERY FUNNY WALK!

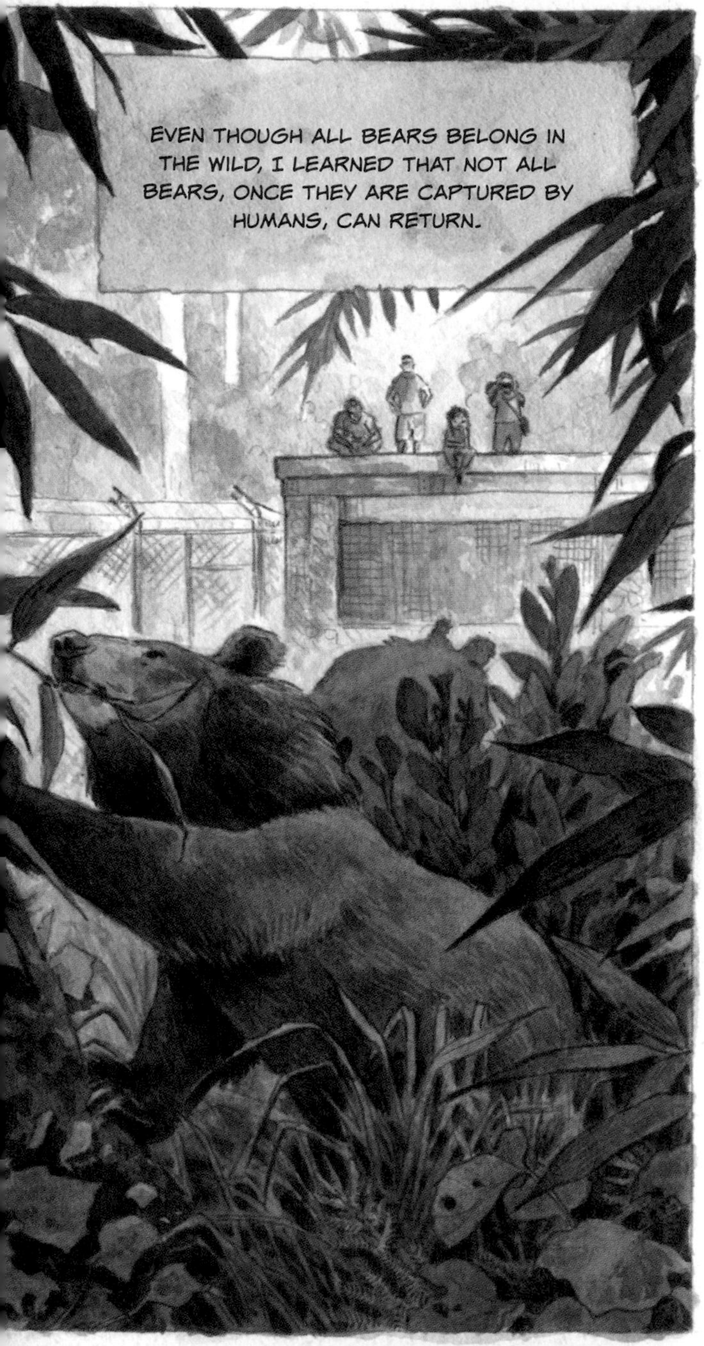
EVEN THOUGH ALL BEARS BELONG IN THE WILD, I LEARNED THAT NOT ALL BEARS, ONCE THEY ARE CAPTURED BY HUMANS, CAN RETURN.

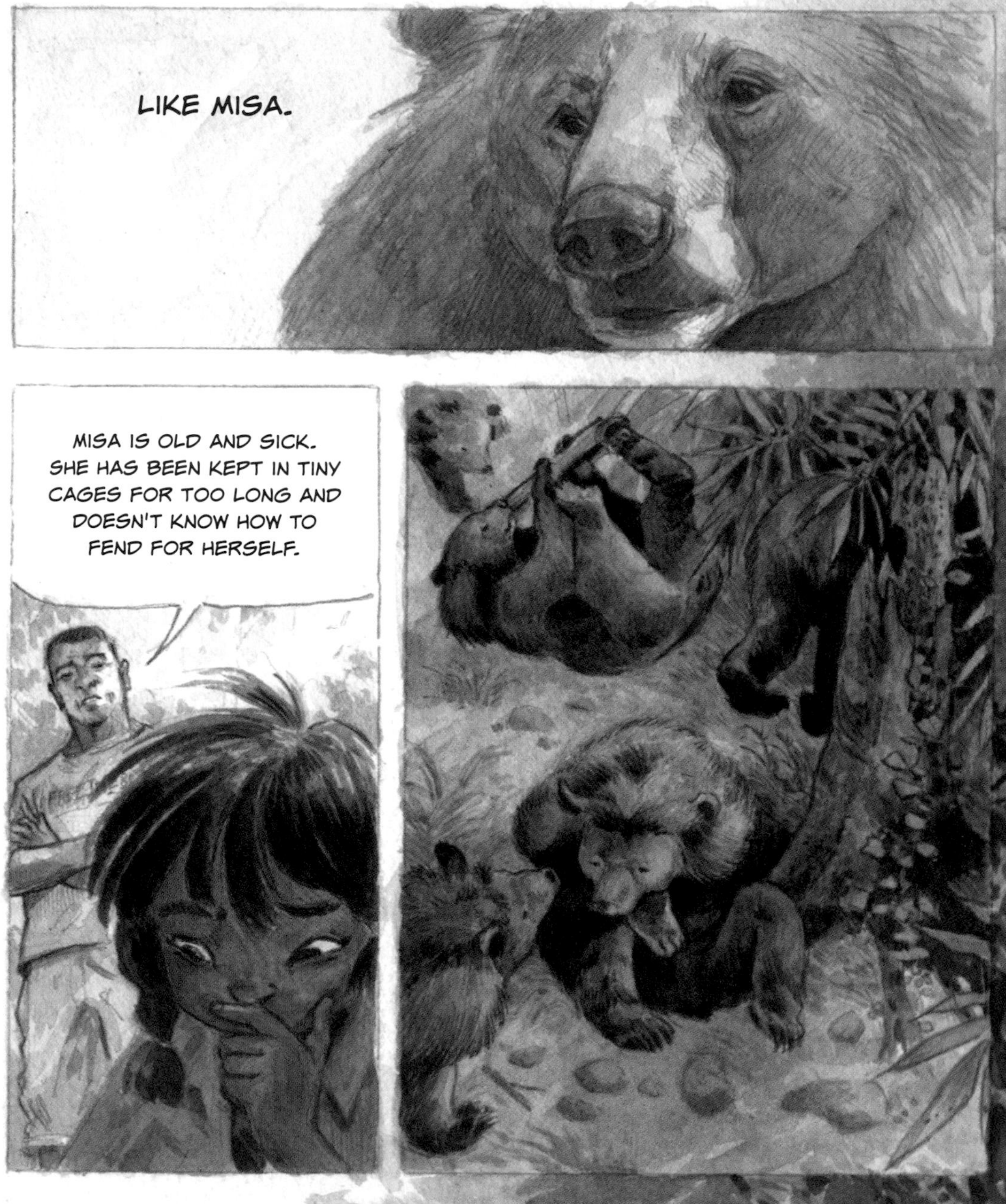
LIKE MISA.
MISA IS OLD AND SICK. SHE HAS BEEN KEPT IN TINY CAGES FOR TOO LONG AND DOESN'T KNOW HOW TO FEND FOR HERSELF.

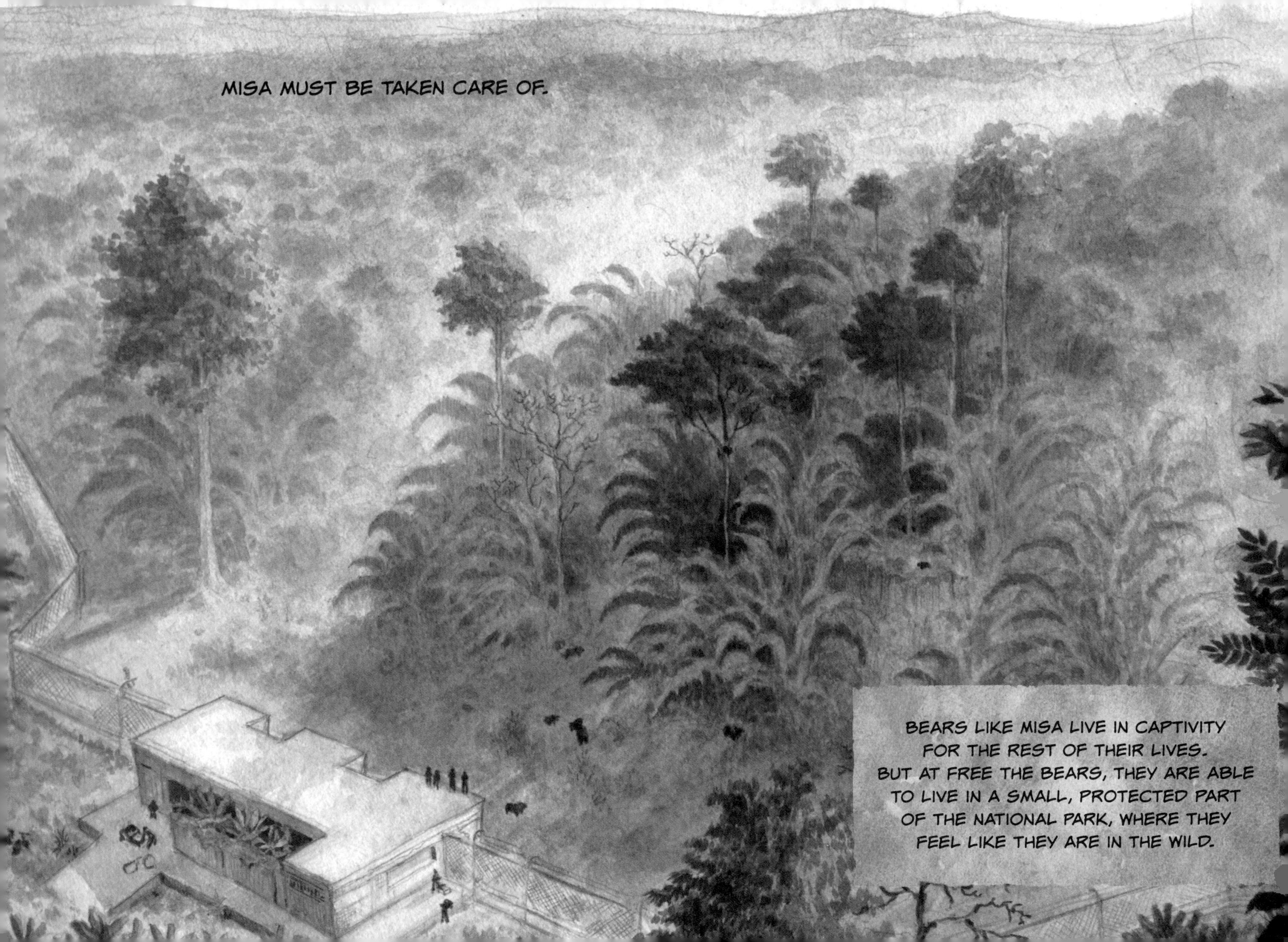
MISA MUST BE TAKEN CARE OF.
BEARS LIKE MISA LIVE IN CAPTIVITY FOR THE REST OF THEIR LIVES. BUT AT FREE THE BEARS, THEY ARE ABLE TO LIVE IN A SMALL, PROTECTED PART OF THE NATIONAL PARK, WHERE THEY FEEL LIKE THEY ARE IN THE WILD.

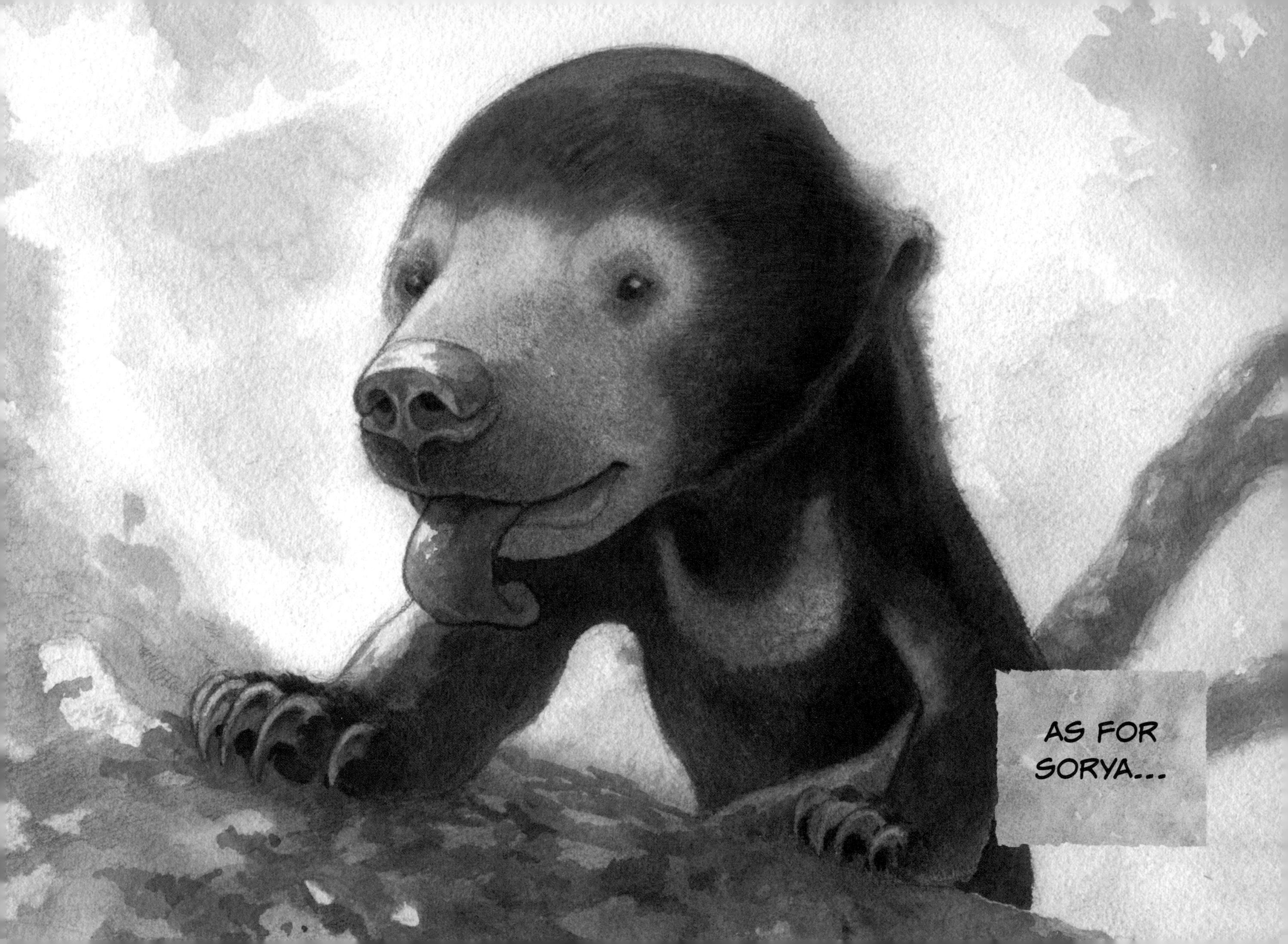
AS FOR SORYA...

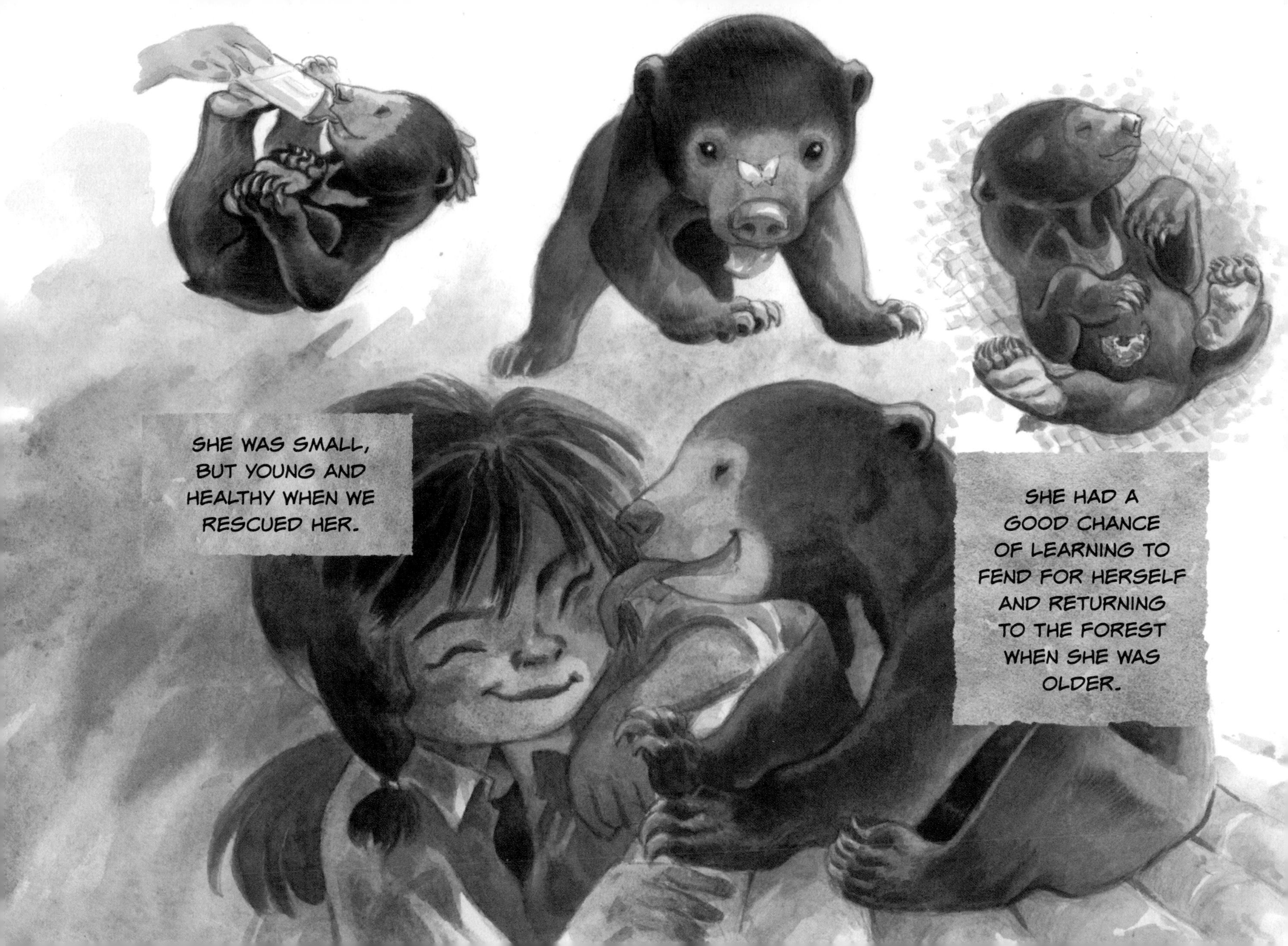
SHE WAS SMALL, BUT YOUNG AND HEALTHY WHEN WE RESCUED HER.
SHE HAD A GOOD CHANCE OF LEARNING TO FEND FOR HERSELF AND RETURNING TO THE FOREST WHEN SHE WAS OLDER.

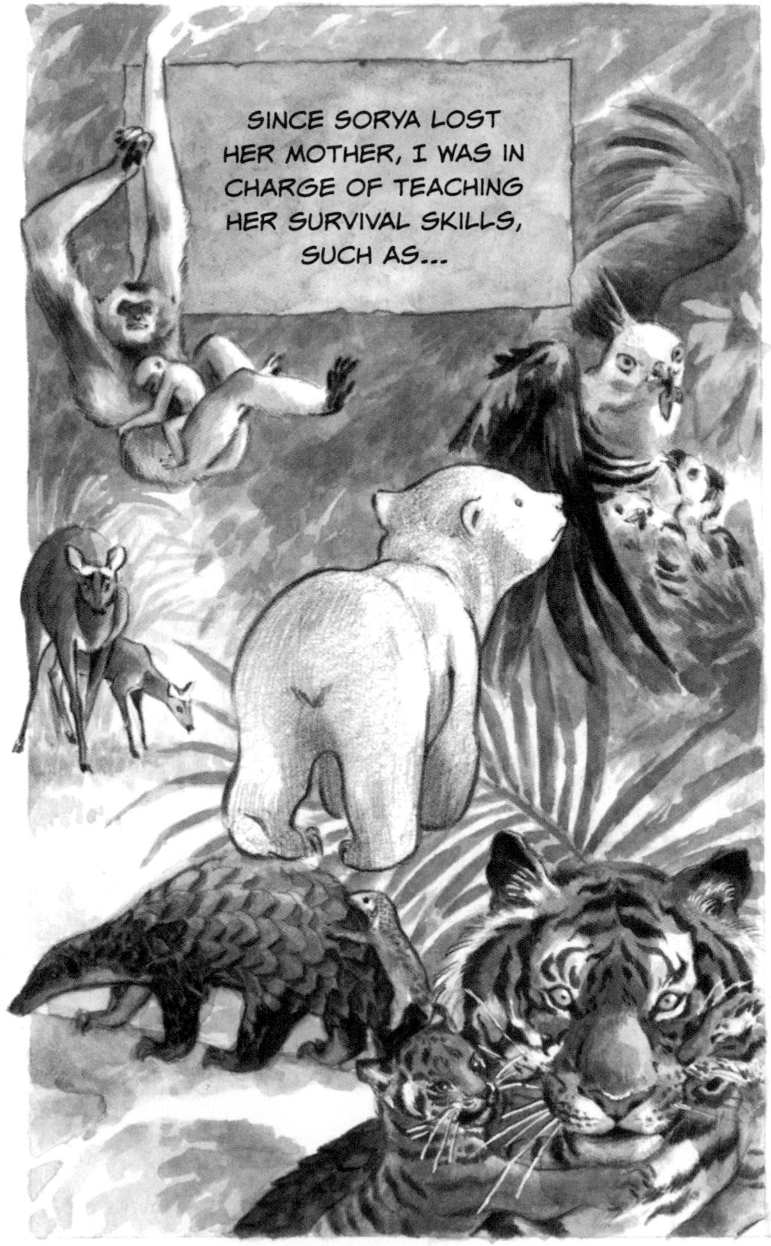
SINCE SORYA LOST HER MOTHER, I WAS IN CHARGE OF TEACHING HER SURVIVAL SKILLS, SUCH AS...

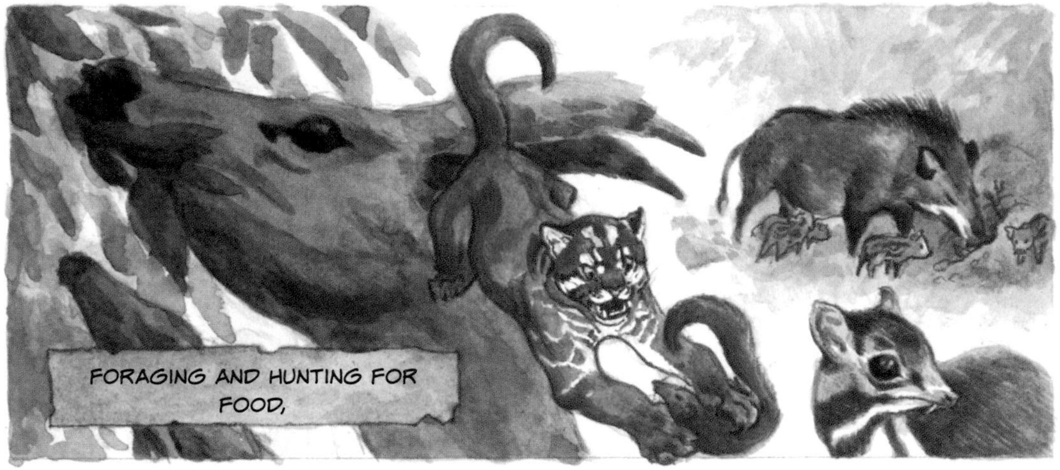
FORAGING AND HUNTING FOR FOOD,

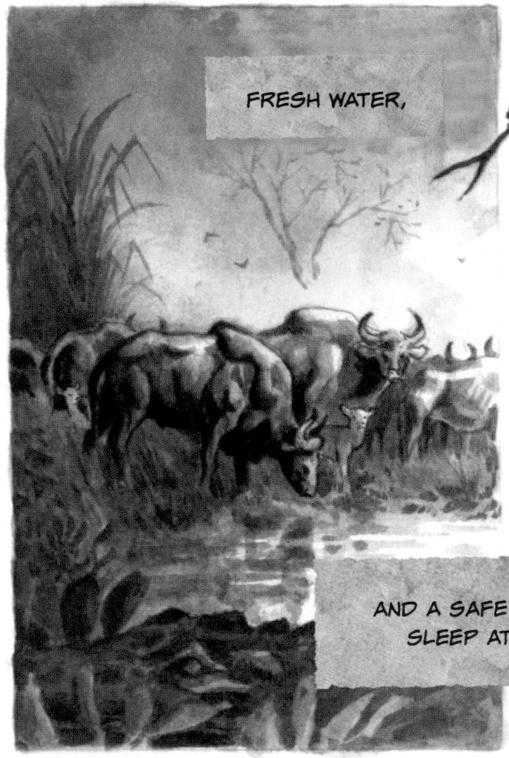
FRESH WATER,

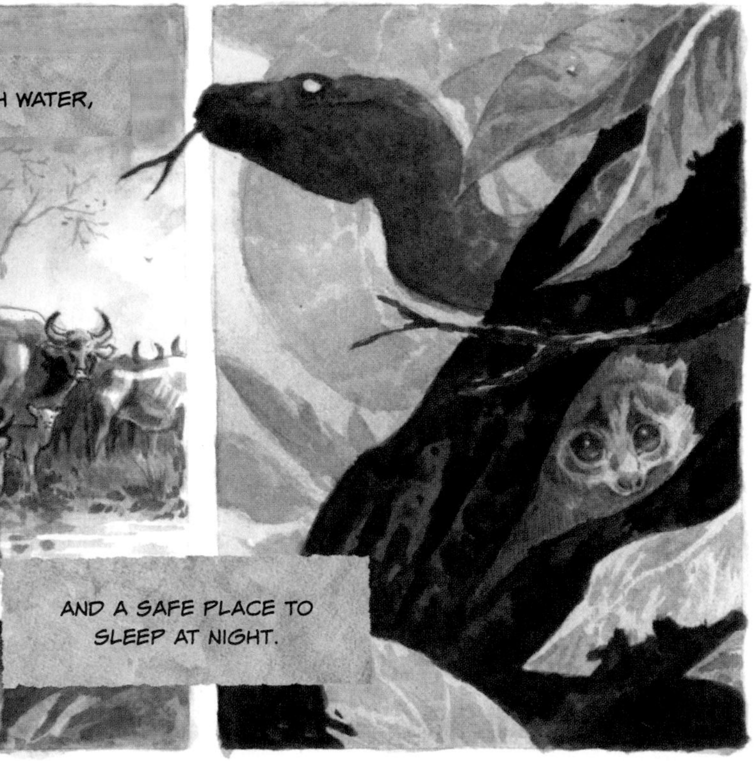
AND A SAFE PLACE TO SLEEP AT NIGHT.

LIKE SOME CUBS
WITHOUT MOTHERS,
SORYA ALSO
DEVELOPED A HABIT
OF SUCKING ON HER
TOES AND FINGERS.

IT WAS CUTE AT FIRST,
BUT EVERY TIME SORYA
DID THIS...

SLURP!
SUCK!

OH NO!
YOUR PAWS ARE
BLEEDING!

SHE'D BREAK THE SKIN
AROUND HER TOENAILS
AND HURT HERSELF.

Rescued bears often behave strangely.

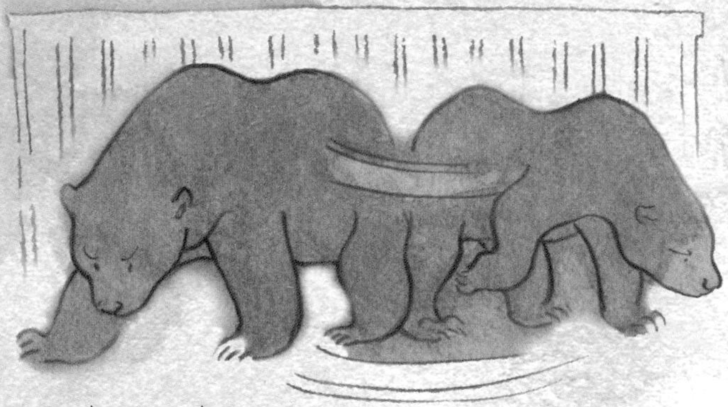

Some walk back and forth, like they are still inside invisible cages.

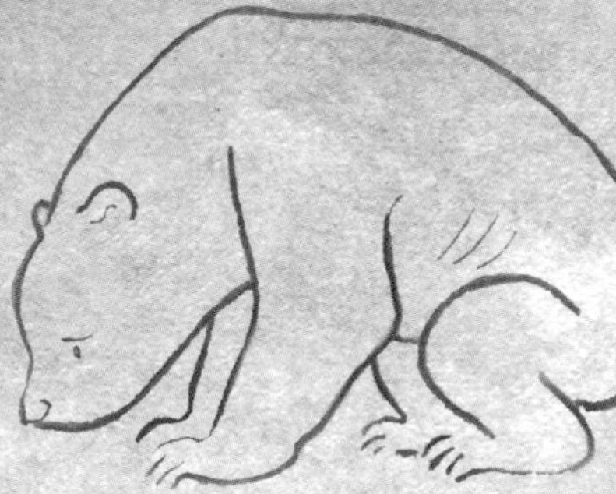

Some of them don't have fur anymore because of stress or a skin condition that hasn't been treated in time.

Some are covered in scabs, from where they have rubbed their bodies on the bars of their cages.

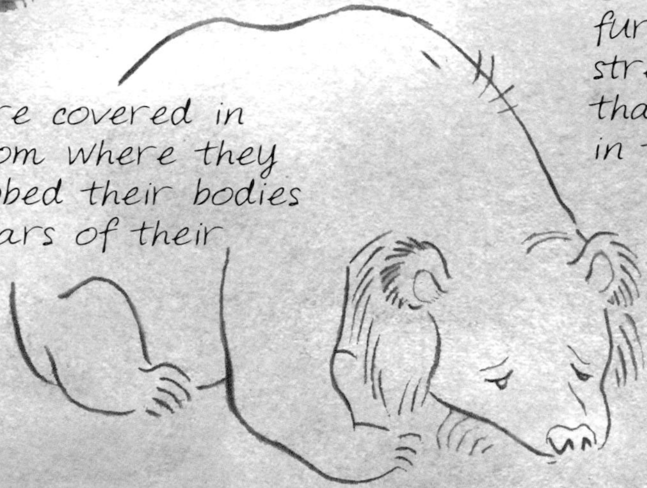

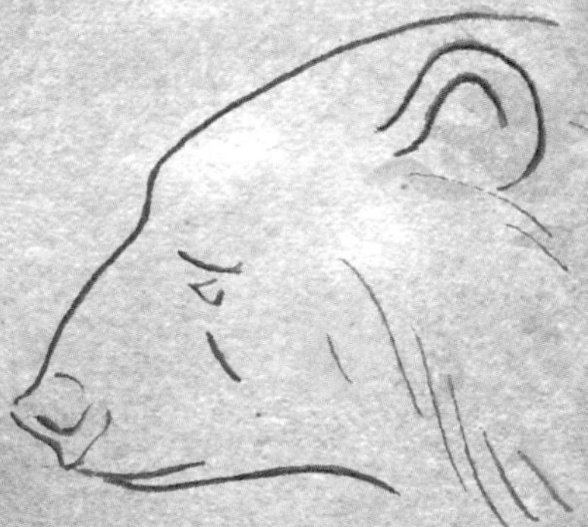

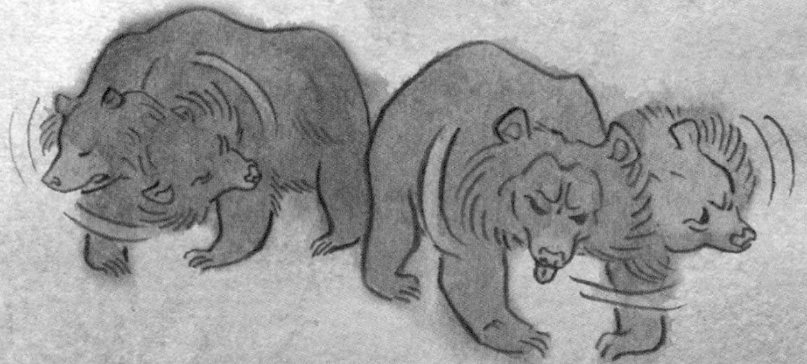

Some shake their heads constantly.

These are all signs that some bears can't return to the wild. They've been suffering for too long, and wouldn't be able to take care of themselves.

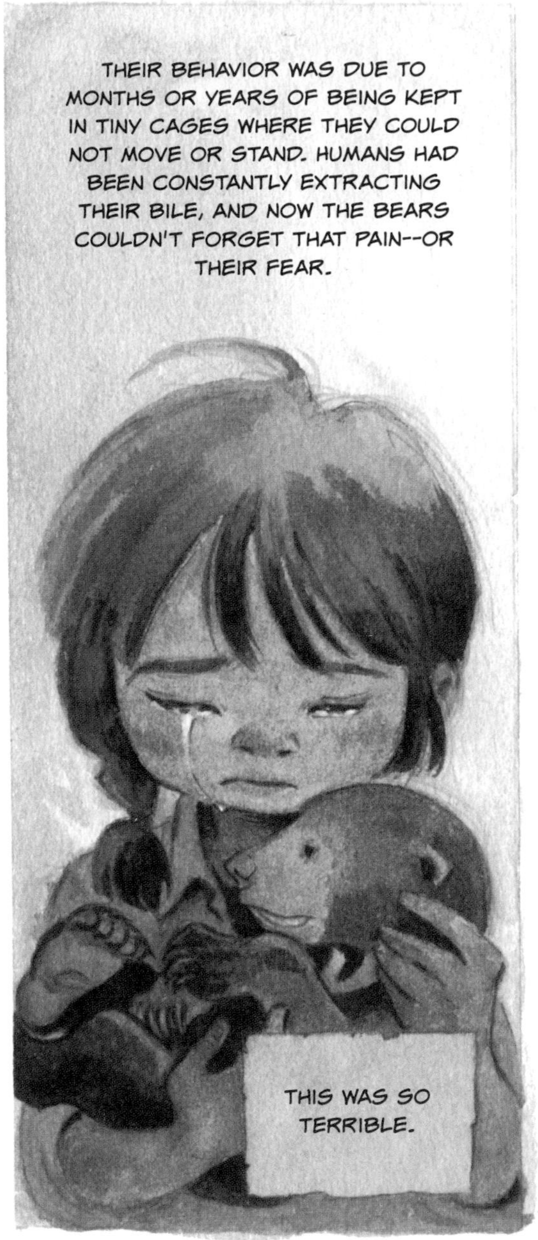
THEIR BEHAVIOR WAS DUE TO MONTHS OR YEARS OF BEING KEPT IN TINY CAGES WHERE THEY COULD NOT MOVE OR STAND. HUMANS HAD BEEN CONSTANTLY EXTRACTING THEIR BILE, AND NOW THE BEARS COULDN'T FORGET THAT PAIN--OR THEIR FEAR.
THIS WAS SO TERRIBLE.

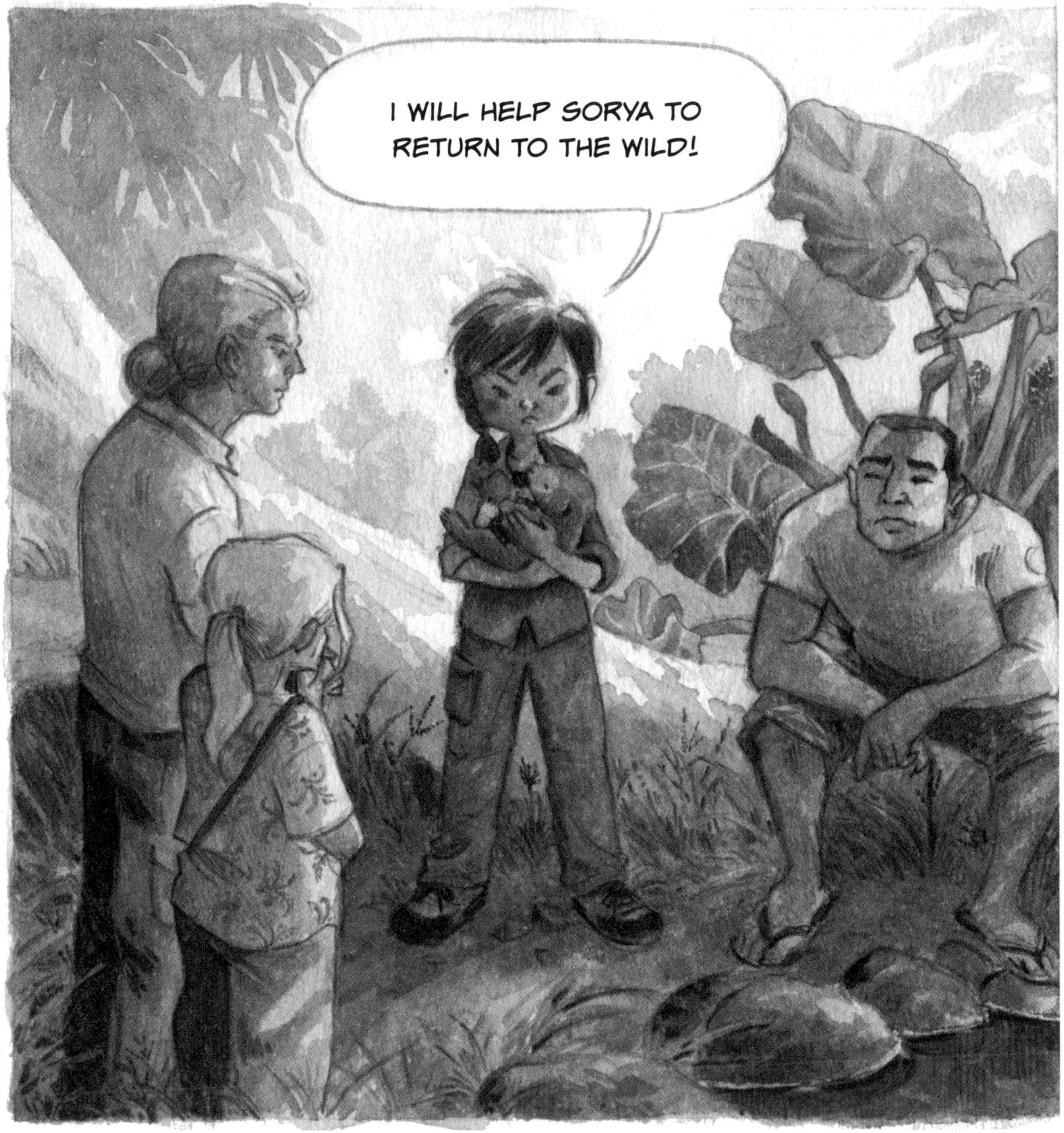
I WILL HELP SORYA TO RETURN TO THE WILD!

CHAPTER FOUR

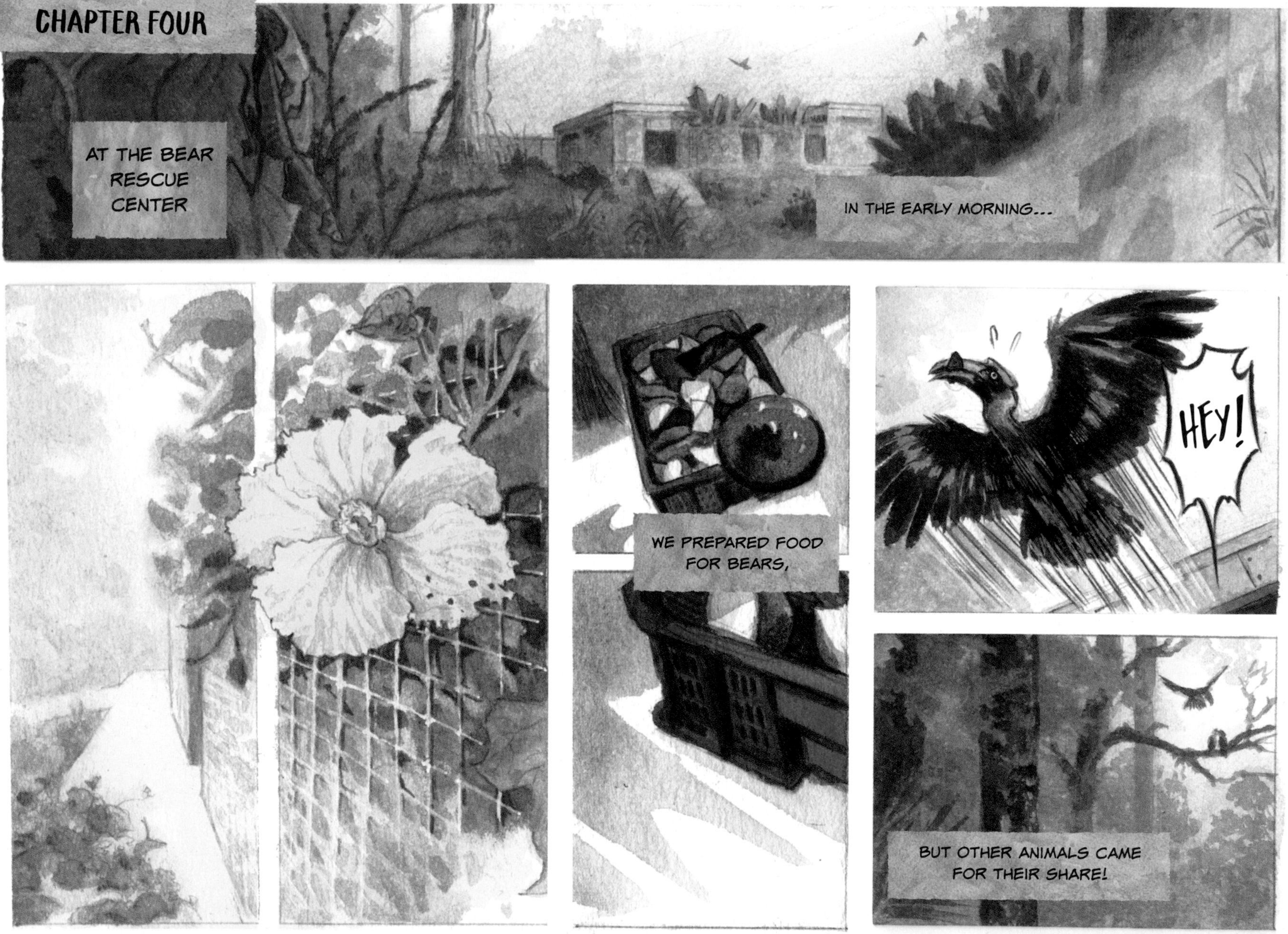
AT THE BEAR RESCUE CENTER
IN THE EARLY MORNING...
WE PREPARED FOOD FOR BEARS,
HEY!
BUT OTHER ANIMALS CAME FOR THEIR SHARE!

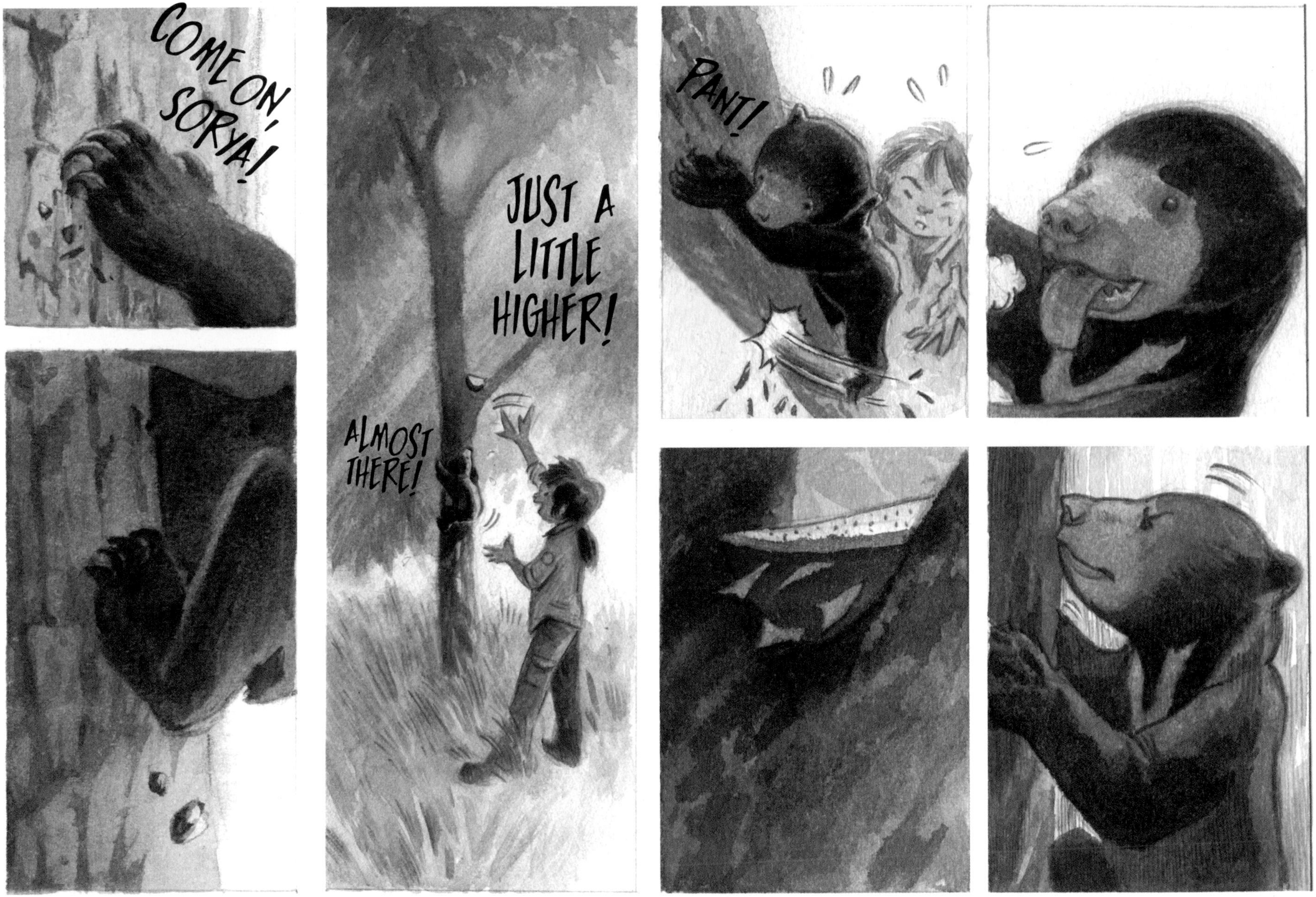
COME ON, SORYA!
JUST A LITTLE HIGHER!
ALMOST THERE!
PANT!

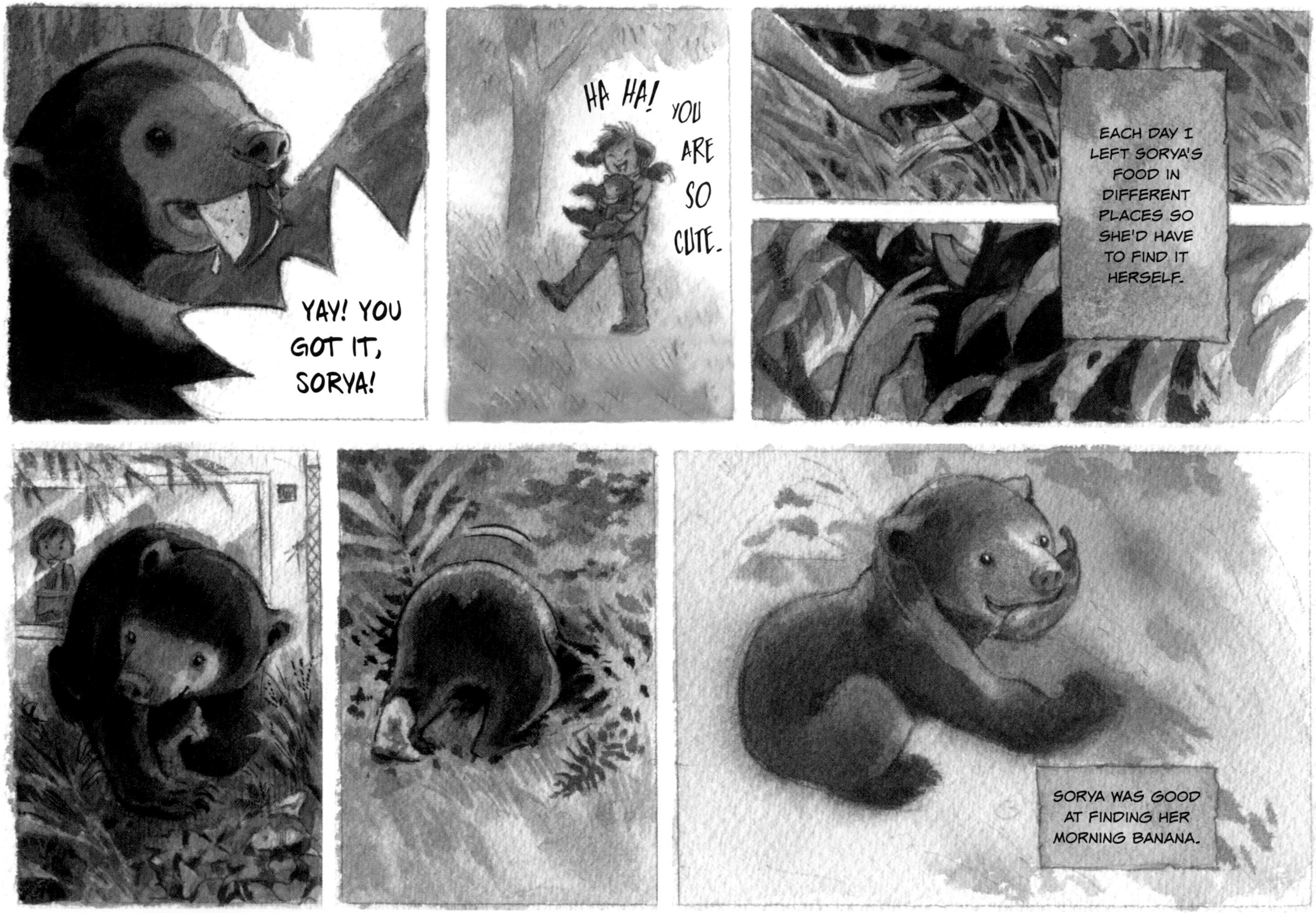
YAY! YOU GOT IT, SORYA!
HA HA!
YOU ARE SO CUTE.
EACH DAY I LEFT SORYA'S FOOD IN DIFFERENT PLACES SO SHE'D HAVE TO FIND IT HERSELF.
SORYA WAS GOOD AT FINDING HER MORNING BANANA.

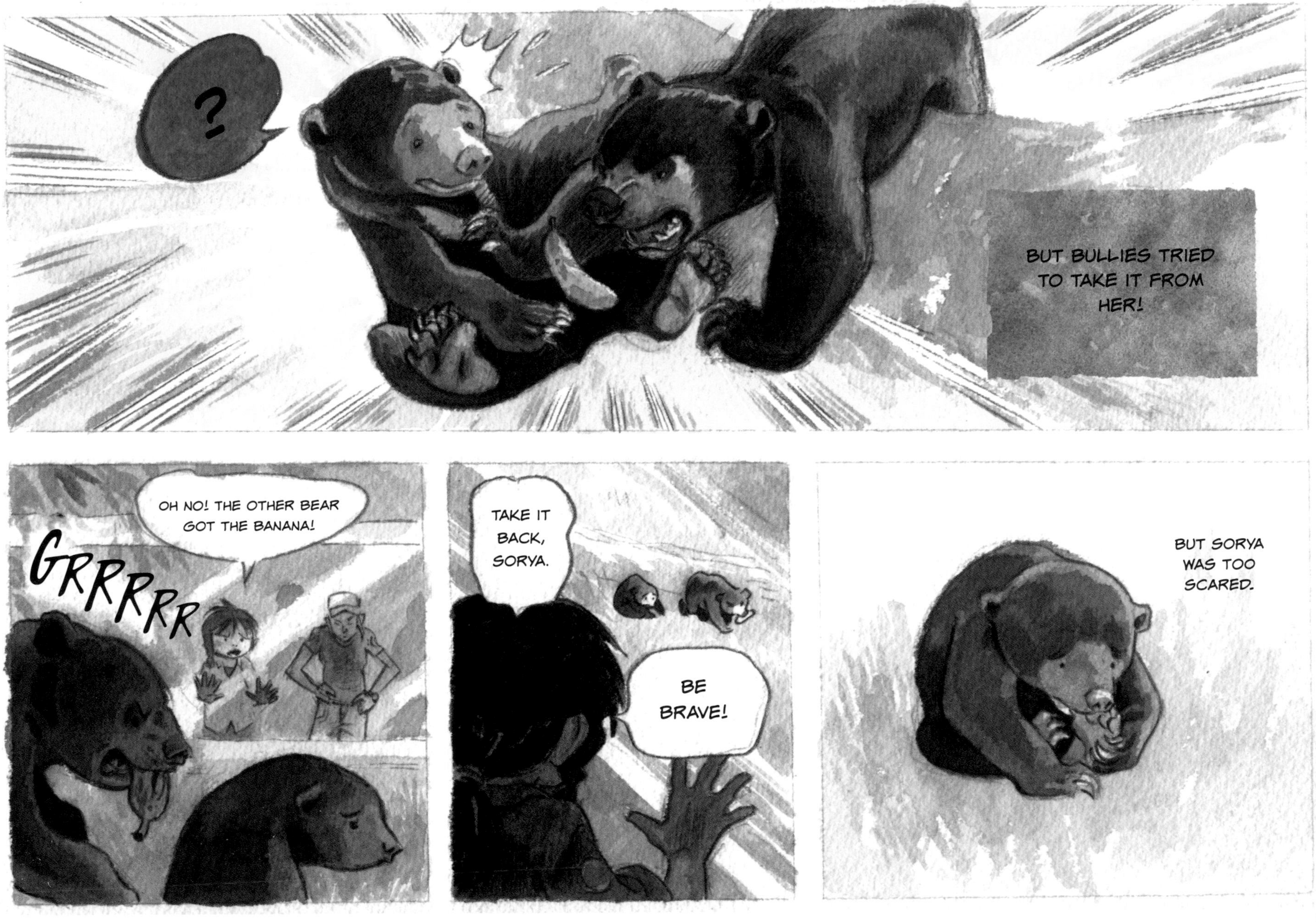
?
BUT BULLIES TRIED TO TAKE IT FROM HER!
OH NO! THE OTHER BEAR GOT THE BANANA!
GRRRRRR
TAKE IT BACK, SORYA.
BE BRAVE!
BUT SORYA WAS TOO SCARED.

I'M SORRY, CHANG. I DON'T THINK YOUR TRAINING WITH SORYA IS WORKING.

SHE'S WEAKER THAN THE OTHER BEARS. IF SHE CAN'T STAND UP FOR HERSELF, SHE'LL NEVER BE ABLE TO MAKE IT ON HER OWN.

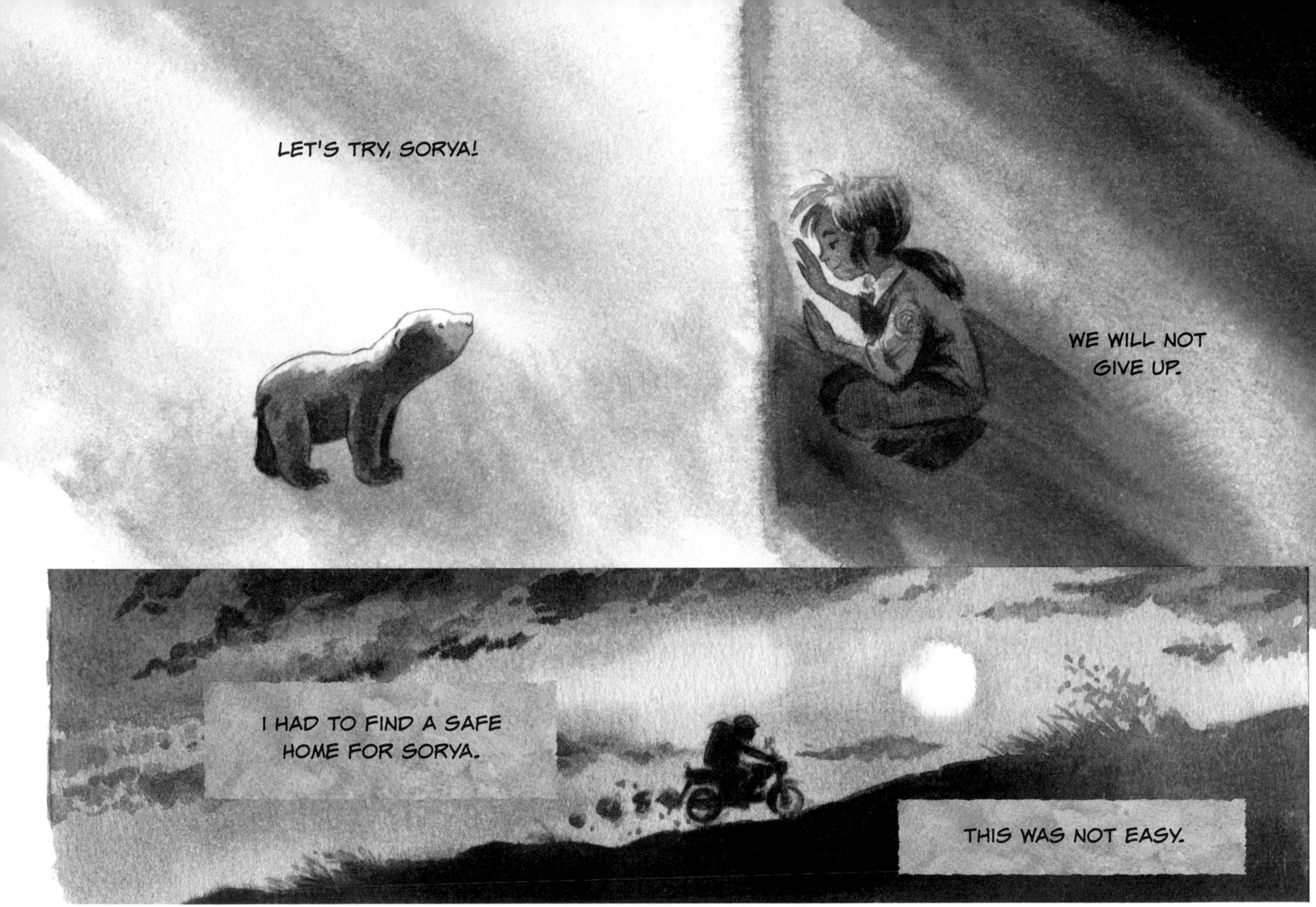
LET'S TRY, SORYA!
WE WILL NOT GIVE UP.
I HAD TO FIND A SAFE HOME FOR SORYA.
THIS WAS NOT EASY.

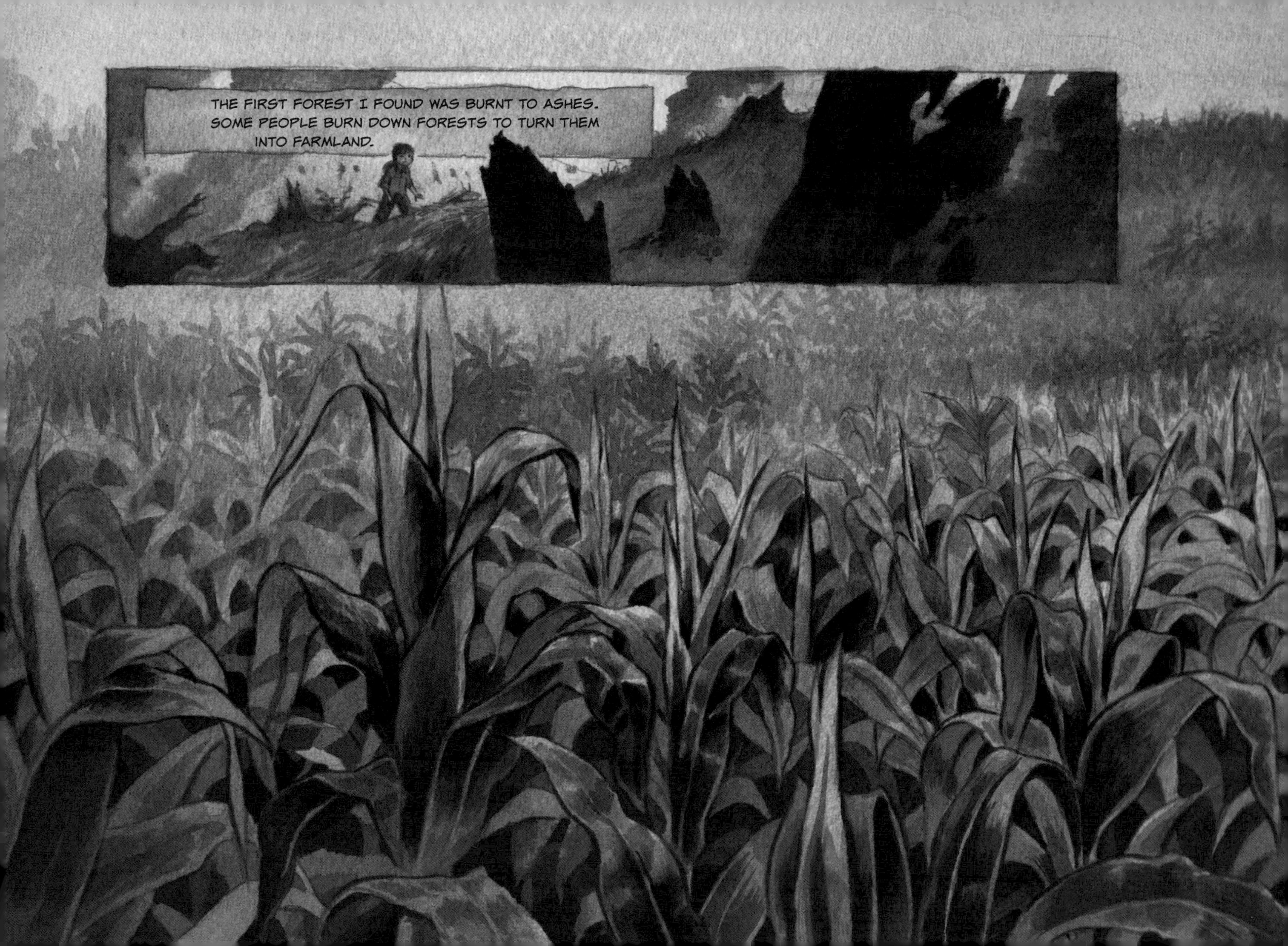
THE FIRST FOREST I FOUND WAS BURNT TO ASHES. SOME PEOPLE BURN DOWN FORESTS TO TURN THEM INTO FARMLAND.

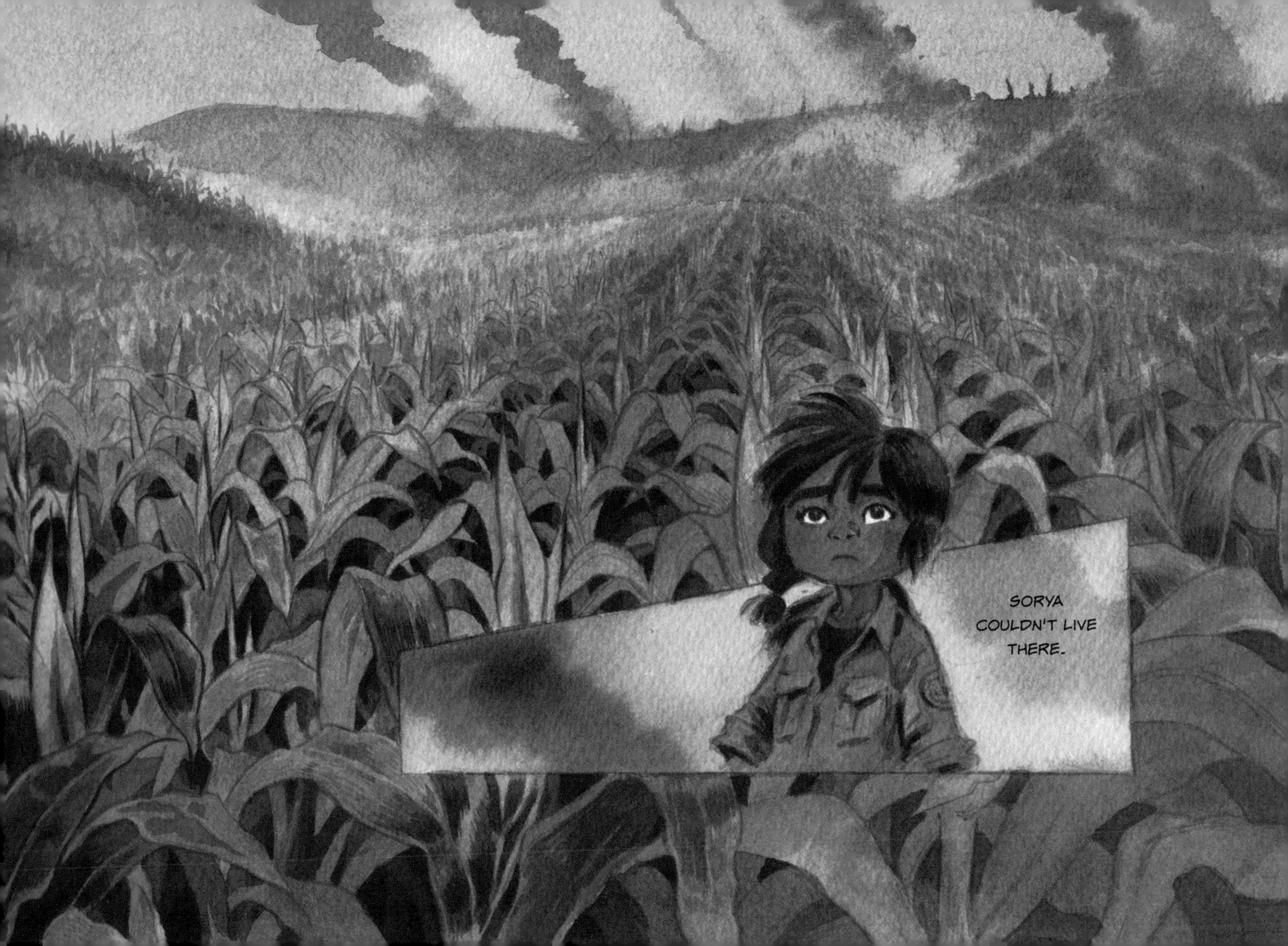
SORYA COULDN'T LIVE THERE.

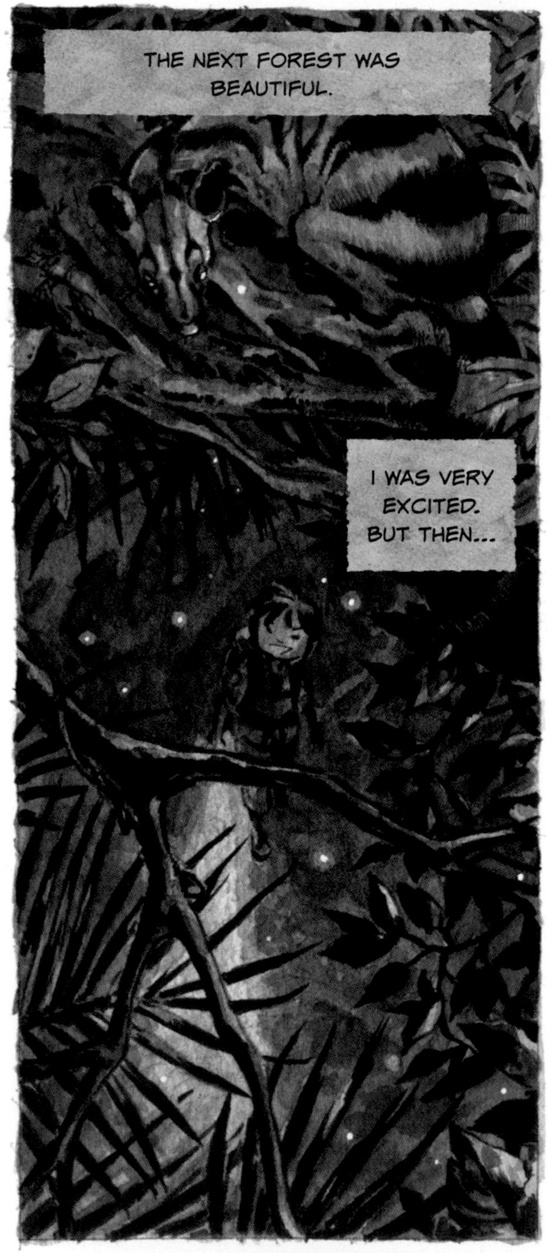
THE NEXT FOREST WAS BEAUTIFUL.
I WAS VERY EXCITED. BUT THEN...

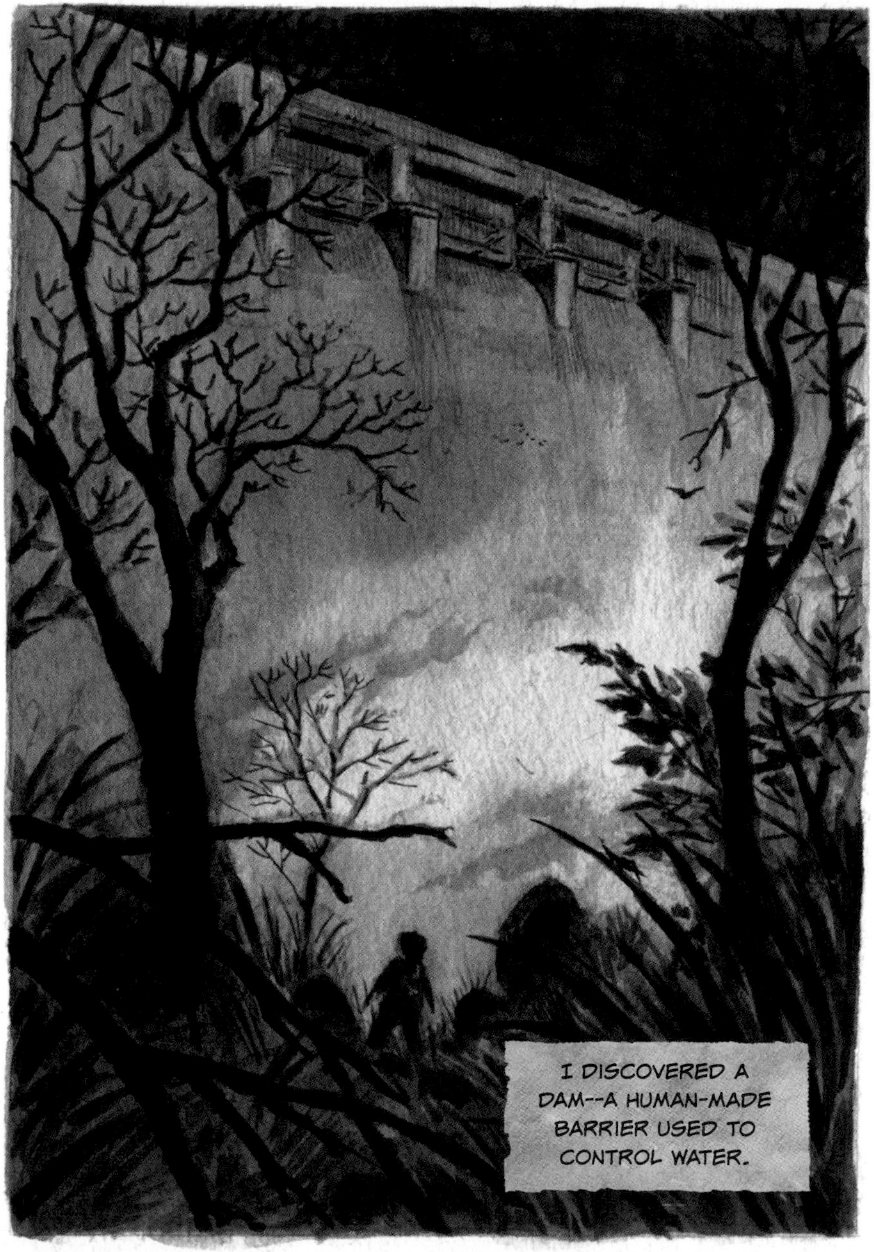
I DISCOVERED A DAM--A HUMAN-MADE BARRIER USED TO CONTROL WATER.

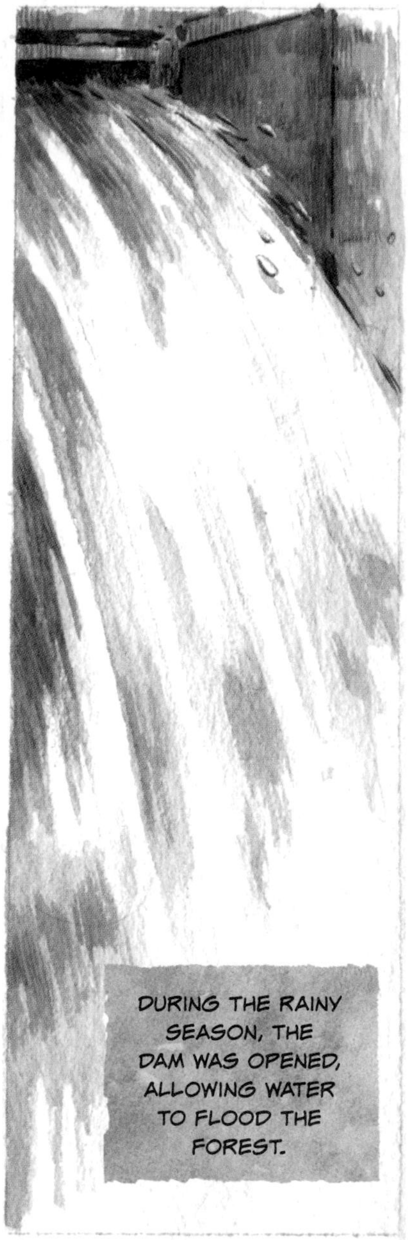
DURING THE RAINY SEASON, THE DAM WAS OPENED, ALLOWING WATER TO FLOOD THE FOREST.

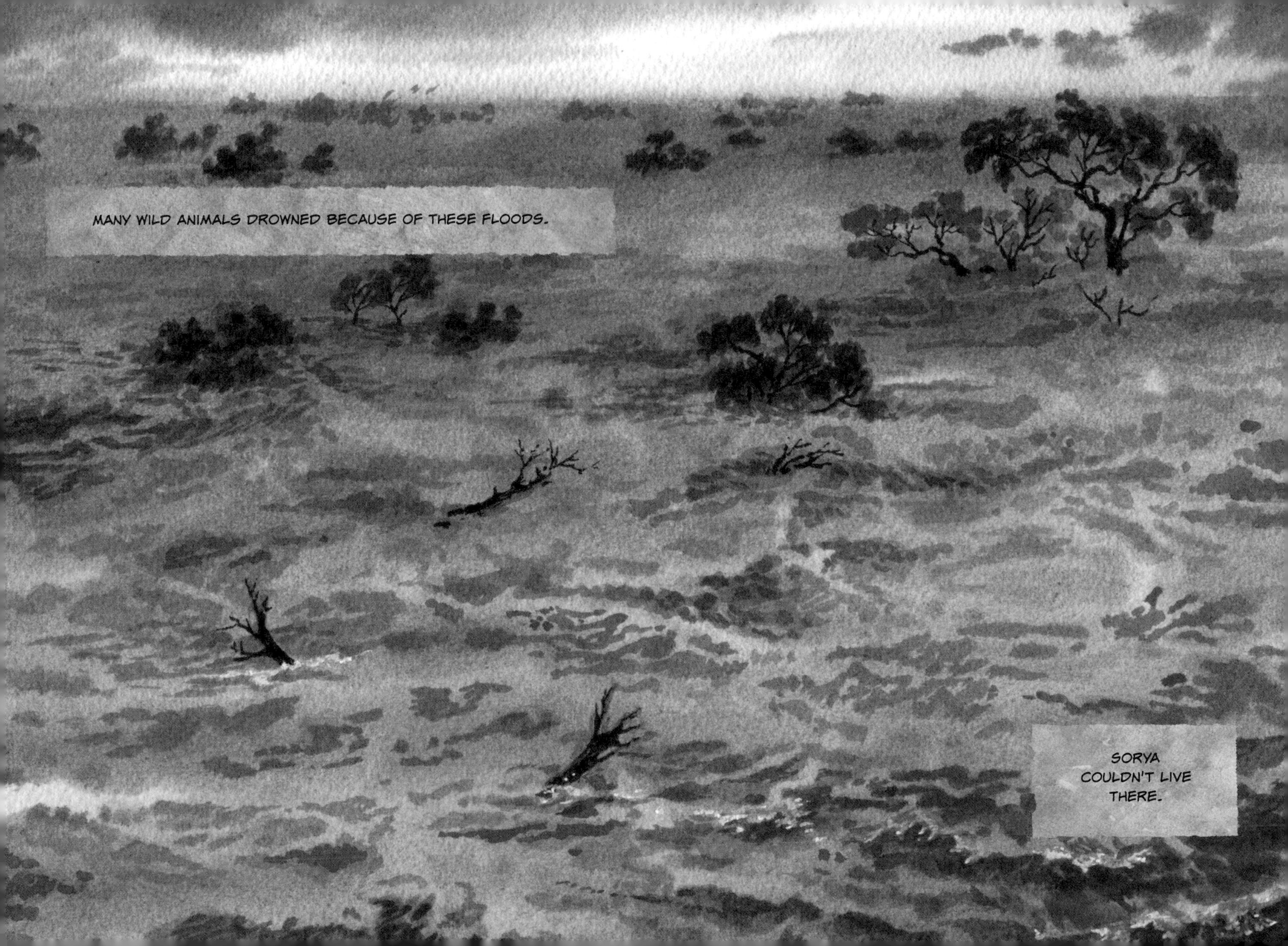
MANY WILD ANIMALS DROWNED BECAUSE OF THESE FLOODS.
SORYA COULDN'T LIVE THERE.

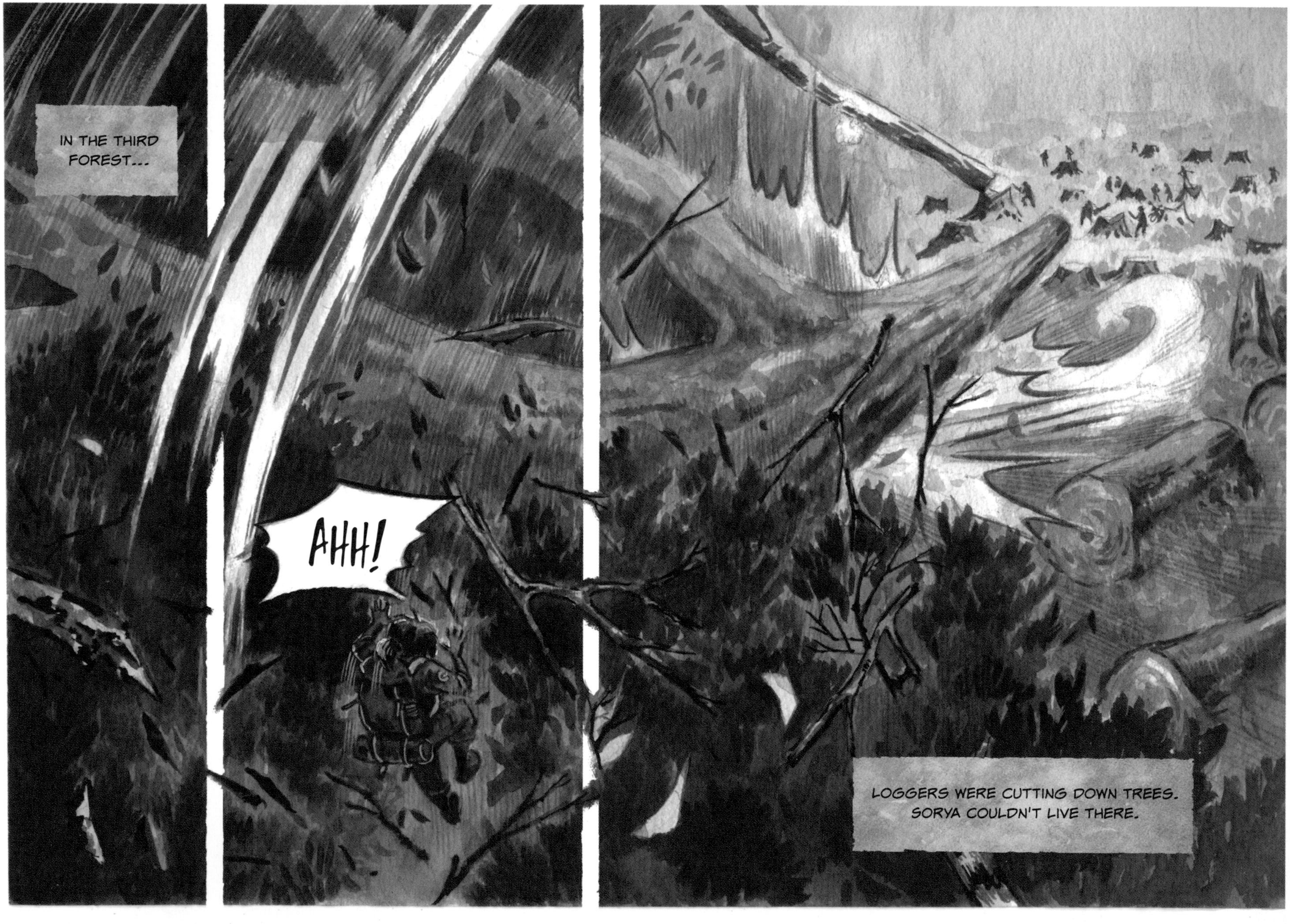
IN THE THIRD FOREST...
AHH!
LOGGERS WERE CUTTING DOWN TREES. SORYA COULDN'T LIVE THERE.

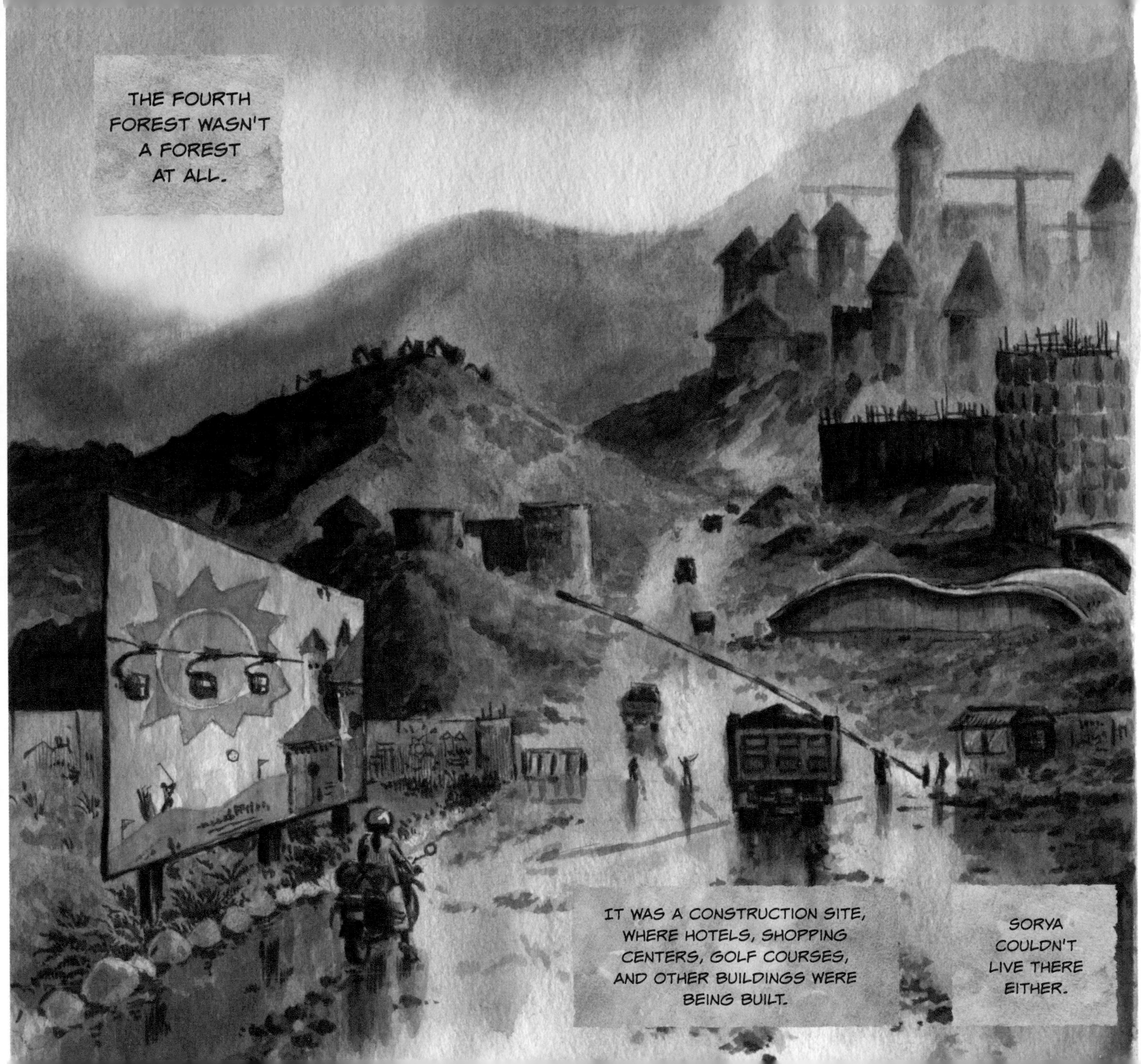
THE FOURTH FOREST WASN'T A FOREST AT ALL.
IT WAS A CONSTRUCTION SITE, WHERE HOTELS, SHOPPING CENTERS, GOLF COURSES, AND OTHER BUILDINGS WERE BEING BUILT.
SORYA COULDN'T LIVE THERE EITHER.

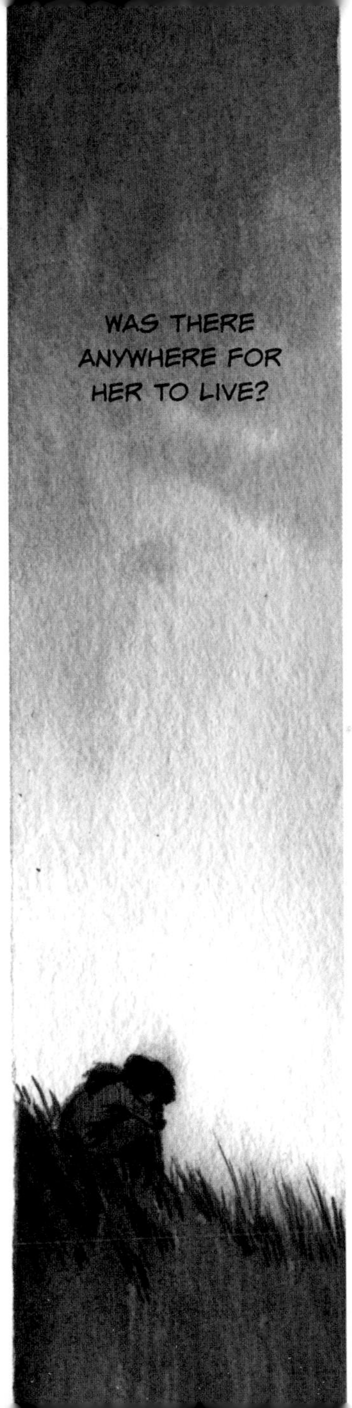
WAS THERE ANYWHERE FOR HER TO LIVE?

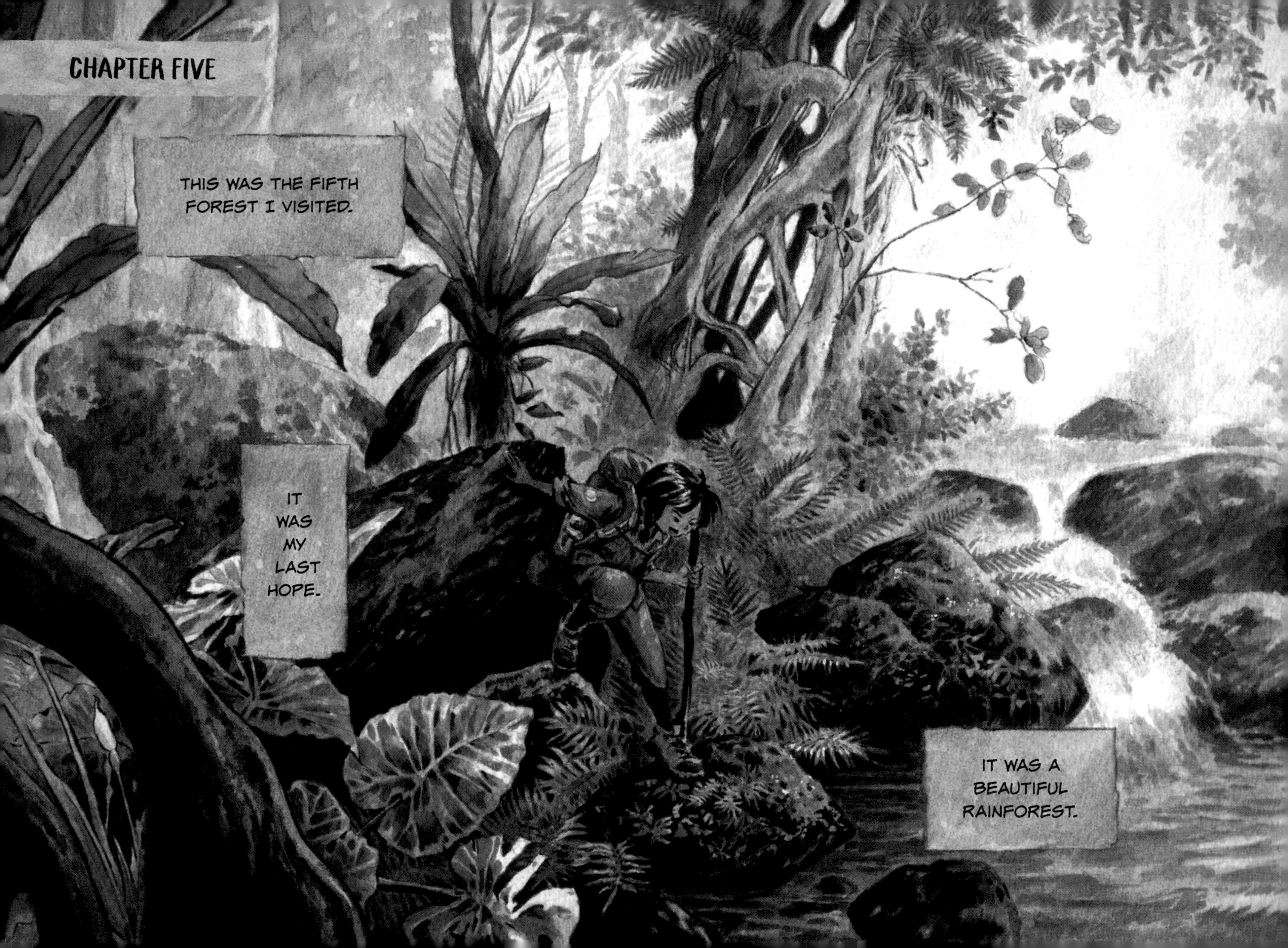
CHAPTER FIVE
THIS WAS THE FIFTH FOREST I VISITED.
IT WAS MY LAST HOPE.
IT WAS A BEAUTIFUL RAINFOREST.

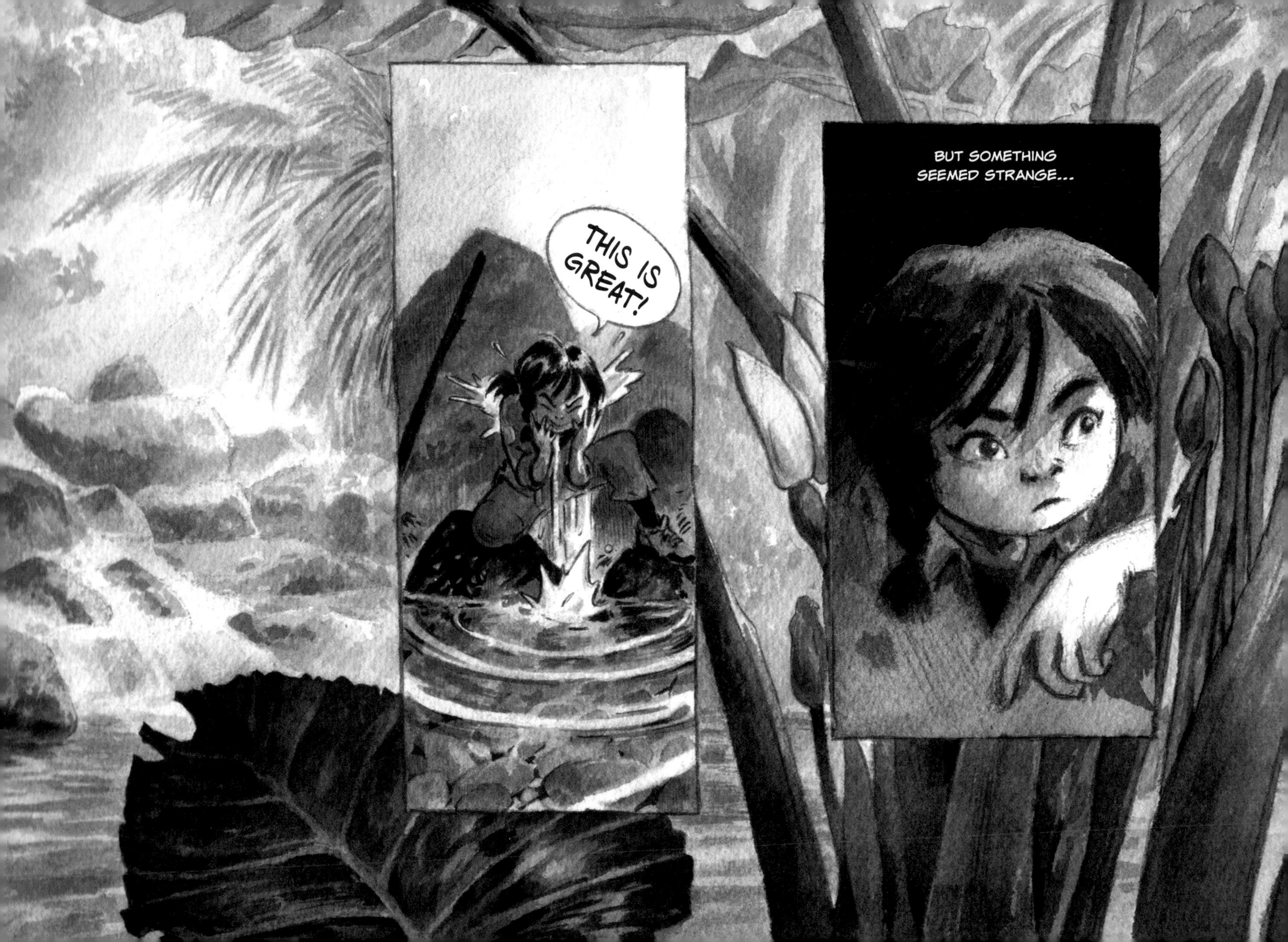
THIS IS GREAT!
BUT SOMETHING SEEMED STRANGE...

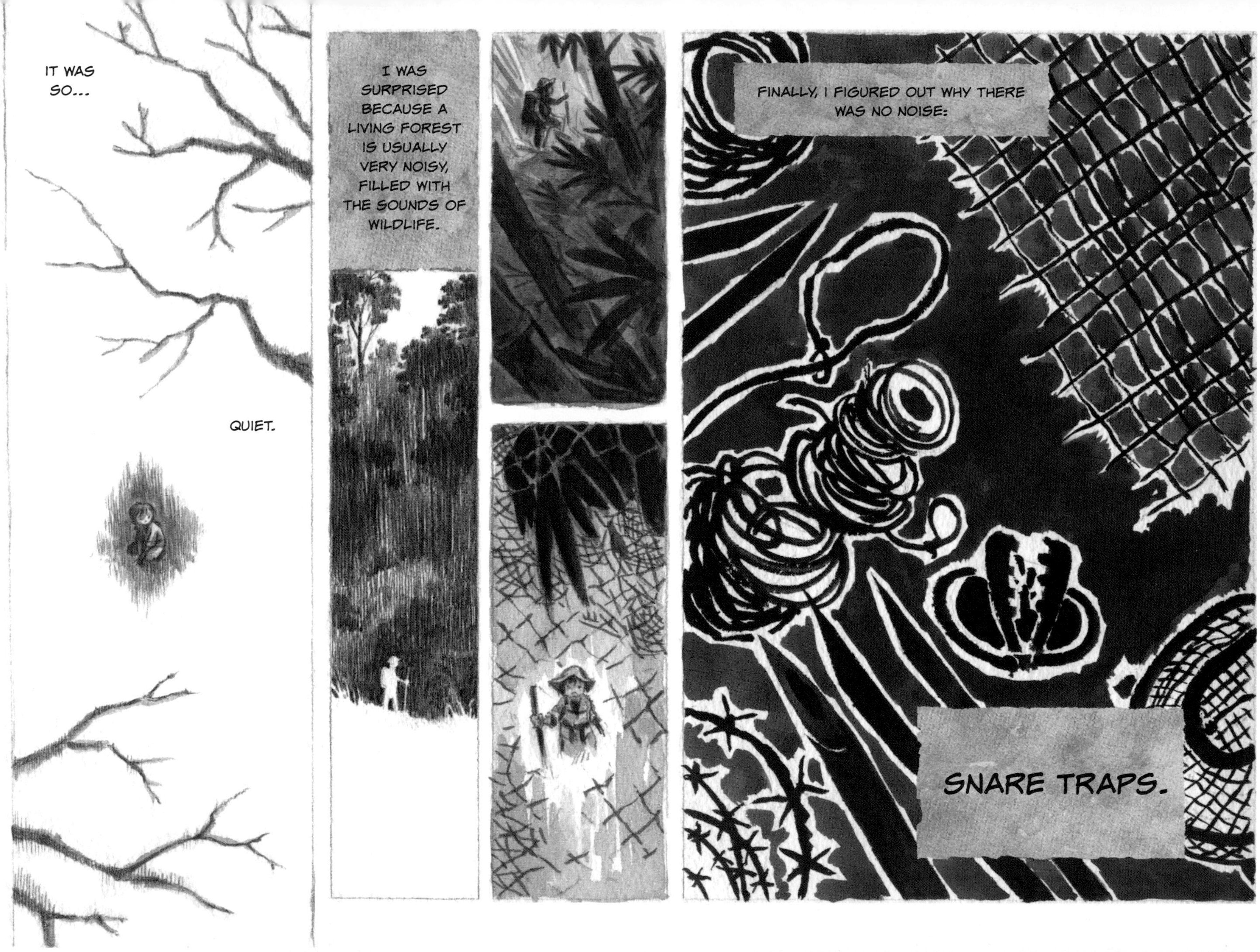
IT WAS SO...
QUIET.
I WAS SURPRISED BECAUSE A LIVING FOREST IS USUALLY VERY NOISY, FILLED WITH THE SOUNDS OF WILDLIFE.
FINALLY, I FIGURED OUT WHY THERE WAS NO NOISE:
SNARE TRAPS.

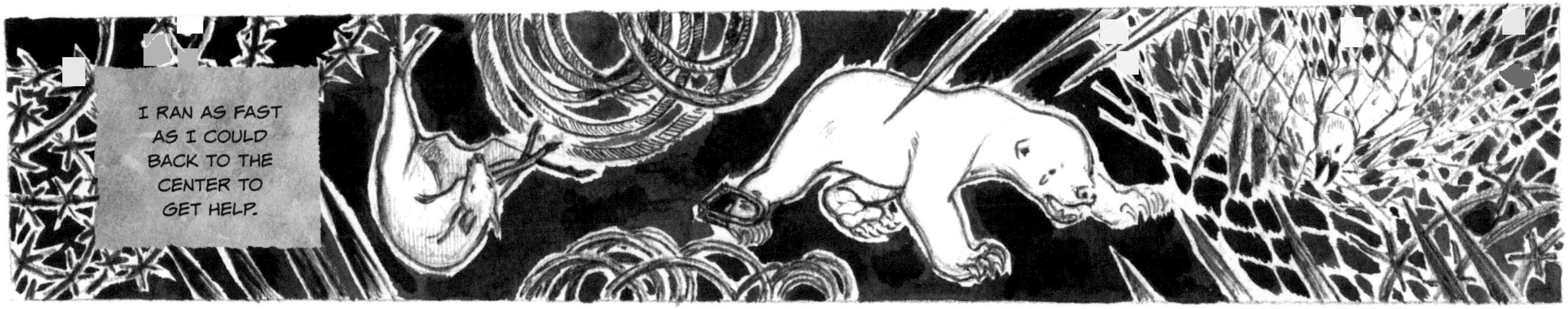
I RAN AS FAST AS I COULD BACK TO THE CENTER TO GET HELP.

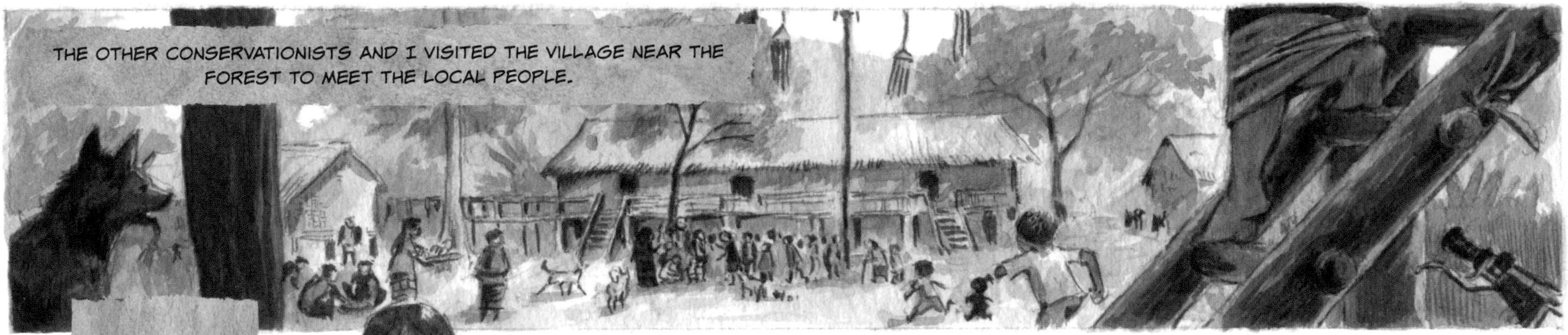
THE OTHER CONSERVATIONISTS AND I VISITED THE VILLAGE NEAR THE FOREST TO MEET THE LOCAL PEOPLE.

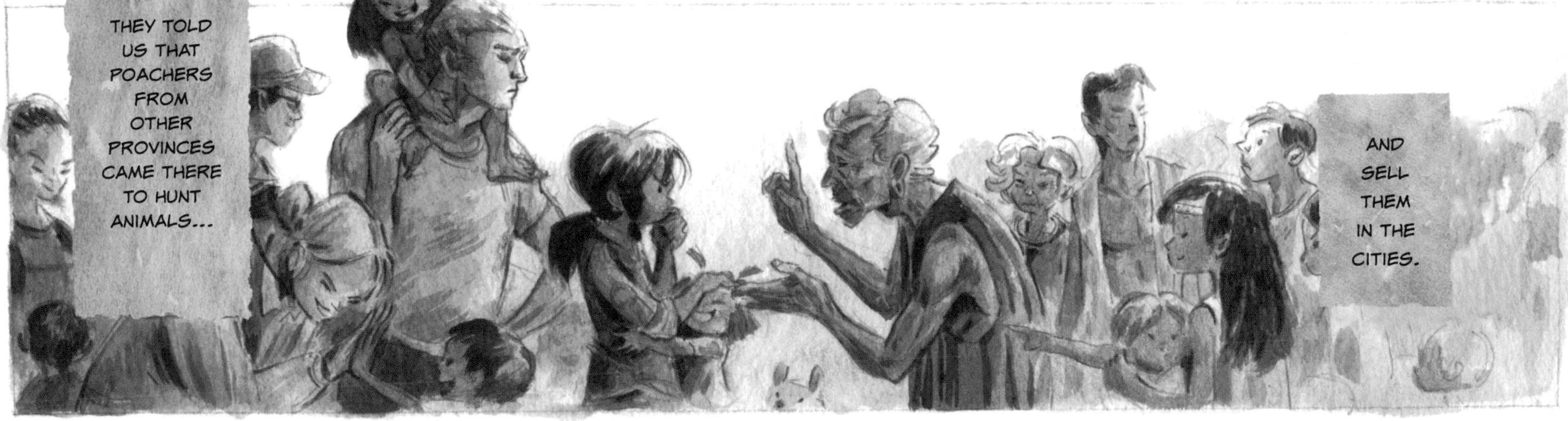
THEY TOLD US THAT POACHERS FROM OTHER PROVINCES CAME THERE TO HUNT ANIMALS...
AND SELL THEM IN THE CITIES.

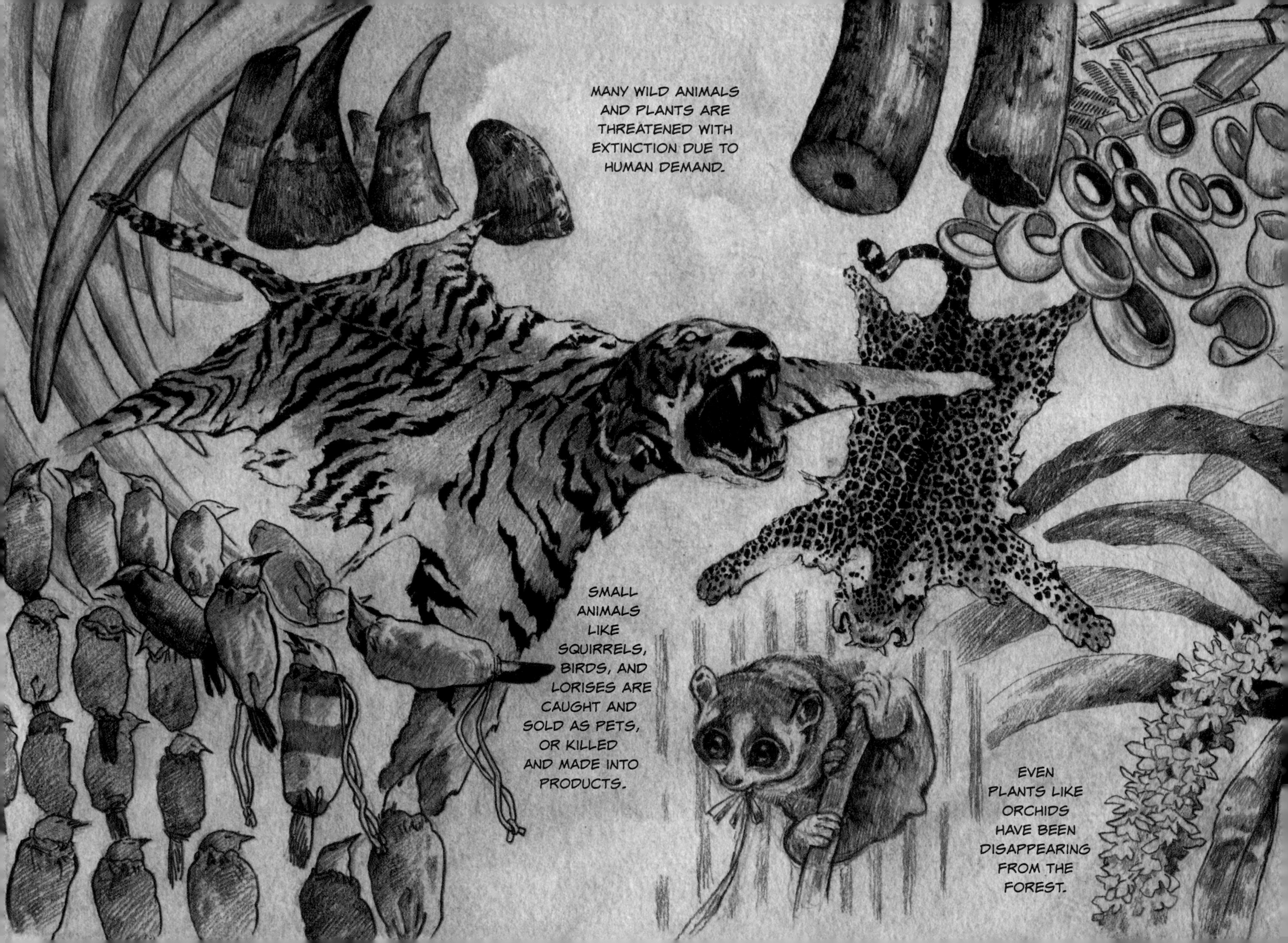
MANY WILD ANIMALS AND PLANTS ARE THREATENED WITH EXTINCTION DUE TO HUMAN DEMAND.
SMALL ANIMALS LIKE SQUIRRELS, BIRDS, AND LORISES ARE CAUGHT AND SOLD AS PETS, OR KILLED AND MADE INTO PRODUCTS.
EVEN PLANTS LIKE ORCHIDS HAVE BEEN DISAPPEARING FROM THE FOREST.

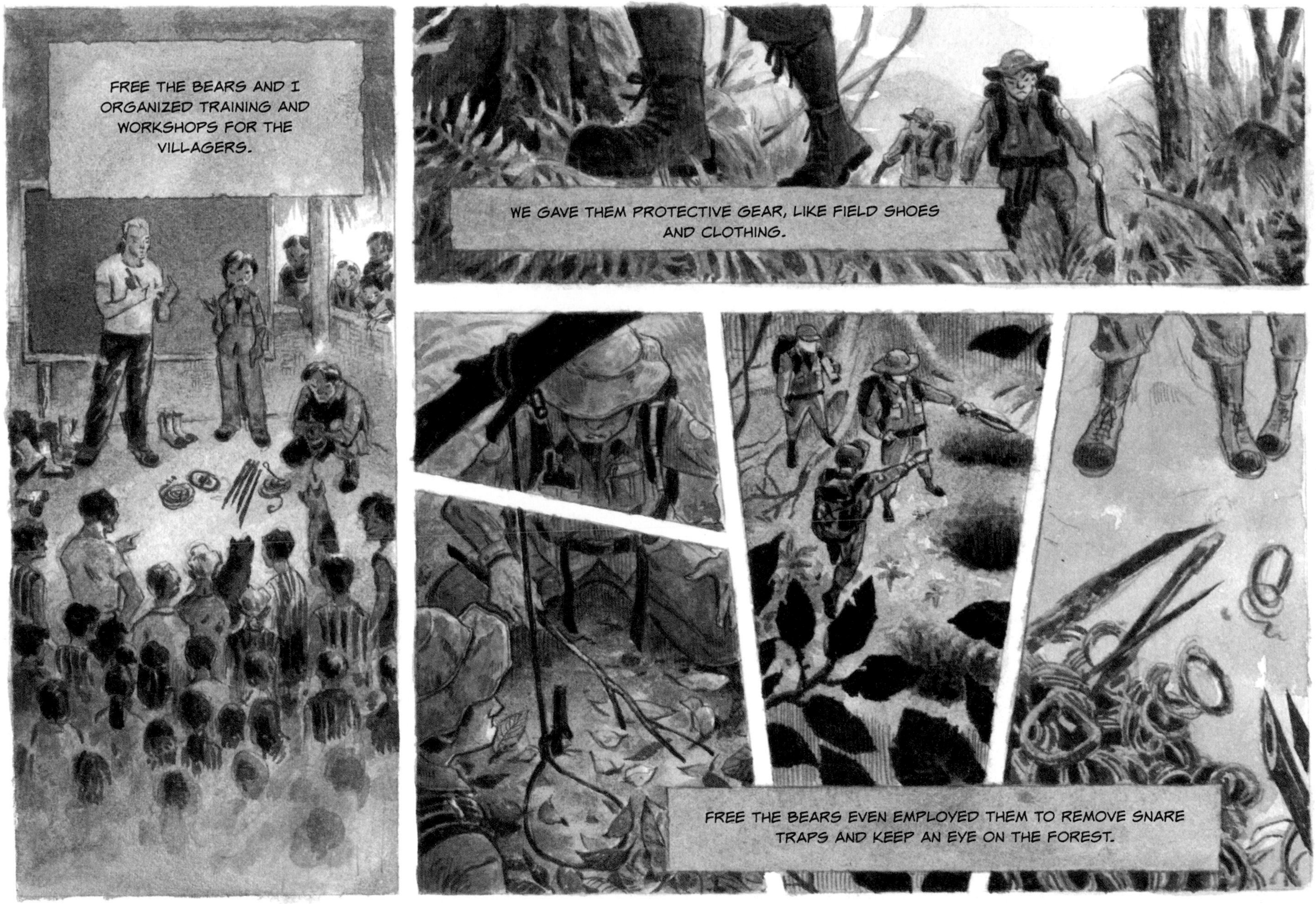
FREE THE BEARS AND I ORGANIZED TRAINING AND WORKSHOPS FOR THE VILLAGERS.
WE GAVE THEM PROTECTIVE GEAR, LIKE FIELD SHOES AND CLOTHING.
FREE THE BEARS EVEN EMPLOYED THEM TO REMOVE SNARE TRAPS AND KEEP AN EYE ON THE FOREST.

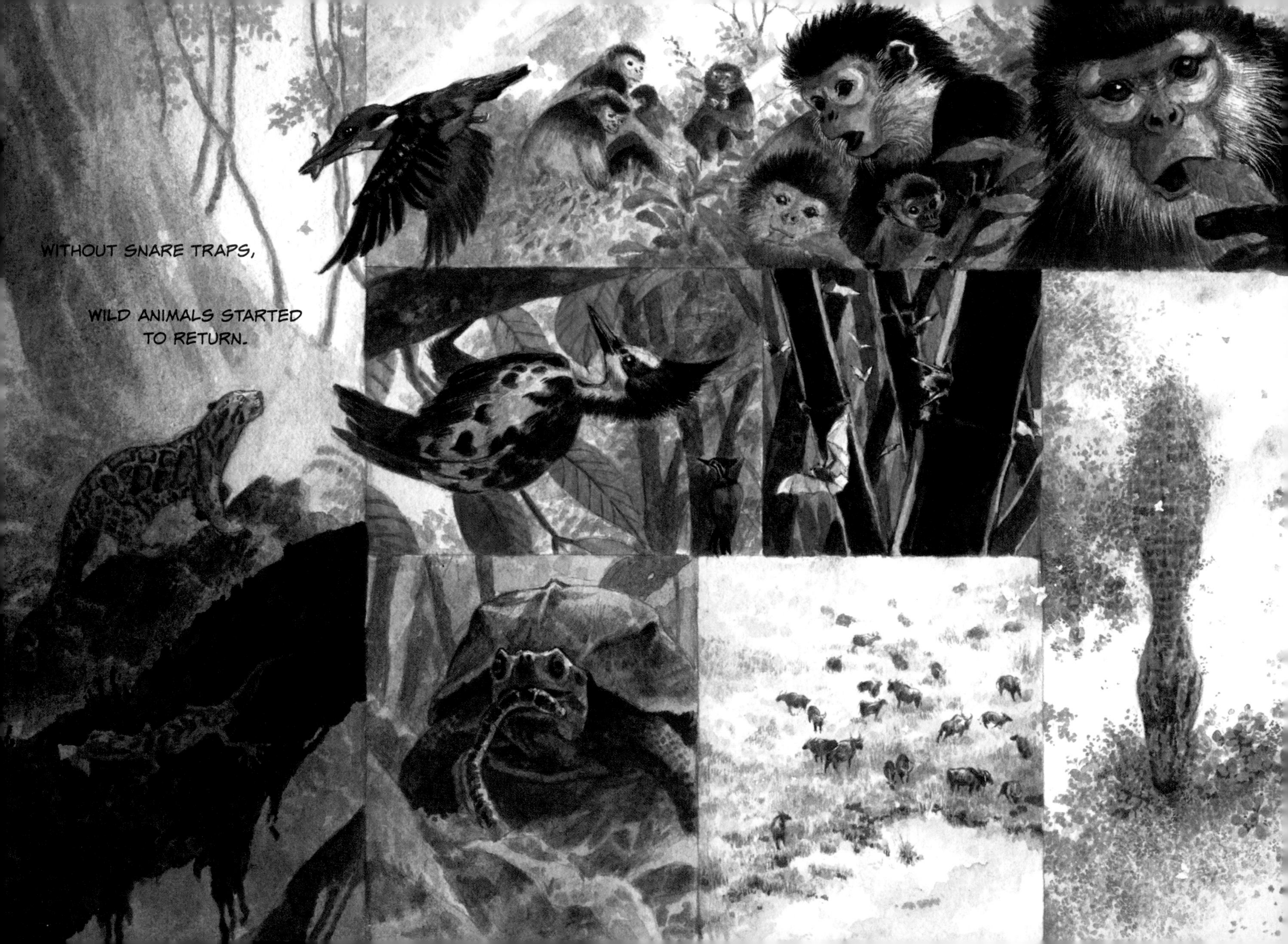
WITHOUT SNARE TRAPS,
WILD ANIMALS STARTED TO RETURN.

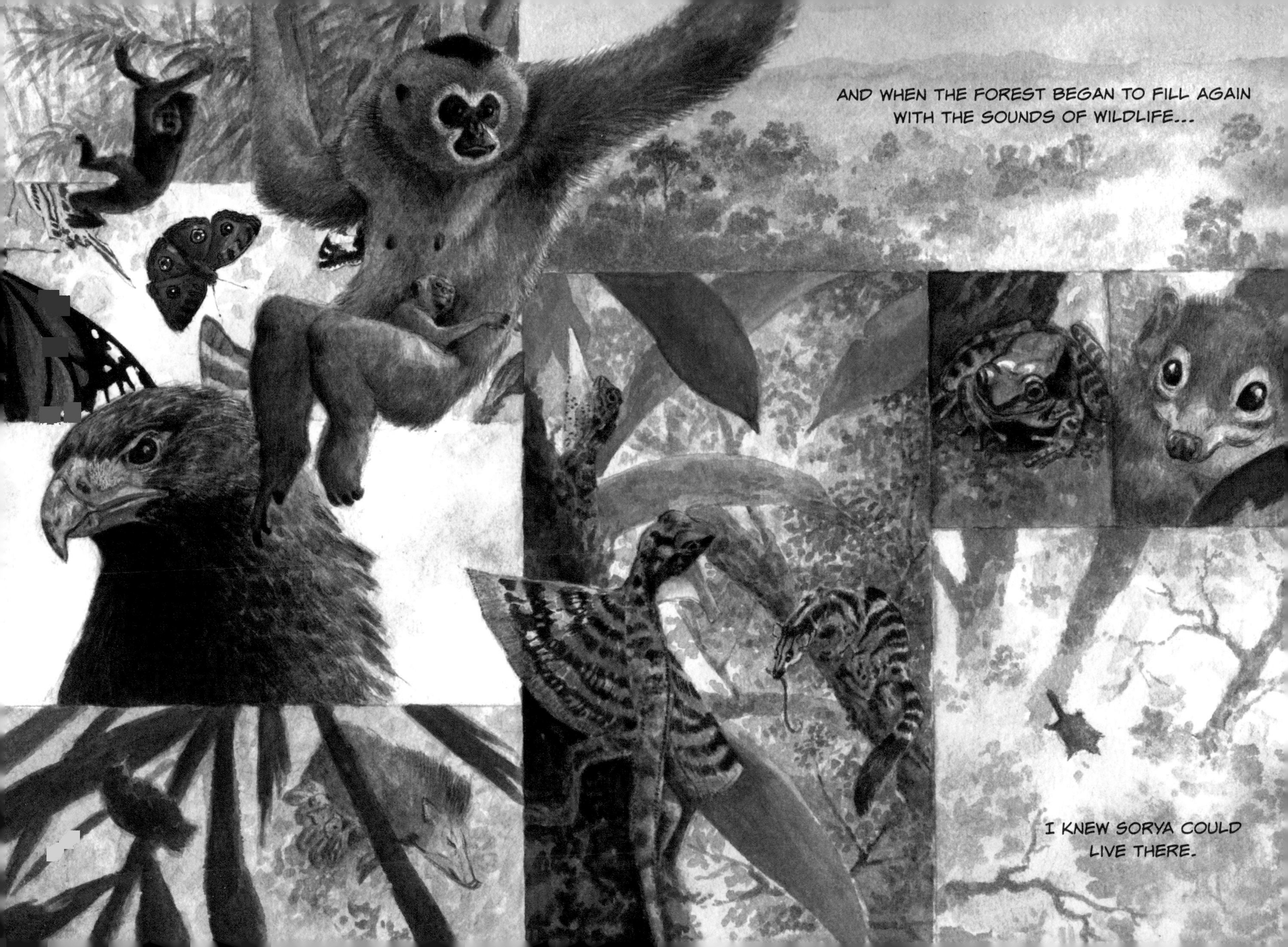
AND WHEN THE FOREST BEGAN TO FILL AGAIN WITH THE SOUNDS OF WILDLIFE...
I KNEW SORYA COULD LIVE THERE.

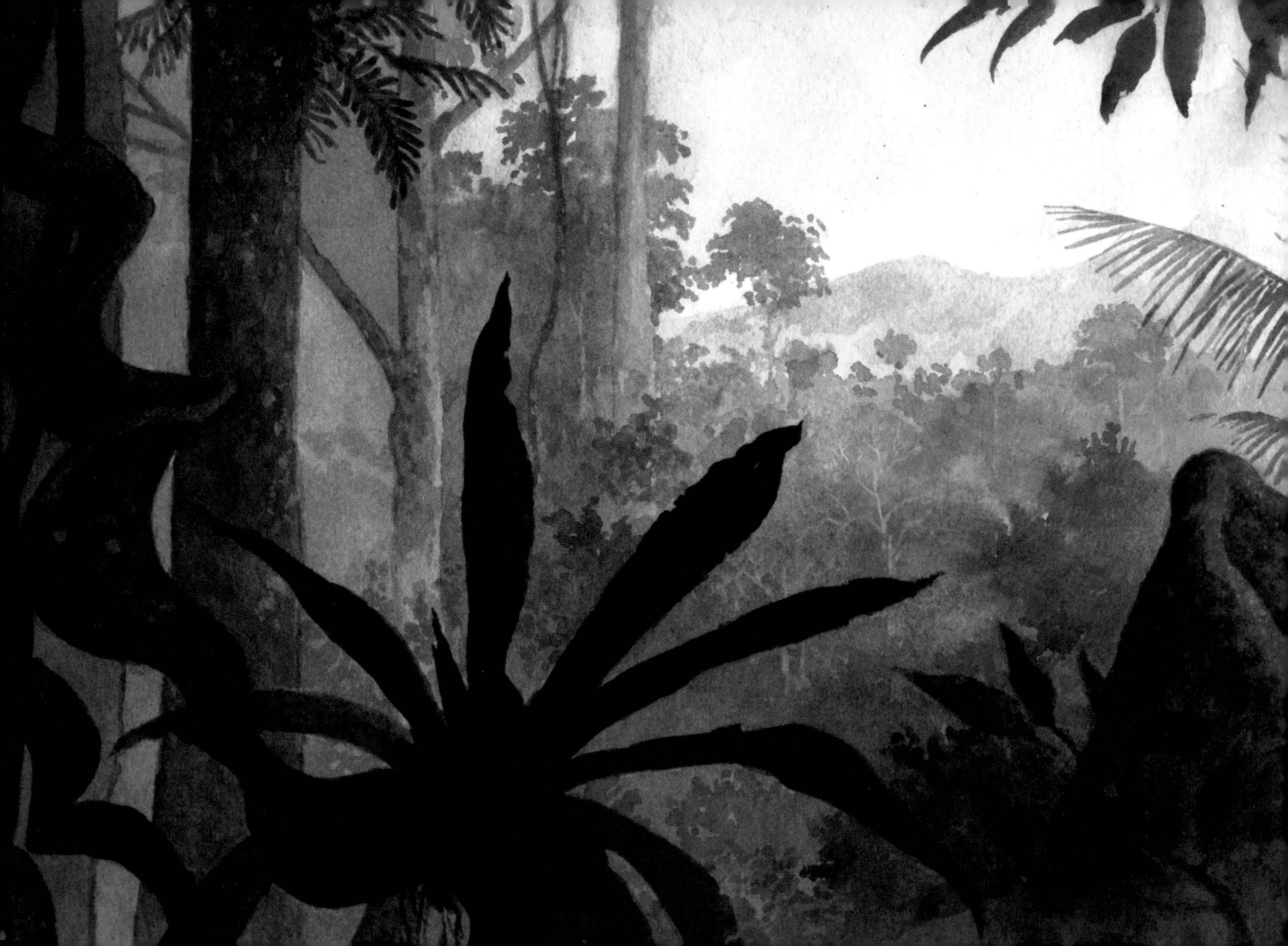

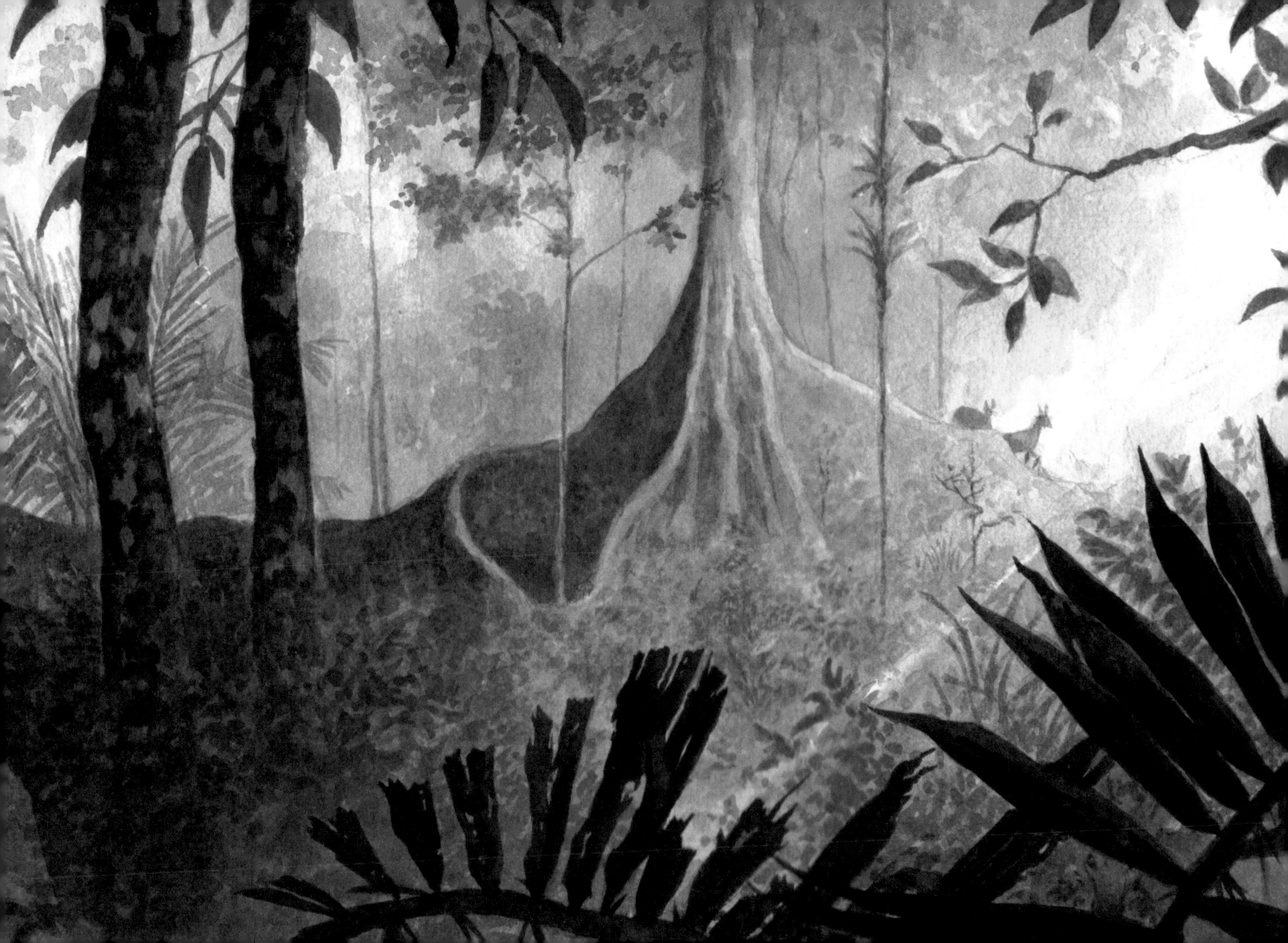

CHAPTER SIX

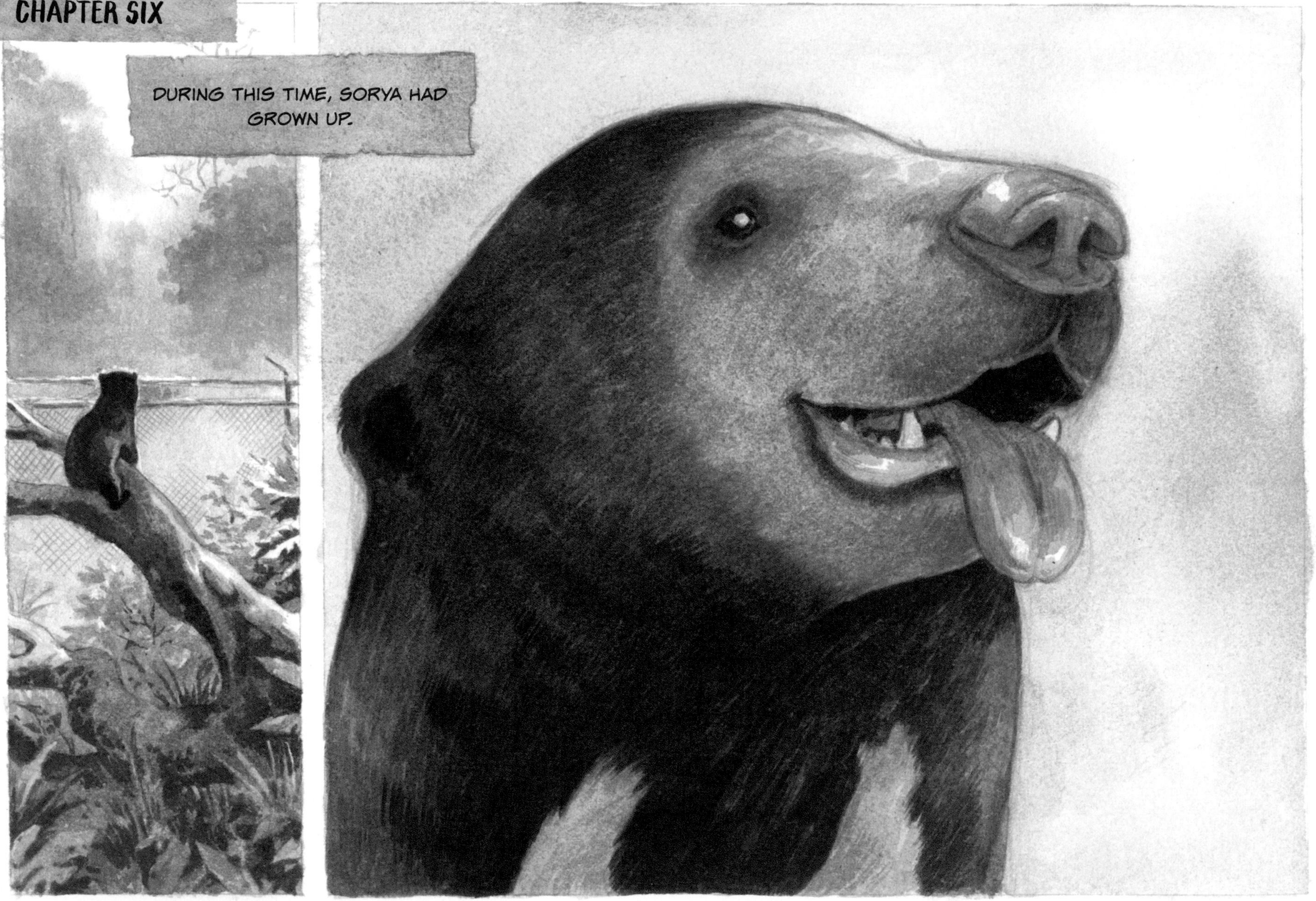
DURING THIS TIME, SORYA HAD GROWN UP.

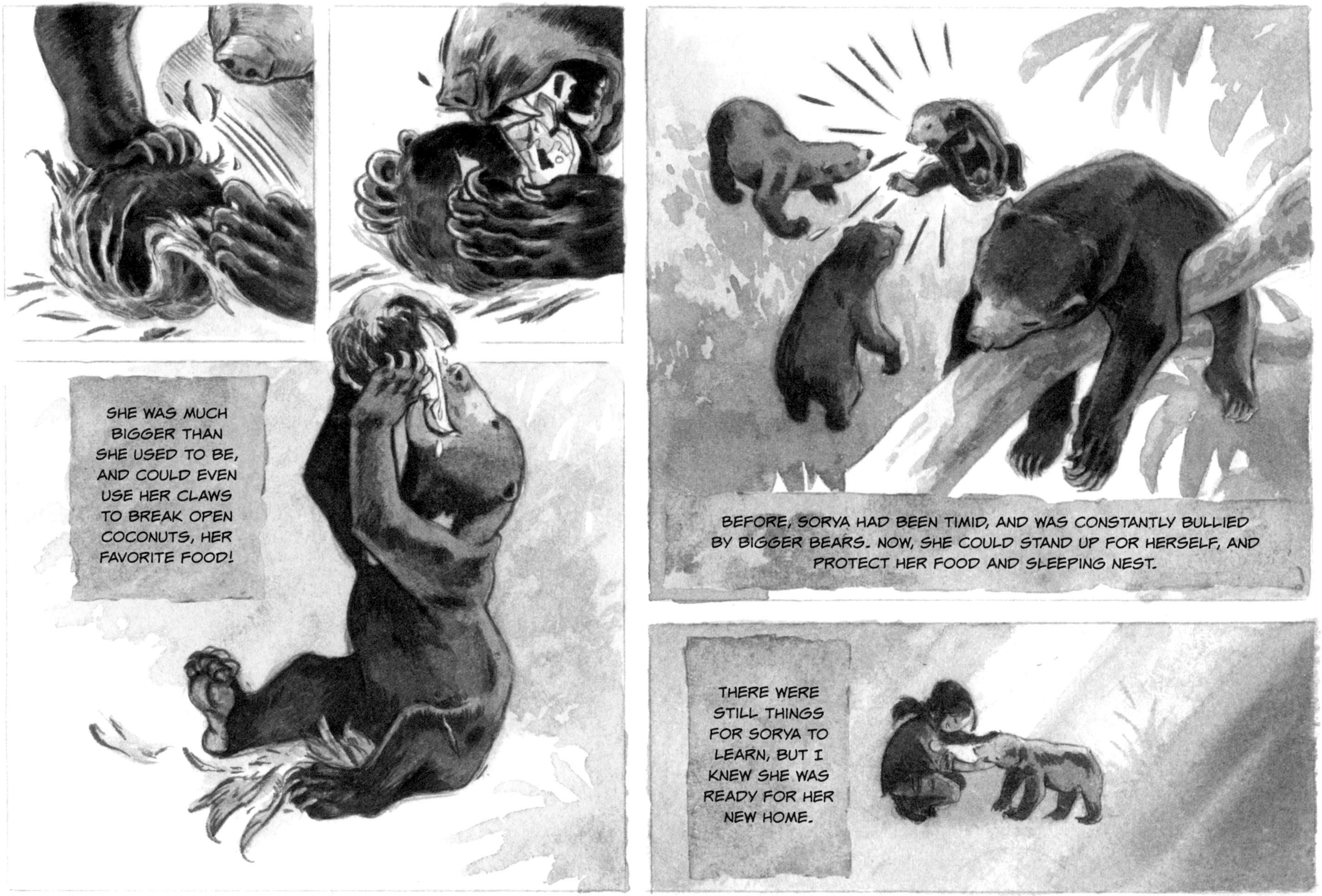
SHE WAS MUCH BIGGER THAN SHE USED TO BE, AND COULD EVEN USE HER CLAWS TO BREAK OPEN COCONUTS, HER FAVORITE FOOD!
BEFORE, SORYA HAD BEEN TIMID, AND WAS CONSTANTLY BULLIED BY BIGGER BEARS. NOW, SHE COULD STAND UP FOR HERSELF, AND PROTECT HER FOOD AND SLEEPING NEST.
THERE WERE STILL THINGS FOR SORYA TO LEARN, BUT I KNEW SHE WAS READY FOR HER NEW HOME.

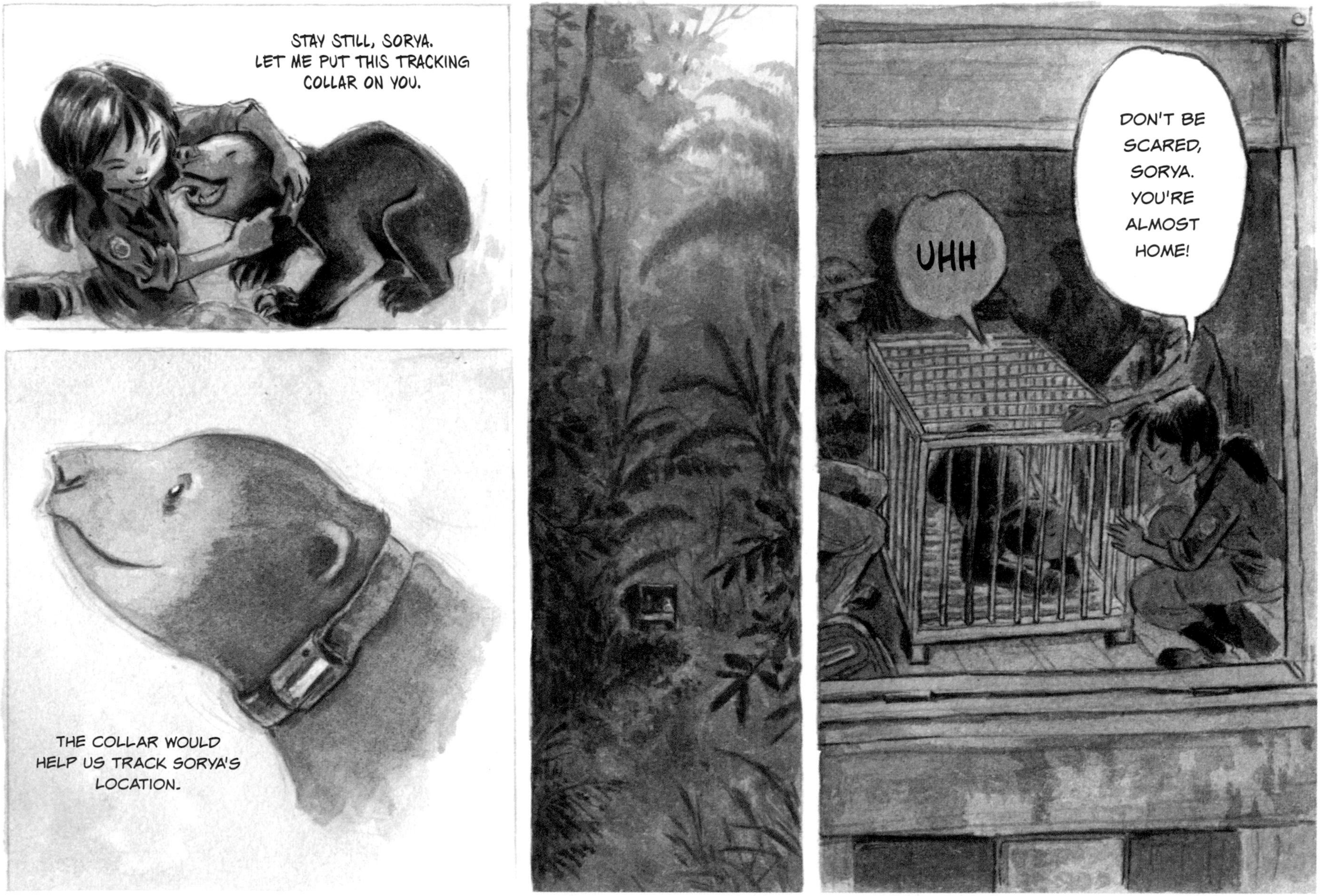
STAY STILL, SORYA. LET ME PUT THIS TRACKING COLLAR ON YOU.
THE COLLAR WOULD HELP US TRACK SORYA'S LOCATION.
DON'T BE SCARED, SORYA. YOU'RE ALMOST HOME!
UHH

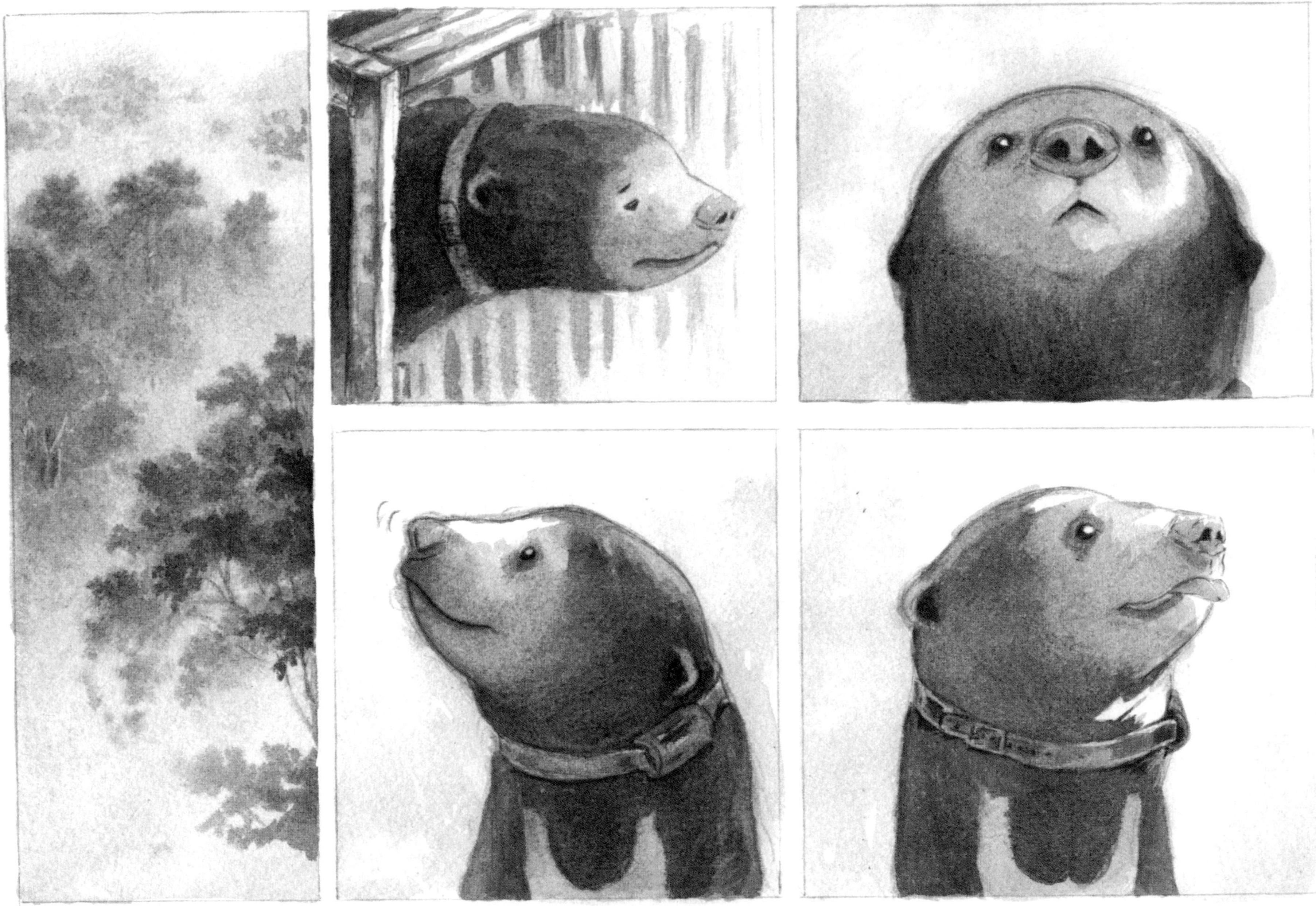

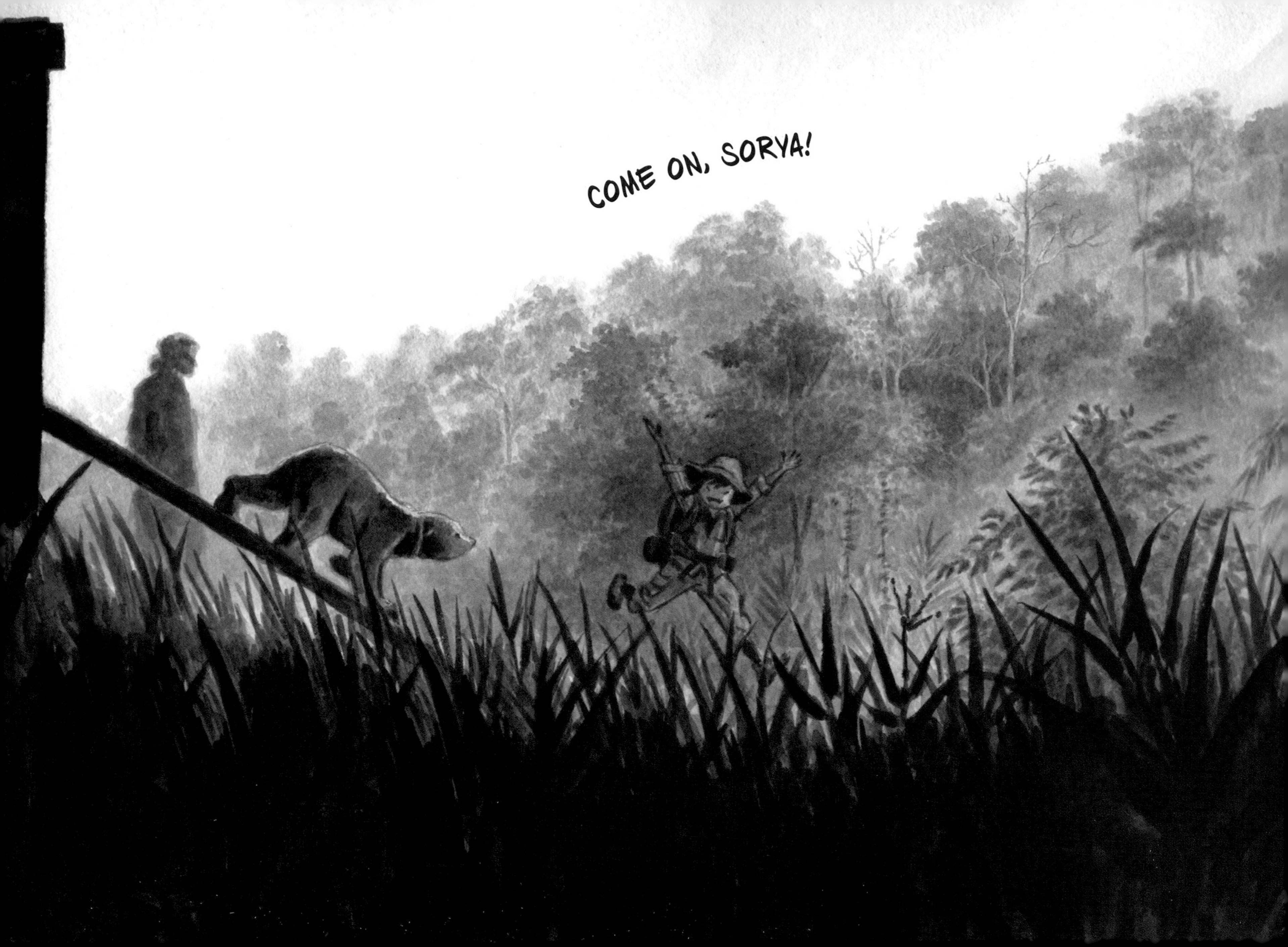
COME ON, SORYA!

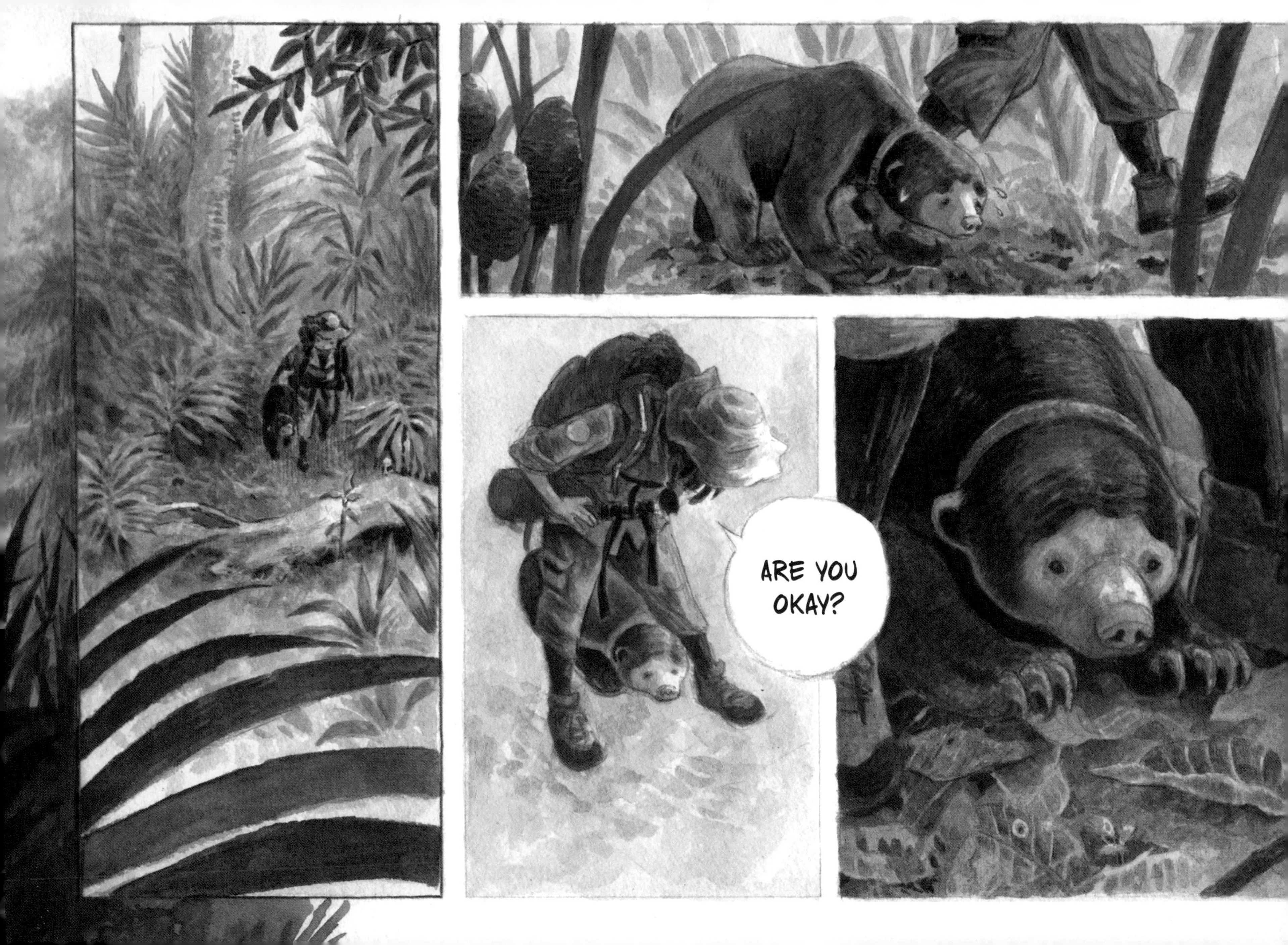
ARE YOU
OKAY?

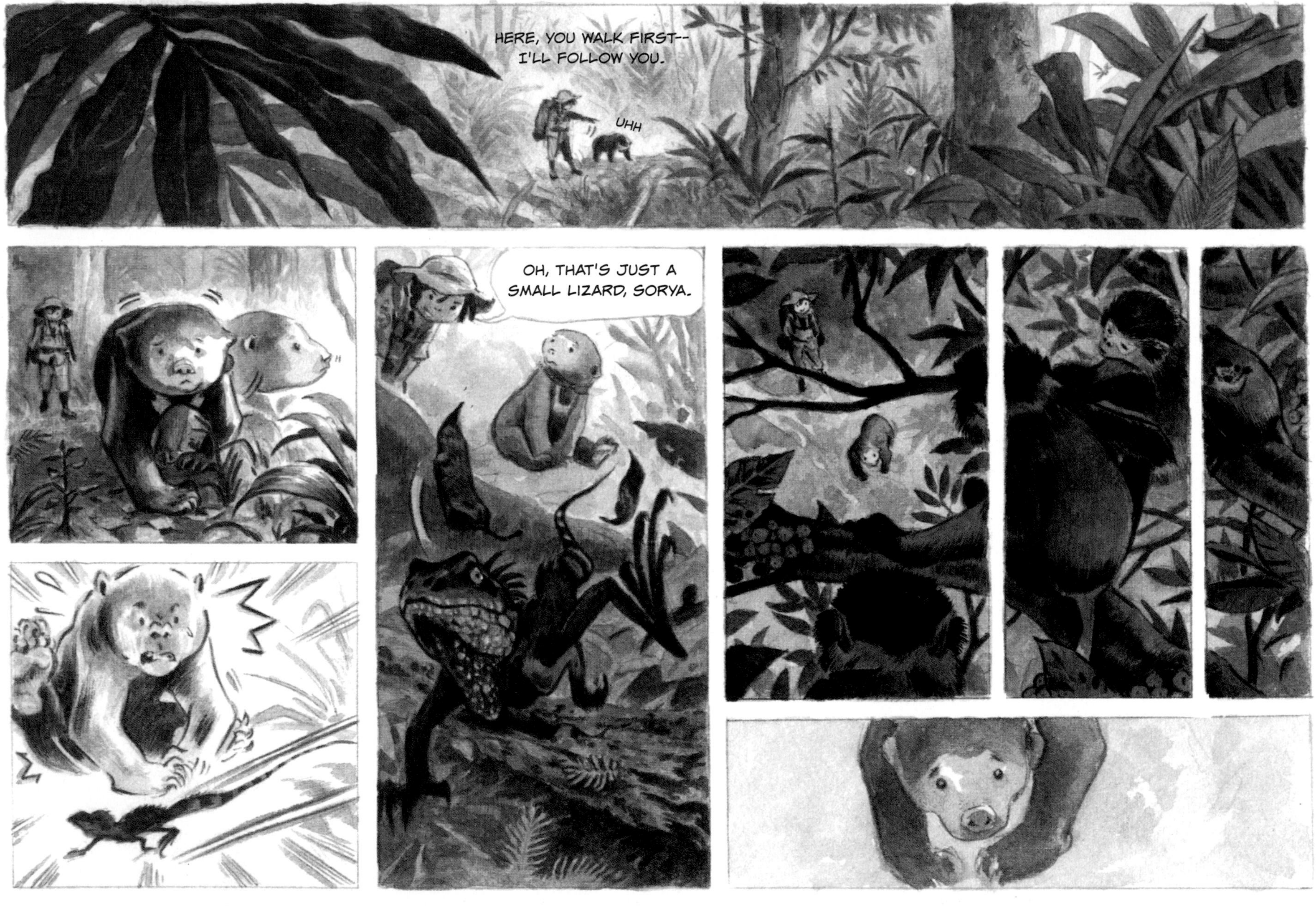
HERE, YOU WALK FIRST--
I'LL FOLLOW YOU.
UHH
OH, THAT'S JUST A SMALL LIZARD, SORYA.

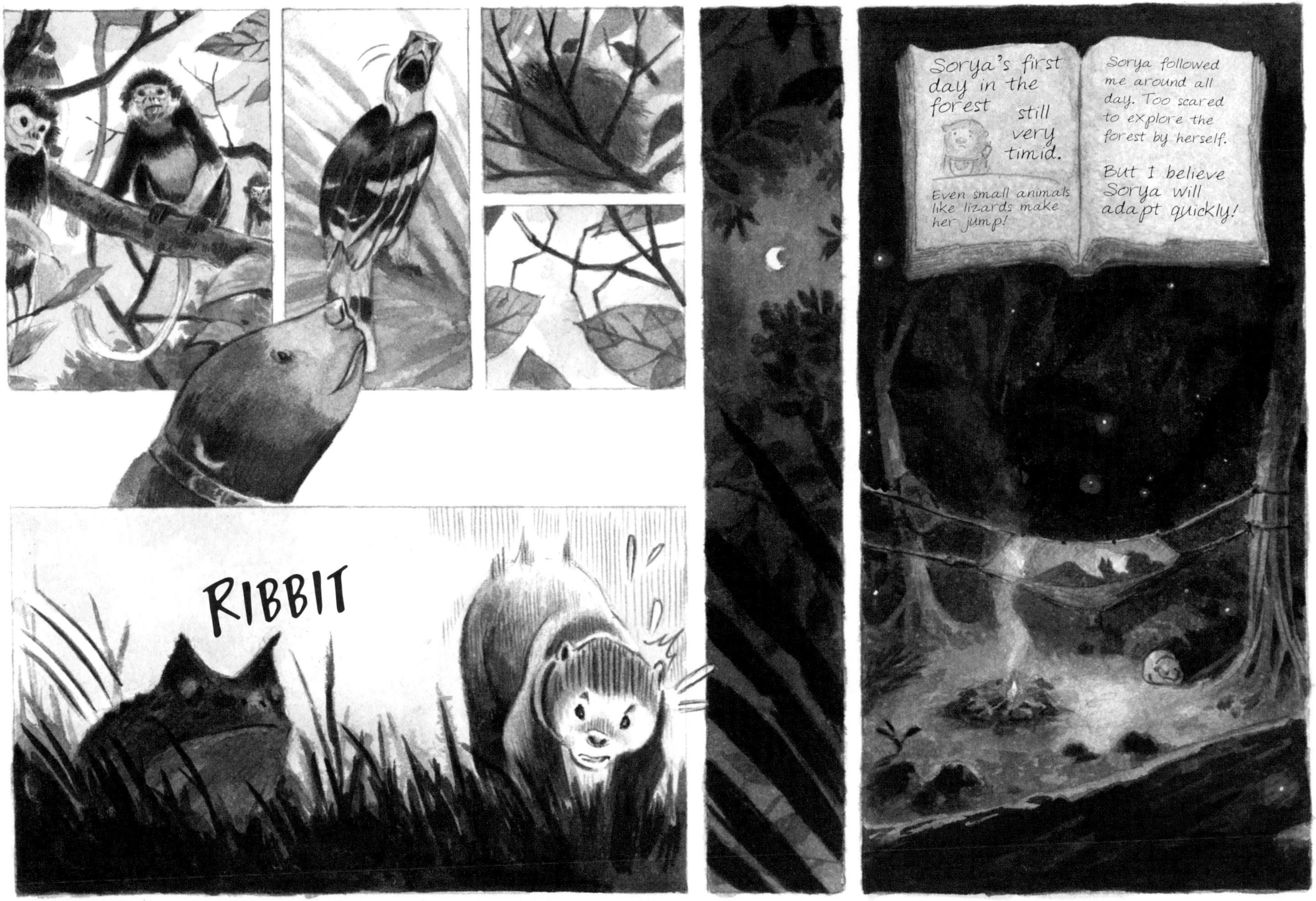

RIBBIT
Sorya's first day in the forest
still very timid.
Even small animals like lizards make her jump!
Sorya followed me around all day. Too scared to explore the forest by herself.
But I believe Sorya will adapt quickly!

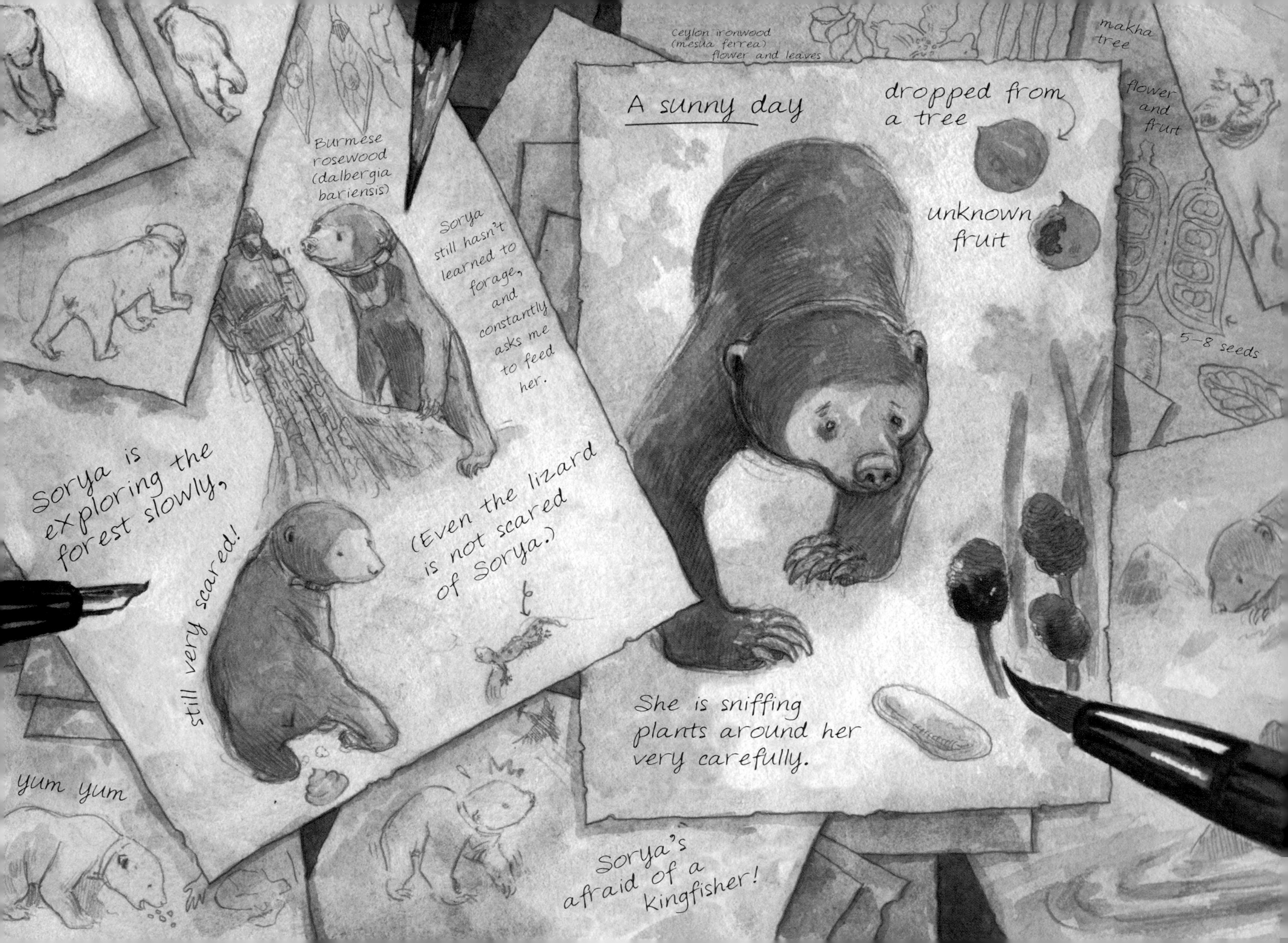

ceylon ironwood
(mesua ferrea)
flower and leaves
makha tree
Burmese rosewood (dalbergia bariensis)
Sorya still hasn't learned to forage, and constantly asks me to feed her.
A sunny day
dropped from a tree
unknown fruit
flower and fruit
5–8 seeds
Sorya is exploring the forest slowly,
still very scared!
(Even the lizard is not scared of Sorya.)
She is sniffing plants around her very carefully.
yum yum
Sorya's afraid of a kingfisher!

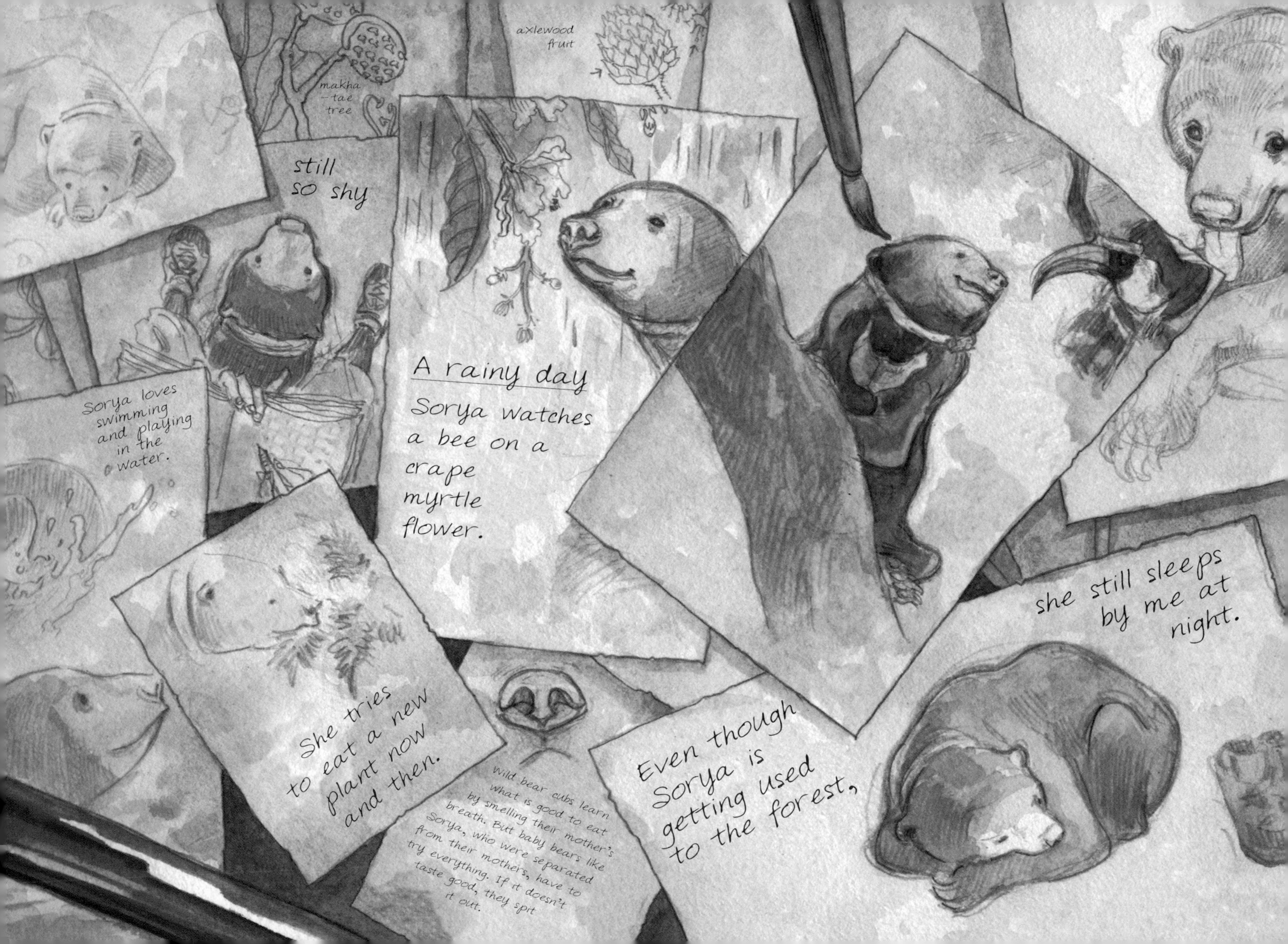
makha-tae tree
axlewood fruit
still so shy
Sorya loves swimming and playing in the water.
A rainy day
Sorya watches a bee on a crape myrtle flower.
She tries to eat a new plant now and then.
Wild bear cubs learn what is good to eat by smelling their mother's breath. But baby bears like Sorya, who were separated from their mothers, have to try everything. If it doesn't taste good, they spit it out.
Even though Sorya is getting used to the forest,
she still sleeps by me at night.

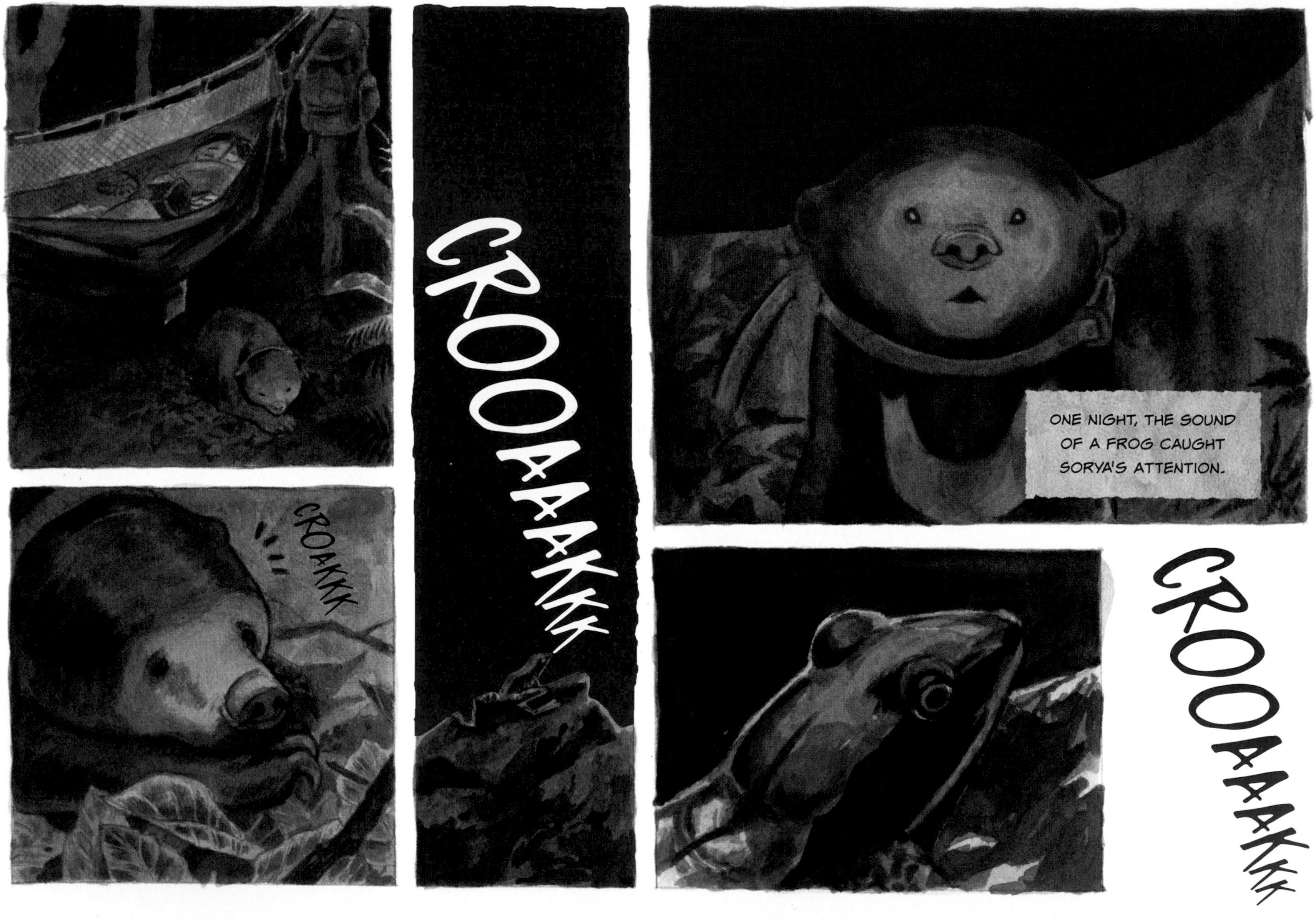
CROAKKK
CROOAAAKKK
ONE NIGHT, THE SOUND OF A FROG CAUGHT SORYA'S ATTENTION.
CROOAAAKKK

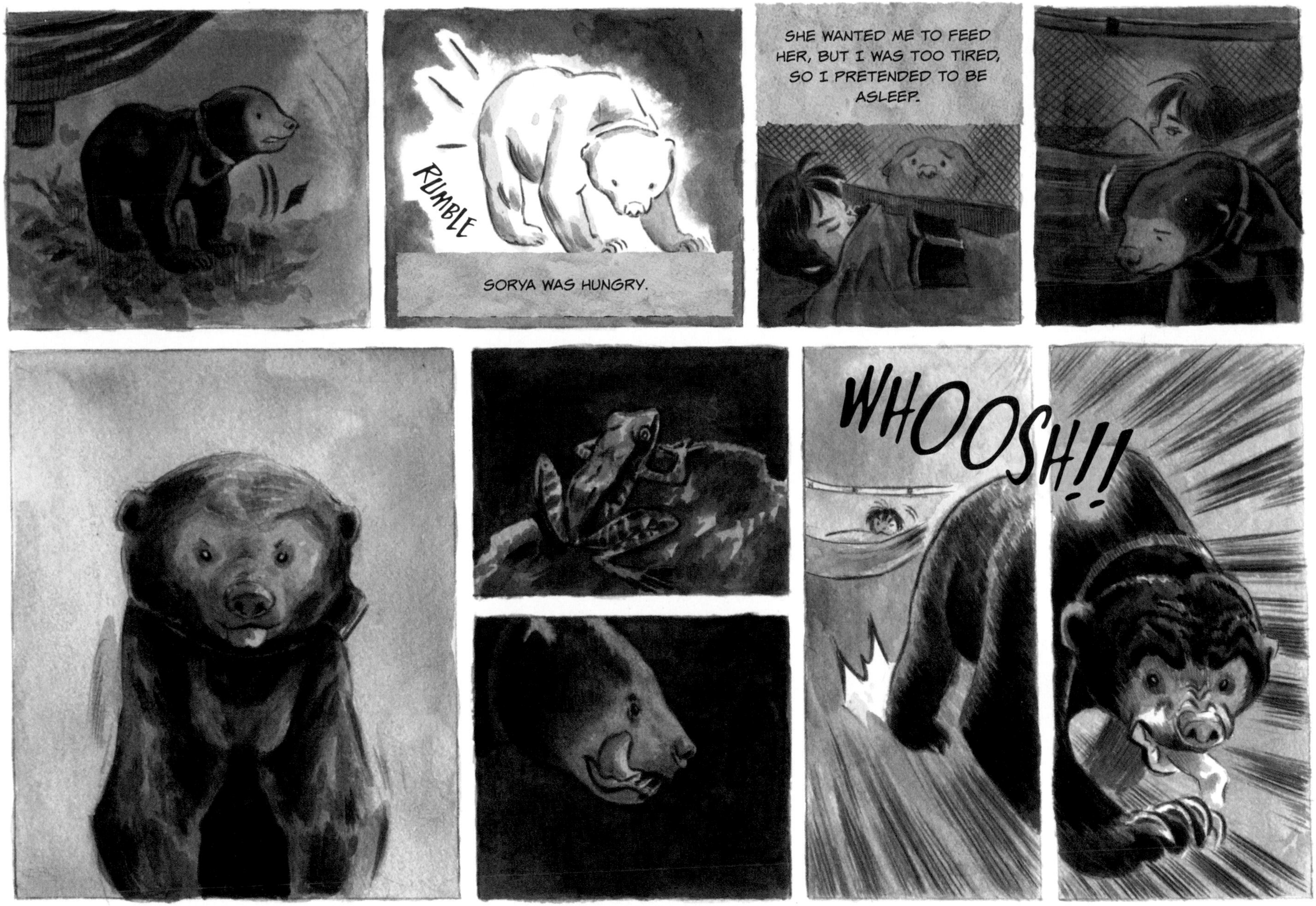
RUMBLE
SORYA WAS HUNGRY.
SHE WANTED ME TO FEED HER, BUT I WAS TOO TIRED, SO I PRETENDED TO BE ASLEEP.
WHOOSH!!

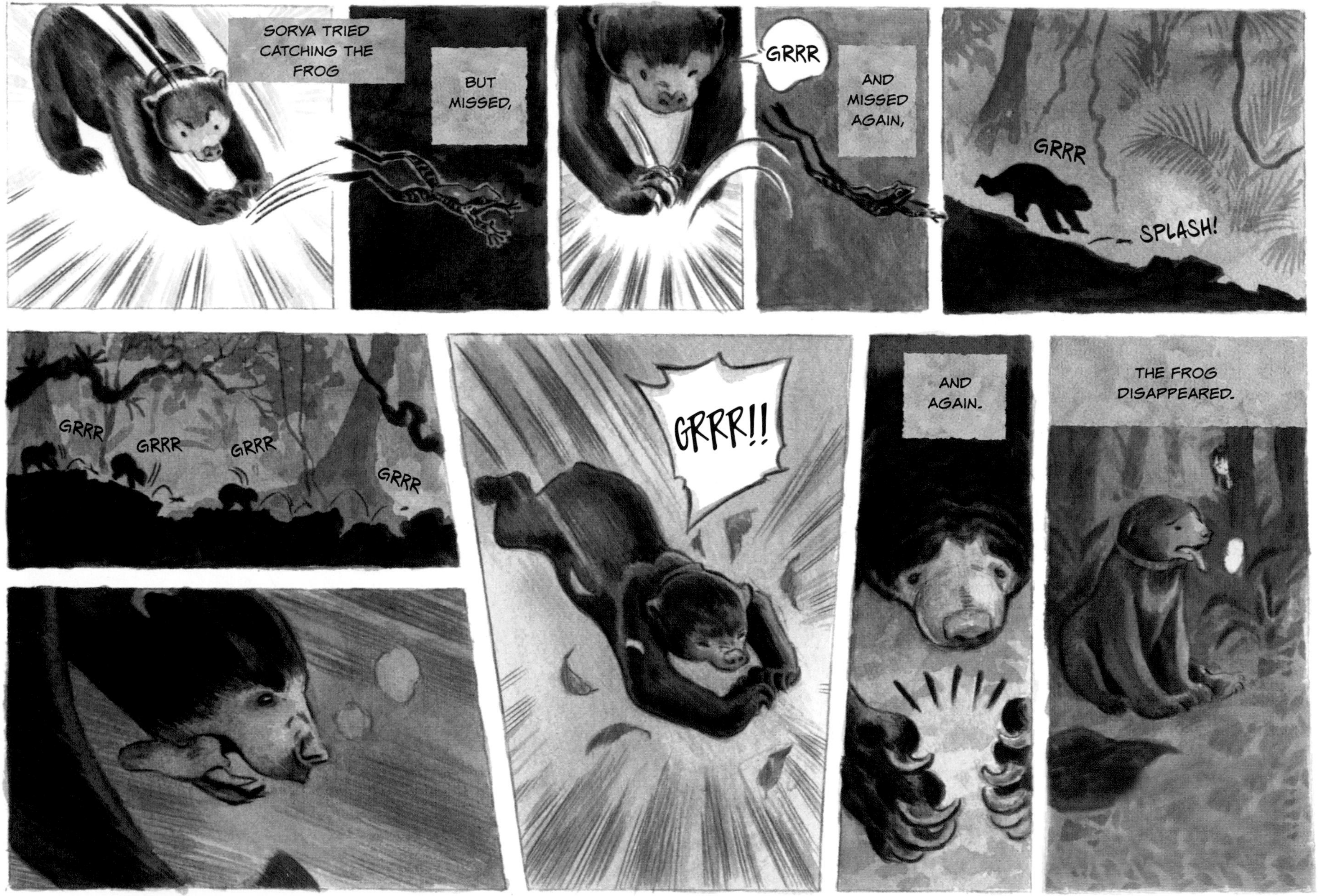
SORYA TRIED CATCHING THE FROG
BUT MISSED,
GRRR
AND MISSED AGAIN,
GRRR
SPLASH!
GRRR
GRRR
GRRR
GRRR
GRRR!!
AND AGAIN.
THE FROG DISAPPEARED.

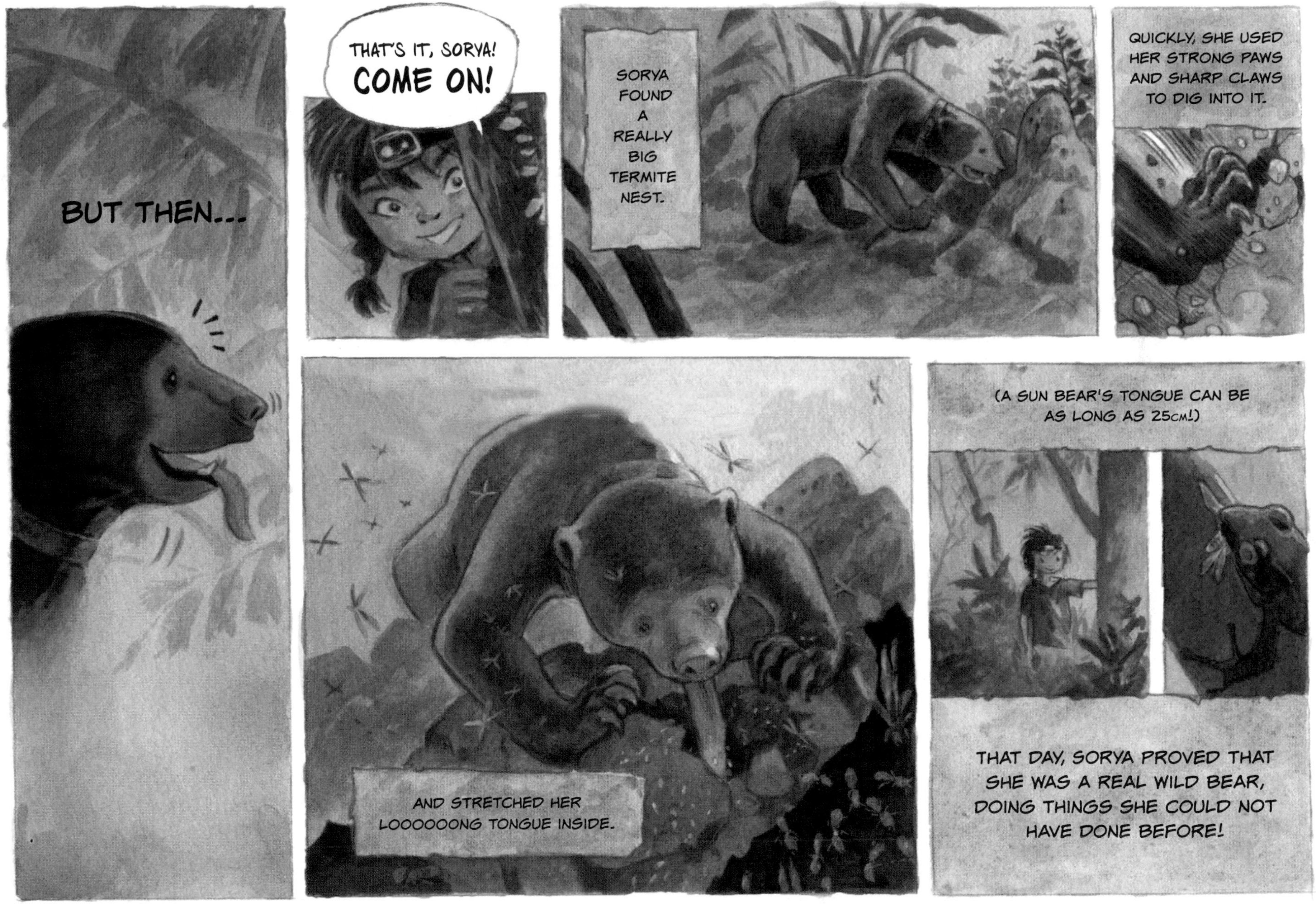
BUT THEN...
THAT'S IT, SORYA! COME ON!
SORYA FOUND A REALLY BIG TERMITE NEST.
QUICKLY, SHE USED HER STRONG PAWS AND SHARP CLAWS TO DIG INTO IT.
AND STRETCHED HER LOOOOOONG TONGUE INSIDE.
(A SUN BEAR'S TONGUE CAN BE AS LONG AS 25CM!)
THAT DAY, SORYA PROVED THAT SHE WAS A REAL WILD BEAR, DOING THINGS SHE COULD NOT HAVE DONE BEFORE!

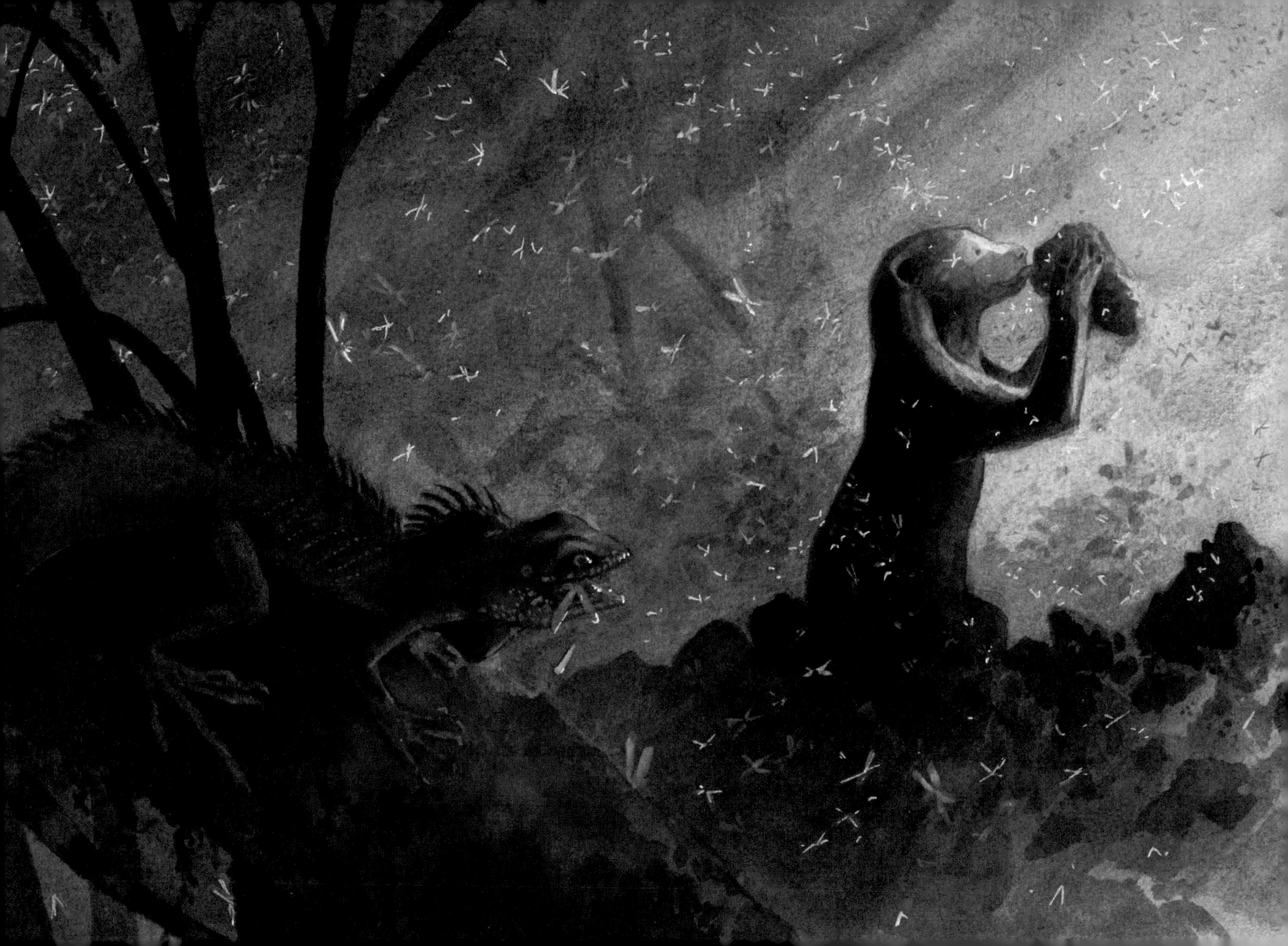

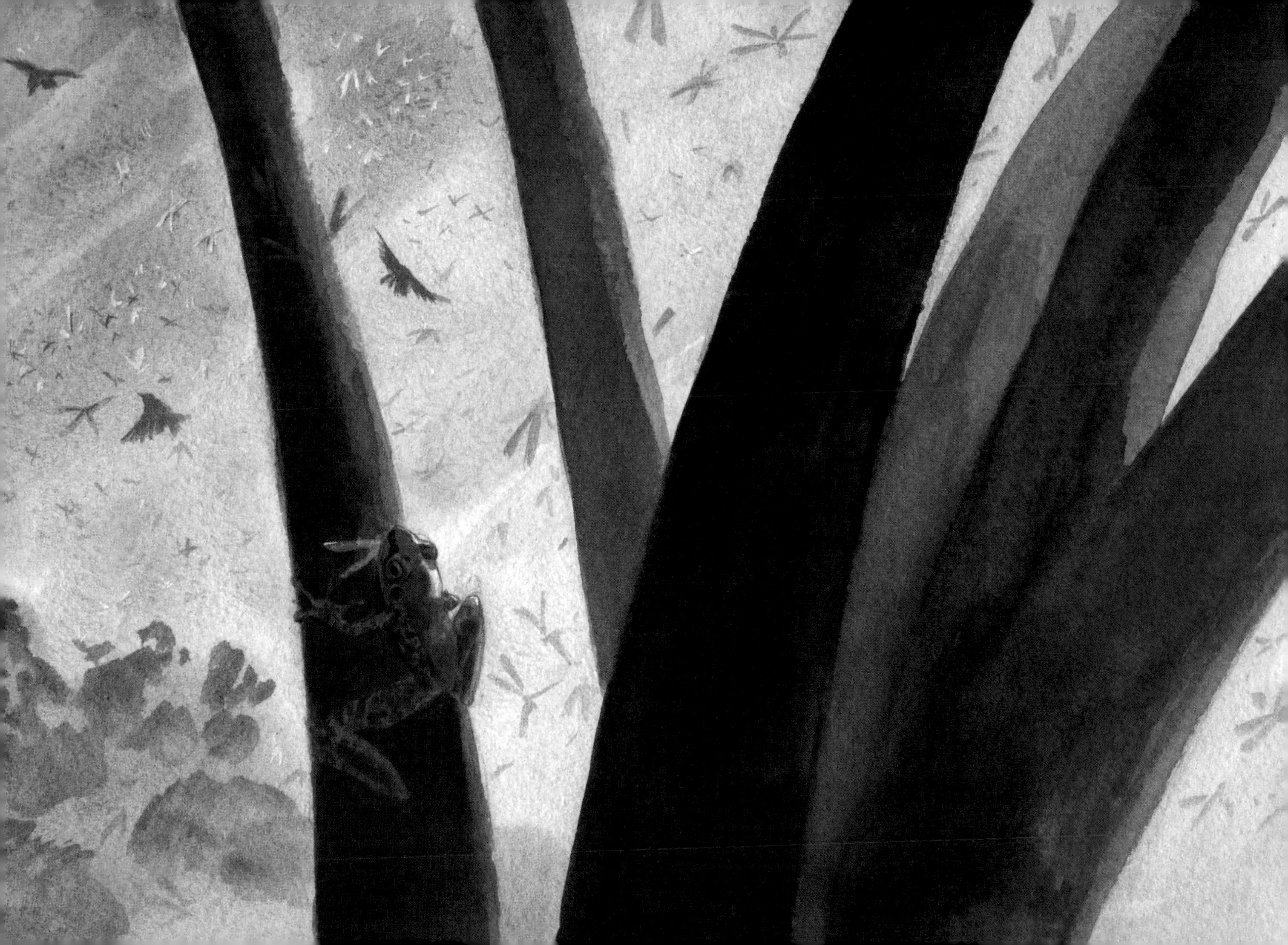

CHAPTER SEVEN

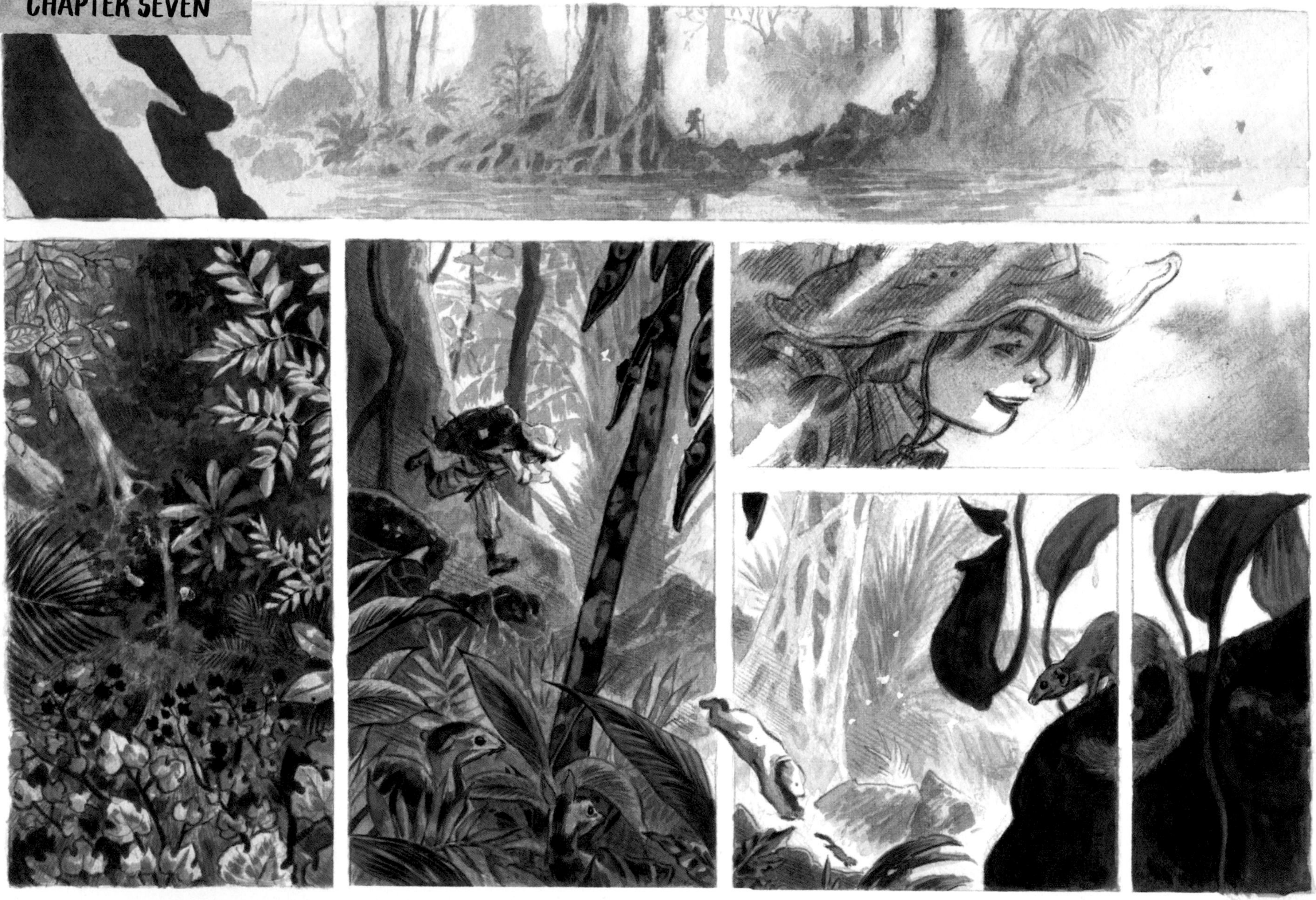

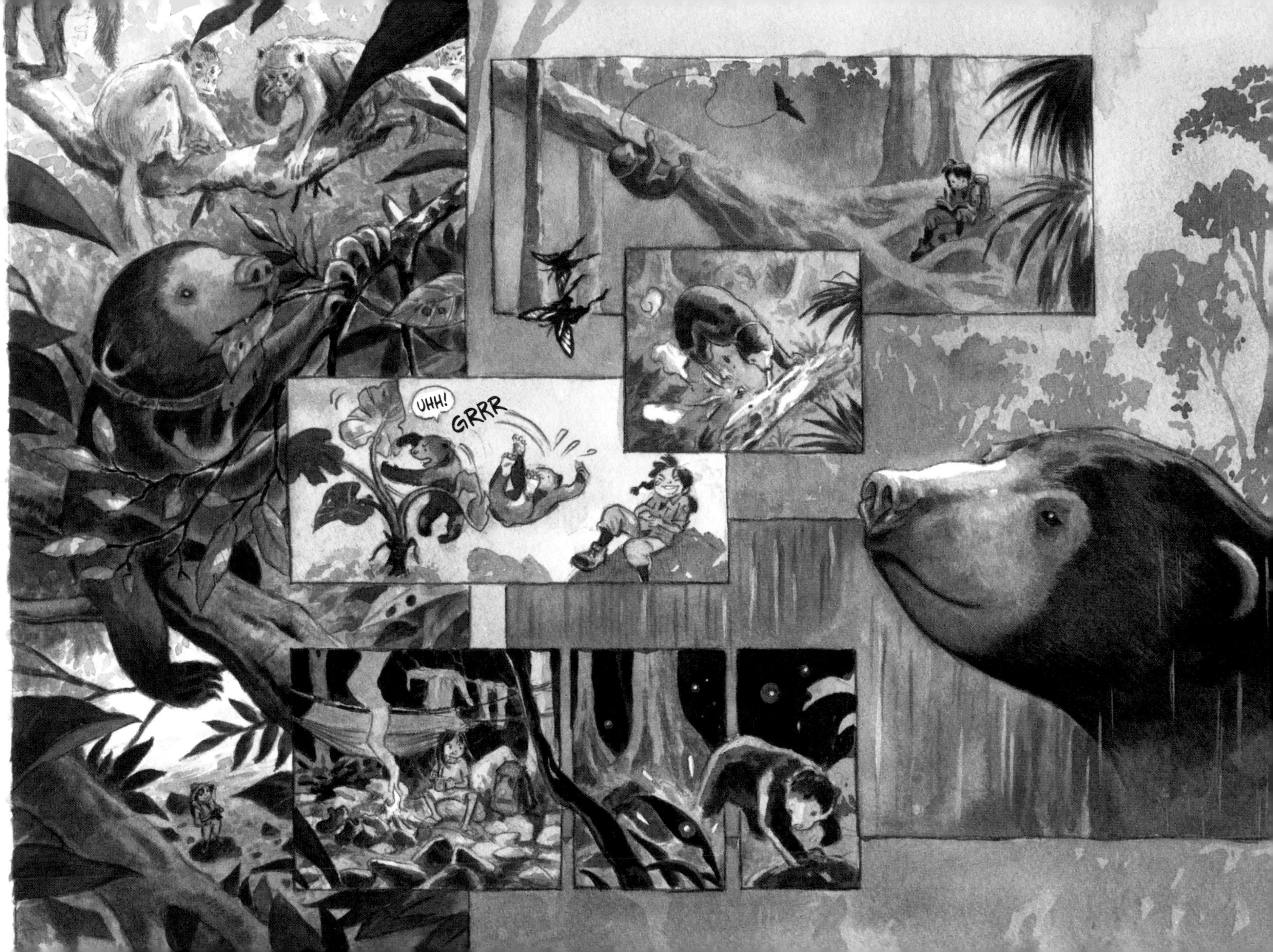
UHH!
GRRR

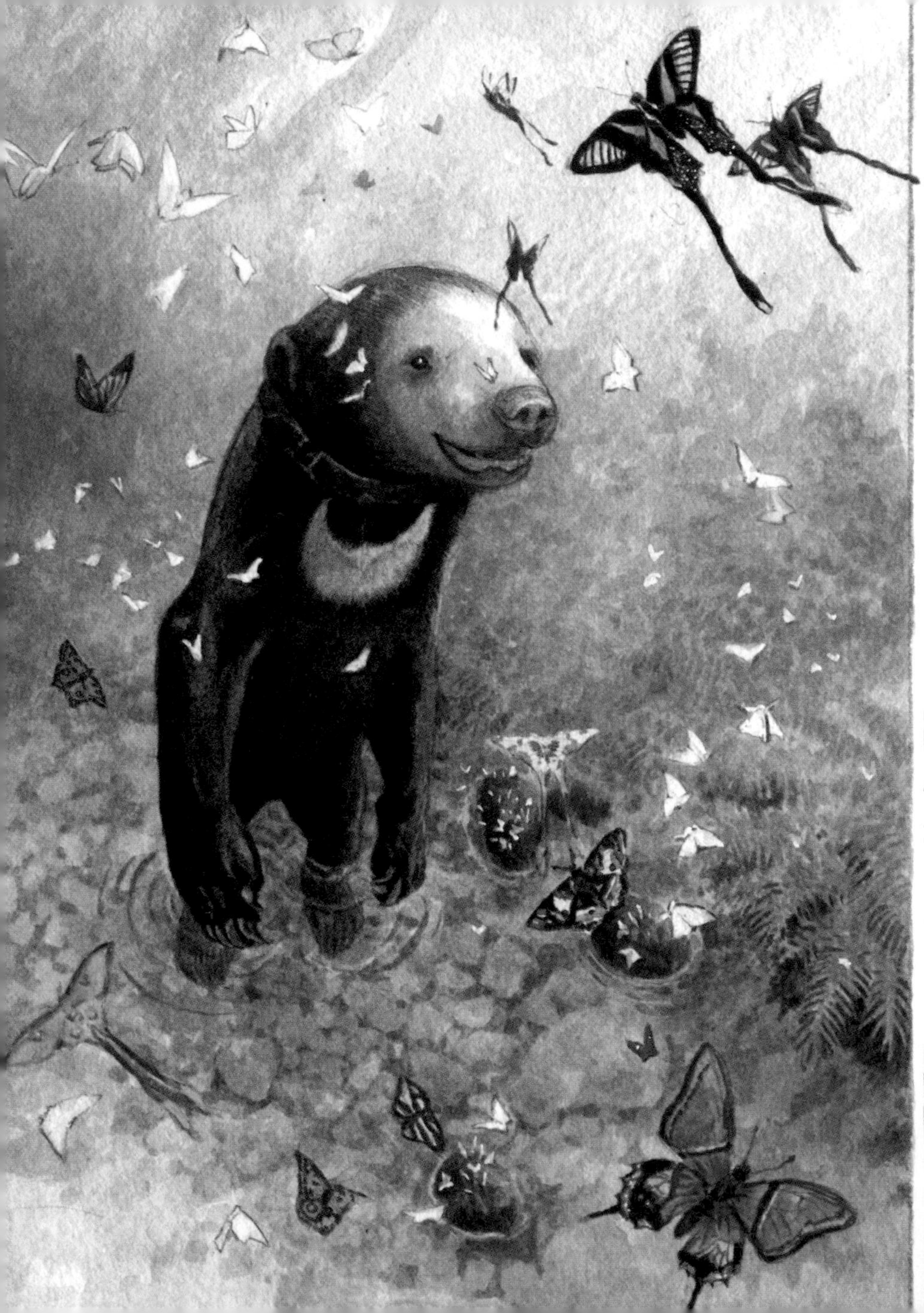

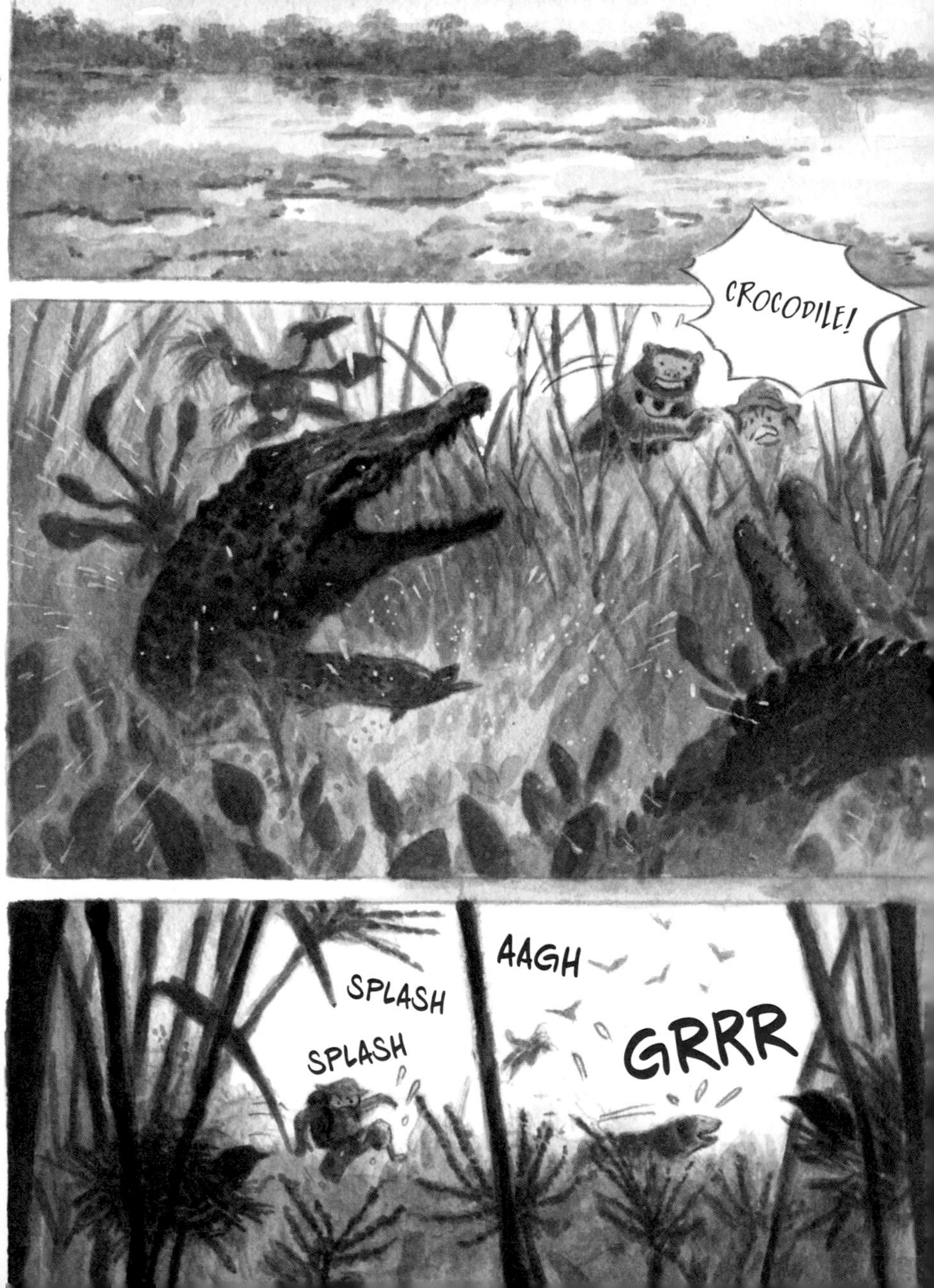

CROCODILE!
SPLASH
SPLASH
AAGH
GRRR

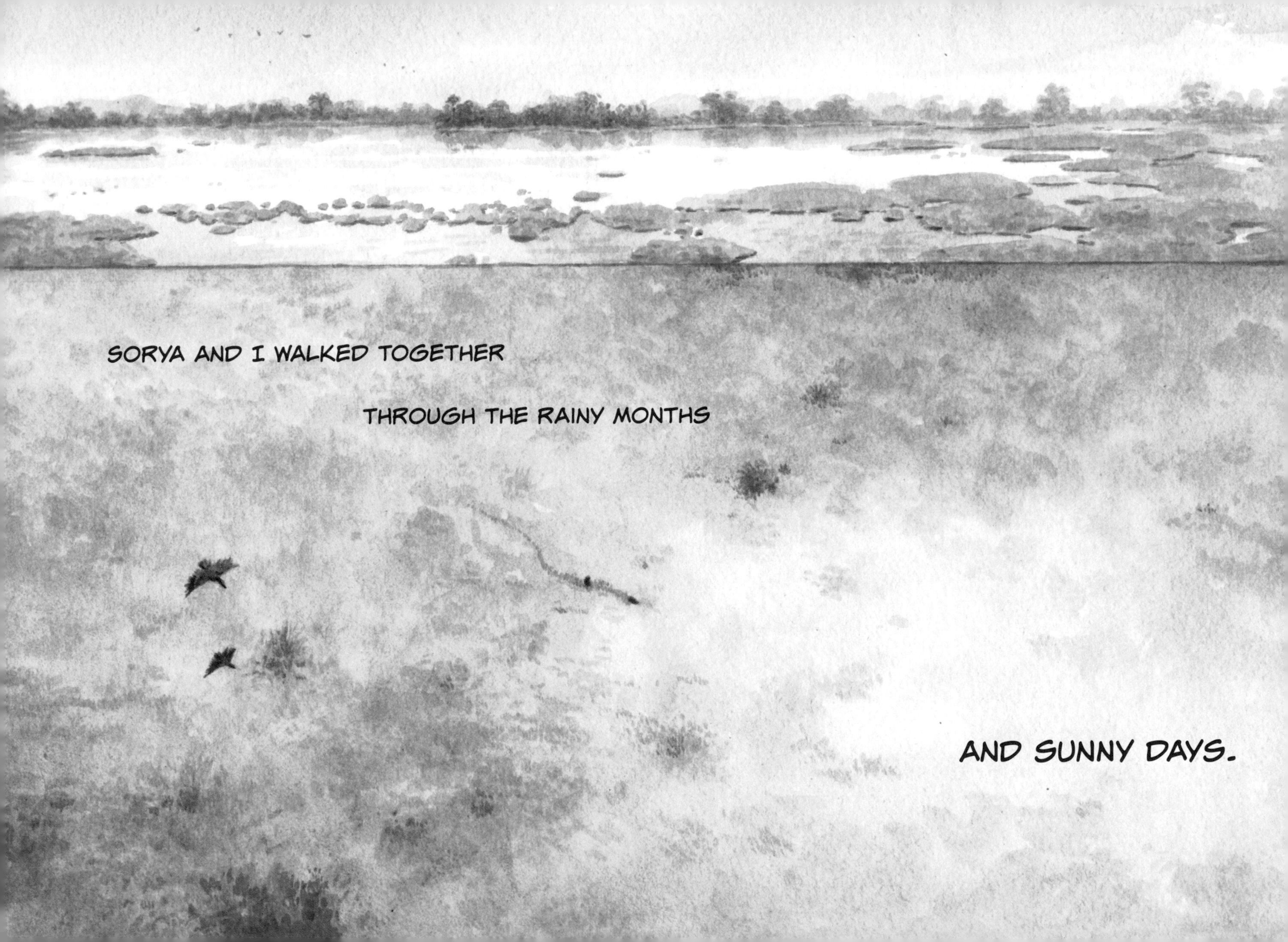
SORYA AND I WALKED TOGETHER
THROUGH THE RAINY MONTHS
AND SUNNY DAYS.

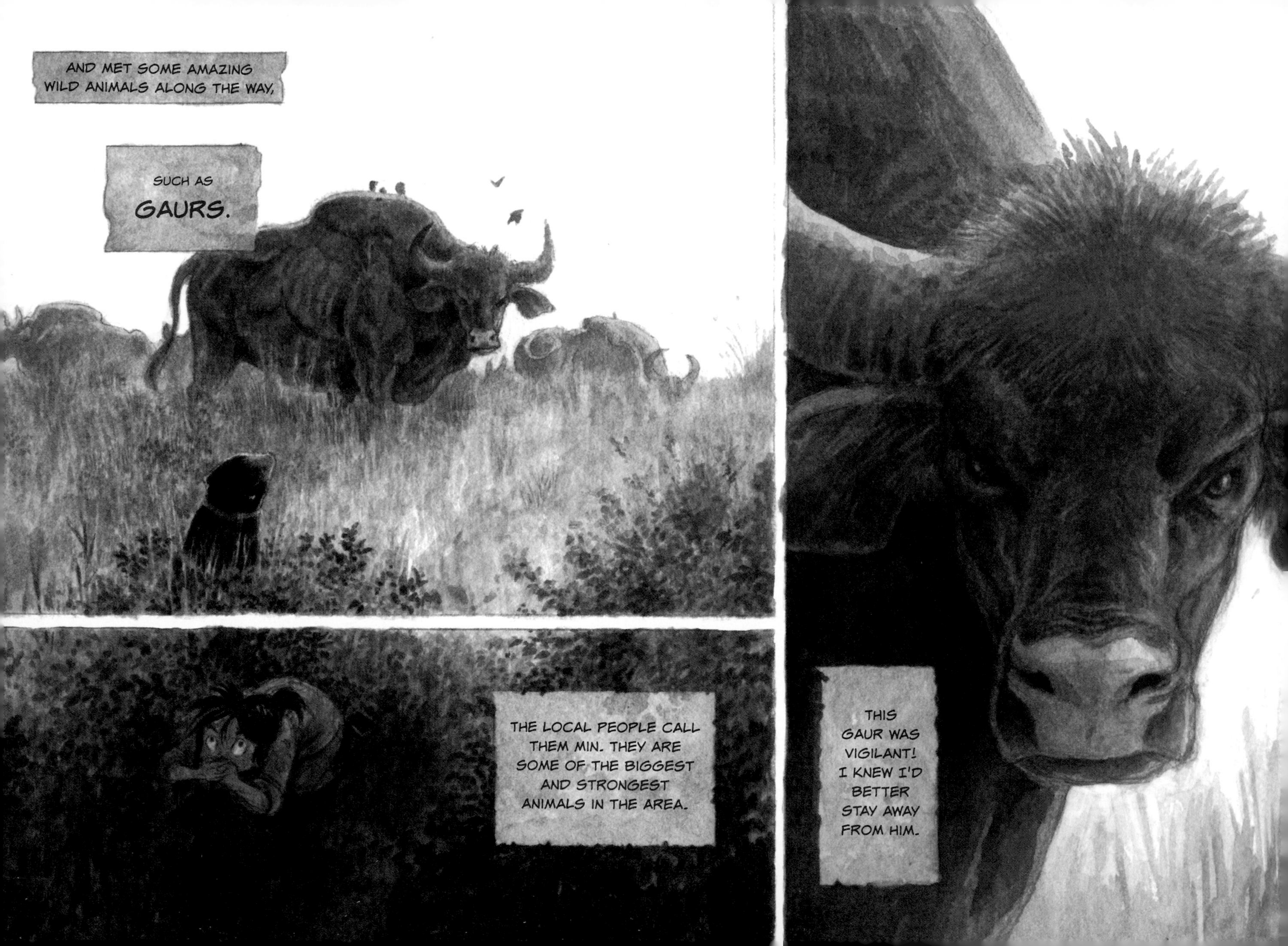
AND MET SOME AMAZING WILD ANIMALS ALONG THE WAY,
SUCH AS GAURS.
THE LOCAL PEOPLE CALL THEM MIN. THEY ARE SOME OF THE BIGGEST AND STRONGEST ANIMALS IN THE AREA.
THIS GAUR WAS VIGILANT! I KNEW I'D BETTER STAY AWAY FROM HIM.

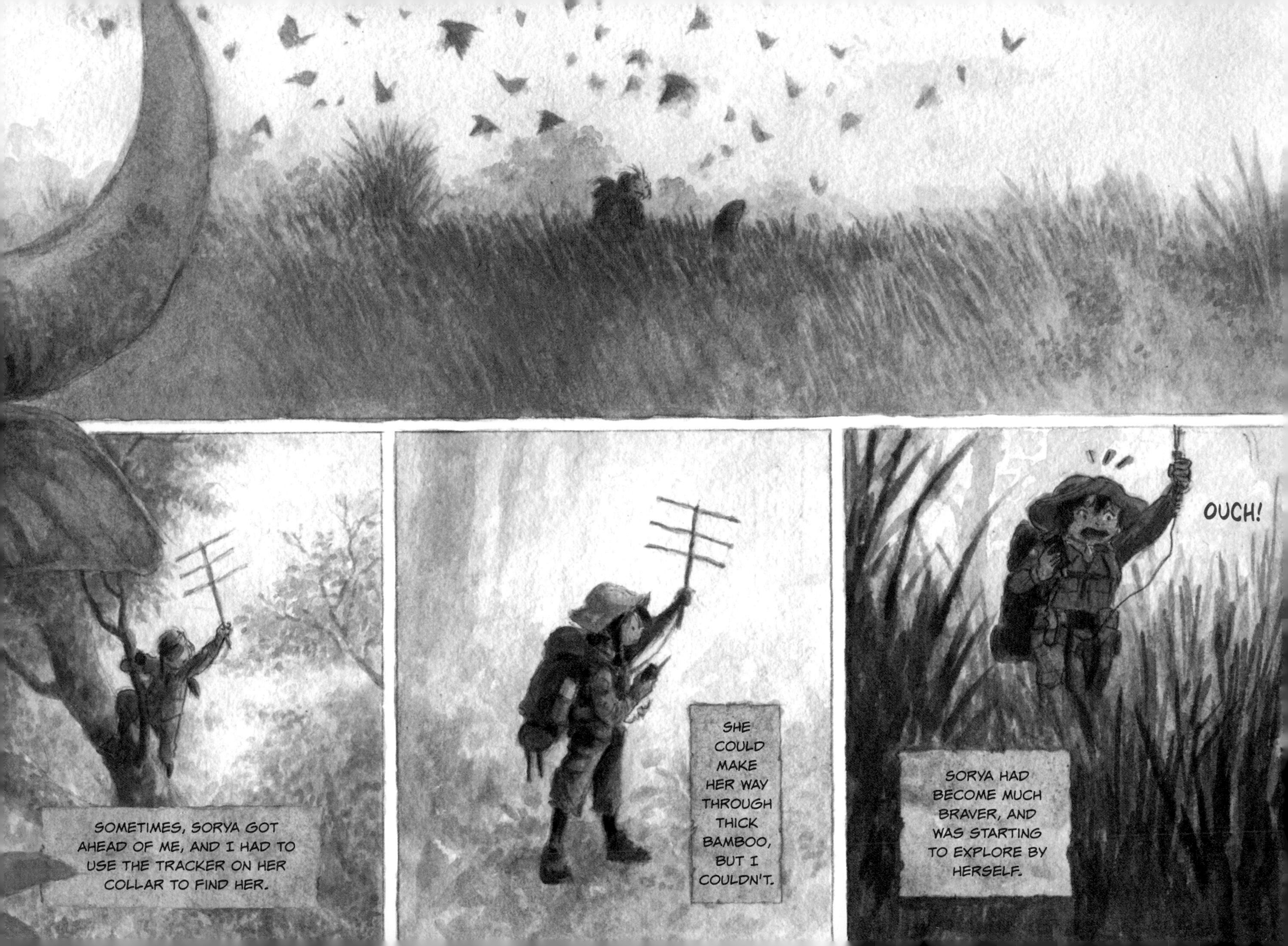
SOMETIMES, SORYA GOT AHEAD OF ME, AND I HAD TO USE THE TRACKER ON HER COLLAR TO FIND HER.
SHE COULD MAKE HER WAY THROUGH THICK BAMBOO, BUT I COULDN'T.
OUCH!
SORYA HAD BECOME MUCH BRAVER, AND WAS STARTING TO EXPLORE BY HERSELF.

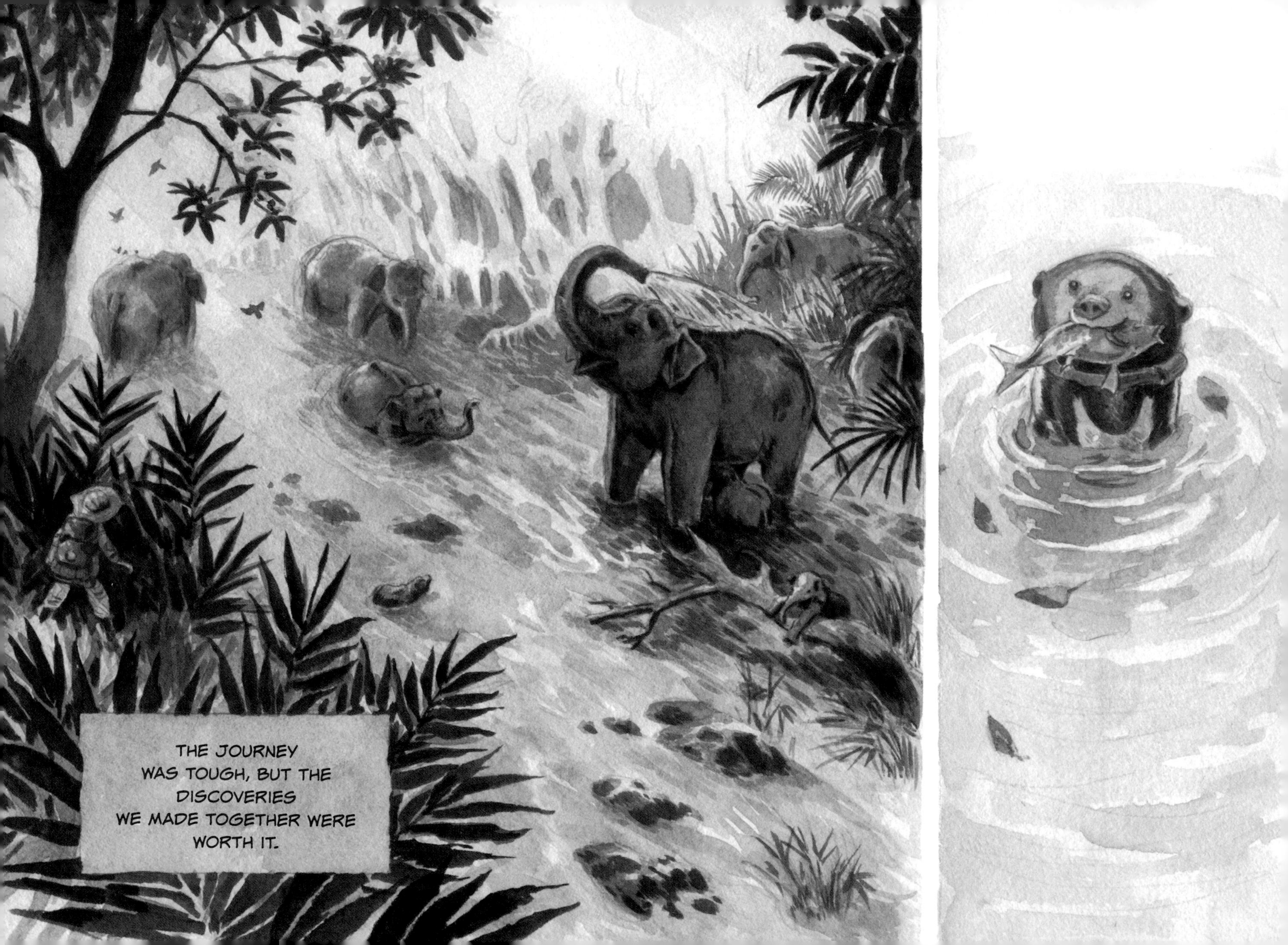
THE JOURNEY
WAS TOUGH, BUT THE
DISCOVERIES
WE MADE TOGETHER WERE
WORTH IT.

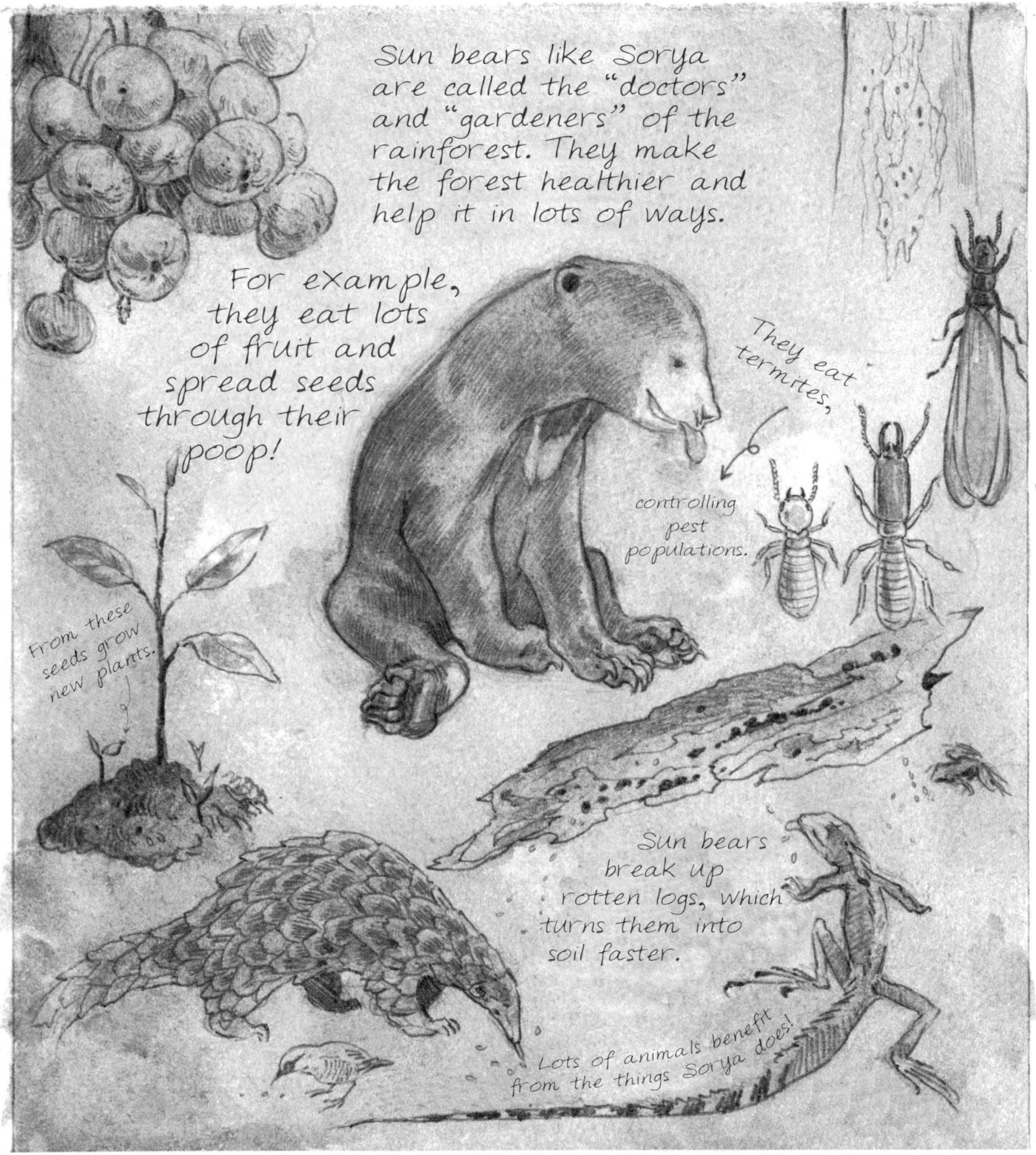
Sun bears like Sorya are called the "doctors" and "gardeners" of the rainforest. They make the forest healthier and help it in lots of ways.
For example, they eat lots of fruit and spread seeds through their poop!
They eat termites,
controlling pest populations.
From these seeds grow new plants.
Sun bears break up rotten logs, which turns them into soil faster.
Lots of animals benefit from the things Sorya does!

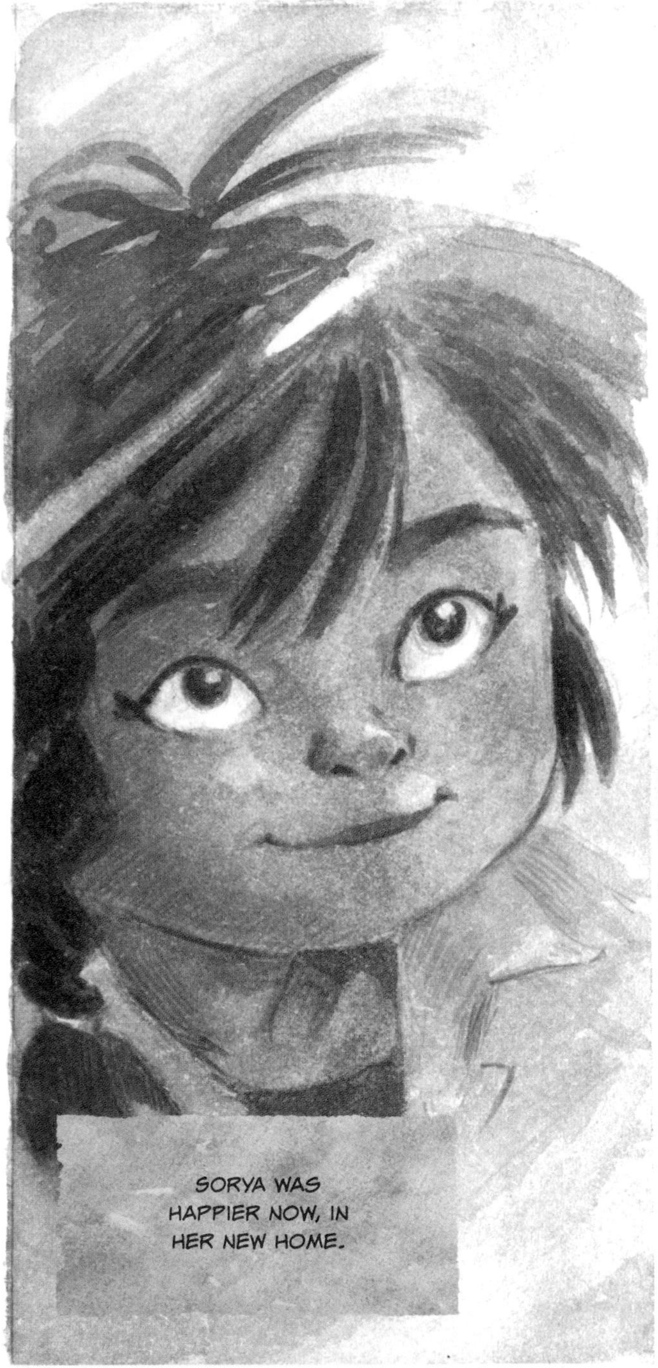
SORYA WAS HAPPIER NOW, IN HER NEW HOME.

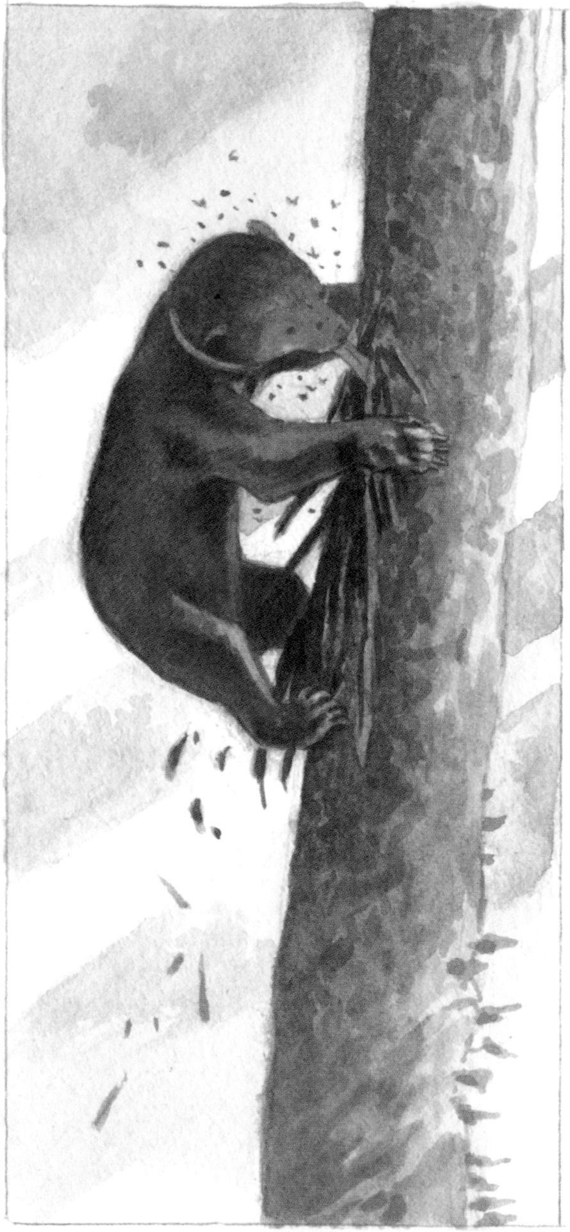

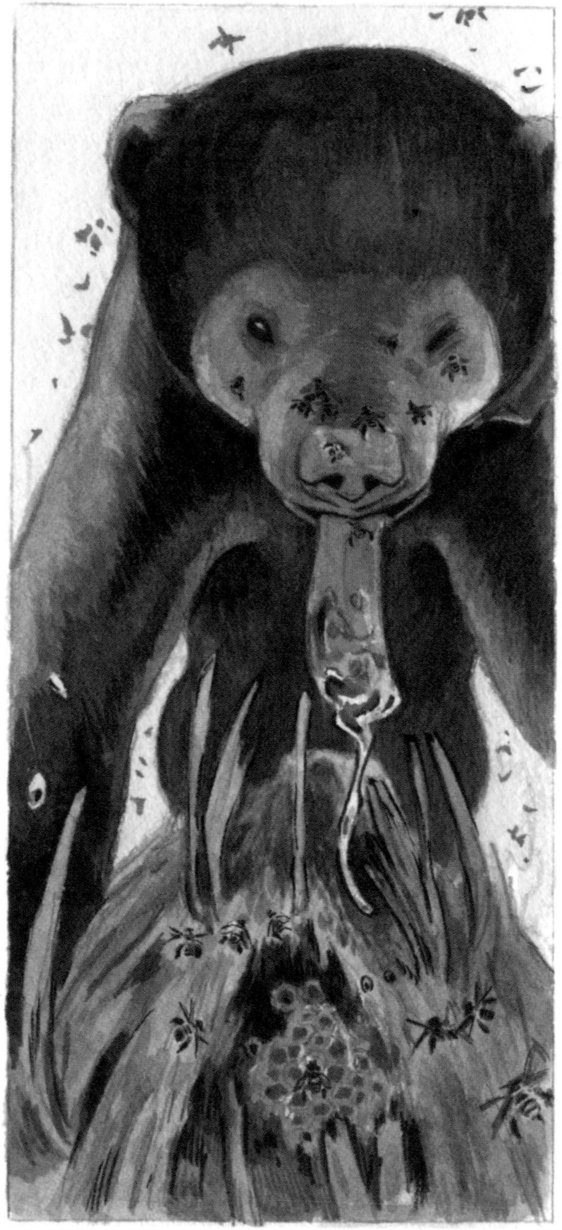

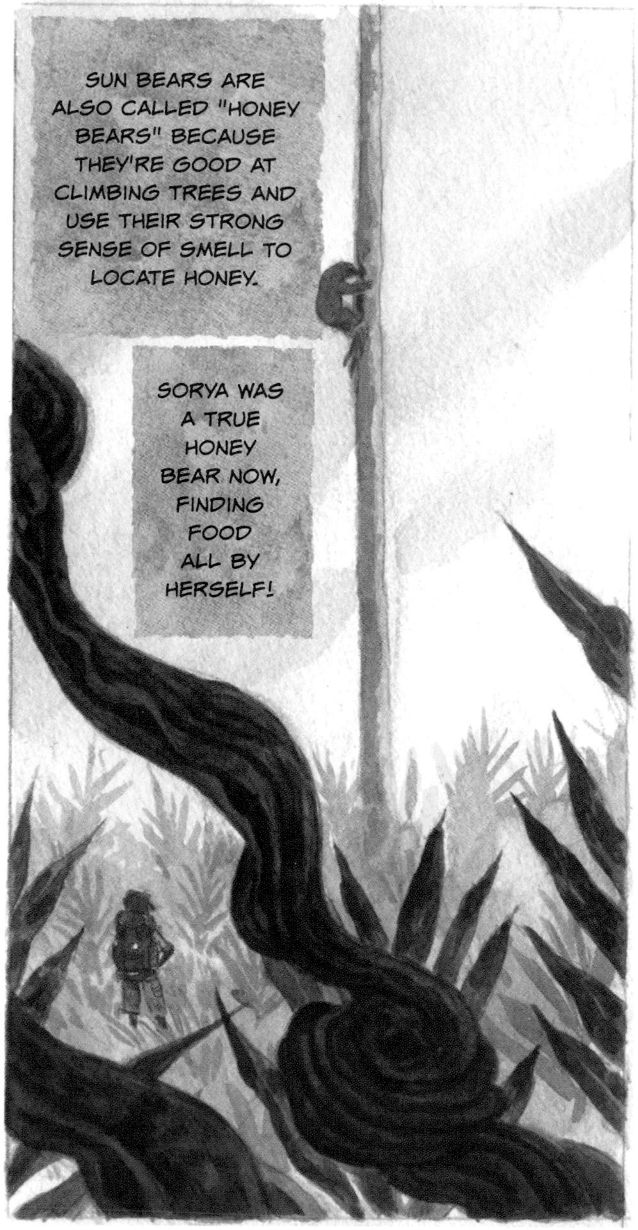
SUN BEARS ARE ALSO CALLED "HONEY BEARS" BECAUSE THEY'RE GOOD AT CLIMBING TREES AND USE THEIR STRONG SENSE OF SMELL TO LOCATE HONEY.
SORYA WAS A TRUE HONEY BEAR NOW, FINDING FOOD ALL BY HERSELF!

AT NIGHT SHE
USED TO
FIND ME,

AND WE'D
SLEEP UNDER
THE STARS.

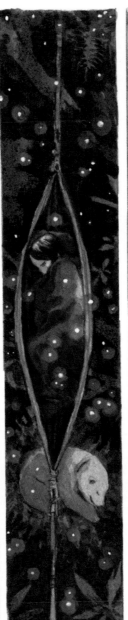

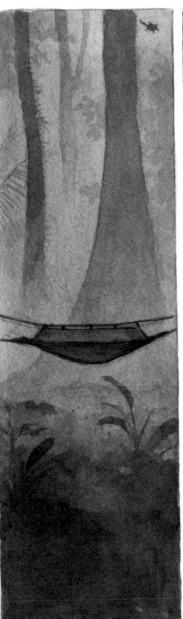

But now, my dear Sorya is a lot more confident.

She makes her own nest in the trees and sleeps there by herself.

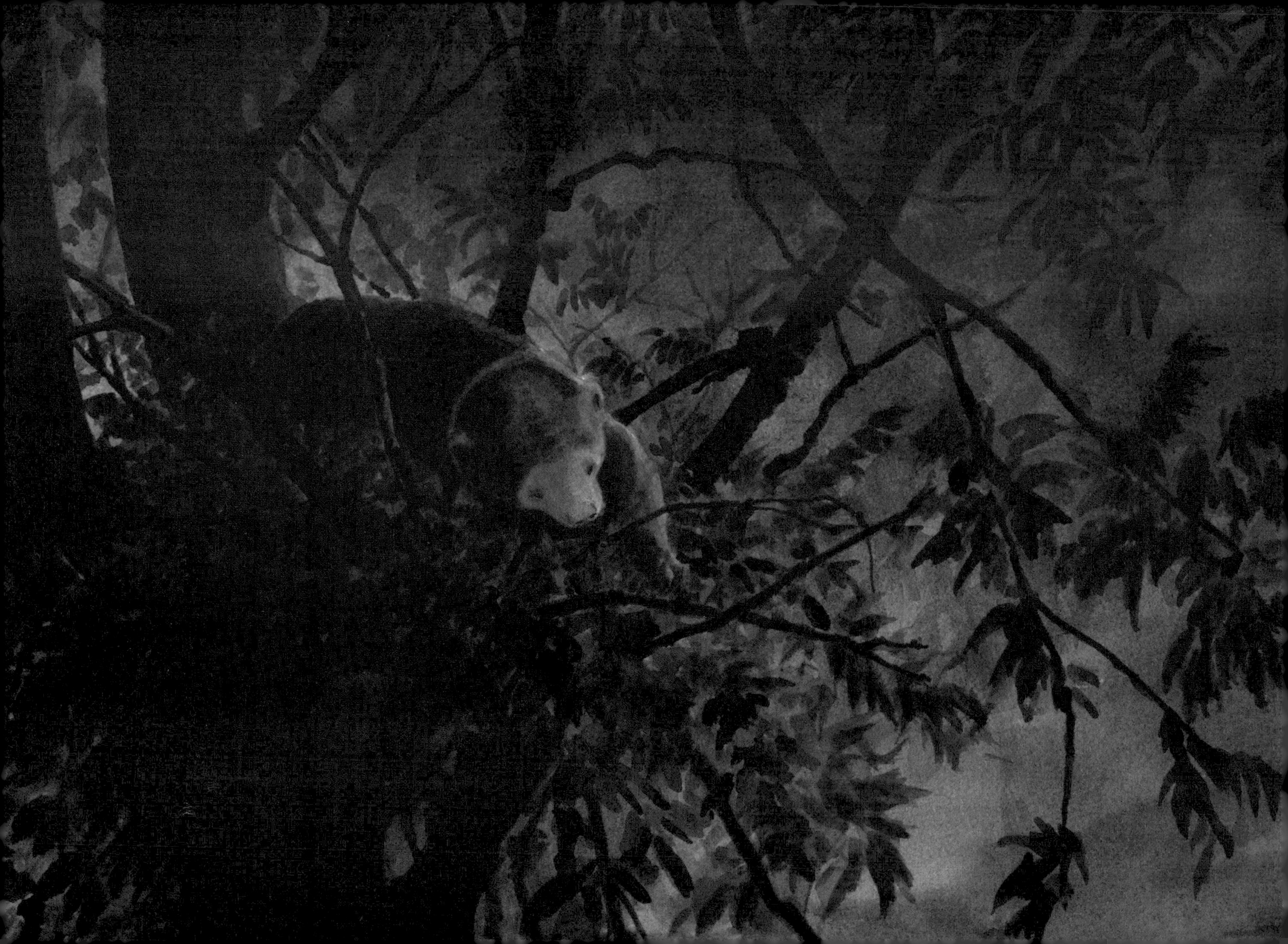

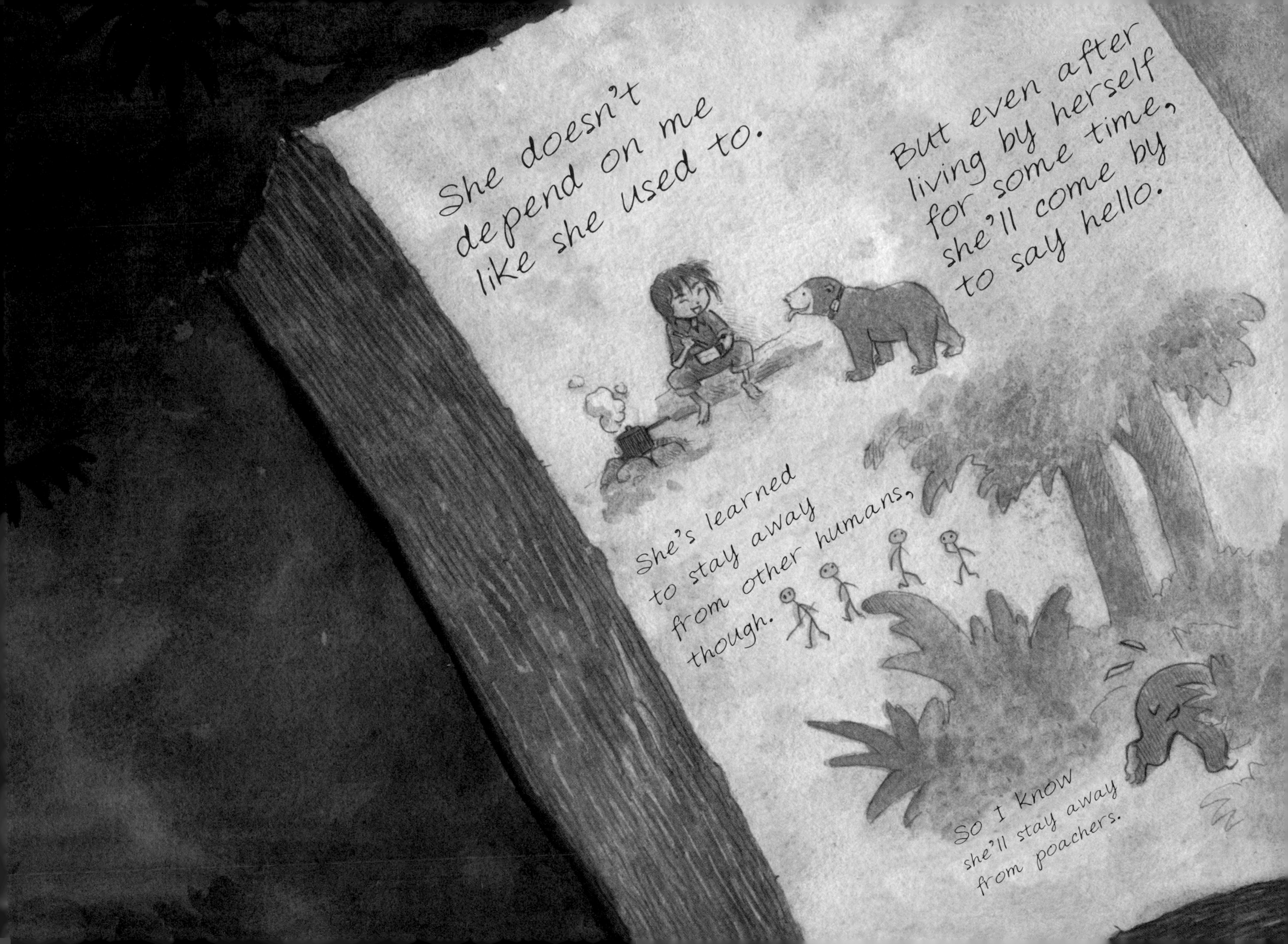
She doesn't depend on me like she used to.
But even after living by herself for some time, she'll come by to say hello.
She's learned to stay away from other humans, though.
So I know she'll stay away from poachers.

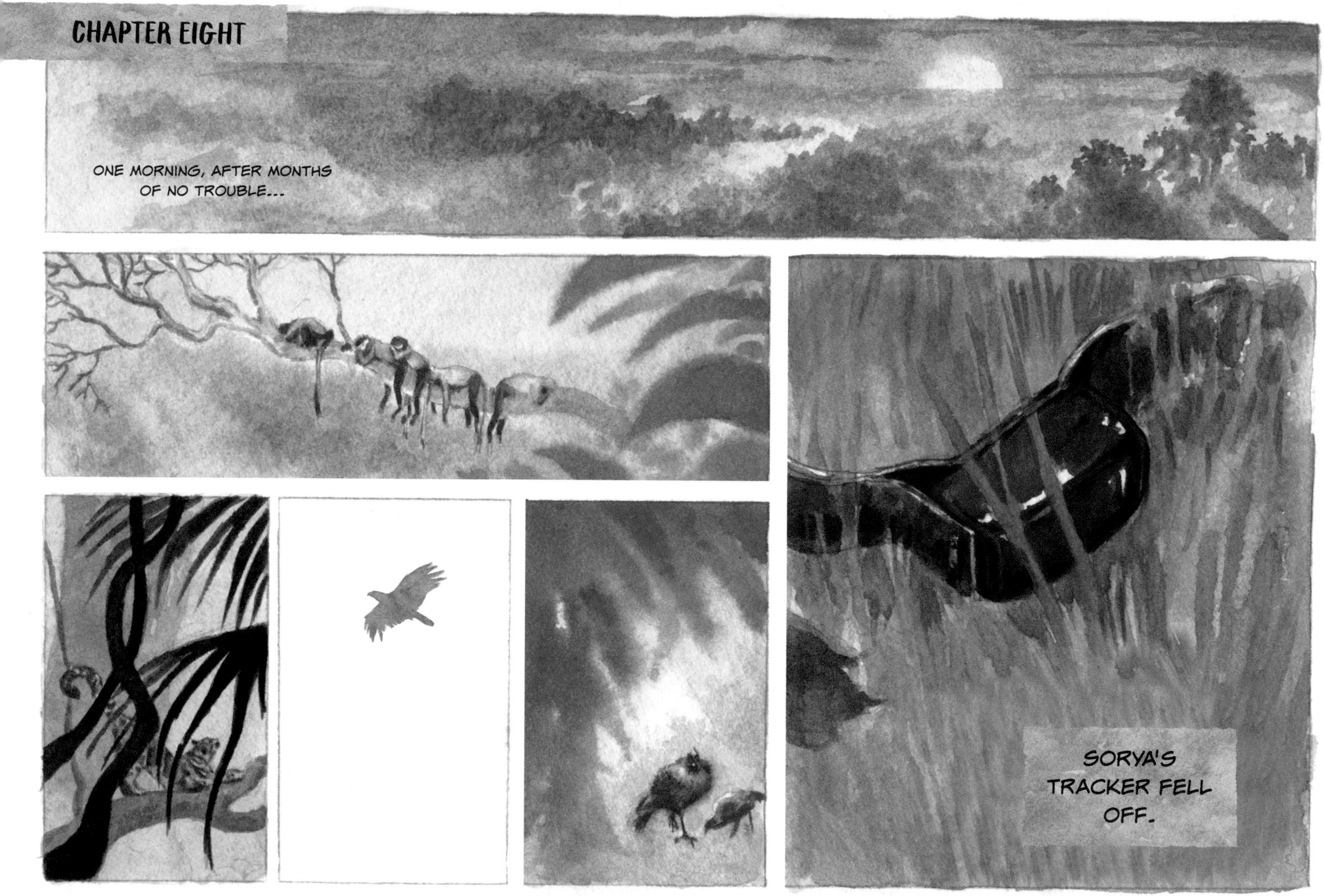
CHAPTER EIGHT
ONE MORNING, AFTER MONTHS
OF NO TROUBLE...
SORYA'S
TRACKER FELL
OFF.

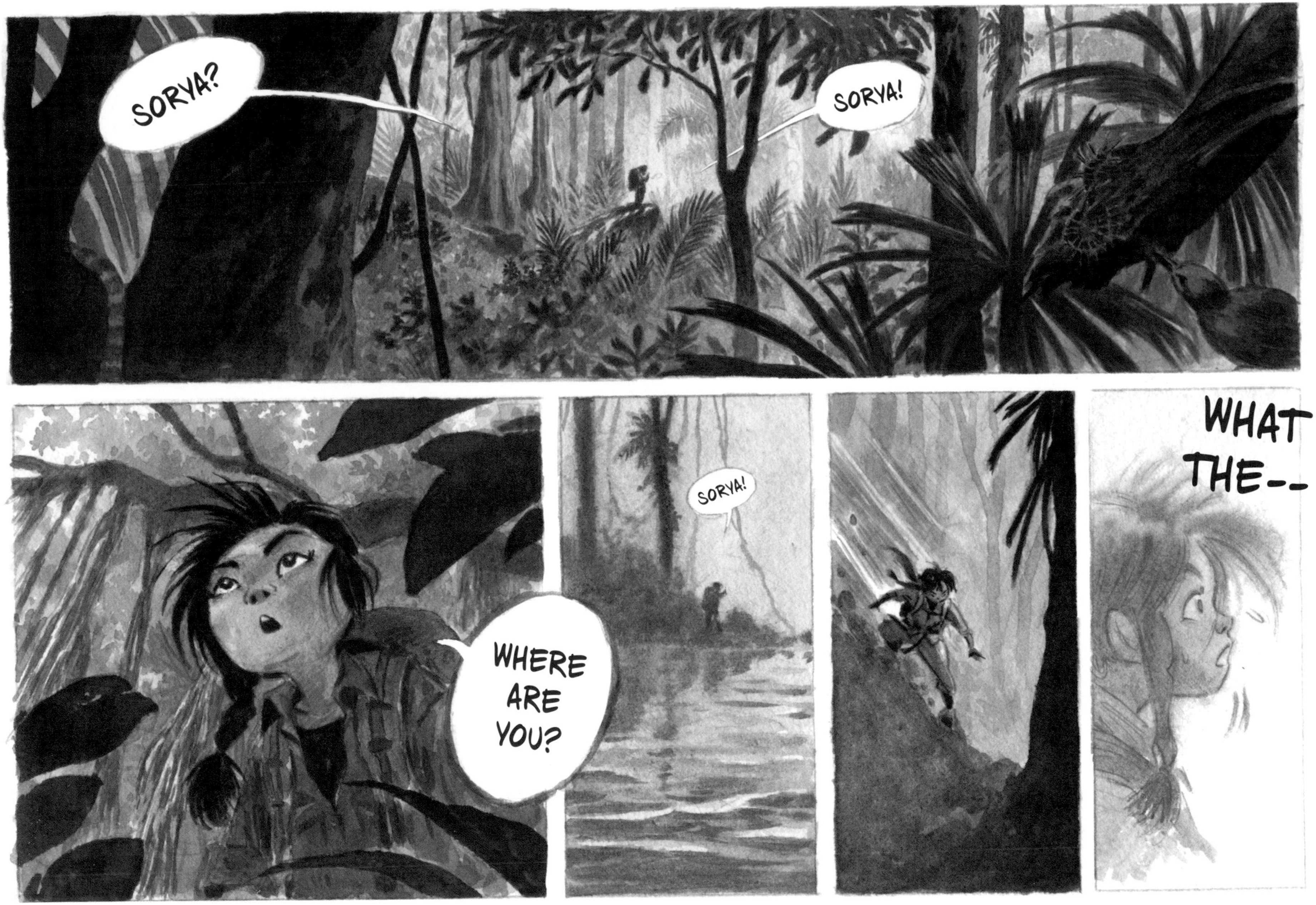
SORYA?
SORYA!
WHERE ARE YOU?
SORYA!
WHAT THE--

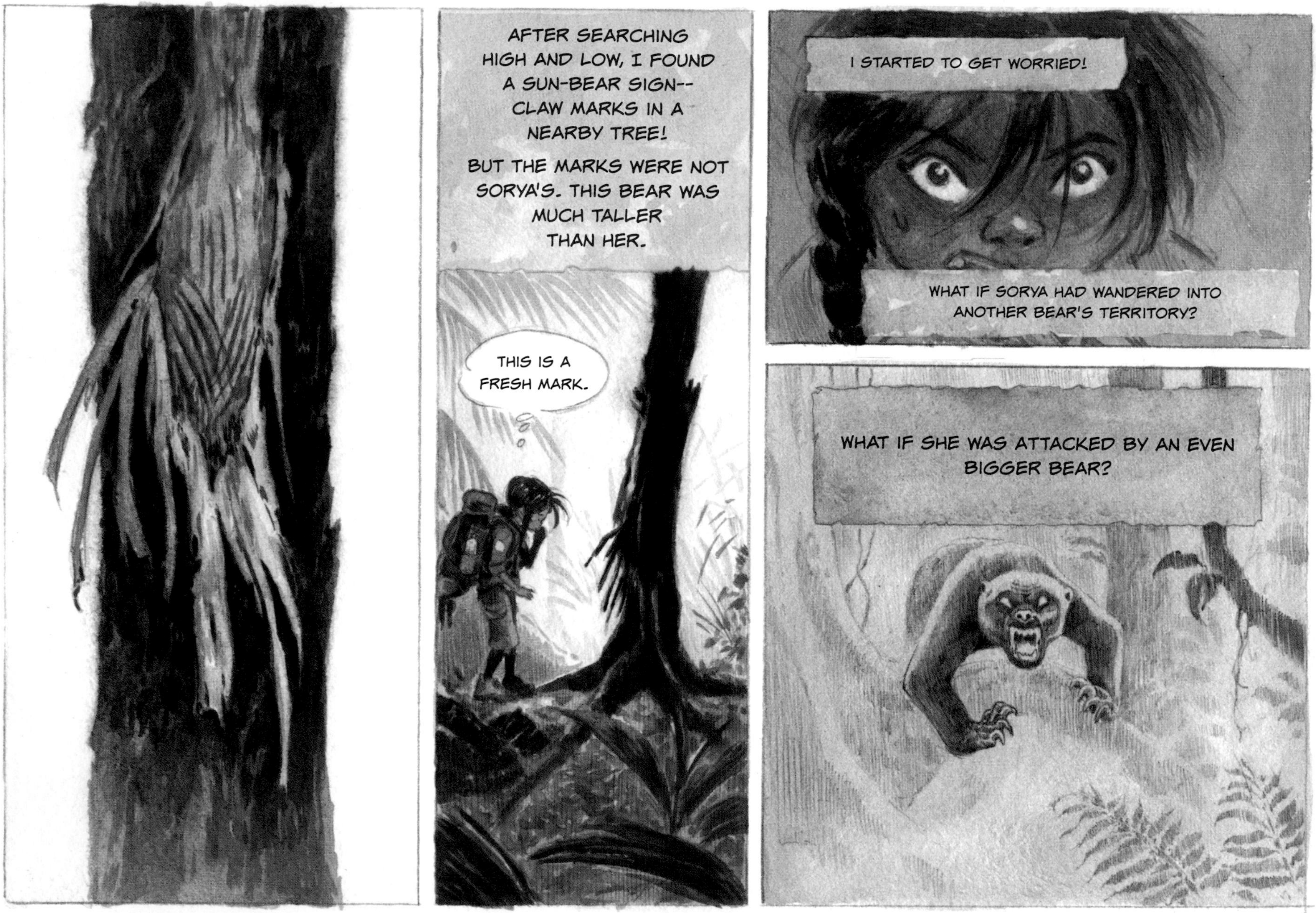
AFTER SEARCHING HIGH AND LOW, I FOUND A SUN-BEAR SIGN-- CLAW MARKS IN A NEARBY TREE!
BUT THE MARKS WERE NOT SORYA'S. THIS BEAR WAS MUCH TALLER THAN HER.
THIS IS A FRESH MARK.
I STARTED TO GET WORRIED!
WHAT IF SORYA HAD WANDERED INTO ANOTHER BEAR'S TERRITORY?
WHAT IF SHE WAS ATTACKED BY AN EVEN BIGGER BEAR?

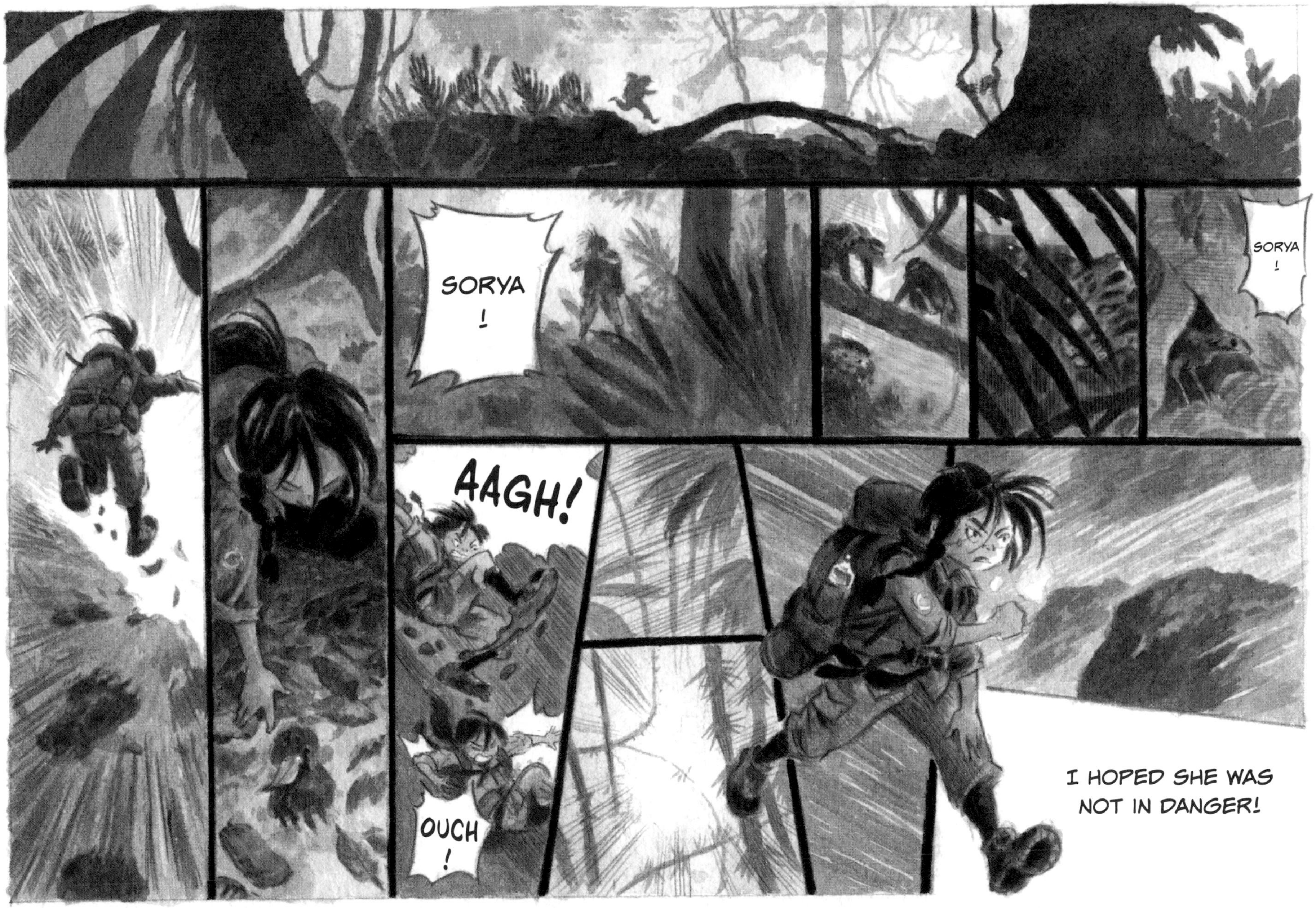
SORYA !
SORYA !
AAGH!
OUCH !
I HOPED SHE WAS NOT IN DANGER!

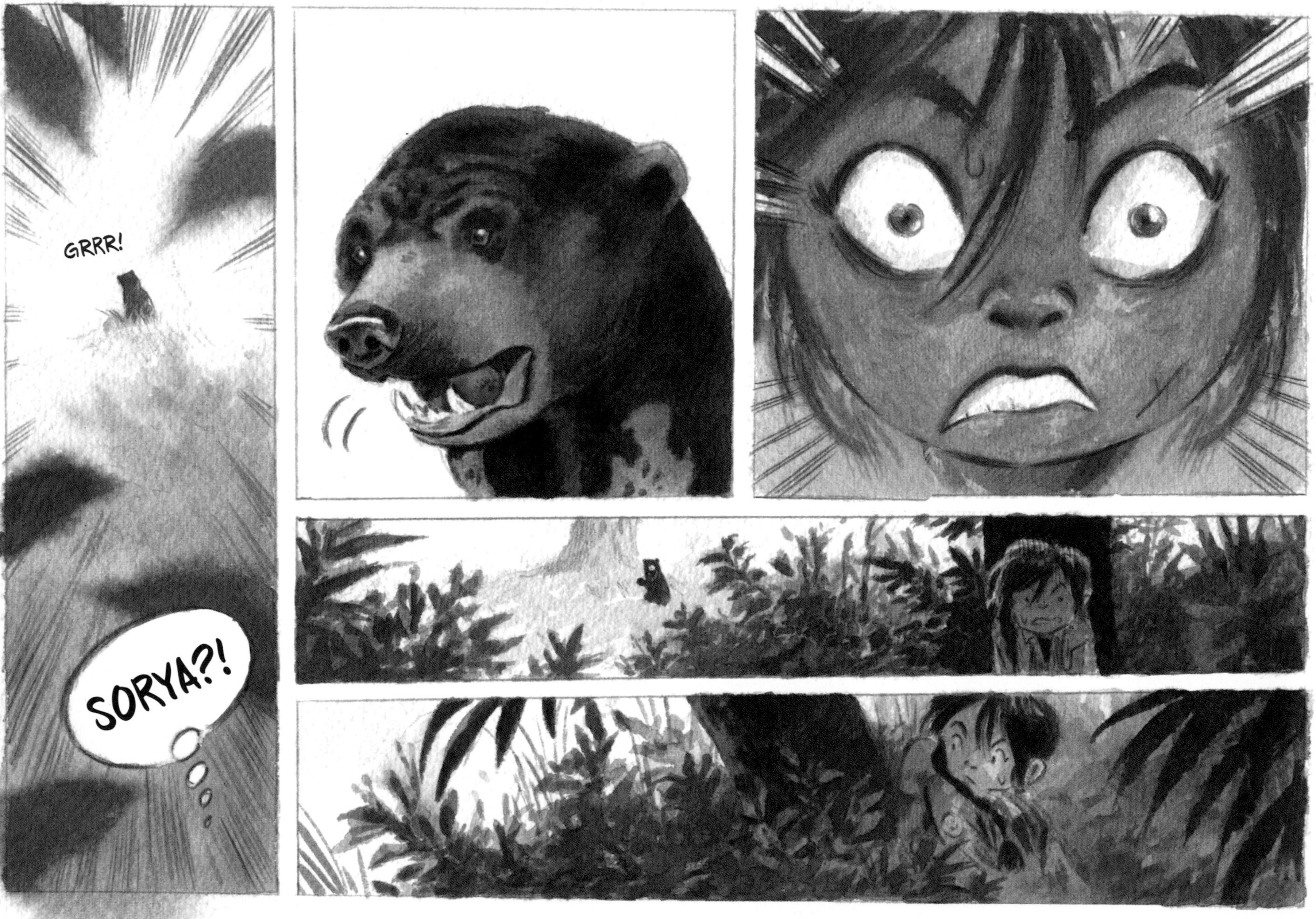
GRRR!
SORYA?!

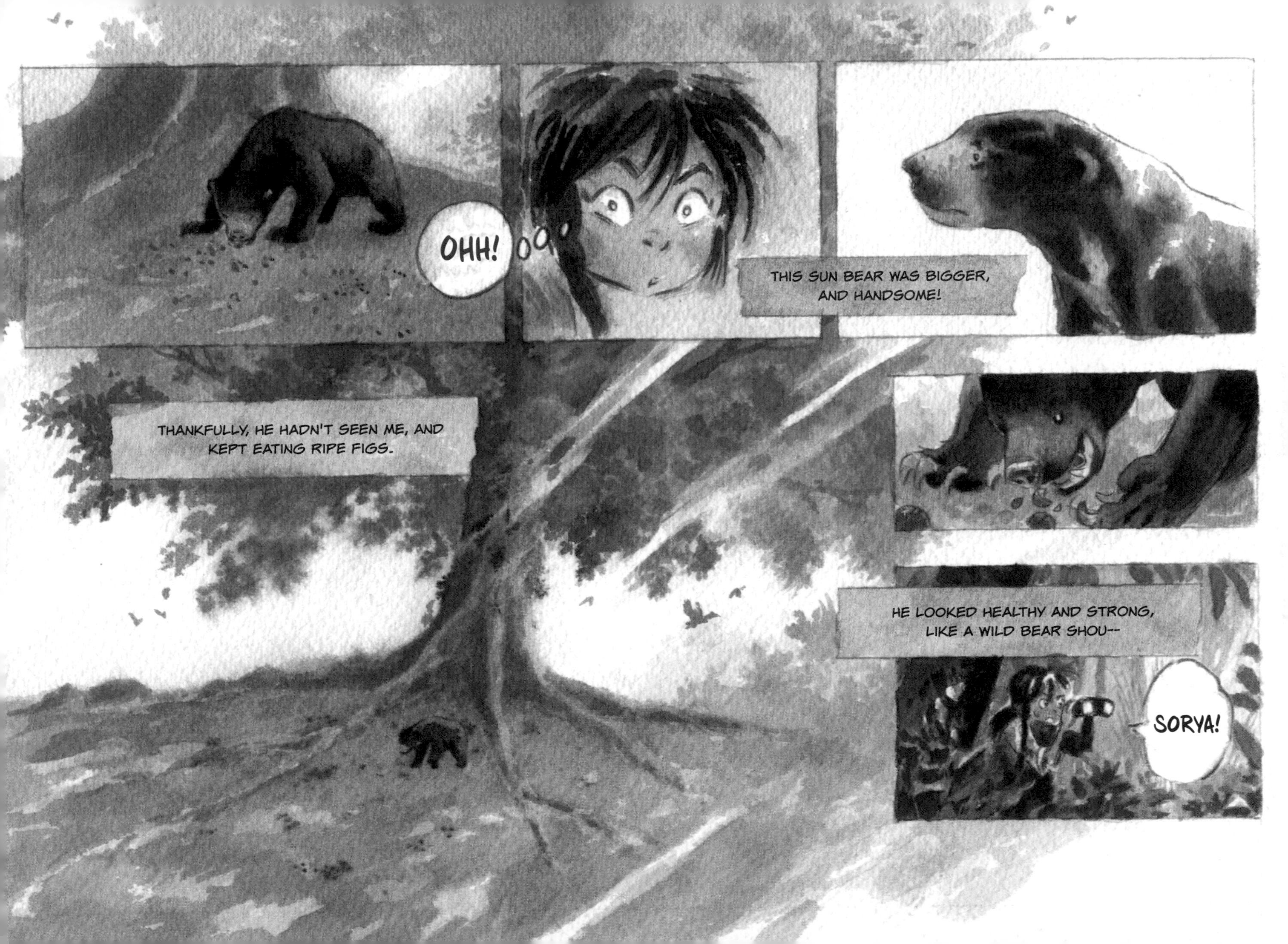
OHH!
THIS SUN BEAR WAS BIGGER, AND HANDSOME!
THANKFULLY, HE HADN'T SEEN ME, AND KEPT EATING RIPE FIGS.
HE LOOKED HEALTHY AND STRONG, LIKE A WILD BEAR SHOU--
SORYA!

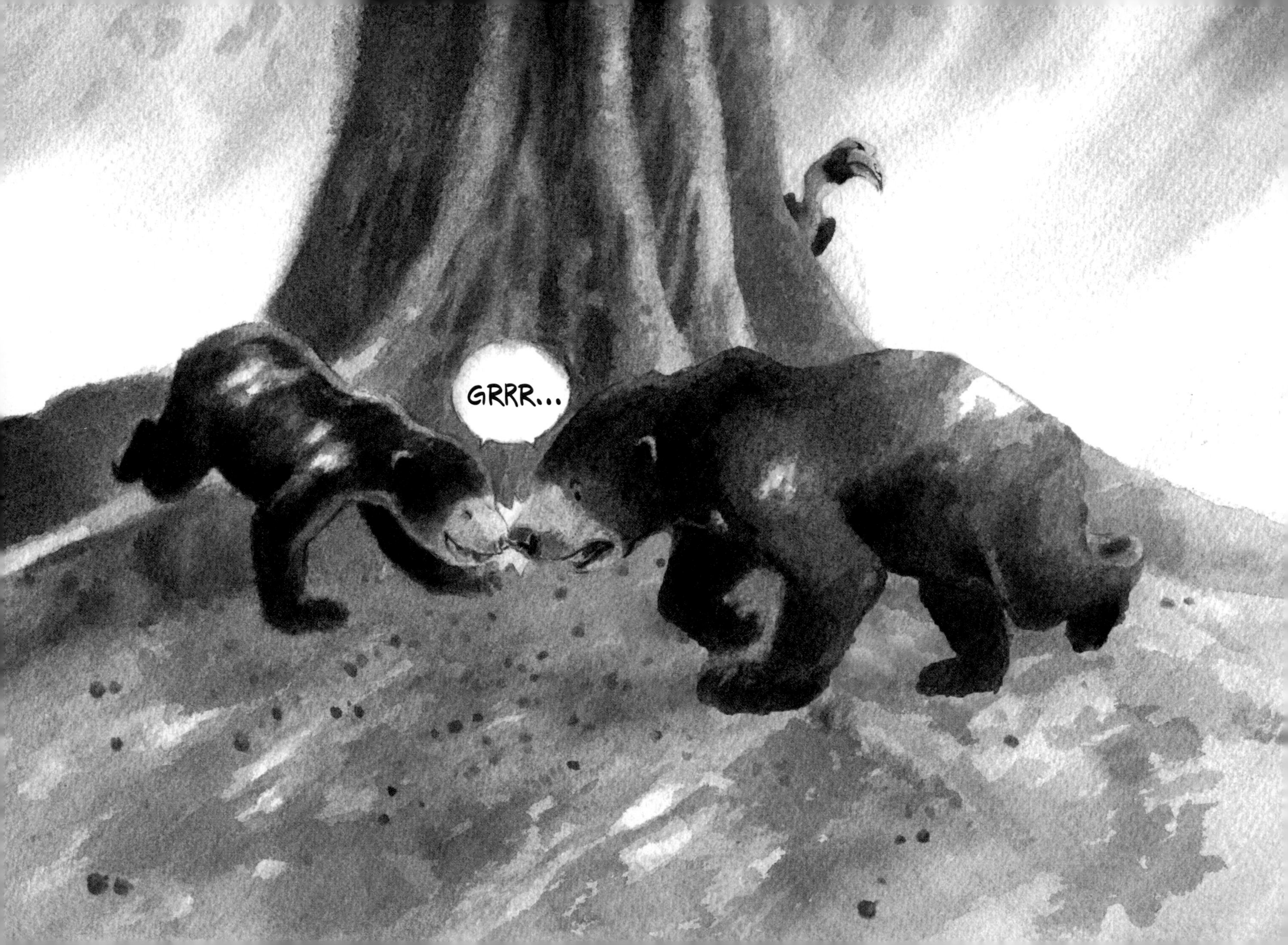
GRRR...

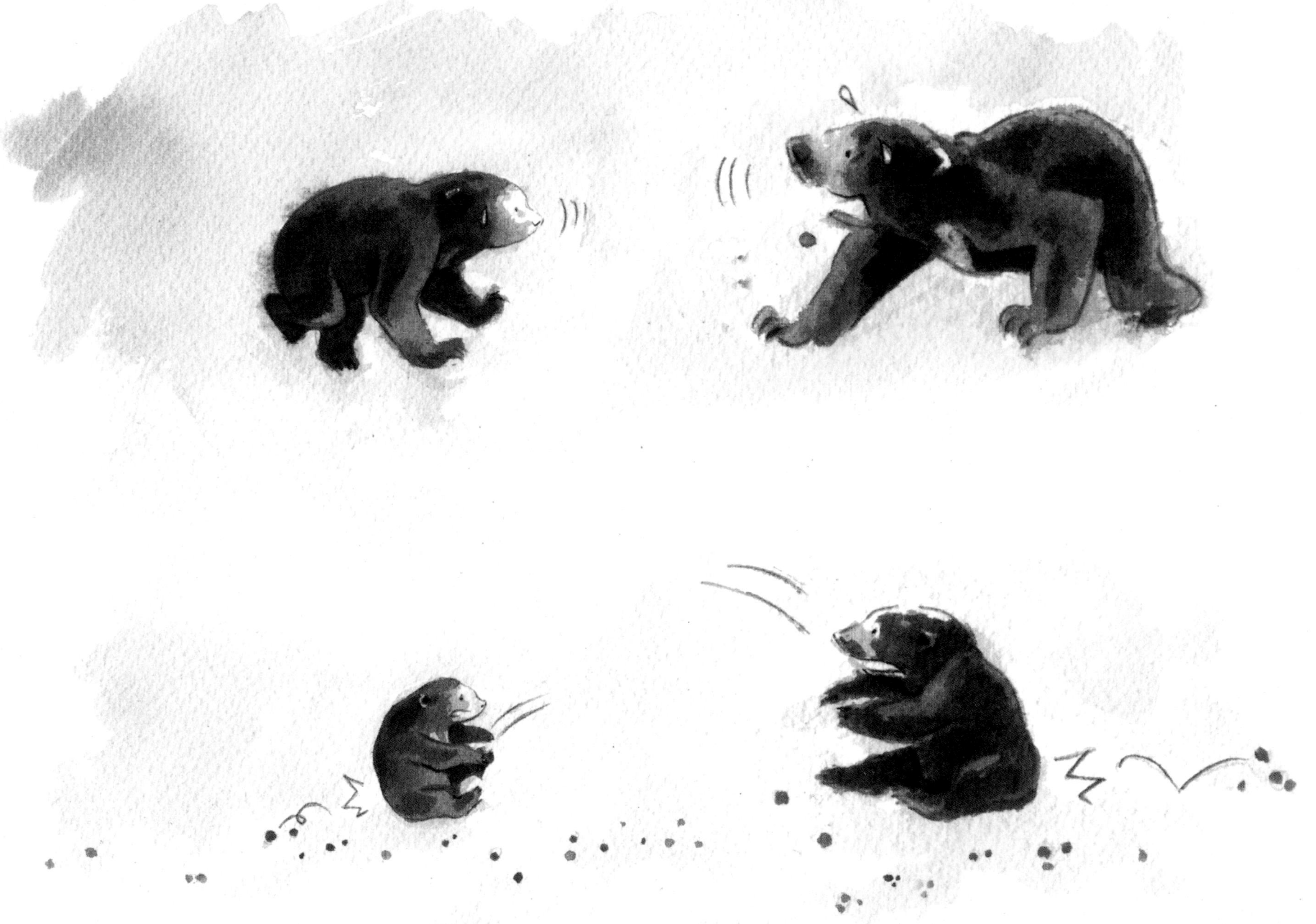

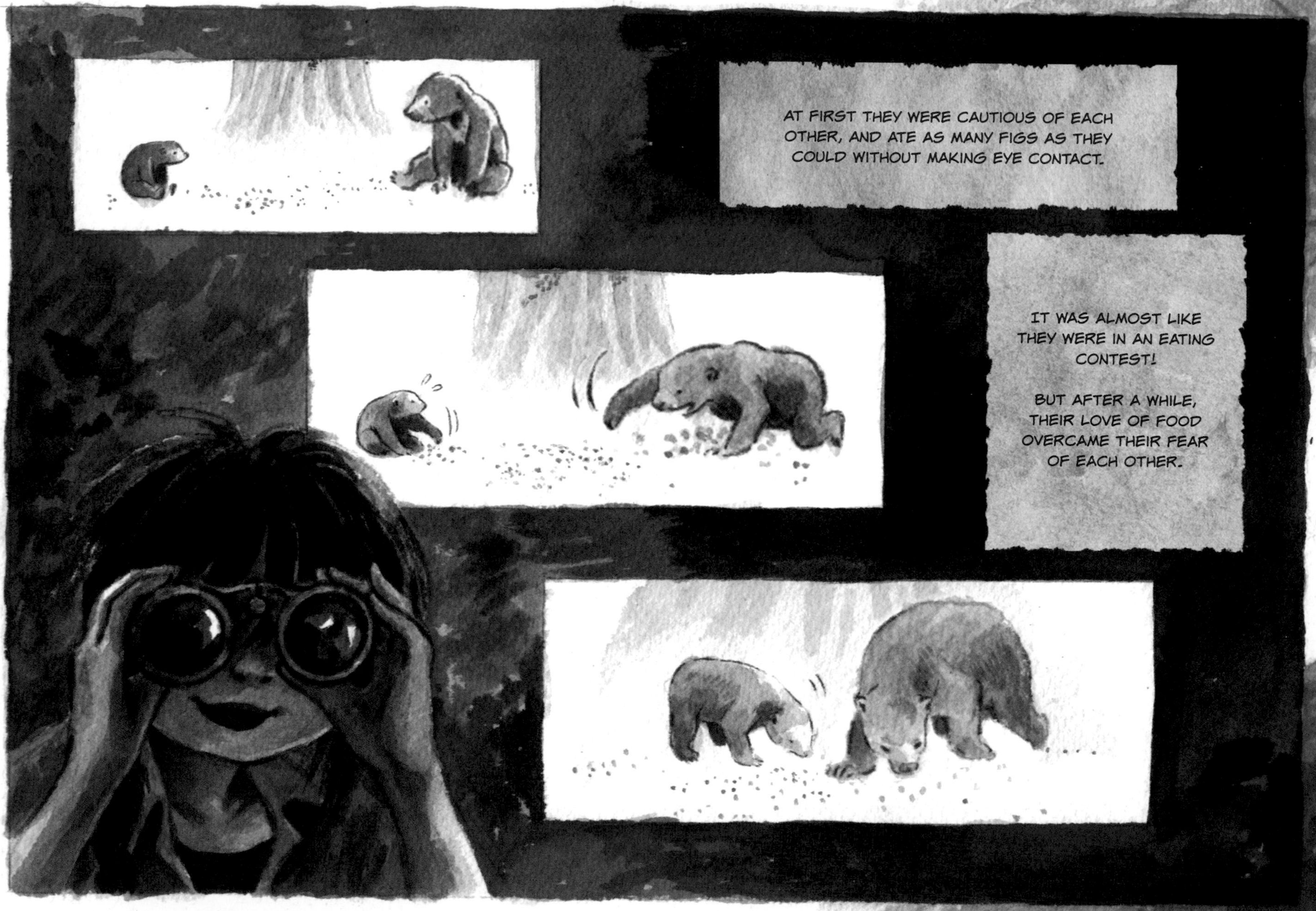
AT FIRST THEY WERE CAUTIOUS OF EACH OTHER, AND ATE AS MANY FIGS AS THEY COULD WITHOUT MAKING EYE CONTACT.
IT WAS ALMOST LIKE THEY WERE IN AN EATING CONTEST!
BUT AFTER A WHILE, THEIR LOVE OF FOOD OVERCAME THEIR FEAR OF EACH OTHER.

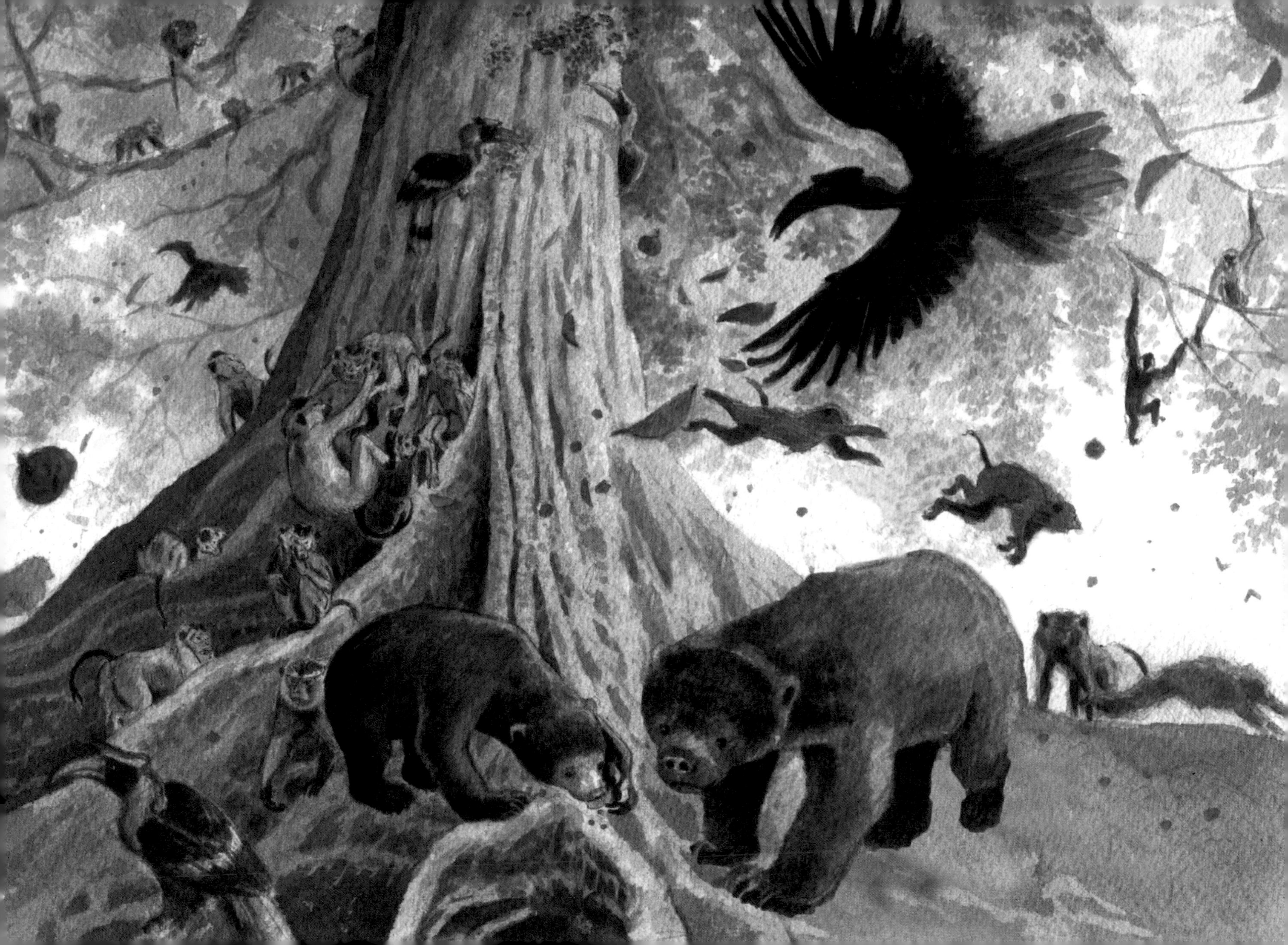

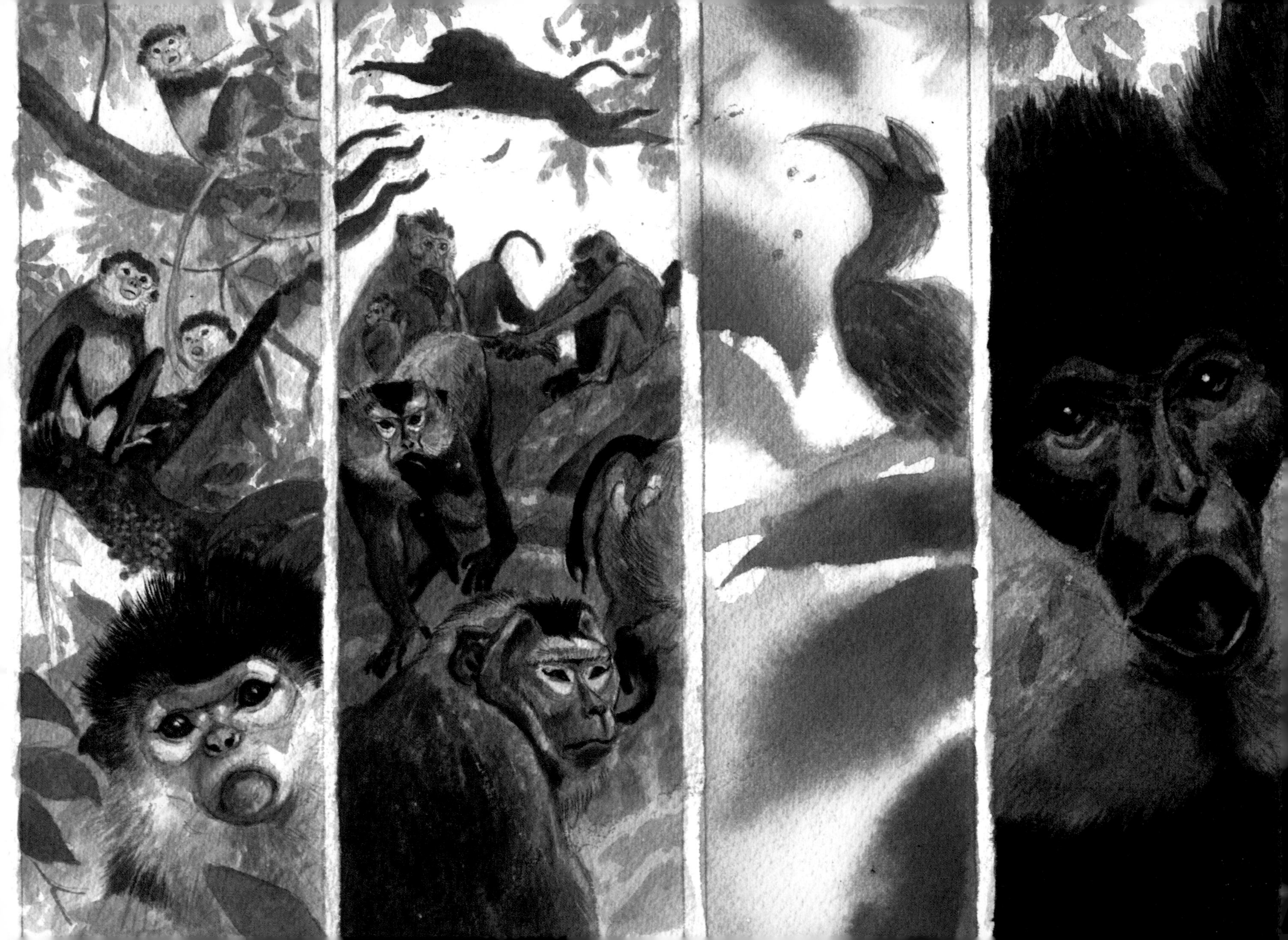

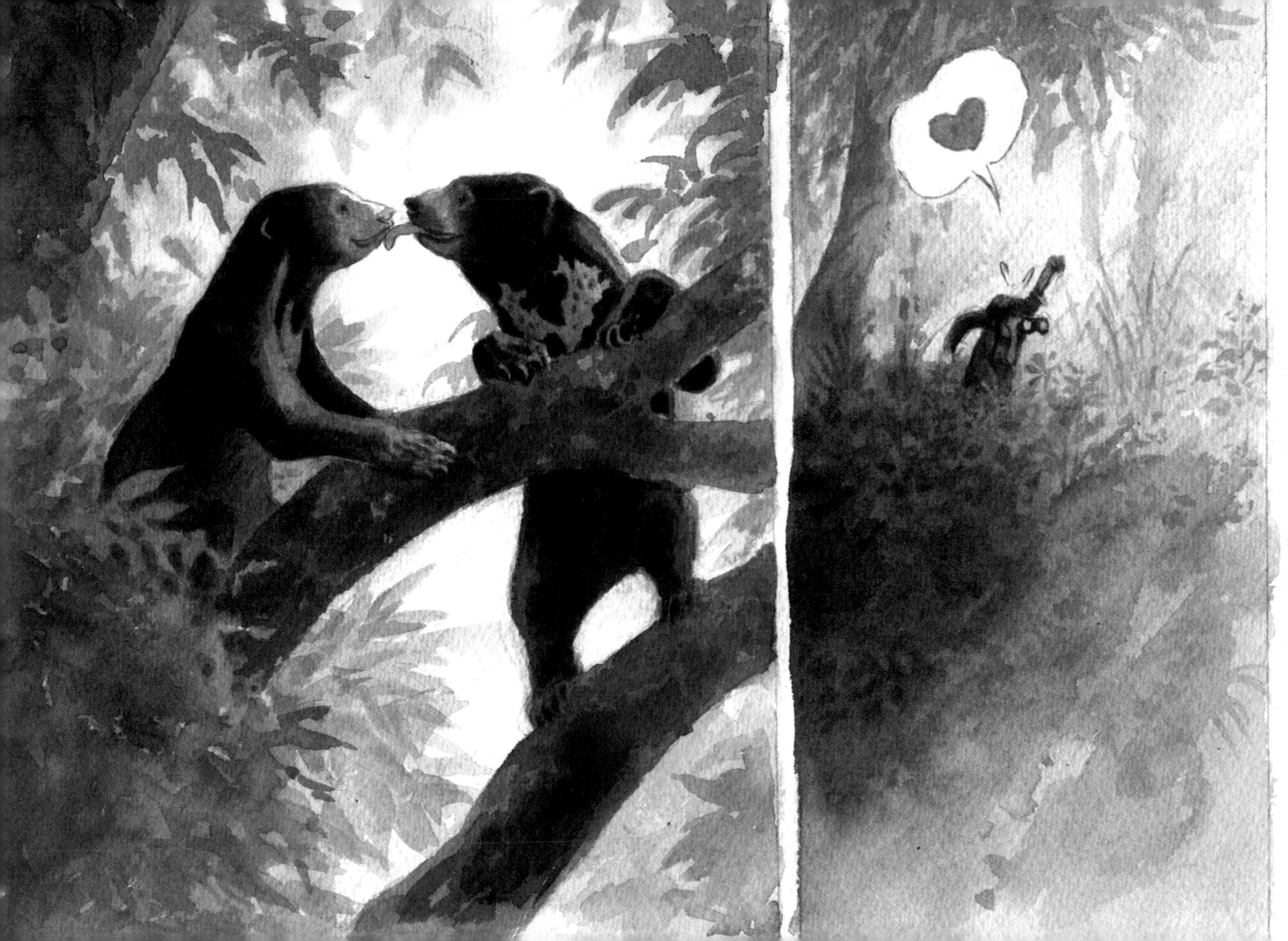

CHAPTER NINE

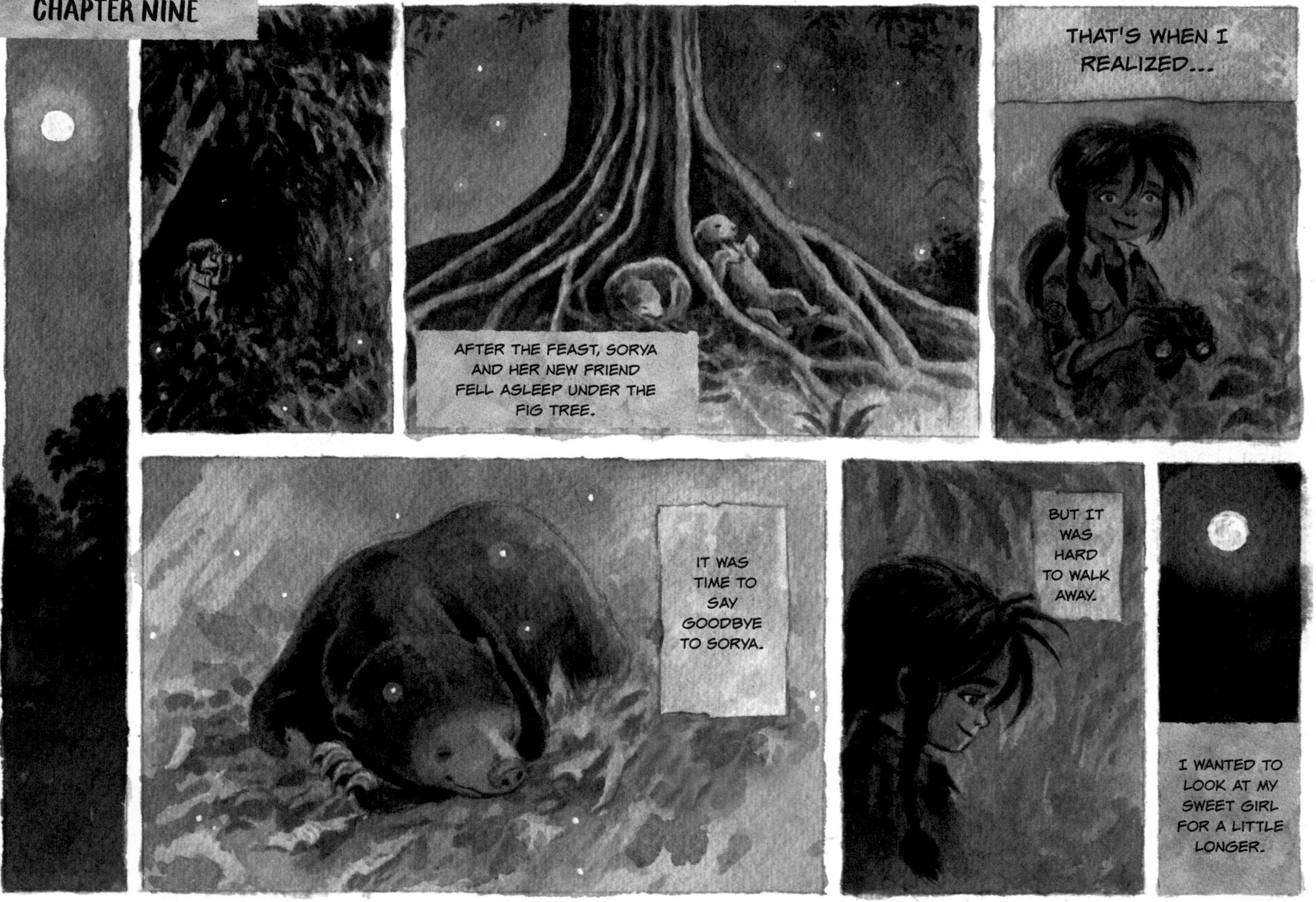
AFTER THE FEAST, SORYA AND HER NEW FRIEND FELL ASLEEP UNDER THE FIG TREE.
THAT'S WHEN I REALIZED...
IT WAS TIME TO SAY GOODBYE TO SORYA.
BUT IT WAS HARD TO WALK AWAY.
I WANTED TO LOOK AT MY SWEET GIRL FOR A LITTLE LONGER.

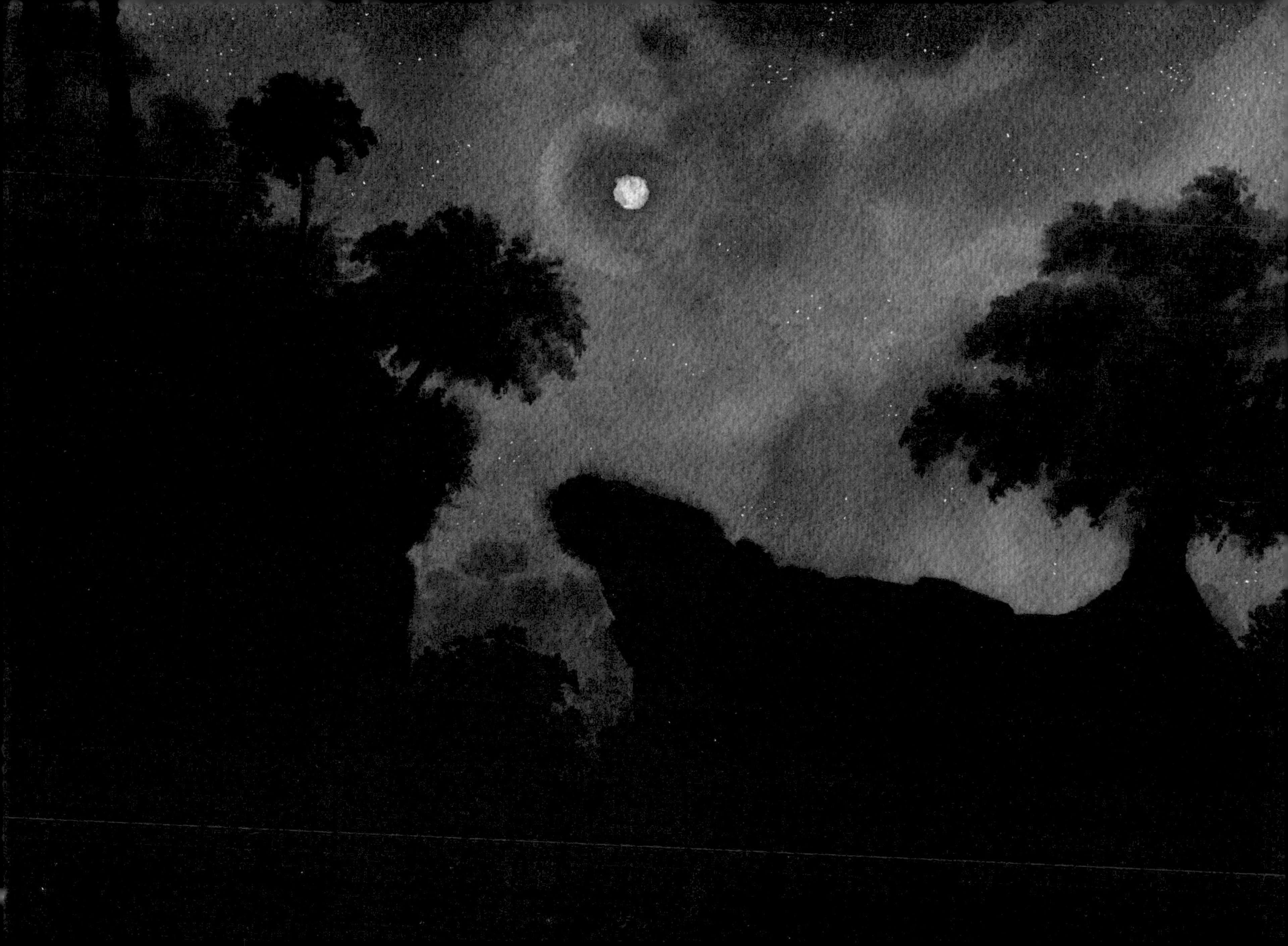

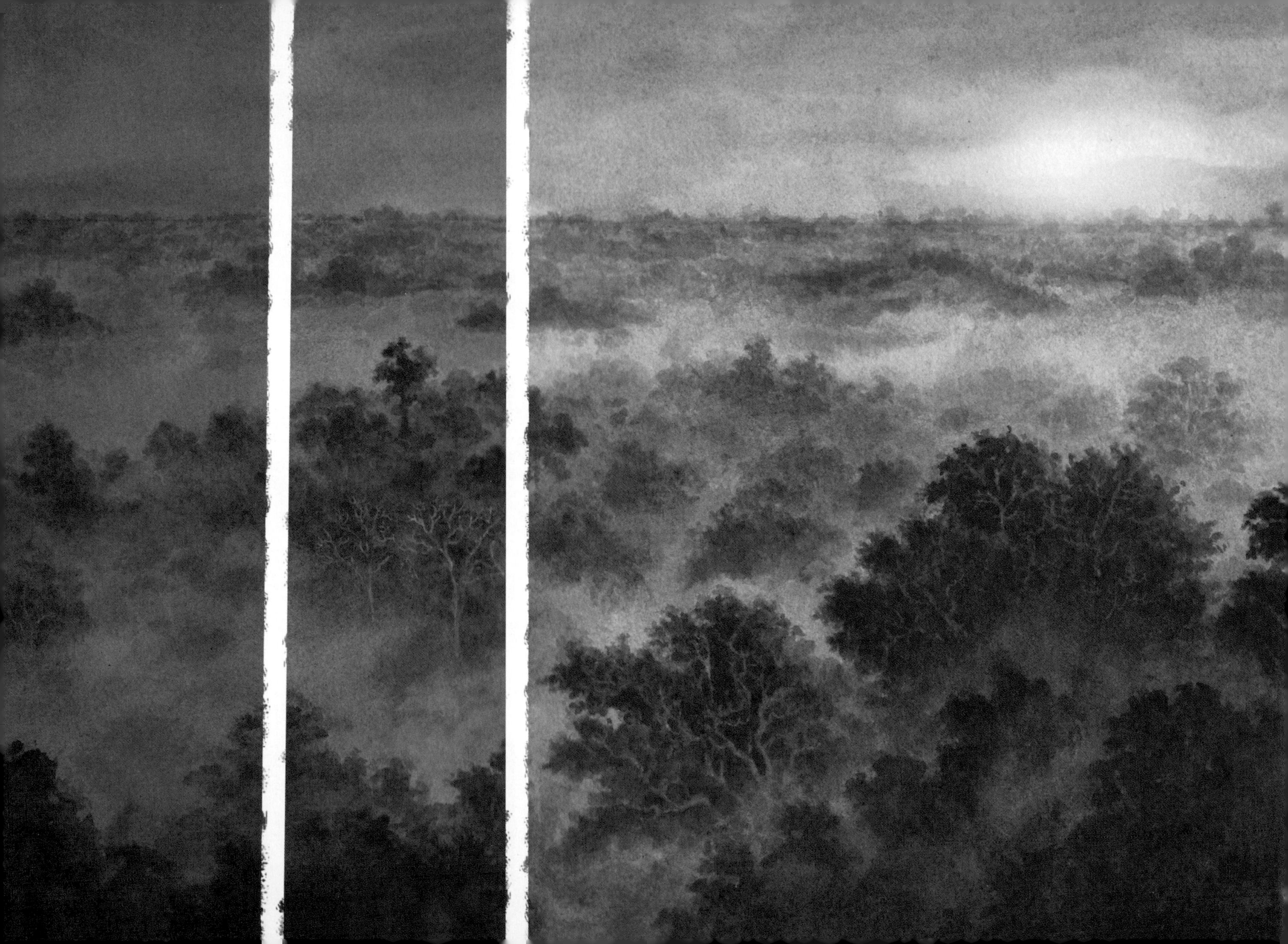

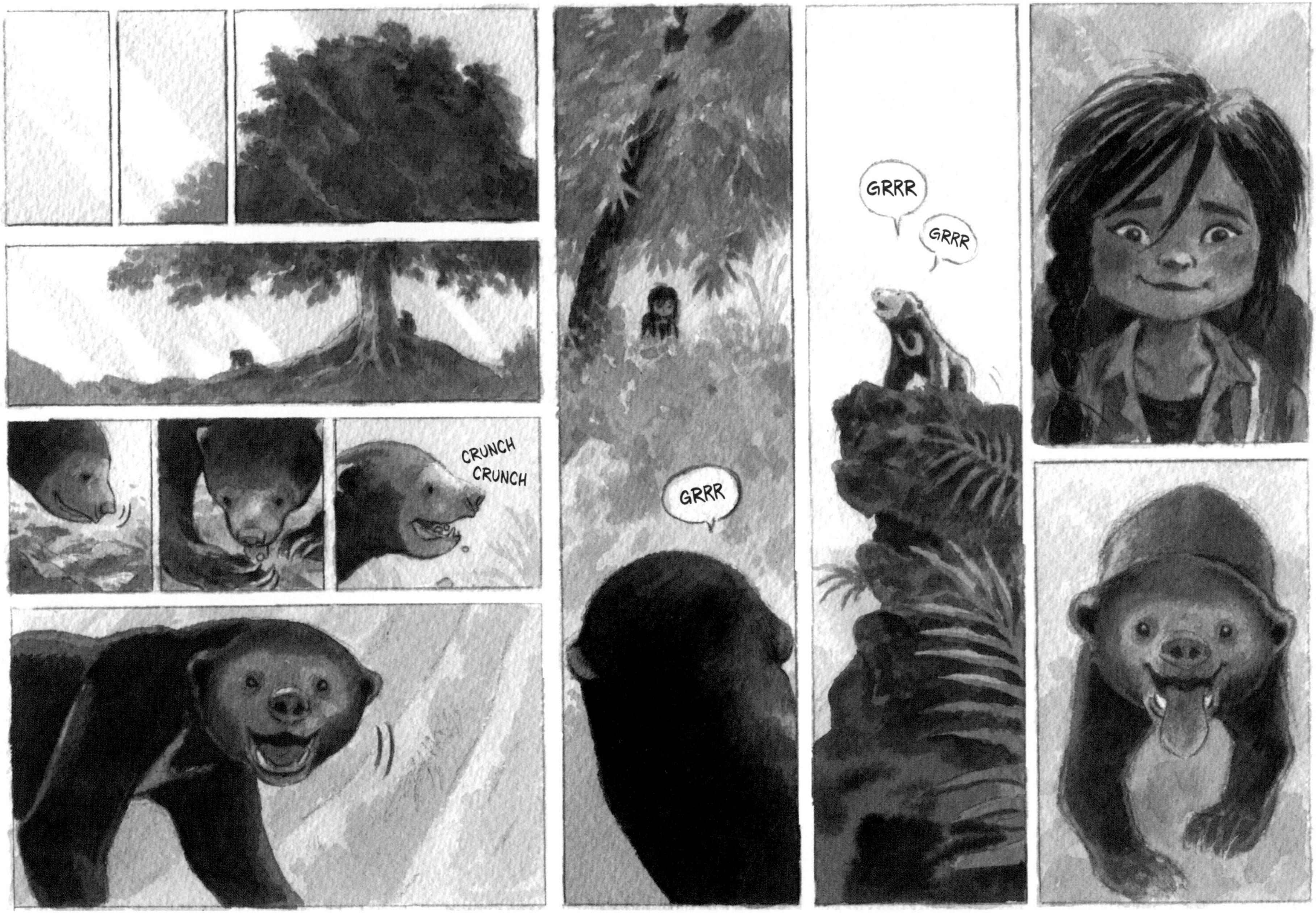
CRUNCH
CRUNCH
GRRR
GRRR
GRRR

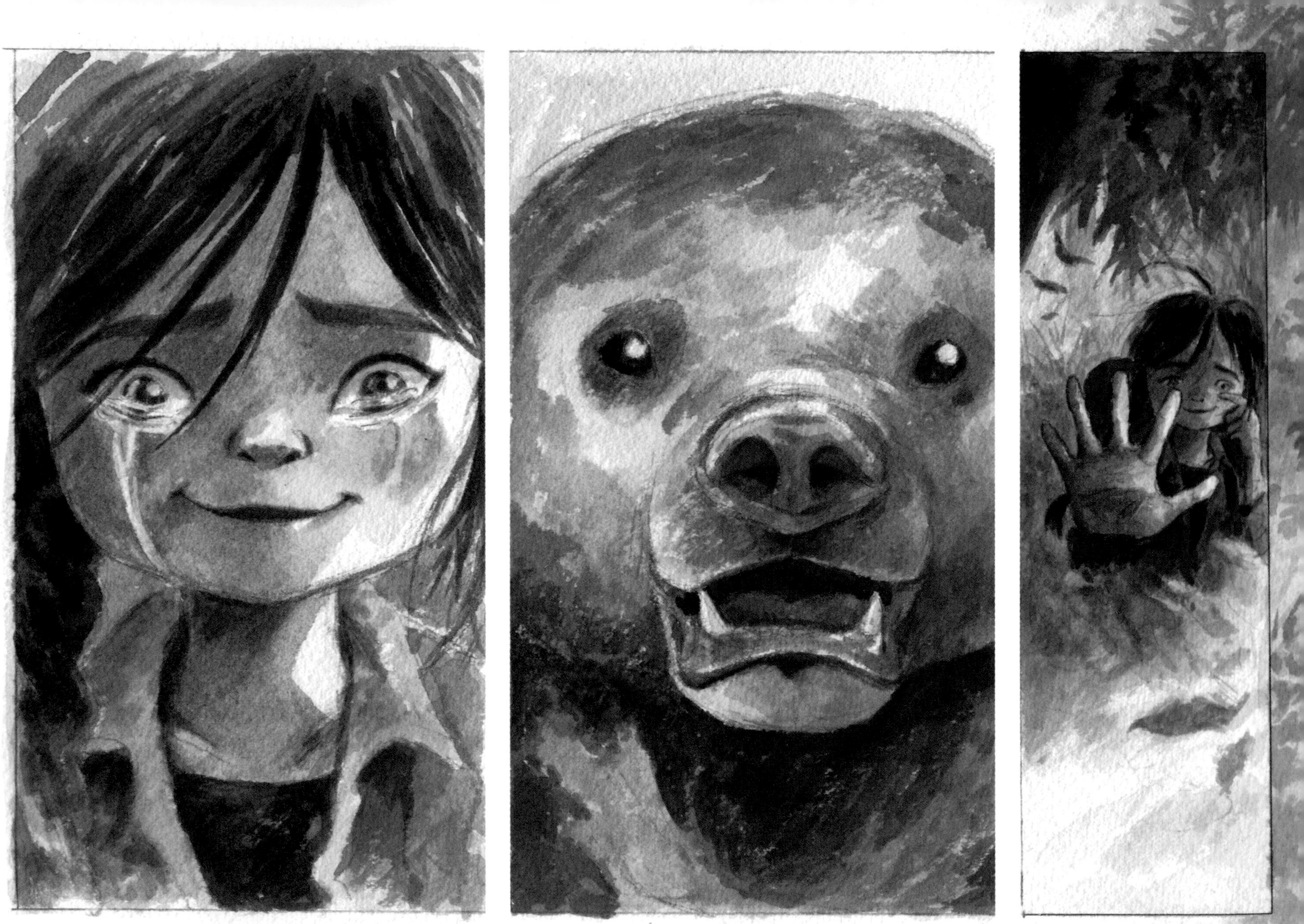

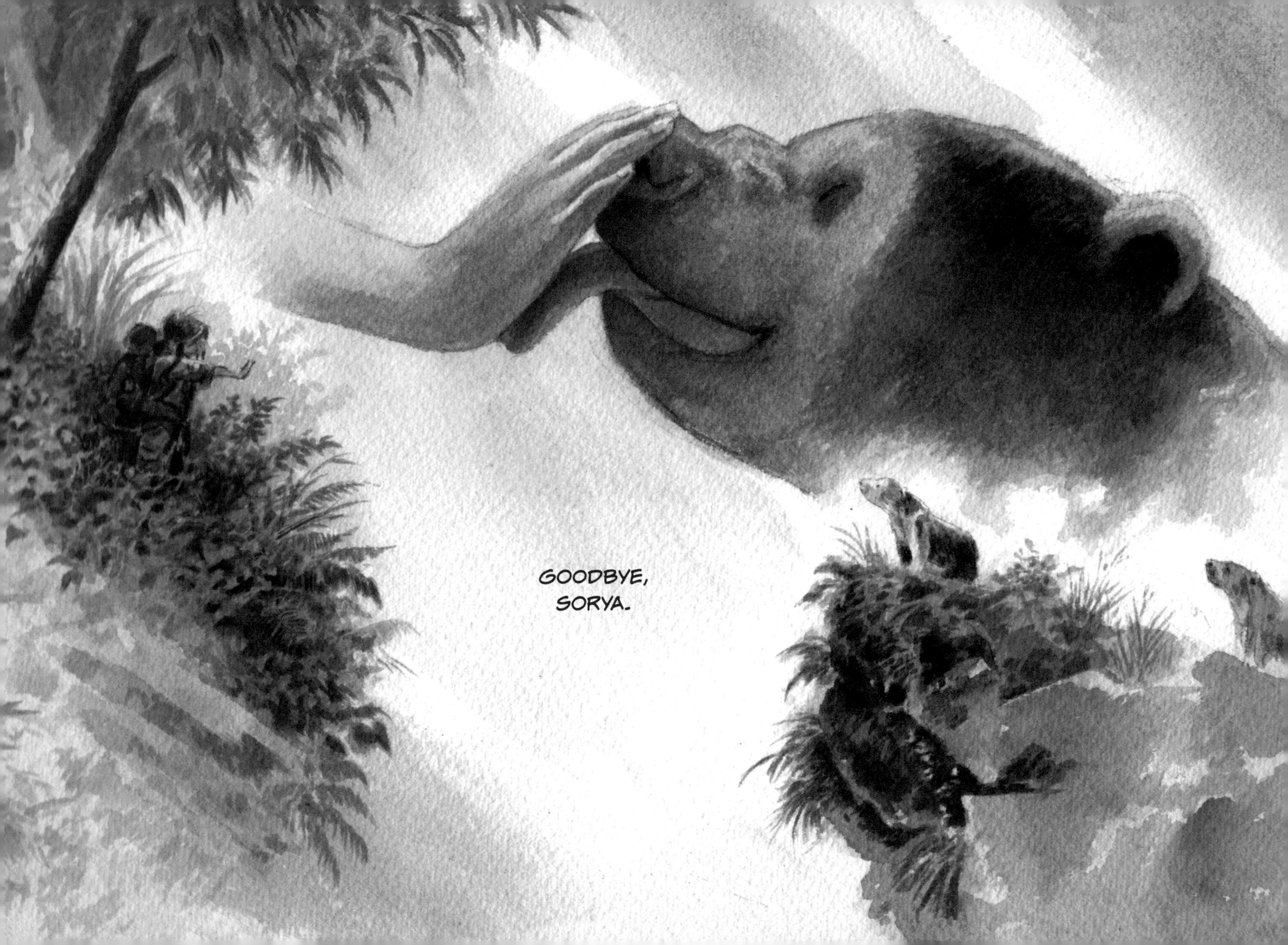
GOODBYE,
SORYA.

EPILOGUE

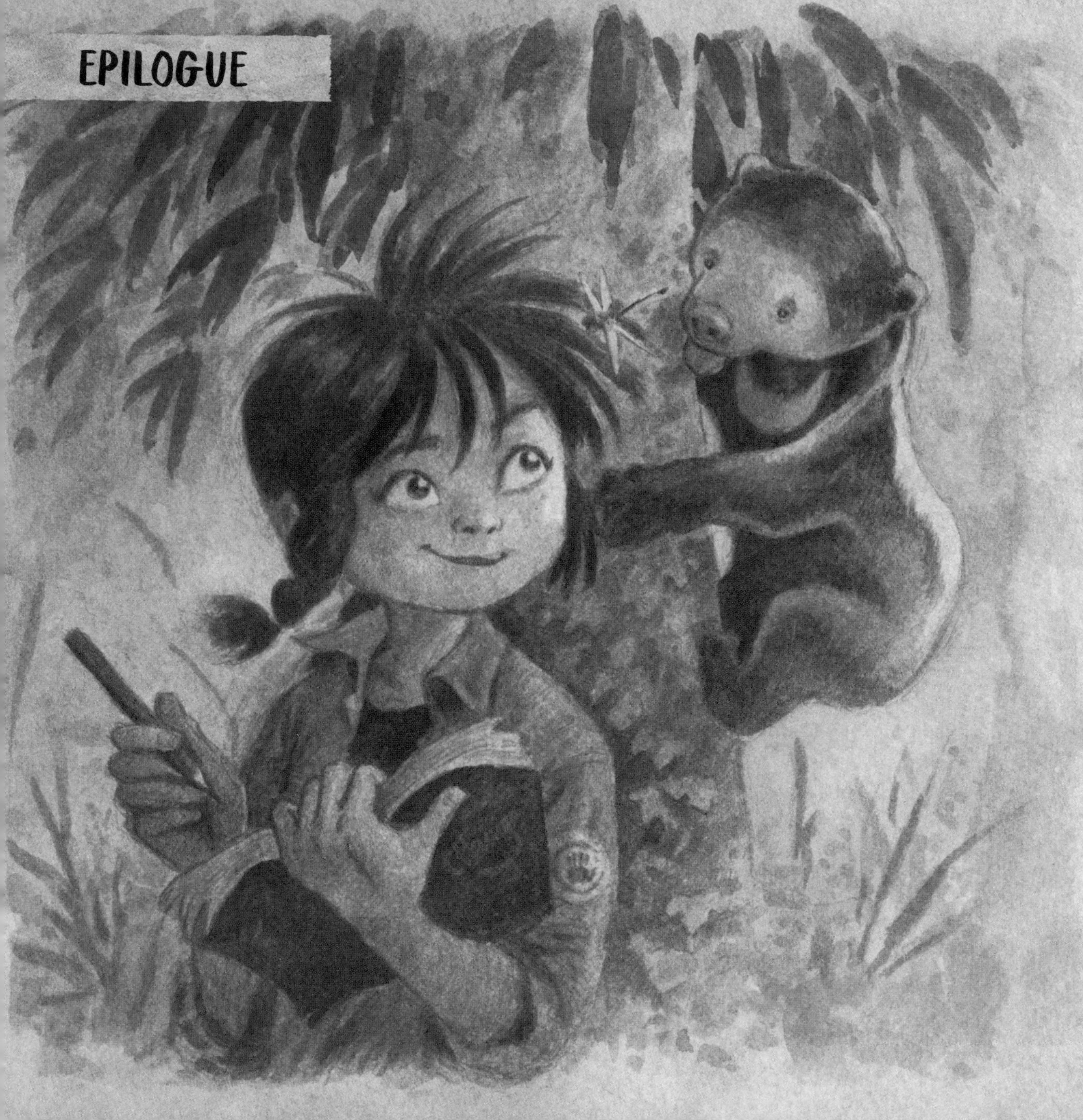

MY NAME IS CHANG.

I AM A WILDLIFE CONSERVATIONIST.

MY GOAL WAS TO FIND SORYA
A HOME IN THE FOREST
WHERE SHE COULD LIVE . . .

WILD AND FREE.

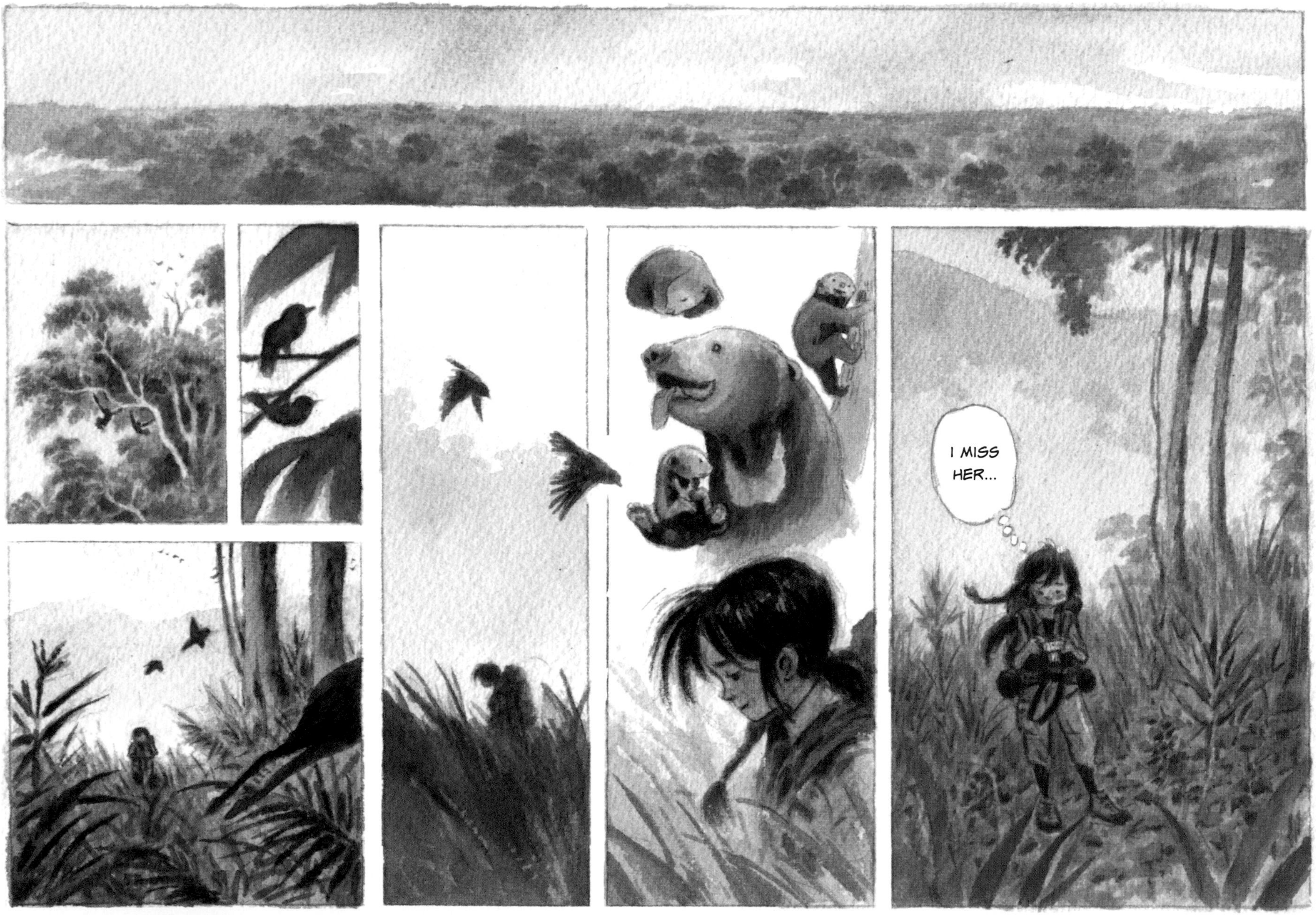
I MISS
HER...

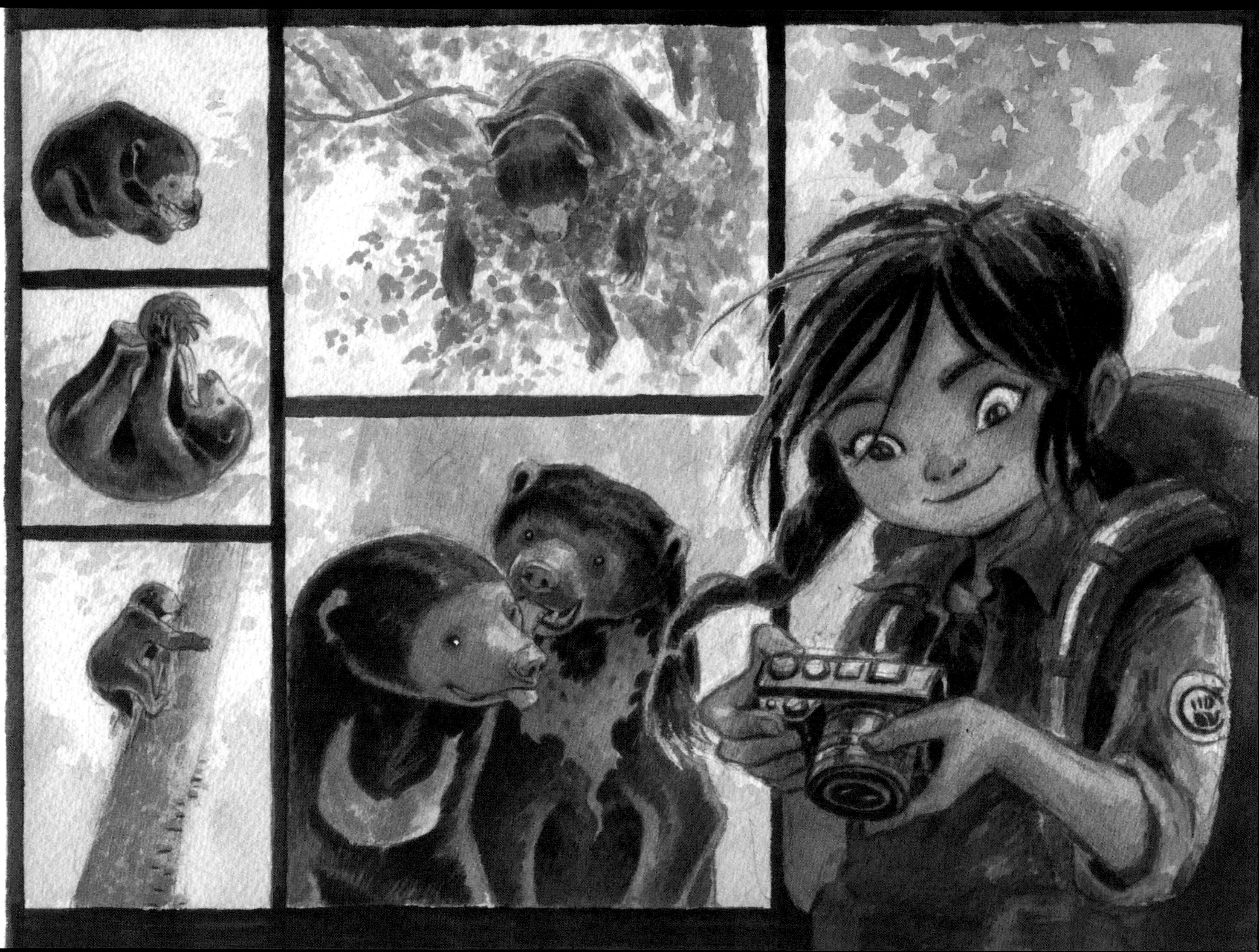

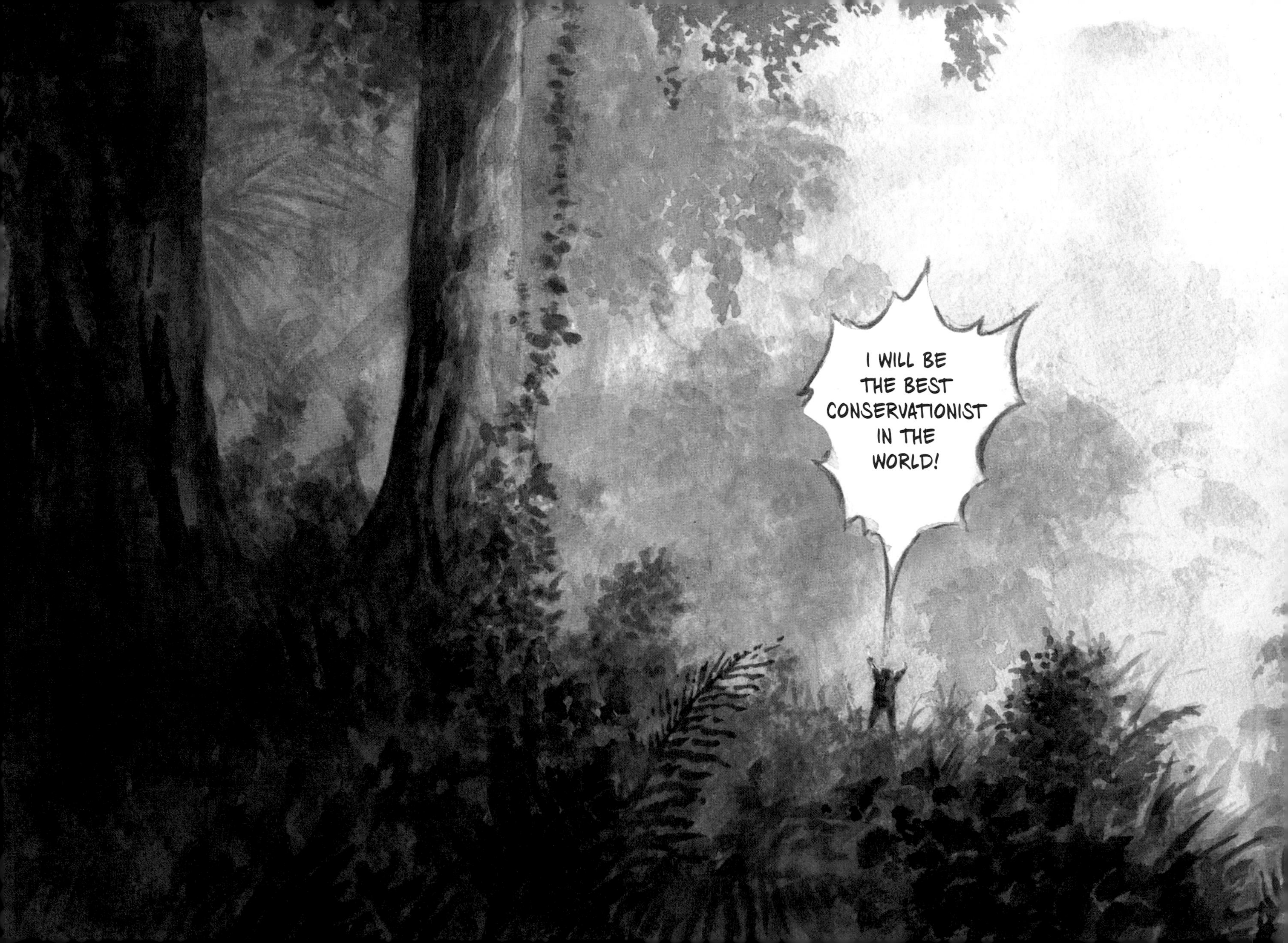
I WILL BE THE BEST CONSERVATIONIST IN THE WORLD!

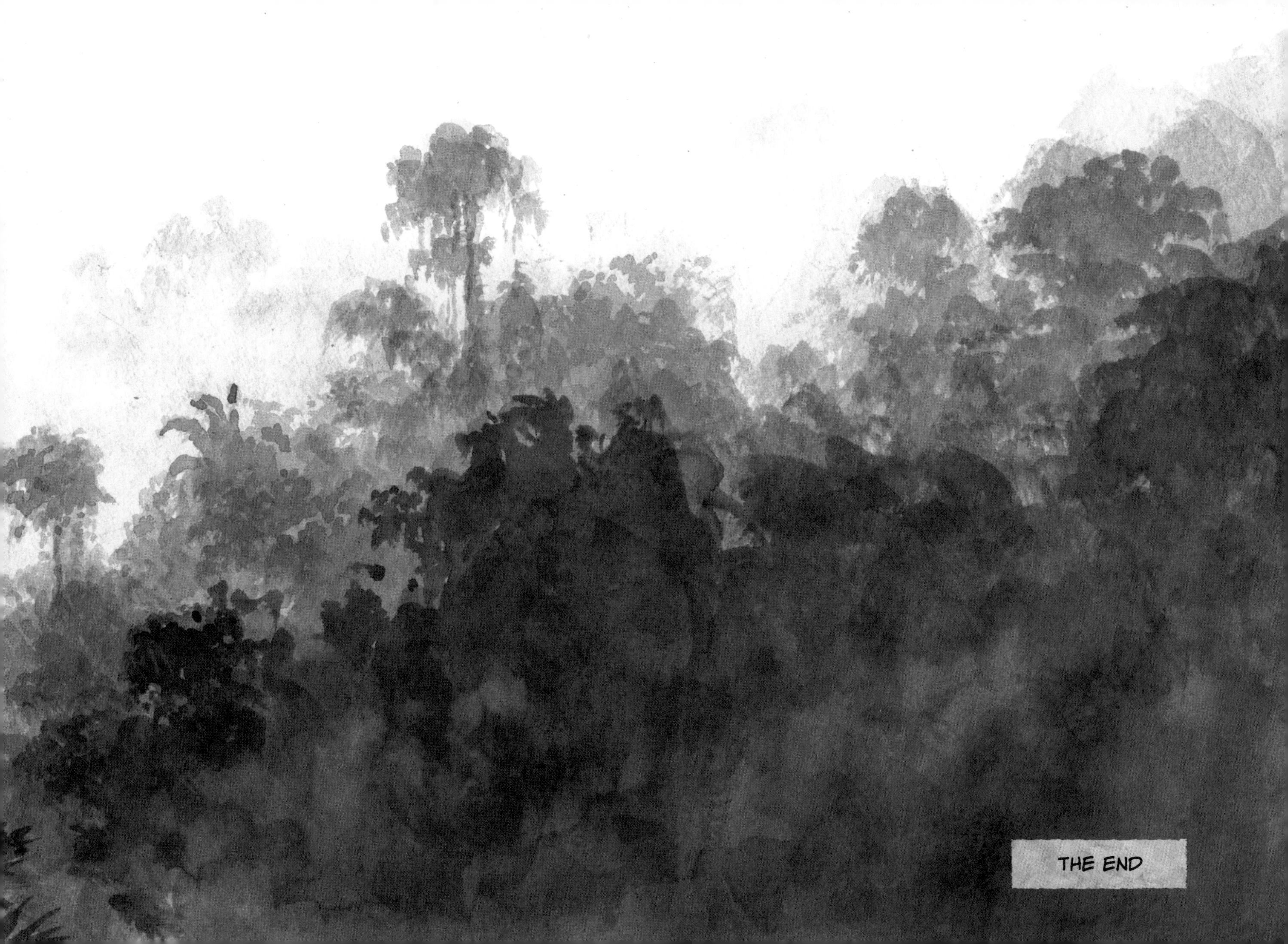
THE END

A MESSAGE FROM TRANG AND JEET:

WE WOULD LIKE TO SEND OUR SINCERE
THANKS TO MATT HUNT, BRIAN CRUDGE,
MARION SCHNEIDER, AND "FREE THE BEARS"
ORGANIZATION, WHO GAVE US A WONDERFUL
OPPORTUNITY TO CREATE THIS BOOK. PLEASE
VISIT "FREE THE BEARS" RESCUE CENTER IN
CAT TIEN NATIONAL PARK, VIETNAM, AND
SUPPORT THEIR WORK!

FREE
THE
BEARS

WWW.FREETHEBEARS.ORG

ILLUSTRATOR'S NOTE:

I WOULD LIKE TO THANK TRANG NGUYEN, THE BRAVE AND KIND-HEARTED CONSERVATIONIST, A FRIEND OF MINE. I WOULD NOT HAVE BEEN ABLE TO CREATE THIS WORK WITHOUT HER STORIES, HER KNOWLEDGE, AND HER REAL-LIFE EXPERIENCES. THANKS TO TRANG, I HAD THE CHANCE TO VOLUNTEER AT WILDLIFE RESCUE CENTERS AND DO FIELDWORK (THANKS MATT HUNT FOR SUPPORTING ME EVEN THOUGH WE'VE NEVER HAD THE CHANCE TO MEET). I SINCERELY APPRECIATE BRIAN CRUDGE AND MARION SCHNEIDER, THE TWO EXPERTS ON BEARS WHO SHARED THEIR VALUABLE KNOWLEDGE OF BEAR CONSERVATION. IT WAS A PRIVILEGE TO WORK WITH THEM. I WOULD ALSO LIKE TO THANK THE STAFF AND VOLUNTEERS AT "FREE THE BEARS" RESCUE CENTER IN CAT TIEN NATIONAL PARK, VIETNAM, AND PHNOM TAMAO WILDLIFE RESCUE CENTER IN CAMBODIA.

MY GRATITUDE GOES TO PHUONG AN (PAN) AND NGUYET HANG (MOCHI MUN), MY TWO LOVELY AND DEDICATED ASSISTANTS. BESIDE THE HARD WORK OF SEARCHING, CATEGORIZING, DRAWING, AND TAKING DETAILED NOTES ON PLANTS ENDEMIC TO VIETNAM, THEY ALSO PROVIDED ME WITH DRAWING PAPER AND FOOD WHEN TIMES WERE TOUGH.

THANKS TO TA LAN HANH FOR INTRODUCING ME TO LINH PHAN, THE TALENTED DESIGNER WHO WAS FULLY DEVOTED TO THE PROJECT.

AND ONCE AGAIN, THANKS TRANG, FOR YOUR PATIENCE.

JEET ZDUNG

ABOUT THE CREATORS:

TRANG NGUYEN IS A VIETNAMESE WILDLIFE CONSERVATIONIST, ENVIRONMENTAL ACTIVIST, AND WRITER, KNOWN FOR HER CONSERVATION WORK IN TACKLING THE ILLEGAL WILDLIFE TRADE IN AFRICA AND ASIA. TRANG GRADUATED WITH HER PHD IN BIODIVERSITY MANAGEMENT AT THE UNIVERSITY OF KENT, ENGLAND, RESEARCHING WILD ANIMAL PART USE IN TRADITIONAL ASIAN MEDICINE AND ITS IMPACT ON AFRICAN WILDLIFE. IN 2018, TRANG WAS FEATURED IN THE DOCUMENTARY FILM *STROOP: JOURNEY INTO THE RHINO HORN WAR*, ALONGSIDE JANE GOODALL. SHE WAS SELECTED BY BBC FOR THEIR 100 WOMEN OF 2019 LIST AND BY FORBES FOR THEIR 2020 30 UNDER 30 ASIA LIST. TRANG IS THE FOUNDER AND EXECUTIVE DIRECTOR OF WILDACT, AN NGO THAT MONITORS THE ILLEGAL WILDLIFE TRADE MARKETS AND PROVIDES CONSERVATION EDUCATION PROGRAMS FOR VIETNAMESE YOUTH. SHE IS ALSO A MEMBER OF THE IUCN SSC BEAR SPECIALIST GROUP, WHICH STRIVES TO PROMOTE THE CONSERVATION OF BEARS LIVING IN THEIR NATURAL HABITATS AROUND THE WORLD. *SAVING SORYA: CHANG AND THE SUN BEAR* IS HER FIRST CHILDREN'S BOOK.

JEET ZDUNG IS AN ILLUSTRATOR WHO FUSES TRADITIONAL VIETNAMESE ART WITH MANGA, USING PENCILS, WATERCOLORS, INK, AND OTHER DIGITAL MEANS TO CREATE WORKS OF BEAUTY AND INNOVATION. HE HAS WON SEVERAL AWARDS, INCLUDING A SILENT MANGA AUDITION EXCELLENCE AWARD FOR HIS MANGA *STAND UP AND FLY*. *SAVING SORYA: CHANG AND THE SUN BEAR* IS HIS FIRST CHILDREN'S BOOK PUBLISHED IN THE US. HE LIVES IN HANOI, VIETNAM.

WILDACT IS A NOT-FOR-PROFIT CONSERVATION
ORGANIZATION BASED IN VIETNAM, ESTABLISHED IN 2015.
ITS MISSION IS TO INSPIRE, MOTIVATE, AND EMPOWER
SOCIETY AND INDIVIDUALS TO ENGAGE IN THE
SCIENCE-BASED CONSERVATION OF THREATENED
SPECIES AND ECOSYSTEMS.

DIAL BOOKS FOR YOUNG READERS

AN IMPRINT OF PENGUIN RANDOM HOUSE LLC, NEW YORK

ORIGINALLY PUBLISHED IN VIETNAMESE AS *CHANG HOANG DÃ – GÃU* BY KIM DONG PUBLISHING COMPANY, 2020.

FIRST ENGLISH LANGUAGE PUBLICATION IN THE UNITED KINGDOM BY MACMILLAN CHILDREN'S BOOKS, AN IMPRINT OF PAN MACMILLAN, 2021

ORIGINAL TEXT COPYRIGHT © 2020 BY TRANG NGUYEN

TRANSLATION COPYRIGHT © 2021 BY TRANG NGUYEN

ILLUSTRATIONS COPYRIGHT © 2020 BY JEET ZDUNG

VISIT US ONLINE AT PENGUINRANDOMHOUSE.COM.

FIRST AMERICAN EDITION

LIBRARY OF CONGRESS CATALOGING-IN-PUBLICATION DATA IS AVAILABLE.

MANUFACTURED IN CHINA

ISBN 9780593353639 HC   10 9 8 7 6 5 4 3 2 1

ISBN 9780593353622 PB   10 9 8 7 6 5 4 3 2 1

12/21

TEXT SET IN DAN PANOSIAN, JACK ARMSTRONG, AND TWO FISTED